Sex Magick

Sex Magick

The Mapleview Series – Book 3

Tom Raimbault

Published 2015 by Creativia

Book design by Creativia (www.creativia.org)

Cover art by http://www.thecovercollection.com/

Preface

I'm sure in a few dusty, old books of spells that have survived centuries of persecution and burning by those who hunt witches; there might be a recipe or two that call for a broken man's heart. Imagine the power that can fuel and drive a spell into motion if such a broken heart could be won. Thanks to the power that a woman possesses, she can easily win the attraction of any male. And if knowledgeable enough, she might know just the right moment to hex her victim with a terrible love spell that causes him to fall head over heels—so madly in love with her. In many cases this victim might not have ever met the woman who casts such a spell. He only encounters her in public places such as the daily commute on the train, or the morning visit to the coffee shop. Chances are the two never exchanged even the simplest of words with one another. But somehow he falls in love her.

From that moment on he can't eat, he can't sleep and he can't drive the irrational thoughts or feelings of this woman out of his mind and heart. And if a man who falls victim to this spell happens to be previously in love with another woman, she will soon be forgotten. For you see, there is no way to resist the power of terrible love spell.

The answer is clear. Those uncontrollable thoughts and feelings are a calling out from the desired woman. So with heart racing, body trembling and all sorts of chemicals surging through his veins; the man finally speaks out and makes his move.

In just one example out of a thousand, he usually falls flat on his face—figuratively speaking. He's intoxicated with being in love and can't seem to speak or act out appropriately.

But she's so callous and cold, "Such a disappointment; he's not the sort of man I thought he was. You only have one chance to make a first impression with me."

Or maybe a cruel witch of a woman might play the card of being taken off guard and surprised. "I'm so sorry! I didn't mean to make you feel this way. Whatever I did or said was purely unintentional. You seem like a nice guy, but we don't share the same feelings."

She might not even say that much. She might only walk away, never to be seen or heard from again. There is nothing left to do or say. It's simply time for her to hide in the attic during the midnight hours with candles of various colors and a collection of strange items needed for the perfect recipe for a granted wish.

But the most precious, the sweetest of these ingredients is the man's fragile, shattered heart. It causes him to walk the days as a disheveled mess with red, glassy eyes as he struggles in vain to overcome his emotional wreck. Perhaps a witch might even be able to reach across the void in the dark of night, and collect the tears from the pillow of a man whose heart she has broken. Such a precious thing: if the reader is a woman, wouldn't you like to have in your possession a man's tears that have been cried for you?

Fortunately, most witches would never stoop so low—unless, of course, she feels he deserves it. But you can thank the small fraction of a percentage that does use their knowledge in harmful ways for the negative reputation that is often associated with witches. These types disregard any morals or sense for the common good. And this is why witches have been hunted through the ages and given cruel means of disposal—burning, hanging or drowning. Such a shame…

Buried within that small fraction of a percentage of bad witches are the purely evil ones who have seemingly sold their own souls and are merely buying their times here on Earth. Such a witch may only come once every five hundred years (just a guesstimate). They're nearly non-existent, but not completely non-existent!

But to my fellow men, I reassure you not to worry. Most of us will never fall victim to the meddling of wicked witch. It takes a special man who is predisposed, nearly destined to fall victim to a witch. Perhaps he's… well… stupid, and involves himself in things he has no business being involved in. He probably even deserves it!

Tom Raimbault
Hoffman Estates, Illinois
April 12, 2013

Prelude:
Amber Reunites with Trista's Biological Father

Life after being banished from the Dickly castle certainly changed some things for Amber. How could Michael have remained married to a woman who savagely murdered his precious Linsey? Interesting thing; Amber's divorce was slightly different from a woman who is so disgusted of a sour marriage that she wants no association with her ex-husband. Amber had no desire to change her last name back to the maiden. Prior to marrying Michael, she signed a prenuptial agreement as she wanted nothing more than true love and a happy marriage forevermore. Despite the prenuptial agreement, and despite the fact that Michael was deeply saddened and devastated over the terrible things Amber had done, he was compassionate enough to give his ex-wife some money for purposes of establishing herself. But money runs out, of course. Everyone needs more of it; even Amber, who in younger years lived in a universe where only the intangible things were important.

Life hadn't corrupted Amber too badly through the years. But she had gotten wiser and realized that plenty of people would be crawling out of the woodwork after Michael's death. As far as Amber knew, outside of paralyzed Paulette, there were no close relatives to claim Michael's fortune. Shouldn't an ex-wife have claim to some of this? She would be a fool not to at least try upon his death.

Michael was an old man. His life on Earth was running out. Amber wasn't sure of the laws; but given the right attorney who would charge a percentage of her possible fortune, anything was possible. Would you change your name back to your maiden if you were once married to the highly successful and extremely wealthy Michael Dickly?

Amber went through some radical changes in her physical appearance. She no longer possessed her long, beautiful head of naturally flowing brown hair. It was cut short so that it hovered shoulder-length and then dyed light-blond—nearly white. Amber had been light complexioned throughout her whole life and maintained strict avoidance of harmful sunrays. But her nearly-white hair accentuated this complexion so that she appeared radiant, almost like a ghost! Already thin and on the petite side, Amber lost a considerable amount of weight from unnecessary, strict dieting and exercise. If you've ever seen a woman in her thirties lose more than her fair share of weight, you might have noticed that the healthy collagen that once maintained that youthful appearance is soon gone. Although still pretty, alluring and sexy; the new ghostly Amber possessed an element of frightfulness. It might have been easy to have an unexplained fear of the woman.

Throughout the years, Amber maintained a sense of regret for what she had done; feeling that she truly deserved the punishment along with appreciating the lesson well learned. Being that Michael had adopted Trista, Amber imagined it was possible to have him provide child support or even alimony. But she was so disgusted with herself, while at the same time having a sense of pride in the fact that she established herself and supported her daughter throughout the years after divorce.

As for Trista's biological father; Amber probably could have made a claim for child support, even retroactive child support. Any woman in her right mind would have attempted this! But shortly after the divorce, Amber's heart suddenly softened towards Trista's biological father. Imagine that; how unreal! Still dreamy, ethereal and full of wishes; Amber recalled the days when she loved him more than anything. Really all she wished for was to somehow have Trista's biological father in her life—perhaps as a close friend and definitely involved in Trista's life. Just having him live down the street and visiting throughout the week would have made Amber happy. And surely he must have changed through the years as well. If reconnected with a renewed bond, wouldn't he be willing to help out a beloved friend; provide a little money when times were difficult for Amber?

If you've come to know Amber, then you know that all of her wishes come true. Only a few details to iron out and not completely surrendered to Amber,

Trista's biological father had, in fact, returned to Amber! In fact, he often lay beside her in bed!

But Trista's biological father didn't live in the house with Amber and Trista just yet. Mother was working on these small details. Aside from that, now 2009 and Trista being a sixteen-year-old girl, Trista had yet to be informed of this new man's identity who was increasingly becoming a part of Mother's life. Oh, she had her suspicions. But unsure and bit uncomfortable with this man's sudden existence, Trista waited for the official announcement from Mother.

It should also be mentioned that there was the small detail of Trista's biological father being married to another woman with children of his own. But don't be so quick to shake your head in disbelief while pointing the finger of shame at Amber. Amber certainly had her work cut out for her in luring this man home. After initially discovering his whereabouts, she purchased a home right down the street from him. Then for many months she would slowly drive past his house with a hungry look and desperate eyes. Any man would become intrigued by this!

Then one Saturday afternoon, Trista's father stopped at Walmart to purchase some new tools for work. That's when Amber sort of "bumped into him".

He immediately recognized and greeted her. "Oh, hi!"

Amber's wasted not a moment. "I forgive you Matt."

"Excuse me?"

"You don't have to pretend, Matt. It's me, Amber. I dyed my hair. I searched for you a while back and know you spent some time out in California. But you're back in Mapleview, now. I saw you a few years ago and followed you back to your house. As luck had it, there was a house down the street for sale. I'm not here for back child support or anything. Just need a..."

He immediately interrupted. "Whoa, whoa, whoa; first of all, my name is not Matt! And I do not have any children outside of marriage!"

A look of outrage and disbelief fell across Amber's face.

He pulled out his wallet and removed his state driver's license. "See, my name is Jim. Apparently you had me confused with someone else."

Amber put her hand to forehead, partially covering her eyes. "I'm sorry! This is so embarrassing." Then she turned and walked away.

Jim only trailed behind her. "Wait! Wait!" Now aware that he reminded Amber of someone she was once in love with, Jim speculated that he could pretend to be that person. It might have provided a chance to have a piece of the sexy, intriguing blond who lived down the street and often drove slowly past his house.

But Amber kept walking, pushing her hand behind her in a motion for Jim to stay away.

And that should have been the end of whatever game Jim and Amber were involved in. But hopes and dreams die hard. For so long Amber had a sense of relief that a possible fatherly role—Trista's actual father—lived down the street. To make matters worse, Amber's daughter was slowly being made to understand that this man was, in fact, her father. Amber didn't come right out and say it. She was more subtle in her approach. "That man standing out in his driveway; he looks very much like your father." With the continued interest that Mother had in this man, it wouldn't take long for Trista to realize the closeness that she should be sharing with him.

Anything is possible in Amber's world. By merely renewing her overwhelming sense of belief while amplifying desires through fantasy, Jim truly could be Trista's biological father who happened to live down the street and even be part of mother and daughter's life! Can you finally see that Amber was not being so unreasonable with Trista's biological father? The odds were stacked up against Amber, yet somehow she was managing to work everything out in her favor.

* * *

Now what married man in his right mind would allow a strange woman to consecrate him as the biological father of her child, and even aim towards making him her new husband? I'm sure you'll figure a few things out about Jim as this story unfolds. But let me just introduce you to one of the many bizarre facets of Jim's personality.

On any given day of the week a cable company utility bucket truck can be seen driving the roads and highways of Mapleview. A bucket truck, in case you are unaware, is a utility vehicle with bucket ladder that typically rises to utility lines or the top of buildings for accessing equipment. In that utility bucket truck drives a man named Ivan Trovskov. With a name like Ivan Trovskov, one might immediately assume the Mapleview Cable technician to be an immigrant. But he isn't. In fact, his name isn't Ivan Trovskov! His name is Jim—the same Jim who is married and being consecrated as Trista's biological father. He was born and raised in Mapleview; lived there his entire life. Ivan Trovskov is merely a secret persona that Jim created to help accept the fact that he was going bald.

It all happened so suddenly one night while watching TV with his wife, Kimberly. Suddenly, a hair re-growth product commercial appeared with an announcer who wore a grave expression. The camera slowly zoomed in on the announcer's face as he continued to speak, "You might think that the solution to going bald is to simply accept it. Many men lose their hair as they get older, and they seem fine. Why should you be so concerned? Well before you convince yourself that it's nothing to worry about, turn to your wife or girlfriend and ask, 'Honey, will you still find me attractive when I'm bald?' You'd be surprised of the answer! Then call us."

In recent years, Jim certainly lost a lot of hair. There was once a time in his life when he had a full head of brown hair; usually worn wind-tousled and free-spirited. Now in an attempt to have something on his head, Jim had the exact, same hair style as Bert from Sesame Street! In fact, Jim's hair was worse than Bert's. Bert had way more hair on his head. Jim had only a thumbprint's diameter of surviving strands remaining on top. Really it should have been simply trimmed off. But Jim held onto the notion that something adding color on top was better than nothing.

A split second after the commercial, Jim turned to his wife, "Well, will you still find me attractive when I'm bald?"

And how should a supportive wife respond to such a question? Kimberly smirked and then released an uncontrollable giggle. "I'm sorry, but I won't find you the least bit attractive when you go bald!"

"What?"

"Well don't take it personal! I just don't like bald men!" Then Kimberly softened her voice to ensure her husband, "I'll still love you, though. Isn't that all that matters?" Kimberly wasn't concerned with the possibility of Jim calling the number on the screen. It wasn't in the household budget to fund hair re-growth products. And quite frankly, she didn't want Jim to grow more hair. With the couple now in their late 30s, Kimberly needed something to break down Jim's confidence. Although quite beautiful herself, Kimberly struggled with the notion of nearly turning 40. It was comforting for her to know that Jim worried about his appearance in age. Baldness was apparently a sore spot for him. No man wants to hear that he will soon be unattractive. If Jim believed himself to be ugly, then Kimberly had no need to worry of her husband going astray.

Really Kimberly should have simply reassured her husband that he would look fine. For the following morning Jim carefully studied himself in the mirror with a desperate need to reinvent himself. It wasn't Jim's fault that he was losing his hair. Now older and later in life, Jim realized that he had the northern European thing going on. Why, he looked like… like… (A sudden name popped into Jim's head)… Ivan Trovskov! It was best to play the part.

This revelation happened on a Saturday morning. He soon visited the barber and requested that his head be nearly shaved. Afterwards, only a thumbprint receding patch of stubbles sat on his head, outlined by just enough microscopic fur on the sides and the back of his head to give color.

After his shocking alteration in appearance, Jim made a quick trip to the clothing store for some new winter apparel. It was only autumn; but the cold, arctic air would soon rip through the land. Ivan Trovskov needed to work outdoors through those harsh months. That's why he picked out an assortment of baggy, wool pants; various colors ranging from khaki-green to reddish-brown, even checkered-violet. To compliment his collection of wool pants; a large, double-breasted, black, wool coat was added to the shopping cart. For his nearly-shaven head, Ivan Trovskov selected a furry, Russian-style hat. To finish his winter wardrobe, Ivan also visited the shoe department and found a pair of shiny, black, leather boots that nearly went up to his knees! Oh, and he also threw a couple pairs of suspenders in the cart!

Returning from his Saturday morning of personal errands, Jim stormed into the bedroom while his wife vacuumed in the family room. In the bedroom he changed into one of his nifty, new Ivan Trovskov outfits. Some moments later, Kimberly entered the bedroom to see what her husband purchased.

If her husband's nearly shaven head wasn't shocking enough, Kimberly froze in disbelief at the sight of Jim's outfit for the day. He stood in front of the full-length, closet-door mirror; admiring the way he looked in a pair of khaki-green wool pants that were tucked into a pair of shiny, black boots; and wearing a black, double-breasted, wool coat. A closer look revealed that Jim wore only a Fruit-of-the-Loom, white undershirt. For now, the wool coat covered his suspenders.

Had Jim lost his mind? Kimberly was quick to ask, "Jim, why… *are you dressed… like a **polock**?*"

"What?"

"Why, Jim? Why?"

"What are you talking about? I had to pick up some winter clothes. It gets cold out there." Jim reached into the clothing store bag; pulled out the furry, Russian-style hat and placed it on his head.

Kimberly was floored. "Oh my gosh! No! No, you are not wearing that!"

Jim only smiled and tucked the furry hat in his coat pocket before hanging the coat in the closet. That's when Kimberly saw the suspenders over her husband's white, Fruit-of-the-Loom undershirt.

"Jim, take that stuff off! You look like a polock who doesn't know how to dress!"

"What are you talking about? I look fine!" Jim looked in the mirror and smiled at himself while rubbing his clean, nearly-shaven head. "I look like Ivan Trovskov." It was better than looking like Bert from Sesame Street!

For the rest of the weekend, Jim lounged around the house in his baggy, wool pants that were tucked into black, shiny boots and a white, Fruit-of-the-Loom undershirt with suspenders. And while going to church on Sunday, he was sure to sport the brand, new, double-breasted wool coat with his newly-acquired ensemble.

So if there ever comes a time when your husband asks if he'll look attractive upon going bald, it's best to reassure him that he will. Poor Kimberly could only wonder of how long she would have to live with Ivan Trovskov.

Chapter 1

It was 2am Saturday morning in October, 2009—Halloween nearly one week away. Amber lay in bed with her stewing suspicions and growing frustration. For you see, Trista's father had yet to come home. Surely he was with that other woman, or was out running wild like he did in early years. But it would take time to fully win him back. Amber understood this. She was fortunate enough to even have the man in her life.

Suddenly, the Blackberry on her nightstand silently buzzed. It was a text message from Trista's father. "I'm here. Want to let me in?"

Wishing not to clue Trista in of the intimacy shared with him, Amber instructed Trista's father to merely text when coming over late in the evening. She would go to the back door and quietly let him in.

Amber softly walked the darkened hallway, into the kitchen and over to the back door. In recent times she was sure to spray the door hinges with WD-40 lubricant aerosol to prevent any harsh squeaks from waking Trista.

There Trista's father stood, appearing delighted to see Amber. But Amber was smart. She knew he was only acting and attempting to cover where he had been.

"Hey…" greeted Amber.

"Hey…" whispered and smiled Trista's father in return.

The door was quietly closed behind them and the man was carefully escorted into the bedroom where Amber shut the door to prevent Trista from hearing.

Amber was already in her sleepwear. As for Trista's father, he removed his coat and stripped down to his boxers before slipping under the covers. Immediately, Amber pulled close and laid her head at his breast.

The closeness and cuddling removed any and all frustration and doubt for Amber. This is what she wanted. This is the way it was supposed to be. The man she originally loved who helped create a child was to lay in bed with her. The house was to be a home, alive with the activities of a loving family. It would soon all materialize for Amber.

Trista's father softly combed his fingers through Amber's hair. He made it feel so real, like he loved her and had always been a part of her life. In fact, maybe he really did love her; just not realizing how much at the moment.

Don't think for one second that this would be a moment of careless, casual sex between friends. It was careless sex that resulted in losing Trista's father for so many years. There are plenty of ways to love without sex. For now, the safest means of exchanging affection was allowed. It didn't take long for Amber and Trista's father to engage in nothing less than a steamy, late-night make out session. This lasted for a little over an hour until the flames settled down and both could lay close for some dreamy cuddling.

Unfortunately, however, Trista's father might have to wake up before dawn upon an emergency call for his job. And Amber might not see him for a number of hours... even days. Still, for the moment, the man she loved lay beside her, hopefully receiving Amber's dreams through some romantic, in-bed-together telepathic connection.

Some men deserve every bit of misfortune that comes their way. As luck would have it, by half-past four on Saturday morning, the outdated palm pilot styled phone buzzed a couple times on the nightstand next to Jim's side of the bed. It awoke both him and Amber.

Amber softly exhaled and then whispered, "Another outage?"

Jim whispered in return, "Yeah, it would appear that way. Time to go to work."

Amber watched as the man she loved get dressed and then look over to her. The look was a sign that he would surely return, not abandon her like years ago.

"Well, give me a call or text me." whispered Amber.

"I will. Sorry I've got to go."

How badly Amber wished to make her feelings known and receive some affirmation that Trista's father felt the same. Sometimes the words nearly slipped out, "I love you." But Amber bit her tongue and waited for the day when the two could finally speak this.

Yes, some men truly deserve every bit of misfortune. And perhaps it's men like this who fall prey to an evil witch's spells. Now free from Amber's home and stepping out into the crisp, autumn air; Jim walked some distance down the street and stepped back into his utility cable truck. Jim was the lineman technician for Mapleview Cable. It wasn't a rare occurrence for him to be awoken in the dead of night to answer some outage or failure in the town's cable infrastructure. And this was the excuse Jim used to escape the confines of his own home where his wife, Kimberly, lay beside him and two children slept down the hall. In fact, his outdated palm pilot styled phone awoke him shortly before two in the morning.

At that moment; his wife, Kimberly, asked the same question Amber did over two hours later. "Another outage?"

And just like he would do with Amber two hours later, Jim whispered, "Yeah, it would appear that way. Time to go to work."

Driving only seven doors down in his Mapleview Cable utility truck, Jim pulled into his own driveway and crept back into the house—as if not to awaken his wife Kimberly. He would be safe once in the shower where any scent of Amber could be washed away.

Chapter 2

In the year 2009, six years after Amber savagely murdered Linsey, Halloween fell on a Saturday. There is nothing significant of Halloween being held on a Saturday. It is only mentioned so that you can use it as reference. But this particular Saturday morning in 2009 was exactly one week before the holiday, and exactly one week since Mary had the small party in the family mausoleum while her husband, Daren, was away on business.

Married just over one year, both Mary and Daren lived in the large, historic Trivelli house which is one of the oldest homes in Mapleview. The home had been passed down in Mary's family throughout the generations since the early 1830s. The residence sits on a private section of forest near the Hidden Lake Forest Preserve. One must travel uphill on a half-block driveway to get to the historical house. The house overlooks the actual lake that is in Hidden Lake Forest Preserve, and has become an icon to residents of Mapleview who gaze up to the old house on the hill.

Mary started off her Saturday morning in 2009 by brewing a fresh pot of coffee. With Daren still sleeping upstairs, she sat before the computer in search of an awesome fajita recipe that was seen earlier in the week. Muffin the Yorkshire terrier rolled around on the floor near Mary's feet.

But what was this? Every time Mary pressed the Internet Explorer icon, the unfriendly message, "Internet Explorer cannot display the webpage." appeared. Mary is certainly no expert with matters pertaining to computers. She knows how to get around—browse sites, compose emails and create simple documents if needed. But the frustrating message indicated a problem. It even included a link that said, "More information". When clicked, it was more of a list of problems to check, sort of a troubleshooting guide. But the only two items that Mary could recognize were loss of internet connectivity and the website being unavailable. To isolate the problem, she manually typed in the address for Yahoo and Facebook just to verify the problem wasn't limited to her homepage. And to Mary's dismay, the unfriendly message, "Internet Explorer cannot display the webpage." appeared.

How unfortunate! Mary hoped to locate the fajita marinade recipe online and mix the ingredients so the chicken could absorb the flavors throughout the day. Hopefully the problem would be resolved in an hour.

After pouring a cup of coffee, Mary sat down on the sofa before the TV. But what was this? Upon pressing the power button on the remote, the TV displayed an unfriendly message. "No signal available. Check antenna."

Mary's Internet and Cable were both provided by the Mapleview Cable Company. With TV and Internet down, it certainly didn't require a technology guru to determine that the cable company was having problems. Hopefully it would be resolved in an hour or so.

Autumn comes early in Mapleview which means that a morning in October can be quite chilly. There was no way Mary would sit outside on the deck to enjoy her morning cup of coffee. With events not in her favor, she opted to go back upstairs for her morning shower.

A half hour later, Mary completed her shower and entered the master bedroom where Daren stirred awake. She greeted, "Good morning."

"Hey, good morning."

Then she informed her husband, "The cable is out."

Daren stretched before sitting up. "What?"

"We have no Internet and no TV."

Seeing his wife wrapped up in nothing but a large towel, Daren wasn't the least bit worried about cable. "Well that's okay. Why don't you come back to bed? I need a little help getting rid of something—if you know what I mean. Besides, we can work on that baby some more." Married just over a year, they had yet to conceive a child. How Mary wished for that exciting moment of learning that she was pregnant.

But there was busy work to be done on that Saturday. "No, not this morning. We've got to clean the cellar, remember?"

Sorting through old boxes, tools and junk wasn't exactly Daren's favorite Saturday activity. But he agreed to help Mary earlier that week. "Oh yeah, that's right. I guess I'll get up. I'll call the cable company, first."

It would be three hours later when a service technician finally arrived to the Trivelli house. As far as Mary's plans for awesome fajitas, she had a backup.

Sunday was to be slow-cooked meatballs and Italian sausage. Mary simply reversed the meals for the weekend by making Sunday's meal for Saturday. She rolled out the meatballs, soon to be browned and then added to the large crock pot. And it was probably best that meatballs and sausage were made. As Mary would later discover that afternoon, marinating meat in bowl on that particular day would have been a very, bad idea!

* * *

Traveling northbound on Mapleview Road, Ivan Trovskov (Jim) crossed the border from downtown Mapleview into the older, historic section in his Mapleview Cable bucket truck. Ivan Trovskov was en route to the legendary Trivelli house; owner called that morning because of loss of service. Now only a couple blocks from the inclined driveway to the historic Trivelli house, Ivan pulled out his outdated palm-pilot-styled phone with an alert to a text message.

The text message was from Amber. "Hello? Were you ever going to get back to me?"

Such is the cost of having a mistress. Many times a mistress seems to forget that a man must rank his family members in order of importance to keep his priorities straight. The wife is on top of the pyramid, followed by the kids, followed by the mistress. Jim was a family man with a demanding career. He didn't mean to leave Amber out in the distance throughout the week. But what did she expect? Amber was a mistress! From her behavior, it could have easily been concluded that she expected Jim to leave his wife and kids to come live with her—maybe even marry her!

It was probably time for a new mistress. A married one would be a better option. But Jim had yet to receive the ultimate prize in bed. It would have killed him to know that he broke up with Amber just before she fully surrendered!

Now only a hundred feet away from the driveway of the historic Trivelli house, Jim completed his text message, "Sorry... busy morning... let me finish this service call & get back to you."

On this Saturday, one week before Halloween, Jim had been acting out this unusual persona of Ivan Trovskov for nearly three weeks. Amber never took much notice of it. I suppose she was so blind in love with the man that she overlooked his sudden, unusual appearance. And Really, Ivan Trovskov was not a polock as Kimberly suggested. Ivan originated from some ambiguous location in northern Europe, maybe Scandinavia or perhaps even Russia. It all depended on how Jim felt for the day.

By 11:30, a bucket truck with the words, Mapleview Cable pulled into the Trivelli driveway. Daren immediately went out to greet the service technician.

One peculiar habit of Daren's is to walk around with a ridiculously-enormous wad of money in his front pocket. There are many occasions in which he pulls this wad out and flashes it before a stranger's face while pretending to count the money. A few 100s, a couple dozen 20s, a dozen 10s and a handful of 5s and 1s certainly looks impressive. Although not bad-looking with a nice physique, Daren often flashes money in front of beautiful women, believing it makes him all-the-more-desirable.

Pulling out his enormous wad of cash and counting it while approaching the cable man surely delivered a subconscious message. For you see, although the service technician was older than Daren with only a shaven, brown, receding patch of hair; he had a large, muscular physique with handsome, rugged face. Jim was a working man, and Daren felt that Jim might have appeared more desirable to Mary. Insecurities made it necessary for Daren to establish the relationship with the cable man. Flashing the wad of cash said, "Okay; I'm the one with money, and I'm the one who has beautiful Mary as my wife."

Jim was the one who spoke first, "Hi, Mapleview Cable. I understand your Internet and TV are out?"

Finally close to the cable man and turning his attention away from the wad of money, Daren had a chance to take note of the peculiar style of clothing worn by the representative of Mapleview Cable. The temperature for the day had gotten warmer in Mapleview as it was approaching noon. As a result Ivan left his double-breasted, wool coat in the truck so that he wore only a pair of checkered-violet, baggy, wool pants that had been tucked into his black, shiny boots; and a white, Fruit-of-the-Loom undershirt with suspenders strapped over his shoulders.

Was this the sort of people that Mapleview Cable sent to customers' homes? The cable man dressed like an overgrown elf on drugs, or perhaps an immigrant who hadn't been educated on American style of clothing. Daren was quick to reply, nearly demanding an explanation. "Yeah, my wife says the cable is out! What's going on? You people have an outage or something?"

Ivan Trovskov only smiled to himself. He already resolved the problem and quickly answered, "Yeah, there was a blown amp up the road. I replaced it about ten minutes ago. You should be fine. Go in the house and see if your cable and Internet are back."

Receiving orders from the cable man didn't sit well with Daren. He was about to ask if personally checking the customer's TV and Internet was part of the job. But then that would have invited a possibility of the lowlife cable man checking out beautiful Mary. How Daren despised it when other men gawked at his wife. And what if Mary liked the cable man?

Reluctantly, Daren walked into the house and yelled out, "Mary? Mary!"

Muffin the Yorkshire terrier began to bark.

Mary was in the kitchen and called out, "What?"

"Go see if the TV and Internet are working. And hurry up!"

Mary was in the middle of flipping the Italian sausage in the frying pan. This was a bit of an inconvenience. She called out, "Is there any reason why you can't do it?"

This only added to Daren's stress. "Just do what I tell you!" It was imperative that someone obeyed him at that moment!

Poor Mary scampered over to the TV with Muffin excitedly barking behind her. She pressed the power button on the remote. Sure enough, cable had been restored. Then she dashed over to the computer and clicked the Internet Explorer icon. The familiar homepage opened on the screen. "It works!"

At least Daren could get rid of the strange cable man who saw it fit to order the customer around. Satisfied that all was well, Daren stepped out and remained near the house. "Okay, everything is fine now! Thanks!"

"You're good-to-go, now?"

"Yup!"

Ivan Trovskov extended a friendly wave and farewell. "Alright! Now you'll be all set for tomorrow's game! Have a great weekend!"

And that was the moment when two unrelated paths had crossed. It was the moment when imaginary hands of a clock might have reached 12:00am. The seconds began ticking away, counting down another mysterious disappearance in the town of Mapleview.

Chapter 3

Jim's work day unofficially ended shortly after twelve o'clock, noon, He hoped that the remainder of the weekend would be uneventful. On salary and given the responsibility of overseeing the vast cable infrastructure of Mapleview and Sillmac; in reality, Jim worked 24 hours a day, seven days a week. But with an ability to remotely access the network by computer, Jim could relax and work at home during weekends and off-hours, monitoring cable traffic and predicting possible problems before they arise.

And this is what Jim did shortly after greeting his wife upon returning home. "Hey, what's for dinner tonight?" he asked.

"I don't know. Do you want to go out for dinner?"

"Sure, what do you have in mind?"

"How about Big Boy's Beef and Ribs?"

It sounded like a great idea to Jim.

So careless and cruel-hearted, Jim neglected to text or call his needy mistress as promised. Instead, he simply strolled into the den where a portion had been converted into an office. He sat at the desk and logged into the cable network which soon provided an elaborate block diagram of every amplifier, transceiver, filter, fiber optic cable, utility boxes that fed customers houses—everything throughout Mapleview and Sillmac. No red flags or red warnings displayed on the dialog screen, but there was a mild "yellow caution" provided. At one of the apartment complexes in Mapleview, there was a signal leakage at a utility box.

Jim sighed, "Oh, come-on! Can't those installers make the fittings tight enough? It's probably Joe..." But Jim wasn't going to raise an issue if a leakage was caused by an installer. Jim had the reputation of company screw-up many years ago, and wasn't going to reciprocate that to someone new. Instead, he would visit the utility box on Monday and fix it himself.

For the rest of the afternoon, Jim sat on the sofa with his wife, painfully watching episodes of Bridezillas and Say Yes to the Dress. Both he and Kimberly agreed that Saturday she would hold the remote so that Jim could enjoy the game on Sunday.

Jim and Kimberly's 9-year-old son, Collin, played at his friend's house across the street. Their fourteen-year-old daughter, April, practiced her viola in her bedroom. A viola, in case you don't know, is a bowed, stringed musical instrument between the violin and cello that produces mid-tones. Now a freshman in high school, April was in orchestra and preparing for a concert next Thursday.

* * *

But things weren't so boring an uneventful back at the historic Trivelli house. With the cable problem resolved and dinner stewing in the slow cooker, Mary and Daren finished their lunch on that Saturday in October. While scraping the crumbs from her plate into the garbage, Mary announced, "Well, I suppose we should start on the cellar."

Again, this wasn't exactly an activity that Daren looked forward to. Playfully he responded, "Okay, do we have to?"

But it wasn't playful or a joke in Mary's eyes. "Yes, Daren! Come-on, it won't take long. I mostly want to throw out all those old canned goods and sort through some boxes in the tool room."

Shortly after purchasing the Trivelli house over a year ago, Mary vowed to throw away all the junk that had been stored in that cellar for many decades. But one weekend after another passed, and Mary never got around to it. The cellar weighed increasingly heavy on Mary's conscience, causing guilt and all those unsettled feelings brought on by procrastination. It was imperative that she kept her promise to herself and finally clear out all that junk.

If you've ever been in a basement of an old home, it's unlike the ones we see in modern dwellings. And really the basement of Mary's historic dream-home was not a basement at all. It was a cellar that provided just enough headroom to walk around in and seemed to be made for storage only. The floor was a collection of large, flat rocks joined together with cement. Although a crudely-finished area, the cellar did have two rooms that were past the cistern. One of those rooms held all the tools—many of them antique—that had been collected since the house was first built. The other room contained numerous shelves of canned goods that were probably many decades old.

Mary had no intention of throwing out any of the tools. Again, many of them were antique. The elaborate collection of newer ones was certainly a convenience to have during a home project. But there were dusty, old, stacked boxes lying on the floor along with what appeared to be old pictures at the side of the work bench. And being that the tool room was the first one past the cistern, Mary decided to tackle it first.

Immediately, Mary walked over to the side of the bench where some half dozen pictures in frames rested. Daren was more interested in going through the large tool chest and admiring his collection that was inherited through marriage.

Suddenly, Mary exclaimed, "Oh my gosh!"

Something obviously startled Mary, so Daren quickly looked over. "What? What is it?"

All Mary could do was repeat herself. "Oh my gosh!"

Now Daren was curious. From what he could see, Mary held a framed picture while exhibiting a baffled expression. When finally near, all Daren could see was a portrait of the upstairs piano with vase on top. Seated at the piano was a man dressed in a suit. He commented on the picture, "Probably just an old picture that hung upstairs at one time or another. I mean this house is old. People used to do that back then…"

Mary quickly interrupted, "Daren, that's you! That's you sitting on the piano bench!"

Daren further studied the picture. "Well what do you know about that? It does slightly resemble me. It's sort of a vague representation, but what a coincidence." He pulled the portrait from Mary's hands and held it up against the wall. "I like it. Why don't we hang this upstairs near the piano?"

Mary yanked the picture back from her husband. "Daren, no! Do you see that vase on the piano? That's the vase!" She wanted no part of the portrait, not after the horror of what was discovered at the bottom of the vase.

Although disappointed that the portrait would be disposed of, Daren was empathetic to Mary's aversion. Soon he began sorting through the remaining portraits. There was a portrait of the historic Trivelli house as it would have appeared in original construction prior to the nearly 180 years of additions and renovations. It was only a small cottage, then.

But the remaining portraits were eerie and disturbing. One of them was nothing more than a dark hole filled with what appeared to be tormented spirits. There were two matching portraits. One illustrated an unclothed woman standing upright in a restrained position with a cloth sack over her head. Nearly all the flesh of her lower torso, thighs and legs had been removed so all that could be seen was muscle. A large lake of blood ran throughout the floor. The matching portrait told a further story as it detailed the face of a terribly-distraught woman under the cloth sack.

The final portrait threw Mary over the edge. It was the very tool room that she and Daren now stood in, distorted in color so that it radiated dark overtones. On some of the tools were splashes of blood. And then there were cloudy swirls that floated and stretched throughout the room which further gave it a paranormal effect. Mary could see everything in the portrait with such fine detail. The portrait even included a vague representation of her and Daren, sorting through the collection of portraits!

Poor Mary nearly passed out from overwhelming confusion and shock. She had no choice but to run out of the tool room and back upstairs. Startled at his wife's behavior, Daren trailed behind with the portrait still in his hands. "Mary? Mary? What's wrong?"

By the time he reached the main level, Mary stood near the kitchen counter in tears. She backed away in terror as Daren approached with the portrait.

"What's wrong with you?"

"Daren, please don't bring the painting over!"

"What? Why, what's wrong with it?" He glanced at the photo and could see nothing out of the ordinary, just an eerie representation of the tool room.

Nearly hysterical and in tears, Mary shouted, "It's us, Daren! Why are we in there?"

Again, Daren looked at the painting. "Us? I don't see anyone in this picture. It's just a bad painting of the tool room."

Did Mary's mind play tricks on her? Still frightened, she carefully approached the painting just to further examine the portrait and point out the two people who looked like her and Daren. But much to her confusion, there was no one in tool room.

Mary wiped her eyes and brushed her hair back. She sighed and appeared to calm down. "I saw us in the picture before."

"Alright, you know what? You were just freaking yourself out down there. You know what where going to do? I'll show you what we're going to do." Daren stormed out the sliding, glass door that led to the deck and threw the painting down to the middle of the yard. Then he stormed back into the house. "I'll show you what we're going to do with all that crap." He descended the stairs into the cellar and retrieved all the remaining disturbing portraits of the Trivelli house. Once upstairs he walked through the side door near the kitchen so that he was in the backyard instead of on the deck. Daren carried the stack of portraits over to the fire pit and threw them in. And of course he was sure to grab the portrait that had been thrown over the deck.

In the meantime, Mary stood silently on the deck, overlooking her husband's activities down below. She watched as he entered the garage and returned with a container of lighter fluid and matches. The portraits were saturated before Daren struck a match to ignite them. At the match's impact, the portraits burst into flames as the wooden frames crackled and the oil paint sizzled.

Daren quickly ascended the stairs to the deck and lightly rubbed his wife's back. "There, see? That's what we're going to do with that crap!"

Both husband and wife watched for about a minute as the flames roared and embers floated through the air before dying out. Then Mary made mention of something she recalled from her first weekend of living in the house. "You know something Daren; on the weekend that I moved back to Mapleview, I went out to lunch with Shelly (Mary's best friend). She said that Aunt Loraine had some artist renting the house from her. I bet those were her paintings."

"Well she was a real whack-job if you ask me—people being tortured and bleeding, a hole with ghosts in it." Daren made it all better for his wife. Nothing was going to disturb his precious Mary. But unbeknown to her and Daren, there was more waiting in the cellar!

After returning to the tool room, Mary and Daren opened each dusty, old box on the floor to examine the contents. There wasn't anything worth keeping; just a bunch of rusty nails and screws; grimy, old engine parts or an occasional bundle of magazines from the 1970s. Charged and wishing to make the remainder of the day pleasant for his wife, Daren eagerly carried the boxes up and out to the trash, sometimes carrying two or even three at a time.

Many decades of dust and filth were swept off the floor. Daren cleaned and organized his workbench that had been inherited through marriage. Now he had his own little workshop in the cellar.

Finished with the tool room, Mary and Daren turned their attention to the canned goods room. Immediately, Daren reached for an old can of spinach that could have easily been from the 1930s. He playfully asked Mary, "Need a vegetable for tonight?"

"Sure, let me know how it is."

Daren picked up a few more antique cans of vegetables. "I bet this stuff is worth money now. I mean these cans must be collectors' items."

Mary wanted nothing to do with saving antique canned vegetables in hopes of them being valuable. "Just throw them out!"

Then Daren suggested, "Maybe we can donate them to the church pantry."

"Sure; make some poor, old lady who doesn't know any better sick? Throw them out!"

Then Mary directed her attention to the oversized Mason jar of dark, oily liquid. It had sat there on the shelf ever since Mary could remember, and continued to look as nauseating as ever. Mary's face contorted to disgust, "Start with that jar, first. Get rid of it!"

Of course Daren was curious of the jar. "What's in there?"

"I don't know. Nobody knows. When we were kids; my brother, sister and I would come down here and dare one another to open it and drink whatever is in there."

"No one was ever bold enough to try?"

Mary shook her head, no.

"Well I want to see what's in there."

"No, Daren! Just throw it out!"

"Oh, come-on! It'll be fun! This is your lifelong mystery. Wouldn't you like to finally solve the riddle of what's in this jar?" Daren picked up the oversized jar from the shelf and realized how large and heavy the thing was. It must have been capable of holding 3 gallons of fluid with a top that could easily accommodate a volleyball to pass through!

"Daren, where are you going with that?" Mary nervously trailed behind.

"I just want to check it out."

In horror, Mary watched as Daren ascended the stairs with the oversized Mason jar. "No, Daren! Don't you dare open that thing in the kitchen!"

"I'm not going to open it. I just need some light so we can see what's inside." Once upstairs, he brought the jar over to the piano and gently set it down.

"Oh, real nice, Daren! Just scratch the antique piano with some old jar."

"It's not going to scratch anything! Would you rather this be on your kitchen counter? Here, let's put a blanket underneath." Daren walked over to the sofa and returned with an Afghan blanket. It was soon positioned under the over-sized Mason jar.

Really, calling it a Mason jar is a mistake for it didn't have the word Mason embossed across. Nor did it say Ball, Kerr or Atlas. It was simply an unmarked, glass jar. But had Daren and Mary known more of antique jars, they would have noticed the wax sealer lid. And there was something else that Daren took notice of now that the jar was upstairs in the light. "This jar is colored blue, Mary." Again, had Daren known more of antique jars, he would have noticed that the jar was actually a rare cobalt blue. Colored jars were popular in olden times as they restricted light from entering and possibly spoiling the food.

Daren looked closer at the inner contents. "There's something in here, some kind of organic material."

"It's probably some old, decomposed vegetables or something. Let's just throw it out, Daren."

But Daren insisted on further investigation. "No, no! Let me bring the light over here and get a closer look." There was an antique, reading floor lamp next to the piano with reflector shade that could bend to a desired angle. Daren pulled the lamp closer to the jar and then positioned the shade behind it before turning the lamp on. And once additional light had been provided, Daren grew all-the-more intrigued.

"Hey Mary… It looks like there's a face in the jar… Actually a head!"

Mary didn't appreciate humor at that moment. At least she believed Daren was only trying to be funny. "Daren, knock it off!" She brought her face close to the jar and took sight of the recognizable features of closed eyes… a nose… cheeks…lips… a chin… all surrounded by a cloud of thick hair that floated. It was most certainly the head of a woman in that jar, and it bore a terrible resemblance to Mary!

What else could Mary have done at that moment outside of raising her hand to her agape, trembling mouth? Terror filled her again; resulting in even worse trauma than the experienced hallucination on the painting. But scream-ing wasn't possible, thanks to overwhelming shock. Mary darted across the family room and to the outside deck where the twilight, chilled air restored a sense of physical awareness. Poor Mary was close to passing out in her mo-ment of terror.

Daren quickly joined Mary outside and embraced his wife. "Are you okay? Don't worry; I'll dispose of that."

"No, Daren! We have to call the police! You just don't throw out a dismembered head!" At that, Mary walked back into the house, trembling, yet fully prepared to deal with the situation.

As his wife reached for the phone, Daren called out from across the room. "Mary! Don't call 911! That's your Grandma Trivelli in there, murdered almost 200 years ago. The police already solved the case. Just call the non-emergency number. Have them pick up the jar and store it away as evidence or something."

Mary paused for a moment, considering the truth of Daren's suggestion. But exactly what was the non-emergency number for the Mapleview Police?

Fortunately, Daren had his Android-style smart phone in his pocket. It took no more than 10 seconds to search for the Mapleview police contact information so that he could click the hyperlinked number and hand the phone to his wife.

It was Officer Ralph, clerk of the Mapleview Police, who answered the call on that late, Saturday afternoon in October. Despite his lifelong ambition to fight crime, Officer Ralph worked the beat of traffic patrol early in his career until it was decided that the pudgy and good natured member of the police force was better suited for office duties. He immediately recalled Mary and the Trivelli house from the previous times Mapleview Police had visited the residence. Hearing of the new discovery had Officer Ralph very excited.

Just as many Saturday afternoons, Detective Tom Morehausen and his partner, Larry Copperwright, both sat in their offices doing nothing more than wait for suspicious activity that needed investigating. This particular weekend had been slow. One might think that both detectives would have stayed at home to enjoy their weekends. But for some reason, they found it necessary to hang out at the office. And it was best that Detective Tom had a slow Saturday. Already past the age of retirement, the veteran detective had gotten ill on Friday from the stomach flu or some food poisoning. Still feeling queasy, he wasn't capable of stomaching much at that moment.

With Mary still on the line, Officer Ralph excitedly burst into Detective Tom's office. "Detective Tom! I've got an interesting call for you!"

"Who is it Ralph?"

"It's that Mary from the Trivelli house! She says she found a huge Mason jar with a dismembered head in it!"

Detective Tom winced while rolling his eyes. "Good God!"

Overhearing mention of the Trivelli house, Detective Larry soon stepped into Detective Tom's office.

Officer Ralph continued. "She thinks it's that Trivelli woman who had been murdered back in the 1800s. I guess the husband put her head in a Mason jar, pickled it and then sealed it shut. It's still preserved!"

The very image in Detective Tom's mind nearly caused him to gag and upchuck. "Cool it, Ralph! I'm still shaking this bug!" He paused for a moment, "Alright, I'm not going over there to look at that! Didn't Mary's husband recently build a family mausoleum in the backyard?"

"That's right, he did." said Detective Larry.

"Alright, tell them to take that head and put it in one of the crypts of the mausoleum. Put that woman to rest. That's what a mausoleum is for, right? We don't need to go over there. I wrapped that case up last year."

Chapter 4

It was now five o'clock in the afternoon. Back at Jim's house, little Collin returned from his friend's house. See how uneventful and boring Jim's day was in comparison to Daren's?

Collin returning home served as a cue for the family to put on their jackets and head out to Big Boy's Beef and Ribs for dinner. For nearly 20 years, Big Boy's Beef and Ribs has served Mapleview and surrounding areas, offering the finest grilled menu items. Patrons return again and again for their favorite burgers, Italian beef or sausage sandwiches, grilled chicken, barbecued ribs and even steaks. If it's grilled meat you crave, then Big Boy's Beef and Ribs is the place to visit for lunch or dinner.

Suddenly, Jim's quiet Saturday wasn't so uneventful. While parading through the parking lot with his family up to the restaurant, Jim spotted and soon locked eyes with Amber through one of the windows! What was she doing there? How could she have possibly known that Jim and his family were to eat dinner that night at Big Boy's Beef and Ribs? It had to be coincidence! Trista sat at the same table across from Amber. And from the moment that Amber recognized Jim, she put on an expression that certainly conveyed her scorn. Apparently Amber was a little more than disappointed for being "blown off" for the afternoon.

This was not good! Could Jim suggest eating Saturday dinner at some other place? But why would he suddenly wish to eat elsewhere? It was best to hold his breath and play it by ear. Hopefully Amber would follow the proper rules of engagement for a situation like this.

All appeared to go according to expectation during the first several minutes in the restaurant. After ordering their meals at the counter, Jim and his family migrated towards the dining area. It was Jim's intention to sit somewhat near

Amber and her daughter's table as an indicator that he still cared. But then Kimberly softly urged, "Let's sit over here."

The seat Kimberly chose was near the entrance door. Being October, it would have brought with it chilled air as patrons entered and exited the establishment. Jim brought this to his wife's attention. "Are you sure? There's a better seat over there."

But "over there" was closer to that woman. Kimberly had a strong dislike and an irrational hatred towards the very person that Jim secretly shared a taboo relationship with. Again, she softly urged, "Let's just sit here, Jim. I don't want to sit over there. I don't like that woman. She reminds me of a witch."

Ah, but despite how softly Kimberly mentioned this, Amber overheard it! Jim could see it in Amber's eyes, the shock and resentment of such cruel name-calling. How could he have allowed Kimberly to speak that way about her?

Still, Jim remained loyal to his wife. Feeling it best to follow her wishes, Jim pulled out a chair and sat at the table of Kimberly's preference. April and Collin followed. Soon the large, plastic, white number-ticket had been inserted in the wire stand. This would help a waitress locate the appropriate table as the same number would be printed on the receipt.

And then Jim sat there, silently, watching the kids take sips from their sodas and chat about the happy highlights of their afternoon. Of course his mind and heart were racing with the presence of his mistress and her daughter in the restaurant. In the distance, Amber glared with her fierce eyes. Nobody called her a witch and got away with it. And no man was to treat her as second best, dust her off the shelf when needed and place her back at will.

It was coming! Amber's negative emotions began to spark and discharge into the air. What to do with them was a different matter. Surely they would soon be injected in some terrible fantasy and bring much misfortune to a happy, loving family.

* * *

Back at the Trivelli House, Mary had just handed the Android-style smart phone back to Daren and sighed. "The police say it's not necessary to come here."

"What?"

"I guess Detective Tom wants us to put Grandma Trivelli to rest and place her in one of the crypts of your mausoleum."

A look of near delight suddenly stretched across Daren's face. "Really? Sure, we can put Grandma Trivelli in the mausoleum. Do you want to come with and say your goodbye?"

Mary didn't see the new storage of Grandma Trivelli's dismembered head as a proper funeral and burial. The mausoleum was just a means of disposal. Aside from that, who knows how many more times a piece of Grandma Trivelli would surface in the future? "No, Daren!" Mary answered. "Just put her in there like the detective said."

Alone, Daren carried the heavy, oversized, cobalt-blue jar down the stairs of the wooden deck and across the backyard until reaching the entryway of the mausoleum. It was necessary to set the jar on the grass before reaching for the keys in his front pocket. Once the thick, iron doors had been unlocked and opened, he flipped the light switch inside. The building was just like any small, family mausoleum; except it lacked decaying occupants. A lightly-stained, wooden bench was mounted to the center floor; two lit sconces affixed to the rear-wall; and empty, closed crypts took up the sidewalls of the building. Grandma Trivelli was carried inside and temporarily placed on the wooden bench so Daren could open one of the empty crypts. But then curiosity overtook Daren. He never did get a chance to fully examine the face of Grandma Trivelli.

The word Grandma might bring to mind images of a decrepit, old woman. But Grandma Trivelli was murdered at a young age. In those days, it was common for people to marry at a young age—sometimes as young as sixteen-years-old. Grandma Trivelli had her first child, a daughter, at the age of eighteen. Being that this daughter was thirteen on the supposed night of the disappearance, Grandma Trivelli would have been thirty-one and still very young.

These facts were apparent to Daren as he held the heavy, oversized jar in front of the illuminated sconce. It provided enough light for him to see the young and beautiful face of Grandma Trivelli. She looked so much like his own Mary, sleeping soundly in the early morning light. Daren assumed her voice sounded just like Mary's as she most-likely made the same facial expressions or exhibited the same occasional, quirky behavior. What was wrong with Grandpa Trivelli? How could he have murdered this beautiful woman in such a brutal way?

Well she belonged to Daren, now. Grandpa Trivelli certainly didn't deserve this woman. Daren would care for her and give her the best crypt in the mausoleum, right next to his favorite one. Speaking of which, Daren set the jar back down on the bench and opened his favorite crypt that was closest to the door and on the left wall (left if entering the building). Inside was a cooler that contained partially thawed ice and about a dozen bottles of his favorite, imported beer. Working so hard that afternoon, Daren certainly deserved a cold one. Cracking open the family mausoleum and then cracking open a cold one was a favorite activity of Daren's since having the building constructed.

After taking a few guzzles from the bottle; he set the beer on the corner of the floor and opened the crypt that would soon be Grandma Trivelli's. The oversized, heavy cobalt-blue jar was set inside. Daren finished his beer while admiring the new addition to the family mausoleum. Then he closed and locked Grandma Trivelli's crypt.

Chapter 5

Sunday afternoon, Daren was called out on a sudden business trip. A customer service engineer would be visiting a hospital in Detroit on Monday, possibly Tuesday as well. If Daren accompanied the engineer during this visit, it might have provided an opportunity to establish a relationship with hospital management and hopefully sell medical equipment. It was an opportunity that Daren's manager wouldn't allow to slip by.

But Saturday was a bit traumatic for poor Mary. Concerned, Daren asked his wife, "Are you going to be okay while I'm gone?"

Mary reassured him, "I'll be fine. Grandma Trivelli is in the mausoleum, and you burned those creepy pictures. Besides, I'll be at work during the week."

Mary worked at her best friend, Shelly's, flower shop in Mapleview.

"And I'll have Muffin to keep me company at night. Isn't that right you little munchkin?" Mary briskly stroked the sides of the dog's face. It was interpreted as play which resulted in barking.

How Daren hated when "Rat Dog" barked!

Chapter 6

Amber had the potential to be one of those overly-emotional, temperamental women who softly approach a man while appearing bashful and battered; a real victim of love who sees the man before her as the knight in shining armor to rescue her. Such a woman claims that nobody understands her like that knight in shining armor. She could elevate a vulnerable man above a pedestal and make him feel like the center of the universe; read every aspect of his personality and delve into his life. Any man in this situation would feel as though he died and went to Heaven.

But a man best watch out for these women! Through time she demands more and more of his attention, revealing that she feels increasingly neglected. Soon nothing will make her happy. In the end she hates that knight in shining armor and blames him for every bit of unhappiness. A rats nest of an emotional wreck; she'll drain the very life out of a man, chew him up and spit him out before finished.

Fortunately for Jim, Amber was not this sort of woman! Amber had a certain fortitude along with a degree of self-respect that would nearly make it a sin to be one of those pathetic, wimpy, little women who know not what they want out of life. But Jim should have still watched out. Amber was worse than those emotional wrecks that drain the life out of a man. Where-as a needy woman has no ulterior motive—only wishes to find her idea of true love—Amber knows full well of the damage she can do. She's extremely intelligent and views the world around her slightly different than most women.

In Amber's world, wives are interesting creatures. Once upon a time, any given wife would have found such overwhelming happiness in the presence of her man; declaring how much she loved him and how happy he made her. As the years unfolded, that love lost its novelty and turned into more of a comfy love as both husband and wife tolerated small imperfections; laziness, messiness, grumpiness, moodiness—all spouses contain one or more of these negative characteristics.

Bring the marriage beyond ten years, any given wife has adopted the philosophy, "He drives me nuts! Sometimes I can't even stand him! But I still love my husband." In this stage, a wife will find any opportunity to find examples that demonstrate her disappointments of a husband are mutually shared by many others. Any mistake or shortcoming is highlighted and pointed out to the husband. Why would a wife do this; to destroy her husband and crush his confidence along with self perception? Surely a wife doesn't mean to do this intentionally. But Amber knew just how easy it was to give a man what he so badly needed. Pay attention if you happen to be a wife. It isn't sex that causes a man to stray. Amber knew this.

* * *

It was a Monday afternoon at about a quarter past four o'clock. Jim didn't have to go home until sometime after five. Being that Trista was at the library working on a group research paper with classmates, Jim had an opportunity to visit his mistress.

You might ask how it was possible for Jim to be only seven doors down from his home and remain unnoticeable by Kimberly. This was due to the fact that Amber's home was just past a major bend in the road. Kimberly could have stood outside and looked in the direction of Amber's house and not have seen Jim's Mapleview Cable bucket truck.

On this fine, autumn Monday; Amber served tea in her back screened-in patio. The storm windows were only slightly opened as the October air had a slight chill. Both Jim and Amber sat side-by-side, cuddling and drinking their tea on a small sofa with wooden coffee table a few feet away.

Amber was now the manager of the jewelry department at the Mapleview Department store. Mondays provided an opportunity to leave earlier in the afternoon in comparison to other days of the week.

Being an uneventful day for Amber, She casually stated, "It wasn't such bad day for me. How about you? How was your day?"

Ah, but it was not Jim's day at Mapleview Cable! In comparison to Amber, he had somewhat of a bad day. He now sat with the mistress, wearing his Ivan Trovskov attire; green, wool pants that were tucked into his black, shiny boots and a white, Fruit-of-the-Loom undershirt with suspenders stretched over his chest and shoulders. Small sprouts of patchy hair now growing through the top of his nearly bald head; Jim was lucky that Amber believed him to be Trista's biological father.

Jim set his teacup on the coffee table. "It was kind of a rough day for me. Last Friday I had to bring a fiberglass extension ladder over to a telephone pole in someone's backyard to do some work. In trying to locate the problem, I temporarily left the backyard to check signals at a utility box down the street. Finding the problem was actually at the utility box; I made the repair and signed off on the job. But I left the ladder at the pole in the other backyard!"

Amber exclaimed, "Oh no!"

Jim continued, "Yeah! The customer called the office this morning and complained. They said that their kids were climbing the ladder and suggested some-one could have gotten electrocuted. So I was totally reamed in the boss' office and given a write-up!"

Amber was nearly outraged. "That sucks! What the hell? You didn't mean to leave it there, it was only an accident."

"I know; that's what I kept telling them. But I guess they needed to punish someone."

Amber softly rubbed Jim's shoulder. "They should feel so lucky to have you working for them. Not only are you busting your ass out in the weather, but they use you as their fall guy or scapegoat." Then Amber put the secret icing on her little spell. "And I hope your wife appreciates everything you do each day out there. You work hard for your family."

Amber was right! Jim never looked at his existence in that light before. Maybe there was more to Amber than what Jim originally suspected. She was probably the best thing for him.

Sometime later, after a bit of autumn smooching on the sofa with Amber; Jim returned home with a boosted sense of self-worth and the belief that he had been wronged at work. He nearly floated in the door at home on cloud nine.

"Hey..." greeted Kimberly.

"Hi!" answered Jim in return.

"So how was your day?" asked Kimberly.

"Oh get this!" Jim repeated the same story that was told to Amber about leaving his fiberglass extension ladder at the telephone pole over the weekend. But he added more, his opinion that Mapleview Cable should have been so lucky to have him working there along with accusations that the company used him as a scapegoat. Amber convinced him of this and surely Kimberly believed him as well.

But what was this? Kimberly only stared at her husband in disbelief as he relayed the story in his ridiculous Ivan Trovskov attire. What was happening to her husband? "Jim?" Kimberly finally asked. "What the hell is wrong with you? You left a ladder on a telephone pole? Your boss is right! Some kid could have climbed that ladder and gotten electrocuted. I can't believe you don't see that."

"Oh come-on, Kimberly! It was just an accident! You're over-reacting like everyone else!"

Everyone else, that is, except for Amber...

"You know, Jim, this is exactly how you are. You forget something totally important that could have had serious consequences and you act like it's nothing! You're almost forty-years old! It's time to grow up! I hope you learned your lesson! You deserve that write-up. Hopefully you don't lose your job."

Amber's spell was going according to plan. Now in the kitchen with his wife and supper almost done—kids in the other rooms—Jim longed for the woman who truly understood him, Amber.

While sitting at the table with family and enjoying a home-cooked meal from a loving wife, Jim tried so desperately to replace Kimberly's face with Amber's. Such sadness; such sorrow. Jim's heart nearly ached to be back in the presence of Amber.

Chapter 7

The least favorite activity for Daren was to accompanying field service engineers to hospitals. He had greater success in building clientele and generating sales at conventions and expos. People who attended these were in the market for purchasing new equipment. But when making unsolicited visits to a hospital, prospects were often closed up to any introduction of new equipment. These people weren't in the market for laying out hundreds of thousands— even a couple million dollars for new equipment. Prospects who called out a field service engineer simply wanted the equipment serviced.

Daren could see the rejection in a prospect's eyes from the moment he was introduced by the engineer. And being introduced, not the first person to speak was already a problem for Daren. Daren was second in this situation and considered less important than the engineer. And as soon as the engineer would introduce Daren, "…and this is our sales consultant…" Daren could see the look of disappointment in their eyes and noticed how all attention was given back to the engineer.

In normal circumstances, Daren had the perfect solution to restore his confidence and gain respect from people. It was only necessary to reach into his pocket and pull out the enormous wad of money and count it before people's face. But when visiting a hospital with the intention to build clientele and hopefully a sale, what could be said of a man who flashes a bundle of money before people's faces? Would you have respect for such a salesperson? Might that person see a dollar sign over your head?

Officials at a hospital were polite, however. They played along with Daren and invited him to an available conference room to listen to his presentations— slide shows, catalogs and mentions of lifetime warranties on all biomedical equipment. But how he hated to see people doze off while speaking! Daren was simply not appreciated in that moment. The man was born to be a leader and to be at the very center of attention, not ignored and treated as a nuisance.

Such a day would be considered a "rough one" for Daren. Alone and on the road, it was easy for him to dress sharply, stick an enormous wad of money in his pocket and head down to the hotel bar in search of some woman who was alone for the night. His favorite sort of woman was a thirty-something blond, dressed in her business attire. If available, Daren would immediately pull out a thick wad of cash, "What are you drinking?"

Often such a woman's pheromones would suddenly spike as the scent of fresh bills flipped in the tall, dark stranger's hand. She would sit up and tightly close her legs together, "A strawberry daiquiri!"

Then Daren would yell out to the bar tender, "Get this lady another drink; and I'll have a martini!" Now with his foot in the door, it was easy to lay on the charm and intrigue while offering tales of traveling the globe, people met and activities experienced. Nine times out of ten, the woman of that evening would accompany Daren back to his hotel room. And that's how he repaired his bruised ego after a hard day on the road.

This is what Daren set out to do on his first night (Monday) in Detroit. Seven o'clock in the evening, he strolled into the hotel lounge, dressed in a business suit and flipping through a wad of money. Then he glanced at the surroundings and noticed that there were no "qualified" women to spend the evening with. Outside of a pair of used up business women in their late fifties who sat at a cocktail table, drinking wine and talking of real estate and financing; the lounge was empty. That was okay. Maybe Daren needed alone time that night.

When first dating Mary, Daren was a heavy drinker and nearly lost the woman he loved with his fits of anger and near-violent behavior. In an effort to keep Mary, he admitted that he could do without the booze in his life. But Daren wasn't about to jump on the wagon. As Daren saw it, he should still be able to enjoy a beer or some wine on occasions. Being alone without Mary, tonight, there was no reason not to drown his sorrows in a few bottles of beer. He approached the bar, dropped a ten dollar bill in the tip cup and then made his order. "Give me two MGDs." There was no reason to purchase his beer one at a time.

With his two bottles, Daren sat at a table in a dimly-lit corner and took a few gulps from his first beer. "Ah…" That was better. Daren needed that! How badly he wished to slam the remains of that bottle, but thought it best not to cause a scene.

It was after taking the first swig of the second bottle that Daren suddenly spoke out mentally to Grandma Trivelli. He never knew the woman, but somehow felt connected to her from the moment he noticed her beautiful face inside the oversized Mason jar. "See what I have to go through?" he asked.

The woman was dead; had been since the 1830s. There was no way she would answer Daren. And she certainly wouldn't be able to tell anyone of his confiding in her. Perhaps this was the sort of company that Daren needed for the evening.

Daren continued to mentally speak out to Grandma Trivelli. "I've sometimes hinted to Mary that I had a rough trip and all. She doesn't understand. And really, I don't want to bother her with the problems of my job. A wife shouldn't have to hear that stuff."

By his fourth beer, Daren set down the bottle and mentioned, "I don't even know your real name! I keep calling you Grandma Trivelli, but you sure as hell don't look like a grandma! From what I see, you're gorgeous…! So what was with your husband, anyway? The guy has a beautiful wife and decides to murder her!"

Halfway through Daren's 5th beer, an attractive woman entered the lounge, alone. While approaching the bar she took notice of Daren and casually smiled. But Daren wasn't interested. He found his woman for the night, someone who could do more than treat his bruised ego with a one night stand.

But did Grandma Trivelli understand this?

Daren suddenly changed the direction of conversation. "You know what gets me? I see these beautiful women come in these bars while I'm on the road—and I don't have to cover anything up to you—I have my way with them. But they don't really care who I am. All they see is a guy dressed up with pocketful of money. They don't care about my feelings or the things I think about through the day. But then you don't care about money, right? Well, you probably do care enough for me to bring home money to your granddaughter. But where you live, no one needs money. You don't find money sexy, right? You know people from the inside, right?"

Needless to say, Daren was close to drunk with his aimless rambling. And then he quieted down after his 5th beer, mood obviously changed as he began to feel sorry for himself. No one knew Daren for who he really was. He struggled to bring home money while tolerating disrespect from hospital personnel who weren't the least bit interested in his biomedical equipment. Daren was so lonely on the road and often looked for companionship in one night stands with strange women. But they only cared of the fact that he had money; never bothered to look beyond the surface.

Poor Daren; how badly he needed a hug! He had a beautiful wife at home who would have gladly received a late night call just to hear his voice and hear him vent the frustrations of his trip. But she didn't fully understand; at least this is how Daren believed it.

"See what I have to put up with?" In those 45 minutes alone with Grandma Trivelli, Daren had transformed into nothing more than a pathetic drunk who took pity on himself.

Daren could nearly feel Grandma Trivelli's comforting hand rest on his shoulder. "Why don't you go back up to your room and call it a night. You're tired, and you've had a long day."

* * *

By Wednesday afternoon, Daren returned home while Mary was still at work. Rat Dog filled the peace and quiet of the Trivelli house with his ferocious barking. The dog apparently had something wrong with its memory, as it required a couple days to get used to Daren's returned presence.

Barking and barking and barking; every time Daren stood up or walked to a different area of the house, Rat Dog would snarl and ferociously bark. And Mary wouldn't allow a de-barker collar, claiming that such a thing was cruelty to animals.

Daren finally had enough. He picked up his shoe and whipped it at the stupid dog, probably injuring it. "Shut the hell up!"

Rat Dog ran off and hid. It was best to wait for Momma to return home.

That blasted dog brought the very jerk out of Daren. He was so calm at his initial return home, but the dog put him on edge. "See what I have to put with?" he asked his newfound friend.

At least Grandma Trivelli understood.

As Mary worked at the flower shop throughout the week, it wasn't uncommon for her to make simpler meals like Shake-n-Bake chicken on weeknights.

On the Wednesday evening of Daren's return, both husband and wife enjoyed this meal with Uncle Ben's instant rice and microwaved, frozen vegetables.

Halfway through the meal, after all the updates of the past few days had been exchanged, Daren suddenly asked, "Hey, I was wondering; what was your Grandma Trivelli's first name?"

It was an unusual question for Mary; but under recent events an appropriate one. "Actually, her name was Mary. Why do you ask?"

"Well, I thought it would be nice to attach a nameplate to her crypt."

But it wouldn't be until Saturday, Halloween night, when Daren paid a visit to the family mausoleum!

Chapter 8

Amber's fresh spell placed on Jim early in the week must have surely worked; for he hadn't a second thought in taking his now more-than-mistress, Amber, to the yearly Mapleview Halloween carnival on Wednesday night. Announcing another inconvenient cable outage, Jim was able to leave his wife and kids at home for a little mid-week date with Amber. He simply picked her up in his Mapleview Cable bucket truck and drove downtown to the haunted festivities. And what woman wouldn't like to go for a ride in a cable truck?

No date at a carnival would be complete without a boat ride through the haunted tunnel of love. Sitting beside his Amber, floating in blood-red water amidst the flicker of black strobe lights, and overshadowed by shenanigans of creepy monster robots; Jim stole plenty of tongue-lashing kisses from her. A few times his fingertips grazed across Amber's cleavage.

Detective Tom was at the Mapleview Halloween carnival that night. In fact, he was always sure to visit local attractions to case out the crowds and take note of peculiar individuals. Just as he walked past the exit of the haunted tunnel of love, he spotted Jim and Amber with beaming smiles and stepping off the boat.

This was interesting for Detective Tom. It immediately brought his mind back to a cold, rainy day in April of that year when he pulled over to visit a small traffic accident already being investigated by two police officers. Detective Tom realized that the officers were rushing through the investigation, already deciding that the female driver simply didn't pay attention and plowed the front end of her Pontiac Grand Prix into a crossing motorists' Dodge Challenger at the intersection.

But on that day, Detective Tom couldn't help but notice the freshly-made aggressive tire track marks near the stop sign that suggested the assaulting vehicle to have torn off and deliberately plowed into the crossing motorist. Not every botched up investigation needs the supervision of Detective Tom. He simply made mental note of the people involved for future reference.

And there they were, the female driver of the assaulting Grand Prix and the unfortunate motorist whose beautiful Dodge Challenger had been plowed. Maybe the accident merely served as fate to bring two lovers together. But Detective Tom knows how people are. He knew that Jim wasn't supposed to be with Amber. A married man in the act of betrayal always sticks out in the crowd.

Time froze for a split second as Jim locked eyes with the seasoned Mapleview detective. From now on, Jim and Amber had better keep their noses clean. Detective Tom was watching and taking notes.

As far as Jim was concerned, the detective could have watched all he wanted. Jim wasn't committing a crime and certainly not about to. Plenty of men have mistresses. As-if Detective Tom never had one himself!

Some hot chocolate to warm up and a shared bag of cotton candy, Jim and Amber walked arm in arm just like lovers do. They rode the Ferris wheel while Jim teased Amber by rocking the cart. Amber isn't really afraid of heights, but playing the frightened little girl is all part of the seduction. And then they stopped at an attraction that anyone should visit while at the carnival. Kids and parents lined up for the carousel ride with animals possessing beautifully painted and carved faces that nearly came to life.

"Are you really going to ride the carousel?" Amber asked Jim while smiling.

"Oh yeah! You're never too old to ride a carousel!"

Amber laughed

As the line continued to move forward, Jim and Amber approached closer to the carousel. It provided Jim a better opportunity for a deeper look of the situation at hand. Not only did the faces on the animals look as-if to come to life, but they appeared so frightening, nearly evil.

A strange, old woman operated the ride. Long strands of ratted black and gray hair draped along her shoulders and back. The top of her head was terribly thinned out so that the scalp could be seen. Her dark eyes were surrounded by glassy-red pupils that could either suggest craziness or possibly drunkenness.

And she didn't just operate the carousel. The strange, old woman played a large keyboard that was apparently wired into the speakers. But the pitch of the keyboard sounded to be deliberately off tune. Although the lively organ music matched the dance of the animals, it had an overwhelming hint of being somewhat scary. In addition to playing this disturbing music; the strange, old woman danced from side to side while swaying her long strands of black and gray hair along her back and shoulders. She was clearly out of her mind!

If you've ever stood in line for a thrill ride such as the latest roller coaster, then surely you can recall the slight sense of anxiety before boarding. You might even laugh to yourself upon the secret reminder that there is nothing to be afraid of. Thousands of people had experienced that ride and nothing bad ever happened.

But Jim was suddenly terrified while waiting in line. Why wouldn't he be? The children screamed and cried while going up and down on the animals. The parents who stood nearby or rode with them exhibited extreme anxiety as-if there was something wrong.

"We're next. Are you excited?" asked Amber.

Jim could do this! It was only a carousel ride. "Let's do it!"

Amber straddled a midnight black horse with a dull gray saddle and stirrups. If one looked carefully enough, it would have been noticed that the horse's eyes matched the craziness of the old woman. Next to Amber, Jim sat on what appeared to be a sea dragon with golden gills on its neck, detailed scales along the body and a furious face that roared with sharp teeth and a tongue that lay out on the side.

Going around the carousel the first two times wasn't so bad. Amber giggled at Jim as he smiled in return. Then the organ music evolved into something eerie and haunting. It might have resembled some distorted piano piece by Tchaikovsky that could provoke sweet feelings of a love once known, long for-gotten; but suddenly remembered in a vague sense.

Why would the strange, old woman create those sounds, much less distort them to be eerie and haunted? And after the third time around, Jim suddenly realized that he knew the old woman from somewhere. She lived in town and worked at one of the small businesses that Jim couldn't quite remember. She must have been volunteering for the yearly carnival.

Apparently she noticed Jim as well! Deliberate eye contact with a stretched out face that nearly touched Jim was made by the strange, old woman each and every time he passed. It was as-if the ride was all for him! With each passing, she read him further and further; knowing that he wasn't supposed to be at the carnival and knowing that the woman with him should not have been near. Jim was the man that the crazy, old woman had been waiting for all along! After so many years, he finally arrived!

The music returned to being gay and lively with a twist of fright and of being off tune. The children on the ride began to cry out for their mommies. Finally, Jim understood this phenomenon. Invisible things were touching him. Sometimes they felt like bites or scratches. Out of the corner of his eye, Jim could see the center of the carousel ride that was decorated with nothing more than a mirror. For only split seconds at a time, Jim could see the hellish world being reflected of hideous animals that aggressively bit the children and parents with their large, sharp teeth. The creatures stood on their hind legs and then pounced their front hoofs on the guests, nearly crushing them. The lions swiped their enormous paws across the bloody chests and backs of unfortunate riders. Camels ripped the hair out of children's heads with their nasty mouths. Dragons cocked their evil, serpent heads back and then forced rage-full flames into the faces of people to be nearly cooked alive.

It was a splendid performance by the strange, old woman; and it was all done for Jim. Wouldn't you like to ride a carousel like that?

Chapter 9

Keep in mind that Amber's perception of events is slightly different from what you and I see. For one, we've gotten to know the lineman technician for Mapleview Cable as Jim. But Amber doesn't refer to this man as Jim. From what she understands, his name is Matt and he's Trista's biological father.

In Amber's mind, it was that woman who now lives with Jim who took Trista's father away so many years ago. She looks to be so friendly and such a good person. But looks can be deceiving. Never trust your fellow women! As Amber learned so many years ago, any one of them might see it fit to steal your man in a vulnerable moment of the relationship.

As far as Amber was concerned, Jim belonged to her! He was to live in Amber's house with her and Trista, finally get married and be the proper husband and father as originally hoped. He just didn't belong in that house down the street with those other people who Amber could have cared less about.

Next to Amber, the most important person in Jim's life should have been Trista. And on the night of the first high school orchestra concert of the year, Amber might have played a small part in ensuring that Trista looked her best. Now a junior in high school, sixteen-year-old Trista played the violin so exquisitely. That other daughter of Jim's who lived down the street played in the freshman orchestra. Again, Amber didn't care about her! It was Trista who was to come first.

"Why don't you let me put a little curl in your hair for tonight." suggested Amber to her daughter.

"It's only the first concert of the year, Mother!"

"Trista, you're a junior now. Take some pride in your appearance and stand out." Amber made sure that Trista's hair was done up so fine. And what was wrong with just a little extra makeup to help pull out some maturity in Trista's face? By next year, Trista would be a senior, soon to graduate high school and then off to college. All the years that Jim missed on account of his absence; seeing Trista so sophisticated and beautiful would surely coax his return to the family.

Did he tell that woman the truth, yet? Surely he must have broken the news to her. Surely he must have grown tired of all the deception and lies such as those spoken last night of another cable outage just for a few measly hours alone with the woman he belonged with. She might have pleaded some and maybe persuaded Jim to stay. Maybe this is why another night went by with his side of the bed cold and empty.

These are the things Amber wondered while sitting on the bleacher in the gymnasium of Mapleview Community High School. Trista sat with her violin near the front row of the orchestra with the rest of the kids who waited for the others to arrive. The concert would start in about fifteen minutes.

Just then, Jim and that woman with their two children walked through the entrance door. His other daughter went out towards the center of the gymnasium and took her seat some rows behind Trista. It's where she belonged, some distance near the back and obviously less important than Trista.

What was this? Jim only glanced over towards Amber while passing by and provided a quick, halfhearted smile before looking away. Apparently that woman had yet to be informed of the reality, for she showed no interest or made acknowledgement of Amber's presence. What the hell?

Jim was so far out of touch with reality that he referred to himself as Jim. In fact, he now thought of himself as Ivan Trovskov as he sat down in the bleacher some distance from Amber. As usual, he wore his ridiculous wool pants, shiny boots and double breasted black coat. It was warm in the gymnasium, so he removed his coat. It revealed the white undershirt with suspenders strapped over.

Kimberly was a bit embarrassed over her husband's appearance. "You know, Jim, couldn't you have worn something else for your daughter's concert; something other than those... those strange work clothes of yours? You look like a stupid polock on drugs right now!" Kimberly further examined her husband. "Why don't you un-tuck your pant legs from your boots and maybe put your coat back on?"

But Ivan Trovskov was proud of his fashionable attire. To demonstrate this, he lifted both his feet and loudly crashed them on the bleacher below in a means to stretch out and display his black, shiny boots.

Kimberly buried her face in her hands. "Oh Lord!"

Amber watched the scene play out from a distance. There apparently was some friction between Jim and the other woman. Maybe he was approaching the breakup from a different angle. Perhaps this explained his ridiculous choice of clothing in recent times.

Jim should have savored every bit of fun in those remaining minutes, for things were about to change. He would sense this as the gymnasium filled with more people and peculiar feelings of anxiety overcame him. These moments would become increasingly familiar in the upcoming months; irrational panic, feelings of disconnectedness, strange dreams and...

"Agh!" Jim placed his hand to his left eye.

"What? What's wrong?" asked Kimberly.

Jim removed his hand and looked around. "I'm fine now. All of the sudden I saw this exploding flash of light in the upper, left-hand corner of my eye." He pulled his face closer to Kimberly's. "Is my eye okay?"

"You're eye is fine, Jim. It was probably just a sudden ocular migraine."

Along with sudden waves of panic, disconnectedness and nightmares; Jim would have regular occurrences of unexplained flashes of light in his eye. And they would be followed by peculiar feelings or even flashbacks.

Suddenly, Jim's mind went back to a time when he was in grammar school and rode the bus to school. Pulling out of the flashback left him with a very, strange feeling; almost as-if everything was terribly wrong.

While evaluating his new frame of mind, the alarming flash of light in his eye and considering that perhaps he might have had a stroke; one of the officials from school approached the front of the orchestra. She announced, "Ladies and gentlemen, parents and family of our orchestra students; I want to welcome and thank you for coming out to our first concert of the year. And without anything further, please welcome the Mapleview Community High School orchestra teacher, Ms. Ekaterina Lutrova."

Unfortunately, Jim didn't hear the name spoken. He really should have paid closer attention. For no sooner had the name been announced, a dreadful sight approached the center of the gym as parents, teachers and students applauded. It was the mysterious woman who had operated the carousel the previous night!

To make the moment all the more frightening, before taking a bow towards the audience, the mysterious woman shifted her eyes some several bleachers in the audience, right directly towards Jim! She even smiled at him—smiled like she wanted something from him! It was completely unreal! What in the world did this woman want of Jim?

She turned around and tapped the baton on the podium. This cued the entire orchestra to raise their instruments and begin to perform.

A long note was executed to ensure that all instruments were in tune. And then the performance began.

Some years ago when April was in grammar school and began playing her viola, the early performances were mostly plucked out on string instead of using the bow. They were simple songs like Mary had a Little Lamb or Go Tell Aunt Rhody. Eventually the grammar school orchestra progressed to using the bow. Again, the songs were recognizable.

In recent times, April was playing pieces that were unrecognizable to Jim; probably classical pieces. Jim never had an appreciation for this style of music. But it wasn't necessary to recognize the portions of symphonies or movements. From what Jim could gather, the entire performance was just like the carousel ride—all for him. The music spoke to Jim, revealing a destiny that would soon be shared between him and the mysterious, crazy, old woman that conducted the orchestra.

Easily in her sixties with frazzled gray and dull black hairs along with a cracked, deathly face; the mysterious, crazy, old woman was intriguing Jim more and more. In fact she was beginning to appear attractive!

Sex with a woman of that age who looked like that? She certainly wasn't one of those anomalies such as a supermodel of that age who appears to be in her thirties. No, she definitely appeared old and battered from decades of life. But there was something about her, something that definitely intrigued and (at the same time) frightened Jim. Maybe it was her brilliant performance of conducting the orchestra. Maybe it was the theatrical display from the previous night.

Pieces would end, and the audience was inclined to applaud. But it would quickly die down as another piece whirled its way in. This woman was truly talented in the way she prepared her orchestra for that night. When the musicians finally lowered their instruments and the conductor faced the audience for a bow, it was apparent that the evening's performance had ended.

The entire audience got up from their seats for a standing ovation. And in that moment, the mysterious, crazy, old woman glanced up to lock eyes with Jim just before leaving. The final locking of eyes was the most damaging as it hexed Jim with a terrible love spell! It left him numb and confused for some moments after that. What in the world had transpired that evening? It was like a vivid dream. And the best part, April's orchestra teacher never said a word to the audience!

It wasn't until out in the parking lot that Jim began to come back to Earth. Kimberly's voice called out, "Jim, your car's over here?"

Oops! Jim was walking in some other direction as-if he forgot where the car was parked.

"Are you okay?" asked Kimberly.

"Yeah, I'm fine; just a little tired I guess."

Throughout the ride home Kimberly grew increasingly concerned of her husband. Jim continued to rave on about the performance.

"I mean, you kids were spectacular! I've never even seen a concert like that before."

Initially seen as a just a little "good job" pat on the back; it was soon obvious that Jim had been clearly affected by the performance a little more deeply than he should have been. And it was certainly embarrassing that he was the only one who stood up to whistle and clap while screaming bravo. Half the gymnasium quieted down in the middle of the applause while Jim acted this way.

Chapter 10

For most of us, Friday mornings usually bring with it a sense of energy that another weekend is finally here. This can be felt especially if the weekend involves a holiday. But Jim wasn't feeling Friday as much as should have. Dressed up in his Ivan Trovskov attire and in need of another radical haircut, he sat at the breakfast table already on his second cup of coffee.

"Did you take your blood pressure pill this morning?" asked Kimberly.

"As always." replied Jim.

"How about your blood pressure? Did you check your blood pressure?"

"Yes, it's 135/80… 60 beats per minute."

"I'm still calling the doctor to make you another appointment."

"Kimberly, I'm fine! I just didn't sleep very well last night."

Kimberly had the perfect solution to Jim's problem. "Well maybe it's all the coffee you drink."

"Two cups? Come-on!"

Jim usually slept fine on any given night. Perhaps it was the phenomenal music performance of last night that caused him to toss and turn in his sleep. The remembered music echoed in Jim's mind and seemed to cause a series of bizarre dreams.

Now it was the morning after a hard night of sleep. Groggy and feeling a bit of anxiety; it was almost as-if Jim craved another encounter with the mysterious, crazy, old woman.

Whatever it was that happened to Jim, Kimberly certainly recognized the sickly changes beginning to take place in her husband. But she was still assembling the pieces, trying to establish exactly when Jim began to fall apart. "You know, Jim; ever since you started wearing those ridiculous clothes you've been acting strange. What is going on with you, lately?"

"Ridiculous clothes? What are you talking about? It's going to be cold in Mapleview this year. I need my boots and my long, wool trench coat. I still haven't had a need to wear the furry, Russian hat yet."

Kimberly declared, "I'm burning that thing once I get a chance!"

* * *

It wasn't the doctor that Jim needed; more blood pressure pills or even a change of clothes. Rather, it was candy that Jim needed. He needed the sweet, poisonous candy of some wicked witch; the naughty sort of candy that might be handed out for trick-or-treat and made especially to corrupt the victim with more lies, deceptions, delusions and hallucinations. But it was nowhere to be found—all gone. And in all of Jim's sickness, he seemed to take great pleasure in his painful yearning for that forbidden candy.

Jim drove to work on Friday morning in his Mapleview Cable bucket truck. Then, like a kaleidoscope of serpentine dancing colors that appeared in the upper corner of his left eye, that wicked candy found him. It was so bad and poisonous. Although the mysterious, crazy, old woman was clearly a mature lady and far from Jim's reach, he wanted her so badly. Such is the truth with forbidden candy. If only Jim could have been there with her in earlier years. And who was he in those times? Certainly not someone she would have been interested in!

As Jim remembered from last night's concert; the mysterious, crazy, old woman had a long name, sort of like an immigrant. Could he even speak the same language as her? And he never lived the clichés and catch phrases of her day. How could he even share and relate to the same feelings towards certain events throughout time?

These sudden feelings all created a desire so powerful, a love that could be similar to wishing for someone who is beyond the grave. Jim was developing what could be described as a mystical fascination with the mysterious, crazy, old woman.

By the time Jim pulled into the parking lot of Mapleview Cable, he was experiencing a major crisis. All those intense feelings, the longing and desire to be near the mysterious woman, it transformed into a dreadful panic as Jim realized there was no way to find her!

Friday mornings are the weekly staff meetings at Mapleview Cable. All members of management, office staff, installers and technical personnel grouped in a large room that resembled a pow-wow as the chairs formed a large circle. The plant manager would sometimes address the group at the center of the room and introduce other individuals to discuss certain issues or new promotions. This week the upcoming sales promotion—Something to Be Thankful For—corresponded to the offering of free premium channels throughout Thanksgiving weekend. Halloween was tomorrow, but it was best to mention to new customers of the sales promotion.

Jim barely heard a word of the morning's meeting. He played and replayed in his mind every possible scenario to hopefully find the mysterious, crazy, old woman.

Ask his daughter, April, of her name? This might look suspicious. The best Jim could hope for would be to wait for the next concert.

But he couldn't wait! Time was running out! There was almost an urgency in finding her, now! What could he do?

Soon Jim learned that the universe most-often provides an answer. If you wish for something, it's given to you. And if you look for something, it's certainly found. Whether-or-not that applies to both good and bad things remains open to debate. But Jim thought he found his answer right across the room.

From the surface, 20-year-old Jeanine looked to be just another freaky Goth-chick. On this morning, she wore her usual dark clothing along with her unique style of makeup. But she wore something sparkly and reflective around her neck that Jim was most curious of.

Jeanine had been hired as the radio dispatcher and to assist with callers who inquired of their scheduled cable installs. After the meeting, Jim quietly approached Jeanine's work area and greeted her. "Hey, good morning."

"Hey…"

"I know this might sound strange, but I was wondering about that crystal you have around your neck. What is it?" Jim was referring to a medium-sized, pointed quartz crystal that was suspended by what appeared to be a suede necklace.

Jeanine so nonchalantly answered as-if everyone wore these things, "It's a quartz crystal."

"Quartz crystal? Didn't those go out in the 80s along with mall hair and leg warmers? And aren't you a little young to remember that new age stuff?"

Jeanine was suddenly annoyed. Is that all Jim had come to visit her for, to poke fun of something she valued? He was just like everyone else. She nearly raised her voice in reply, "Okay, maybe they were a big fad at one time or another, but they work! And people still use them for healing, focusing their thoughts or building up energy."

Jim patted Jeanine on the back in reassurance. "I was only teasing you. Where do you get those at, anyway?"

"Over at Sillmac Quartz and Candles."

It was all the information Jim needed. He certainly wasn't going to mention his need to track a woman of obsession through psychic means. And perhaps it was best to keep this intention a secret, even from someone working at Sillmac Quartz and Candles.

Rather than take off from the cable yard on that Friday morning to do some routine diagnostic tests, Jim drove right up Mapleview Road, past Hotlick's Sports Bar and Grill to where it connected to Route 4. From there he continued traveling until reaching Mapleview's neighboring town, Sillmac. Mapleview Cable served the neighboring community, and Jim had every right to be there. But how unusual it must have looked to see a cable utility truck park in front of the store at 8:30 in the morning!

If you've ever been in a bookstore that specializes in new age or witchcraft items, then you might have noticed how peculiar the people behind the counter are. Maybe your aura was off-color or noisy. Maybe everything about you said, "I don't really belong here!" Or maybe the person working there could read your thoughts and detect your ill intentions of using magick.

Quartz crystals? What possible good might have come out of selling a man like Jim an item like this? And his question, "What can you tell me about these things?" had the store clerk all the more mistrustful of him.

She calmly answered, "People use them for healing and energy. Quartz crystals are used extensively in meditation and are very useful for balancing chakras."

Jim didn't care about that new age stuff! He boldly asked, "What if I wanted to build up some psychic power? Can I do that?"

It was a peculiar question for the clerk. "Well, sometimes quartz crystals are used to amplify your thoughts. And thoughts can be measured as electromagnetic energy. I suppose it's very possible to develop psychic abilities with the use of quartz."

The suggestion of amplifying thoughts made Jim all the more interested. "Right! Let me ask you something. If I wanted to track someone down through psychic means, can the quartz crystal help me?"

The clerk was at a loss of words. Surely the customer had some bad intentions when it came to using quartz crystals. It was best to turn this matter over to a higher power, allow the universe to hopefully provide a gentle lesson. It might even help him grow spiritually. There was nothing left for the clerk to do except motion Jim to follow to the area of new age books. She picked out a large text book that instructed the proper use of quartz crystals. Every question Jim had could be answered through this book. It also went for the nice price of $39.99, raising a simple $5.00 sale of a rock to something greater!

Jim pulled out of the parking lot of Sillmac Quartz and Candles that morning while holding his new quartz crystal. Not more than a block down the road he was already forcing the image of the mysterious, crazy, old woman in his imagination. Surely, the thing would work.

Chapter 11

All day, Friday, Jim toyed with that quartz crystal. He mostly noticed what could be described as an invisible, optic pressure that radiated from the stone and could be felt near his forehead. When doing actual work, Jim kept the quartz crystal in his pocket, paying close attention to any new power that might have been felt. By afternoon, he parked at the wayside of Hidden Lake Forest Preserve and opened the text book. Surely he could have gone home early that Friday afternoon and monitored the cable network from his PC. But Jim wanted to read his new book, and Kimberly certainly couldn't be aware of his sudden interest in metaphysics.

There were all sorts of procedures and exercises prescribed in that book. It mentioned that cleaning the quartz crystal should be done on a regular basis by soaking the stone in a mixture of sea salt and fresh water for some period of time. Cleaning the crystal would remove any negative energy brought on by regular use that could reduce its efficacy.

In addition, grounding and purifying one's own energies is important. By laying flat on the Earth with the head pointed north, quartz stones could lay at or near each chakra. This exercise of grounding would eliminate any stagnant, harmful energies in the body and cleanse the chakras.

Meditational exercises could be done as well. By forming a 6-pointed star with 6 quartz crystals, a user could sit in the center with a larger "generator stone". By aiming the points of the crystals towards the body, the effect would be more of a personal, transcendental experience. Aim the points away if wishing to pray for or influence the outcome of another individual. When familiar with the 6-pointed star exercise, 6 more quartz crystals could be added to make a 12-pointed star. For the best effect, begin to associate each stone with an astrological sign. One should mentally run through the entire zodiac while performing the 12-pointed star exercise.

When sleeping, three quartz crystals should be used to form a triangle around the body. To avoid the stones from rolling off the mattress at night, one should construct or purchase wooden pedestals or columns that surround the bed. This sleeping in a triangle enables the open energies of the universe to work with the astral body.

Peculiar things begin to happen when using quartz crystals. Some people remember moments and fragments of past lives. If this happens, it's best to seek the consultation of a qualified past life regressionist. This therapy could take years to endure! One man learned that he was once part of a scientifically and technologically advanced, pre-Atlantean civilization that worked with extraterrestrial biologists in creating the first pair of Homo Sapiens!

Avoid making contact with metallic items when using quartz crystals. This won't damage the stone, but could short out the effects. It's better to rest quartz crystals on natural surfaces such as soil, wood, stone or even glass. If one feels that a quartz crystal has been "programmed" improperly and causing harm—yes, these stones can be mentally programmed—it's best to give them a sea salt bath or even bury them in the ground for a few days.

And above all, quartz crystals should only be used for the best and highest good!

Now you would think that while briefly scanning the text book and learning of these activities pertaining to quartz crystals, Jim would have decided against the use of such an item. But surprisingly, by the end of his afternoon reading, Jim was beginning to doubt any prior beliefs or preconceptions he had of quartz crystals. And outside of simply being bizarre, the prescribed exercises would have made Jim feel stupid—sitting in the middle of a 12 pointed star while thinking of the zodiac. Jim just wasn't into that sort of nonsense. Now skeptical, he tucked the crystal back in his front pocket and slipped the text book under his seat.

Suddenly, there was a knock on the drive-side window. A quick look over yielded a familiar but unhappy face. It was Amber, Jim's now forgotten mistress.

Jim rolled down the window. "Oh, hi! What brings you here?"

But Amber was the one asking the questions. "What are you doing?"

Amber couldn't be made known of Jim's new use of quartz crystals. "Just sitting here wrapping up paperwork for the day. What's up?"

"What do you mean what's up? I haven't heard from you since yesterday morning. I was waiting and waiting for you to call or text me—but nothing."

"Sorry about that. It's been a busy Friday."

There was much on Amber's mind. It could be seen in her face. She asked, "Do you have a minute? Can we talk?"

"Sure, here? You can sit in the passenger seat if you want."

Amber walked around the Mapleview Cable bucket truck. Hopefully no one would see her if passing the Hidden Lake Forest Preserve parking lot. And then she sat down.

Amber sighed, not wasting a minute with all those things on her mind. "Does she know?"

"My wife?" asked Jim.

Amber hated when Jim used that word and wished he would only refer to Kimberly as "she or her". Amber shook her head, yes.

"I haven't said anything. Why, are you on to something? Do you suspect that maybe she knows?"

Amber nodded in negation, "No, I just was wondering if you told her the truth about us."

"The truth about us?" Jim had to be very careful with his choice of words in that moment. "Amber, do you really think that I'm just going to suddenly tell my wife that I have something going on with the woman down the street? That would really screw up the marriage, you know?"

Amber frowned, "So everything is going fine between you and her, huh?"

"Yes, it is. Amber, what's this all about? Did you want to cool it for a while?"

Amber shook her head in negation and held back her tears while looking towards the floor. "I just need to know where you and I stand, that's all. I mean you come and go; I don't see you for a couple days. I'd think you could at least call or text me." Then Amber looked directly over at Jim. "I need to feel like I'm not being used. I just wish you could give me a little more commitment, that's all."

Jim sighed. "Alright, I know what you're saying. I can do that, but I need you to understand that I'm married and just can't come over all the time."

Amber hated any mention of him being married.

Jim continued. "I'll call you and text you and make more of an effort to see you throughout the week. Is it a deal?"

Amber nodded, seeming to be okay with the agreement. But she was quick with her farewell, "Give me a call, later." as she stepped out of the truck and over to her car. Without a kiss and only a quick drive away, she left Jim the impression that not all had been settled. There was still unfinished business.

But it was where Jim needed Amber for the moment; somewhat around but not too close. He wasn't ready to burn any bridges with the mistress as he needed to learn more about the mysterious, crazy, old woman. Could she be found and ultimately had?

* * *

Despite how skeptical Jim may have been that afternoon of quartz crystals; there was an all too powerful phenomenon that happened later that night. Maybe there was a speck of remaining hope that caused him to set the quartz crystal on his nightstand. It was small enough and able to hide behind Jim's alarm clock so Kimberly wouldn't see. And after turning out the lights and wishing goodnight to his sleepy wife, Jim lay there on his back with eyes closed.

15 minutes passed… a half hour. Perhaps he was trying too hard. Perhaps all Jim needed to do was roll over on his side and nod off to sleep. This worked for about twenty minutes. But then, suddenly, Jim was wide awake.

It was no problem. All he needed to do was roll over on his other side and doze off. Again, this worked, but was accompanied by a bizarre dream in which Jim sat in a meditational position before a black television screen, naked. Soon the face of an extra terrestrial appeared on the screen and telepathically communicated with Jim, mentioning that for years "they" had been attempting contact, but all efforts were ignored by him.

Jim awoke upon this nightmarish revelation. It was going to be a long night!

Another dream involved sitting in a confessional and having a bizarre discussion with a priest as he told the story, "I've been to Mars and was not impressed. I found green, foozy hairs in the hotel bed sheets. The water in the shower was never hotter than Lukewarm, and the room service was terribly slow… Before leaving Mars I picked up a crystal from the red, powdery surface. It holds some kind of energy. I can't figure it out, but when held in my left hand while facing east, I am able to hold my breath for over seven minutes."

After waking up from his second bizarre dream, Jim began to suspect that the quartz crystal was responsible for his restless night. But there remained some doubt in him as he simply turned over with intention of falling asleep. Suddenly, the terrifying thought of voices calling from the quartz crystal, "Let us out!" swayed Jim to remove the stone from his nightstand.

Something needed to be done to block the effects of the crystal. Jim was beginning to believe in the notion of "mentally programming" quartz rocks and felt he had probably done something inadvertently-negative while reading the blasted text book. Now in the kitchen at nearly one o'clock in the morning, he carefully set the quartz crystal in a small juice glass and covered it with a mound of sea salt. Fortunately, Kimberly was mindful of her family's health, and used sea salt for cooking in substitution of table salt. Next, Jim partially filled the glass with spring water from the cooler. Finally, the deprogramming quartz crystal was brought into the basement and hidden behind some boxes. He would decide what to do with the thing in the morning.

Chapter 12

Jim had gotten sidetracked; that was for certain. Originally wishing to use the quartz crystal for purposes of tracking the mysterious, crazy, old woman; the blasted text book had apparently flooded his brain with all sorts of occult non-sense. Jim stood in the kitchen on Halloween morning, drinking his first cup of coffee while speculating that the crystal had been "misprogrammed". Although doing more harm than good, the book was helpful to some degree. Simply the very understanding of programming, misprogramming and deprogramming a crystal had been made possible by the book. And there were exercises that Jim was growing most curious of, such as sitting in the circle of stones with a larger, generator quartz. But the rest of it needed to be forgotten and cleared from his memory.

Oh, there was one other important piece of information that stood out for Jim from the book. It was mentioned that people have an innate understanding of how to use crystals. No one really needs an instruction book. It was this very notion that inspired Jim to formulate a new plan.

Breakfast eaten and ready for the day, Jim went downstairs to pull the quartz crystal from its cold, slimy sea salt bath. It was immediately rinsed and dried off and soon perceived as special friend; a genie perpetually at Jim's service. But the crystal needed some more friends to assist in the upcoming task.

After pulling out of the subdivision in the company bucket truck that Halloween morning; Jim followed Mapleview Road north, past the Trivelli house, past Hidden Lake Forest Preserve and beyond the bend where the road transitions east. Soon he crossed Creek Highway, en route to Sillmac.

On Halloween morning, the utility truck for Mapleview Cable pulled into the parking lot of Sillmac Quartz and Candles.

"Good morning! Can I help you find something?" The same clerk from yesterday greeted Jim as he entered the shop.

But Jim needed no further help from her! "Yeah, I just need to get some more crystals."

She studied him carefully as he hand selected a collection of a six stones and brought them over to the counter. "Would that be all?"

"Yeah, that's good for now."

In comparison to the crystal purchased yesterday, the medium-sized stones that he browsed this morning were of high quality with minimal impurities; carefully hand cut and pointed. This made them pricey at a cost of $7.00 per stone. The clerk rang Jim up. "That'll be $44.10."

Jim paid cash, of course and threw away the receipt! Again, Kimberly could not be aware of her husband's sudden interest in the occult.

There was a noticeable difference between the crystal purchased on Friday and those purchased on Halloween morning. Friday's stone was considered less quality as it was simply a smoky quartz that was dull-gray in color and roughly filed to form the point. The six crystals purchased together had minimal impurities, making them clear in appearance. In addition, the points had been carefully cut to form crowns. Jim wasn't sure of any proven difference in effects, but the original crystal possessed a certain vibe or energy, nearly a character of its own. In addition; the invisible, optic pressure that radiated from the original stone continued to be felt and was more detectable than the others. Because of these observations, the original stone was chosen as Jim's generator.

* * *

Throughout Halloween afternoon, the additional six crystals soaked in a sea salt bath. While Kimberly took 9-year-old Collin around the neighborhood for trick-or-treating, Jim and April alternated answering the door to ghosts, vampires and pirates. And although Jim wished to snack throughout the afternoon on candy, he had a peculiar understanding to avoid sugar. There was work of an occult nature to do that night.

The same could be said for dinner. Each year, Kimberly made a spooky, Halloween bake for dinner; a casserole that blended macaroni noodles, peas, corn, ground meat and tomato sauce. Along with this, she would bake a double batch of biscuits. Jim often ate hearty on Halloween, as he did every other night of the year. But not tonight! It was best to eat the minimal amount and avoid any additional food after dinner.

"Is that all your going to eat?" asked Kimberly.

"Oh yeah, that's plenty! I don't want to stuff myself."

A wife never voices this, but she truly feels loved when her husband and children enjoy a home cooked meal. But Jim wasn't eating as he usually did. Was there something wrong with the spooky, Halloween casserole? Poor Kimberly didn't understand that her husband had important work of an occult nature to do that night.

As April was out terrorizing Mapleview on Halloween night with friends, and Collin sat on the sofa beside Mother watching spooky movies; Jim made a quick trip to the basement to pull the six quartz crystals from their cold, slimy bath. They were rinsed off, dried and tucked away for the ritual later that night along with the generator stone.

Some moments later, Jim returned to the family room upstairs. Kimberly was now in the kitchen and took notice of her husband sitting in the recliner seat. Being the thoughtful wife that she is, Kimberly asked, "Do you want me to get you a beer while I'm in here?"

It's amazing how people have an innate understanding when it comes to performing occult activities. "Nah, not tonight. I'm too tired." Alcohol could not affect the work that Jim had to do that night.

One thing was for certain. When it came to romance, Kimberly took the holidays off. Many people might find it silly to expect sex on Halloween night. But the same could be said of Kimberly about Christmas, New Years, birthdays, Valentine's Day, Easter and any little Hallmark holiday in between. In younger years, this holiday observation disturbed Jim. But he eventually understood that wives did that sort of thing. As Jim soon came to believe, a wife should be able to enjoy a holiday without the bother of sex. And tonight this was a good thing as Jim had important work of an occult nature to do.

Five minutes to midnight, with Kimberly sound asleep; Jim quietly rose from bed and made his way to the basement stairs. In nothing but his boxers, he descended the staircase and retrieved his collection of quartz crystals. Jim set the generator stone on the Berber carpet and then laid out the remaining crystals so that they surrounded the original and formed a six-pointed star. Finally, four votive candles in their glass holders that were taken from the upstairs family room were set at four of the sides of the six-pointed star and then lit. With the basement lights off, Jim sat in the center of the star and took hold of the generator.

Considering the fact that the mysterious, crazy, old woman appeared to have stranglehold on Jim's thoughts; considering the nights of strange dreams along with unusual cravings throughout the day for whatever power she had over him; and considering the fact that she quite possibly hexed him with a terrible love spell, it was most wise to engage in the activity that Jim was about to perform, especially when surrounded by items of magick on Halloween night.

He closed his eyes and let his imagination journey to a place that (for purposes of purely fantasizing) would have been the mysterious, crazy, old woman's house on a midmorning in spring. The temperature was mild, but with a light drizzle outside. Inside a bedroom, two lovers stood naked and embraced while passionately kissing before the open window. Light mist occasionally spiked against their naked flesh. Soon they found their way over to the bed and wrestled naked, their passionate play increasing in intensity as the drizzle outside turned to a heavy rain.

Back in the basement on Halloween night, Jim succeeded in elevating his sexual energy with the use of that dreamy fantasy along with manipulating that which originally was underneath boxers. It was fully out with no intention of going away. But Jim wasn't there to find relief in finishing a fantasy. Instead he eased his grip so that only his fingertips lightly tickled. It was an interesting sensation he had experimented with throughout the years. Usually this couldn't be done for too long because of the madness brought on by teasing.

This was not the way it should be done! At least this was how Jim's orgasmic wiring understood things. The peculiar touch caused craziness, an increase in heart rate and frantic breathing. Through all this madness, Jim brought to mind the face of the mysterious, crazy, old woman. With eyes closed, he released the madness that echoed through his body by way of mouth, physically kissing her imagined lips in the darkness, saliva nearly dripping from his own mouth. Then he called out in a sexy whisper as-if repeating some mantra, "I want you... I need you... I need to know who you are... Come to me... I need to know your name... Where can I find you...?" While doing this, the generator stone nearly broke in half as it sat tightly in Jim's palm. Through the overwhelming orgasmic sensations and softly-whispered mantra, Jim wasn't the least bit aware of the quartz receiving every bit of programming at midnight, Halloween.

Chapter 13

Back at the Trivelli house, things were about to really heat up in the family mausoleum...

Outside of Mary elaborately decorating the Trivelli house with jack-o-lanterns, ghosts and other fun displays for the holiday, Halloween wasn't much of a big doing for her and Daren. It was Saturday night, and a chance for Mary and Daren to go out for dinner and catch a movie. Afterwards, they went to bed and worked on that baby that Mary so wished for.

By 11:54 pm, Daren stirred awake from his first REM cycle. Mary lay on her side of the bed, sleeping soundly with Muffin nearby. It was the perfect moment for Daren to sneak outside, crack open the family mausoleum and crack open a cold one. But perhaps his sudden need for a late night beer only covered his hidden motive for visiting the mausoleum.

Once inside the building, Daren did open his favorite crypt and pulled a bottle of beer from the cooler. And while taking a few guzzles, he occasionally glanced over to Grandma Trivelli's crypt, or Mary's crypt as he now called it. It had been a week since he looked upon her beautiful, sleeping face. But she was Mary's grandmother—prefixed by several greats—and it would have been quite a disrespect to disturb her crypt, not to mention eternal rest.

One beer was never enough for Daren. He soon cracked open a second, and began speaking mentally to Mary. "Well, I found out your name. I hope you allow me to call you Mary. I hope you don't feel like I'm disrespecting you by ignoring your title of Grandma. I just feel like you've become a friend. I mean you don't look like a grandma!"

Daren set down his beer and did the unthinkable! He carefully approached Grandma Trivelli's crypt and nearly hesitated before unlocking it. After some moments with the crypt finally open; the oversized, cobalt-blue Mason jar sat before Daren. It was only necessary to carefully lift the jar and bring it before the sconce on the wall to provide enough illumination to take sight of her beautiful face.

There she floated, sleeping so peacefully and surrounded by a tranquil, blue lighting effect. Daren discovered that it was possible to interact with her beautiful face by carefully tilting the jar, thereby shifting it to the glass. Mary had such young, smooth, collagen-enriched skin as evidenced by her lovely cheeks that were easily influenced by making contact with the glass. They probably felt exactly like his wife's. As-if able to delicately hold Mary's face in a moment of love, Daren stroked his thumb against the glass, near the area that made contact with her cheek. One could have heard the theme song to Somewhere in Time at that moment—a young man desperately in love with a woman who was separated by many decades; so many, in fact, that she was now dead. But a beautiful love goes beyond the grave. And to make this love all-the-more bittersweet; only a terrible tragedy made possible the bringing of two forbidden lovers together.

Was it possible to stir Mary awake? Daren gently shook the glass in an effort to agitate her eyes open. They probably looked as beautiful as his own Mary's. But sadly, the eyelids remained shut. Old man Trivelli must have glued them before dropping his wife's head in the jar.

Before ending that tender moment of Halloween night, Daren gently kissed the glass near Mary's cheek then set the jar back in the crypt. "Good night, Mary. Sleep well." Then he closed and locked the crypt.

Chapter 14

The morning following Halloween (All Saints Day), Jim woke early and waited as the coffee pot brewed his first cup of coffee for the day. Not expecting immediate results from the previous night's ritual, he was curious as to whether or not it was effective.

Jim is a sensible man, as difficult as that might be to believe. I suppose having a job that involves troubleshooting might result in the scientific method being second nature. It certainly was his intention to establish a deliberate, psychic link to the mysterious, crazy, old woman. And it was his intention to ultimately track her. But what exactly happened last night? Did elevating his sexual energies amplify psychic abilities so that the mysterious, crazy, old woman could sense his thoughts and desires? Was contact actually made, or did Jim simply have an intense fantasy?

A witch might be able to tell you what Jim was doing. Although sloppy and maybe not a very organized ritual, Jim was using a form of sexual witchcraft in which he channeled all that sexual energy towards a specific desire while calling out to it.

And as Jim later found out, such rituals really do work. The results most often occur when least expected. After a late night of performing sex magick, Jim returned to the ordinary world and followed his weekly ritual of attending 8:30 am mass with family at the Trinity Lutheran Church. On this morning; by the time Jim, Kimberly and the two kids loaded into the car; Jim had forgotten the previous night's activities. But out of habit, he kept the generator stone in his left pocket, neglecting to recognize that it maintained and amplified a subconscious calling to the woman he desired.

The family exited the subdivision and traveled northbound until crossing into the old, wooded section of Mapleview. Trinity Lutheran Church is located some distance past the Hidden Lake Forest Preserve parking lot oasis. Jim had a few miles to travel before reaching the church, and for now was only a couple blocks before the historic Trivelli house. If you recall, this section of town has old, historic houses embedded along the surrounding forested wilderness highway.

Just then, the mysterious, crazy, old woman that Jim called out to Halloween night walked along the shoulder of the highway. Wearing simply an old, black dress that might have appeared antique—possibly from a hundred years ago—she spotted Jim's approach and locked eyes with him through the windshield. With such a devious smile, her face nearly touched Jim through the windshield. He called last night, and now she was there for him.

The sudden appearance and strange behavior of her orchestra teacher caused April to gasp and shriek as if nearly frightened out of her mind.

Kimberly called out to her daughter, "What? What is it April?"

"It's Ms. Lutrova! I don't know why, but she scares me!" As the car traveled further away and Ms. Lutrova was some distance behind, the sudden irrational fear faded from April as logic restored and she found her own behavior silly. "I don't know why she scared me. It was only my orchestra teacher. I guess I was just surprised to see her, that's all."

Kimberly smiled and shook her head, "Maybe you were just out a little too late last night and need some more sleep."

In the meantime, Jim carefully studied the mysterious, crazy, old woman in his mirror and made note of which house off the highway she walked in front of. The mischievous smile and eye contact was a message; an answer to his calling and a hint as to where he could find her. Then Jim asked, "What's her name?"

"Ms. Lutrova." answered April.

"Miss? Is she married?"

Kimberly smacked her husband's arm. "What difference does that make?"

"Just wondering…"

Chapter 15

The autumn months of 2009 and the early part of 2010 were marked as a time of emerging "hyperdimensionality" in Jim's life. Often bizarre and very confusing, it felt as though he were in multiple places at one time. And why wouldn't Jim feel this way? Not only married with a secret mistress on the side; there was also some strange, old woman that he was obsessed with.

Which brings us to an additional phenomenon in Jim's life that would have once been considered impossible: Just how well can one get to know another person without maintaining contact? No daily encounters with conversation, no telephone calls, no letters exchanged through the mail, no emails, no text messages; without any of these mediums of communication, becoming acquainted with a stranger is impossible. But despite the fact that weeks would pass before another encounter with Ms. Lutrova; Jim was getting to know her quite well. She was becoming a deep, personal friend of Jim's; even closer of a friend than his mistress, Amber! In fact, she was creating a gradual pull of Jim towards her direction; giving the man a sense that Amber was nothing more than a silly, little girlfriend who should soon be forgotten as he became more deeply involved with Ms. Lutrova. Initially, Jim believed these sensations to be nothing more than a series of overpowering thoughts and fantasies. But they turned real as reality itself.

* * *

Since her banishment from the Dickly castle, holidays were a time of hidden depression for Amber. No contact with her mother and father and no significant other to share her life with; Thanksgiving, Christmas and New Year were often times to hide tears. Oh she had her daughter, Trista, to be with. But the holidays lacked that special magick of sharing it with a significant other. Still so young and beautiful, it would be nice to experience some holiday romance in Amber's life.

When would the time come when Trista's father fully surrendered and returned to the family? So many times Amber considered giving him the ultimatum, "It's either her or me." But she had come so far and wished not to risk losing him. For now, it was necessary to play the little game of being Jim's secret mistress.

It was a Friday evening in mid-November, Thanksgiving being the following week. Despite the undesirable circumstance, it was necessary for Amber to make the best out of this evening. Dreamy and ethereal with a symbolic, poetic approach; tonight would have to be her Thanksgiving celebration with Trista's father. Surely he couldn't be with her on Thanksgiving. Another holiday would go by without Trista being with her father.

On this night Trista was out with friends. Being the case, Jim had been invited over and soon knocked at Amber's door. He was greeted by her warm and friendly smile. This was a special Thanksgiving dinner between Amber and Jim. For that matter, the home was illuminated by the soft glow of candlelight with the sounds of ambient music echoing from the living room speakers.

Just like a real American boy, Jim drinks beer. But tonight was a much, too special for beer. In the kitchen, Amber cracked open a bottle of Winking Owl Merlot from Aldi and carried it to the family room table along with a tray of sliced up Happy Farms cheese and roulades of salami and cream cheese—an appetizer called pinwheels.

"Mmm! Look at that! You went all out, tonight." Jim was sure to be extra nice. It was kind of a stupid appetizer tray. Whoever heard of cream cheese rolled up in salami? The wine was probably cheap, too. But again, Jim was going to be nice.

Amber smiled while placing a few appetizers on Jim's plate and pouring him a glass of Merlot. The man had better show some respect towards the hostess. Years ago, Amber made special dishes like braciole to win the heart of the man she loved. But thanks to purchasing a home in Maple Sap just to be down the street from Trista's father, finances were a little tight for Amber. Pinwheels and slices of Happy Farms cheese along with a couple cheap bottles of wine were the best she could do for tonight.

"So, the holidays are finally here." said Amber while sitting down next to Trista's father with her glass of wine. She clinked her glass against his, "Happy

Thanksgiving!" and then took a sip. "Soon we'll be putting up the tree. You know, I was thinking that maybe you could sneak over here next weekend and help me put up the tree. Do you think you might be available for that?"

Jim took a sip from his glass of wine. He was never a big fan of wine, but assumed he would get buzzed shortly. "I suppose I could get a sudden call on Saturday and drive over here. It sounds like a date."

Amber smiled.

Wine has an interesting effect on the mind. Those unfamiliar with wine assume that the quest for the buzz is the reason for drinking it. But if one can see beyond the initial stages of wine's effect, it would soon be noticed that it stimulates the imagination and pulls out our more sensitive emotions while at the same time smoothing them out. While sitting side-by-side with Amber and hearing of how her week at work went, Jim couldn't help but wonder just what Amber's intentions were. Was it really wise to assist her in putting up the tree for the holidays? And what if Trista were to participate in this ritual?

That's when Ms. Lutrova manifested herself in Jim's imagination in some fantasy as they sat beside one another. She so strongly reassured Jim, "At least I'm not here to ruin your marriage. I not a home wrecker."

Wine enabled Jim's emotions and concerns to bleed over into the psychic link shared with Ms. Lutrova. Wine enabled Jim to receive her intentions and convert them into a daydream. It was time for him and her to have a heart-to-heart talk, just to clarify some things.

"Just what does she want?" asked Ms. Lutrova. "You should watch out for those young women who are in need of nothing more than a close friend. She already has close friends, family members or even a best friend. But always remember that a close, male companion is something different for a woman."

In the meantime, Amber continued to babble on about the week while pouring some more wine for her and Jim. "So I asked my cashier to just get a ladder from maintenance and reach up to the ceiling and hang the Black Friday Jewelry Sale sign. How hard was that to do? I came in the store the following morning and found it lying near the cash register, still rolled up."

"You want to know who she is?" Ms. Lutrova asked with a hint of soon to provide advice. "She's been through plenty of romantic relationships with other men, probably even a marriage or two. After some time, it's nice to simply be close to someone of the opposite sex; enjoy a relationship without a purpose or practical goal in mind. You might be the ideal man to share such a relationship with. Or what do you want to bet that she's had a dark past involving drugs and an eventual turn towards prostitution? Or maybe she spent some years as a sex addict. In either case, it's very possible that she's recently gone through a sudden transfiguration, now devoting her life to celibacy—a woman of chastity for a lack of better words. Then again, it might not be all that dramatic; just a realization that sex played an all-too-important role in her relationships with men. For her, it's now time to put sex on the backburner, learn to enjoy a close and loving relationship with a man in ways that don't involve wrestling naked under the bed sheets. That's dangerous, Jim! She's trying to launch an emotional affair with you! These are the types of women who wreck marriages!"

Chapter 16

Two nights after his unofficial Thanksgiving dinner with Amber, Jim suddenly noticed that the psychic link shared with Ms. Lutrova was beginning to wear off! Perhaps there is some time limit when it comes to magick, dictated by the passing of celestial events or the unraveling of seasons. Whatever the reason, Jim could feel the power wearing off which caused him to feel distanced from Ms. Lutrova. With no recent school orchestra concerts and no sightings of the woman out in town, Jim was beginning to sorely miss her.

It was time for some more of that sex magick. It seemed to work quite well on Halloween. Now Sunday night Jim arose slightly before midnight to head down into the basement. You're already familiar with his protocol of avoiding sugar, alcohol, sex and excessive eating. The mind and body must be clear when following through with a magick ritual.

Just as before, Jim placed a quartz crystal at each of the imagined points of a six-pointed star and then lit four candles to surround it. In the darkened basement at midnight, it was the soft glow of candles and the reflected light from the quartz crystals that illuminated Jim's private space.

He sat in the center of the six-pointed star and closed his eyes. Wearing only his boxers, Jim touched and fondled that which he expected to grow stiff and swell with excitement. But what was this? After about a minute's worth of play, Jim's penis remained flaccid!

The play grew more frantic as Jim began to panic. What was wrong with him? Why couldn't he initiate an erection? Thoughts of sex and naked women were of no help. For now, it would appear that poor Jim was to experience an unpleasant moment of sexual dysfunction. And when there is sexual dysfunction, there can be no sexual magick. This would further mean no calling out and summoning the woman of his desire.

Deeply saddened with desperate thoughts of losing Ms. Lutrova; Jim extinguished his candles and broke down the six-pointed star. He returned to bed where Kimberly lay beside him sleeping. But Jim could not get to sleep. Almost forty years old, his penis was beginning to show signs of impotence. How could he make love to his beautiful wife? What if Amber suddenly felt it was time to have sex? And what of the time when he and Ms. Lutrova finally made contact and attempted intimacy? As Ivan Trovskov was finding out, it's not easy being a real ladies' man, especially when approaching middle-age.

It was a long night of tossing and turning, awakening every couple hours in self-absorbed thoughts and dreams of his penis.

* * *

Monday morning, after reporting to the office and heading out into the field in his Mapleview Cable bucket truck, Jim pulled over to the wayside oasis of the Hidden Lake Forest Preserve. He removed the outdated palm-pilot-styled smart phone from his pocket and entered "remedy for impotence" into the search engine.

As Jim discovered in several articles, Ginseng is an excellent supplement for ensuring stiff and sensational erections. Ginseng stimulates the production of nitric acid in the blood which can relax the blood vessels in the penis and allow for solid, sustainable erections. Not only that, Ginseng is helpful in combating the harmful effects of stress.

Wasting not another moment, Jim peeled off for Mapleview Walmart where he stormed into the store and clicked his Ivan Trovskov black, shiny boots down the tiled floor over to the vitamin aisle.

For only five dollars, a bottle of Korean panax ginseng was very affordable.

"Panax?" Jim softly spoke out. "Is that like panic attacks?" Considering his daily consumption of coffee and need to take blood pressure medication, Jim wondered if ginseng was really safe. But he would never know unless he tried.

A good sign of stable, mental health: when we can step outside of ourselves and question our behavior, we know that we are not crazy. Jim must have had some degree of mental stability, for he obviously questioned his recent behavior. Feeling as though a bad love spell had been casted on him; performing sex magick in the midnight hour of his basement; and dressing like an immigrant named Ivan Trovskov; was Jim really in his right frame of mind? Was he okay? What if the ginseng triggered further delusions?

But it was best that he throw caution to the wind and solve this sudden plague of impotence. He walked down the aisle with a bottle of Korean panax ginseng and then stopped dead in his tracks at something far, more interesting.

Stocked at one of the endcaps were glass vials of panax red ginseng extract. At first glance, the vials would remind someone of an eerie potion mixed up by a witch. Slightly more costly than capsules, they were obviously of greater quality. The boxes and vials contained Chinese lettering with English translations below. "Adaptogen that possesses the qualities of yang." Yang was a good thing for Jim. From what Jim knew; yang is the force in nature that defines hardness, maleness, aggression and all things opposite to being passive. Maybe Jim needed more yang in his life.

The information listed all the benefits. "Has a positive effect on central nervous system, brain, circulation, stimulation and arousal, curing depression, diabetes, boosting immunity, libido, and much more."

The directions were simple. "Consume one to two vials per day." Then it said the most peculiar thing that would make one imagine a Chinese Kung-Fu instructor who spoke with broken English, "The cooler the better taste!"

For the time being, Jim could store his vials of red panax ginseng extract in the back of the Mapleview Cable bucket truck. He put the original bottle of pills away and then grabbed six vials of the extract from the endcap shelf. This would provide a fair three days of testing.

Upon returning to the truck, Jim opened one vial and downed the extract. Containing nine-year old ginseng, honey and royal jelly; it didn't taste terribly bad. Although maybe "the cooler the better taste"?

* * *

Monday night, Kimberly made tacos for her family. As she cut up the tomatoes, shredded the cheddar cheese, and warmed up refried beans in the microwave while the seasoned ground meat cooked on the stove; Jim sneaked outside to down another bottle of red panax ginseng extract. As he learned, there was certainly truth behind "the cooler the better taste". In fact, it was like having a little before dinner cocktail. The second dose, however, was immediately felt as Jim walked back into the house. Maybe it was because he consumed this just at twilight while thinking of Ms. Lutrova. While stepping into the house, Jim saw the peculiar flash of serpentine colors in the upper portion of his left eye. He felt apprehensive for a moment, then silly and giggly while sitting down before the table.

"Taco Tuesday!" Jim announced in his sportscaster voice.

"It's Monday, Jim." Kimberly set the pan of meat on the table and opened a box of taco shells.

"But I thought we have tacos on Tuesday."

"We're having meatloaf tomorrow."

"Meatloaf tomorrow? Shouldn't we be having that tonight?—Meatloaf Monday and Taco Tuesday."

Kimberly had no comment and was in no mood for Jim's silliness.

Midway through dinner, Jim announced that it was time to follow the yearly winter sleep schedule. Being that the winter months caused cable outages late at night, it was best that he go to sleep shortly after dinner in case of being interrupted at one o'clock in the morning. This way, he wouldn't be losing sleep during the winter months.

But there was another reason for retiring early. Jim needed to try the efficacy of Ms. Lutrova's sex potion. Would it work? Maybe he could do some sex magick while laying in the dark before falling asleep.

And the potion definitely worked! If the reader is a male and ever tried ginseng, then surely you know of its sexual effects. Under the blankets and in the dark, Jim marveled at the incredible stiffness with a mushroom head that felt as-if nearly to explode. And it felt so good! It felt so good that Jim forgot his original intention of performing sex magick. It could wait another night. For now, Jim focused on all that sensational pleasure. At some point, he pulled down the blankets to adore his erect penis. Pulling it down to watch the springiness return to 90 degree stiffness, Jim celebrated with more stroking while whispering, "I love masturbating!"

Then all that energy saved up for Ms. Lutrova was finally released as Jim took deep breaths in and out as his heart rate finally slowed down.

But Ms. Lutrova wasn't done with Jim. That Monday night just before the Thanksgiving holiday, the moon was a waxing crescent; ideal for casting spells and magick not only for development or emerging knowledge, but for drawing and attracting people or situations. As Jim slept soundly in the early evening hours, he was unaware of the visitor who would appear later that night. No, it wasn't his wife, Kimberly. Sleeping soundly, Jim was oblivious to her presence as she slipped under the sheets and blankets to drift off for the night.

But with the waxing crescent moon fully set and a considerable distance below the horizon, Jim's night of sleep grew shallow as he had already completed some hours of the deepest REM. It was during this time that he became aware of a dark apparition that suddenly appeared before his bedroom window. With the room on the second level of the house, the shadowy figure obviously had the ability to float and hover as-if suspended by nothing more than the soft, November breeze.

There was a click that definitely resembled the window unlocking, soon to be carefully opened. Sleep paralysis prevented Jim from awakening. As for Kimberly, she was deep in the first night's REM and unaware of anything taking place.

The apparition briefly morphed into a small flying creature such as a bat. Whatever the entity was, it certainly had all the qualities of being a vampire. Oh, but it was far worse than that! Once in the bedroom with the window carefully closed, the dark shadow approached Jim's side of the bed. It was female and dressed in blackened robes, an evil sorceress with demonic qualities. She made her identity known by finally presenting her face close to Jim's. It was Ms. Lutrova, here to answer Jim's call. If Jim wanted sex magick, he was definitely going to get it! Whether or not he enjoyed it was a different matter. But he would soon learn the power of two bodies toying with a build-up of sexual energy.

She pulled back Jim's covers and then straddled him. Apparently her sex potion in the glass vials worked as expected. Jim was nice and hard while sound asleep, just the way she needed to work all that great sex magick.

Ms. Lutrova undid her black, sorceress robe to pull it down midway and expose her bare shoulders, arms and breasts. She was an old lady, but still possessed somewhat smooth skin. Her breasts were rather large, but had been unflatteringly altered by gravity through the years. Still, they were breasts and enough to arouse a man at their exposure.

Ms. Lutrova gave Jim a soft kiss to his lips and then pulled away so that her face was inches close. What was her mouth like? An old lady might have teeth that are badly stained or even rotten along with bad breath brought on by gum disease. Most of the lips' collagen becomes depleted through the decades so that an old lady possesses wiry, dry lips that occasionally become wet through excessive licking. Still, the kiss from Ms. Lutrova was enough to ignite a small flame of desire.

Through Jim's sleep paralysis, she held the man's arms against the pillows and then kissed his forehead. Such a teasing game; her warm, naked body soon covered Jim's. Her breasts touched his while her strands of black and gray hair grazed along his face and shoulders. And the only sensual thing provided was a delicate kiss to his forehead?

But there was more. Miniature kisses were slowly placed on Jim's forehead, down his temple, his cheek, the region above his upper lip and finally a sweet one to land on his lips. But not too much! She held Jim down while slowly and teasingly giving one, gentle kiss after another to his lips. With every kiss, Jim tried so desperately to draw more of the sexual sorceress in. She only beamed with a psychotic smile. There was no rush.

Feeling Jim had received plenty to his lips, Ms. Lutrova moved down his chin and to the neck. Now where was one of those erogenous zones? Do men have any of these? Of course they do; Ms. Lutrova knew this. It only required a bit of exploration, some soft and teasing kisses to the sensitive region on the side of his neck. When goose bumps present themselves and nipples become aroused, rest assured an erogenous zone has been found. She next glided her warm, silky tongue along this area while exhaling hot air. For being an old lady with possibly a stinky, yucky mouth; Jim suddenly wanted that tongue!

Sweet nothings are best whispered in a man's ear in this moment. But Ms. Lutrova knew not to say anything, specifically. Any words might alter the moment. And it's not the words that mean most to a man. It's the sound of her lips and tongue that slightly move as hot hair is exhaled through her teeth. Only a simple exhale with a barely-heard whisper of, "Ah..." should be spoken. Ms. Lutrova knew all the right things to chant and all the right spells to place Jim under.

This was the sexual sorceress' world, her moment and her game with her own rules. Feeling Jim's hardened and aroused nipples, there was no rule to say that she couldn't suddenly attack one of them. It wasn't necessary to slowly kiss down Jim's neck, his chest and to a nipple. She simply moved her face over and kissed one of them, soon to aggressively bite and then pull away with a hard suck. Don't think for one second that a man doesn't enjoy this. He actually craves it and wishes for more of it. For just as a woman loves to have her nipples sucked, lightly pinched and nibbled; a man does the same.

Returning to his lips for more teasing kisses, Ms. Lutrova wouldn't allow Jim to make intimate contact with any part of her body. Of course the same rule didn't apply to her. It was all her pleasure; really all her own!

How badly Jim wished to finally penetrate her, sting like a honey bee and spew his venom. And rest assured, Ms. Lutrova wished for the same. But as a soap bubble softly blows and drifts through the wind, it immediately bursts when touched by a human hand or landing on an object. The same could be said of this moment. Jim could not touch the sorceress; much less sting her for she would die. She floated through the wind across dream world to Jim's window, and was fueled by her own sexual desires. The essence to take from this moment was the build-up of sexual tension, craziness and torture. This is the energy that can fuel magick.

So did Jim enjoy sex magick?

Would you?

Chapter 17

On the third day following Jim's introduction to Ms. Lutrova's magickal sex potion; the moon had grown from waxing crescent to first quarter, and was in transition to a waxing gibbous. By the time Jim entered the office of Mapleview Cable on Wednesday morning, he had downed 5 vials of panax red ginseng extract since Monday morning. He was definitely feeling the effects and much, more confident with the functionality of his penis.

Jim softly knocked on the doorframe of his boss' office. "Ryan?"

"Yeah Jimmy! What's up?"

"Just to let you know, I've got a doctor's visit at one o'clock this afternoon. It shouldn't be long."

"Take as long as you like, Jimmy! I hope it's nothing serious."

"No, just a check-up."

* * *

Now Jim knew very well that the visit was more than just a regular check-up. Kimberly was concerned with his behavior in recent times and swore that his face and breathing revealed someone with possible elevated blood pressure. It was Kimberly who scheduled the doctor's appointment for Jim. And just to appease his wife, Jim followed through with it.

Jim sat in the waiting room at five minutes to one o'clock. Suddenly his name was announced by Nurse Corrine, an attractive thirty-something with natural flowing brown hair and brown eyes.

"We'll have you stop here to get you weighed in." mentioned Nurse Corrine.

Jim didn't bother to remove his black, shiny Ivan Trovskov boots while stepping on the scale. Any possible weight from the boots really didn't matter.

"281 pounds!" commented Nurse Corrine. With your height, that's certainly in the range of obesity.

But that's not what Jim heard. Instead, he heard Nurse Corrine compliment his physique. "Such a nice, big boy and in fine shape; surely you eat plenty of your wife's sausage and potatoes. You look so healthy!"

Nurse Corrine next directed Jim into the patient room and then ordered, "Have a seat." Without a second for his heart to resume a state of rest, she immediately strapped the blood pressure cuff on Jim's arm and began to pump. Unfortunately, Nurse Corrine was so good looking that her appearance caused Jim's heart to pump harder while activating all that chemistry of attraction.

"162/91... 74 beats per minute... Do you have hypertension?"

"I take blood pressure medicine, so yes, I'm being treated."

Just as Nurse Corrine wrote the information on the clipboard, Doctor Millheimer knocked and entered the room.

"Hello?" announced Doctor Millheimer.

"Hi, Dock!" replied Jim.

Doctor Millheimer appeared very concerned with Jim's appearance. "Oh, my! Look at you! Have you gained weight?"

"Um... maybe a few pounds."

Nurse Corrine gave the clipboard to the doctor.

Upon viewing the notes, Doctor Millheimer exclaimed, "281 pounds??? Blood pressure of 162/91??? Jim, come-on! What are you doing to yourself? Stand up for a moment."

Jim did as asked.

"I mean you really want to look like this? Go ahead and look in the mirror. You're obese, Jim!"

But that's not what Jim heard. Rather, the doctor further complimented his physique. "Ah, Ivan Trovskov: the pride of the motherland; and looking in such fine shape for winter!"

Ivan Trovskov agreed with the doctor's imagined compliments, "Well, I've got to put on my fluff for the winter."

Doctor Millheimer would put an end to these delusions so that Jim could finally see reality. "Well, let's just see about that." He placed the stethoscope in his ears and ordered, "Take off your shirt so I can listen."

Still standing, Jim removed his suspenders and white Fruit-of-the-Loom undershirt so that Nurse Corrine could see his thick, beefy chest with love handles that drooped over the sides of his waist. Then he sat down.

But before Doctor Millheimer placed the stethoscope on Jim's chest, he immediately asked, "Jim? What's that?"

"What?"

"That!" Doctor Millheimer motioned towards Jim's chest. "Do you see what I'm talking about, Nurse Corrine?"

"I most certainly do." confirmed the nurse.

Doctor Millheimer wasted not a second in calling the unpleasant fact to Jim's attention. "Jim, you have man boobs!"

Jim looked so surprised, nearly terrified. "Man boobs?"

"Yes, Jim, man boobs! Do you have gynecamastia?"

"Uh, I don't know what that is."

"It's a condition in which men grow larger than normal breasts so that they resemble a woman's pair of breasts. Do you have this? Are you aware if perhaps you have a hormonal imbalance?"

"Uh... not that I know of."

"Do you eat a lot of dairy products? That can trigger gynecamastia."

"I don't eat an excessive amount of dairy, no."

Doctor Millheimer sighed. "Well, unfortunately we're going to have to examine your breasts to eliminate the possibility of this being hormonally related." He looked over to Nurse Corrine. "You might as well put on a pair of latex gloves and give me a hand."

Standing over the patient, Doctor Millheimer took hold of both Jim's breasts and lifted them in the air. "Do you ever notice spontaneous lactation coming from your nipples?"

"No..."

Doctor Millheimer ordered the nurse, "Go ahead Nurse Corrine; lift and feel Jim's left breast."

Nurse Corrine did as directed.

"Do you see what I mean? See how the patient's breast is flabby with an excessive amount of subcutaneous fat?"

Nurse Corrine agreed with the doctor. "Why, yes; it's very soft like a woman's breast. It feels like my own breast."

It appeared as though Doctor Millheimer was providing the nurse training of gynecamastia exams. "Now, next we need to aggravate the gland behind the nipple to confirm no lactation. You position your finger and thumb to encompass the entire areola and follow the pinch and roll technique. Go ahead, pinch and roll... pinch and roll..."

Both the doctor and nurse each had their fingers on Jim's nipples and painfully pinched to aggravate whatever gland was behind.

"Pinch and roll... Pinch and roll..."

The procedure was proving painful for Jim. "Ouch! Ah! How much longer?"

"Be patient, Jim." the doctor urged. "It's not comfortable, but it has to be done."

"Pinch and roll... Pinch and roll..."

After about two minutes of titty-twisting-torture with no response from Tokyo, the doctor appeared satisfied. "Well, I can see no visible signs of lactation." He used a tissue to dab around both nipples to absorb any possible liquid that could not be seen. "Nothing!"

The doctor stood back and sighed in deliberation. "Well, I think it's safe to conclude that your man boobs are brought on by starch muscle. Do you know what starch muscle is, Jim?"

"No..."

The doctor explained the phenomenon of starch muscle. "See, maybe in high school you played football and maybe worked out shortly after graduating. Obviously you've been a big boy your whole life. But you're older, now. You probably sit on the sofa to watch Sunday afternoon football and believe that you actually are the athletes you see on TV. But that muscle you think is behind your shirt is not really muscle. It's actually fat that's accumulated from compulsively eating pizza, pretzels and cookies while watching the game. You stand up and admire yourself in the mirror at how you resemble your favorite football athletes. But it's only starch muscle, not the real thing."

Doctor Millheimer paused for a moment. "Well, as long as you're here, we might as well give you the rectal exam. Pants and boxers off, please."

Now it certainly isn't my intention to completely offend and assault the reader with unpleasant literary imagery. Let me just say that the next five minutes proved to be even more humiliating for Jim than his gynecamastia exam.

If being naked and on all fours before Nurse Corrine wasn't degrading enough, Doctor Millheimer asked the most dreadful questions of them all. "Do you ever experience episodes of sexual dysfunction or impotence?"

And this is why Jim and the doctor engaged in a discussion of ginseng while finally redressing. While on the examination table, Jim made mention of his sudden use of panax red ginseng extract.

Doctor Millheimer now explained why ginseng was not an option for Jim. "The use of ginseng is strongly advised against for patients with hypertension. Not only that, but your blood pressure medicine is an ACE inhibitor. The ACE stand for angiotensin-converting-enzyme. Ginseng can actually affect and counteract against the ACE inhibitor. I urge you... In fact I order you to no longer use ginseng."

Jim stood silent and motionless. Life was so cruel. Ms. Lutrova's sex potion was actually doing wonders for Jim. It was helping him rediscover his penis. But unbeknown to Jim, Ms. Lutrova had something far, more powerful brewing and ready to try.

Doctor Millheimer suggested a new, experimental drug that would improve Jim's occasional episodes of sexual dysfunction. "Jim, I think you would be the perfect candidate to test a new male performance drug on. It hasn't even hit the market. It's been researched for five years and proven to be safe on monkeys. The name of the new drug is called ErexBoost."

As the narrator, I laugh at the thought brought on by the previous, two sentences. For five years, medical researchers apparently specialized in triggering impotence in monkeys, and then caused erections with the ErexBoost drug. Amazing...

The doctor unlocked one of his cabinets and removed a sealed, cardboard box. "This box contains thirty days worth of medication." The doctor pulled an exacto-knife from his desk drawer and sliced open the sealing tape on the box. Then he carefully removed a small, glass vial containing algae green liquid. It looked to be exactly the sort of stuff made with lizards, toads, strange plants and then mixed in a black cauldron at midnight during a time of desirable celestial events. The person mixing the liquid might have even sounded a hysterical cackle.

"You drink one vial per day." the doctor instructed. "One vial is all you need! This will actually work *with* your blood pressure medicine and help keep it down. But I should also tell you that the medicine has a peculiar psychoactive effect that can best be described as those moments when you were about thirteen-years-old and sat in class during a boring lecture. Do you remember how you sort of drifted off to some other place and suddenly developed an erection for no reason at all?"

Jim smiled. "Oh yeah!"

"Well, this can happen to you. Most often it will happen while driving or maybe when you're sitting at an office meeting. To help prevent these undesirable moments, maybe take the medicine before dinner. You probably have sex in the evening, right?"

Jim nodded.

"The effects start to kick in an hour or two later and wears off in about twelve hours. It's perfectly safe, don't worry."

Chapter 18

It was the night before Thanksgiving, and a very important one for April. This evening was solo and duet stringed performance night at Mapleview Community High School. For the past week April had been practicing a duet with her friend, Stacy, so that the two could perform on this special evening.

While Kimberly put the finishing touches on dinner, she glanced out the side kitchen window and took notice of her husband reaching for something in the back of his truck. It was one of those mysterious vials of medicine that the doctor had prescribed. But why was it necessary for Jim to store them outside in his cable truck? And apparently it tasted bad as Jim involuntarily convulsed while swallowing.

He had turned into such a strange man, recently. This transformation seemingly took place when Jim changed his style of clothes (the Ivan Trovskov wardrobe). Maybe "that woman" who lived down the street (Amber) caused this alarming change in Jim's appearance and behavior. He seemed obsessed with her ever since she moved in the neighborhood.

But Kimberly didn't understand the full picture surrounding her husband. For you see, it wasn't Amber who was foremost on Jim's mind. Instead it was April's orchestra teacher! For Jim, attending the performance opened the possibility of an encounter with the strange, crazy, old woman. Perhaps Jim could even pay attention and learn of her first name.

And so Wednesday evening came in much the same way that the Thursday before Halloween performance did. But this time as the rest of the family finished their dinner; Jim quickly stood up, cleared the scraps from his plate into the garbage and then loaded it in the dishwasher. The he announced, "I'm going to wait in the car."

Secretly, Jim was freaking out really bad. And it would certainly show as the evening progressed. As for his blood pressure, it was most likely elevated to sky-rocketing levels as he fretted and considered the possibility of what Ms. Lutrova would do that night. She had been raping Jim in his own bed every night since Monday.

Jim waited impatiently in the driver's seat with the engine running and examined himself in the rearview mirror. It was time for Ivan Trovskov to get another hair cut so that he looked like... well, Ivan Trovskov!

Where the hell was Kimberly, April and Colin? What was taking so long? Didn't they understand that the bleachers were filling up, fast? Jim needed to be close to the performance—as close to Ms. Lutrova as possible. He nearly pressed the horn on the steering wheel, but then spotted his wife and kids walking from the garage.

"What took you so long?" asked Jim as Kimberly and the kids loaded in the car.

"I had to find a better shirt for Collin to wear. He had food stains on his other shirt."

Jim only sighed and resisted the urge to shake his head while clicking the garage door remote. He quickly backed out of the driveway and thudded over the curb. It was the first sign for Kimberly that Jim was in a hurry.

"Relax!" ordered Kimberly "We've got enough time!"

"I just want to make it there."

What was Jim's rush? In Kimberly's perception he had a need to sit near "that woman", probably to make goo-goo eyes at her. How much longer would poor Kimberly observe Amber's control over her husband?

Some minutes passed as Jim cruised through downtown Mapleview, traveling 50MPH in a 35MPH zone. Several car lengths before a traffic light that suddenly turned yellow, Jim floored the accelerator so the car open throttled through the light that had quickly turned red.

Kimberly had enough. "Jim, slow down!"

"What? I want to make it there in time!"

Again, she ordered, "Slow down! We don't have money for a ticket! Nor do I want us to get in an accident. And do you want to get us all killed?"

Jim eased on the accelerator, but then took sight of the horror while approaching Mapleview Community High School. Traffic was backed up as parents and family entered the school parking lot. "Awe jeez! What the hell is this?"

Now at ropes end with her husband's impatience, Kimberly nearly shouted, "Jim would you relax? Look at you! You're face is all red and it looks like you're sweating. What's wrong with you? Are you sure that medicine the doctor prescribed you is working?"

"Yes, I just don't like traffic backups."

More like Jim didn't want to sit too far from "that woman" (Amber). At least this is what Kimberly believed.

Kimberly sighed, "Jim did you drink coffee, today?"

"Just my usual two cups."

Kimberly didn't understand. It wasn't the traffic, the backup in the parking lot, Amber, or the coffee that affected Jim's behavior. Instead, it was the dreaded anticipation of encountering Ms. Lutrova while at the same time possibly missing an opportunity to sit nearby.

Although the school parking lot was filled like a shopping mall on Black Friday, there were spots for Jim to park. It only took four minutes of caravanning behind other motorists before finding one. And sure enough, Jim exited the car with heart rate up and excessive steam blowing through his nose. His biorhythms matched that of a fighter pilot who was moments from soaring into the skies for battle. To make matters worse, no one could walk fast enough for Jim!

"Jim, slow down! Are you going to leave your family behind?" asked Kimberly.

It was best that he calm down and accept the fact that the gymnasium was already full of spectators.

Parents and family of other orchestra members were filing into a side door that apparently led directly into the gymnasium. This was probably done to reduce the amount of excessive hallway traffic. Seeing that the side door was the quicker way in, Jim instinctively lined up behind the trail of people. Within a few moments, he and his family were finally in the gymnasium and approaching the bleachers.

And who do you suppose was waiting for Jim and family? It was the mistress, Amber. She sat in her usual spot. And despite how careful Amber was to make inconspicuous eye contact with who she believed to be her secret husband; Kimberly (that woman who Jim lived with) noticed it.

Kimberly already had a dislike towards "that woman". But as the months passed, she began to hate Amber with an irrational jealousy. It almost felt as though the woman had in mind to take Kimberly's husband away. This is why she was beginning to pay closer attention to Amber during school concerts, and felt an alarming rage when the woman turned around to look at Jim.

To be on the safe side Jim chose a spot no more than twenty feet away from Amber. She appeared closed off, but it didn't terribly bother Jim as he was more interested in seeing Ms. Lutrova and confirming that she had a psychic connection to him.

The anxieties: What if the evening splashed Jim with a cold bucket of reality, an unwelcome reminder that for some weeks he had merely been lost in nothing more than an overpowering fantasy? What if there was never any telepathic communication between him and Ms. Lutrova? What if Jim had merely blown a possible mutual attraction way out of proportion while tampering with mystical forces he knew nothing about?

The gymnasium bleachers filled with more parents. The few rows of folding chairs for performers were becoming increasingly occupied with soloists and duettists. In these moments, Kimberly paid close attention to Amber's daughter, Trista, who sat quietly in her seat. Unlike the other kids, she would only briefly exchange a few words with a neighbor before returning to a reflective, deep-in-thought sort of state. She was such a peculiar girl, looking very much like her mother. Surely Trista had a similar personality to that strange witch-of-a-woman.

It disturbed Kimberly to see Amber's daughter appear so focused on the evening. It was as-if playing in the orchestra was a ticket to a scholarship, or some other recognition. In a way, Trista was one of those grown up girls who were not only beautiful, but destined for success with her peculiar, mysterious nature similar to Amber's. Not only was Kimberly jealous of Amber possibly stealing her husband, but she was becoming envious of Amber's daughter as well.

Only a dot after six o'clock, the school principal stood at the podium and welcomed the parents and family while announcing the overall performance for the evening. Introductions weren't necessary. Jim knew why he was there; to see Ms. Lutrova and possibly learn of her first name.

"At this time, I'd like to turn the stage over to Mapleview Community High School's orchestra teacher…" The first name was so terribly drowned out. It sounded like, "Ms. Arecibo Lutrova."

The audience applauded, including Jim.

Arecibo; as-in the Arecibo Observatory near Puerto Rico? That would be ridiculous! No one names their kid after a stellar radio telescope!

Ms. Lutrova stood at the podium and spoke. It was the first time, ever, that Jim got to hear her voice. The woman spoke somewhat of broken English with a foreign accent; perhaps Polish or maybe even Russian. I'll spare any attempt of emulating her manner of speaking while telling this story. But apparently, Ms. Lutrova was an immigrant.

"Thank you for coming to our concert, tonight. We have a nice show for you tonight. The kids have been practicing very hard. The first part of our evening will be solos. Then we will have duets. Let's have our first solo."

Something was wrong! Ms. Lutrova was not focused on Jim like she was last time. While speaking up at the podium, she made no eye contact with him. He didn't feel her presence and there was no telepathic communication. As the audience applauded and welcomed the first performer, Ms. Lutrova merely sat down at a chair with her back turned to the audience.

While the first performer for the evening played her violin solo, Jim struggled for any favorable theory as to why Ms. Lutrova was so cold that evening. Her mental energies must have been preoccupied with something of greater importance—perhaps overseeing the individual performances.

Of course, that was it! Ms. Lutrova wasn't deliberately being cold to Jim!

Still, he maintained a subtle persistence of calling out to her. Only a deliberate lock of eyes would be necessary to "dust off" the mystical link shared together. Jim focused on his generator stone while forcing his mind into a deeper state of relaxation. "Look at me... Look at me... Look at me..." He repeated this while nearly staring at her.

But Ms. Lutrova remained with her face forward, not so much as a slight turn of her head to inconspicuously glance with her eye. In the meantime, soloists took turns standing before the microphone to deliver their performances. The kids had worked so hard in recent weeks and were proud to finally execute the much-practiced pieces before an audience. And for them, this was merely a "dry run" as shortly after the holiday they would meet for regional competition with other schools.

"Look at me... Look at me... Look at me..." Jim would take rests from his attempt of telepathic communication to watch the performance of the moment. As the audience clapped at the completion of a stringed solo done so well, Jim turned back to her and continued his chant, "Look at me... Look at me... Look at me..."

If only Jim knew of her first name, a telepathic calling would be all the more effective. Perhaps it was on the program handout. Jim reached for it just as the next performer was announced.

The timing was all wrong! From Kimberly's perception, Jim reached for the handout at the moment Amber's daughter was called. To further bring out Kimberly's jealousy, Amber turned her head and looked directly at Jim with eyes deeply set into his with an expression that appeared to be saying something.

Kimberly did not like this. "*What the hell?*" she thought.

Kimberly nearly yanked the program handout from Jim's hand and then pointed out where in order April and Stacy were. Duets would begin shortly. In Kimberly's belief and silent insistence, this is where Jim's mind should have been—not in trying to learn the last name of "that woman" who kept looking at him!

Kimberly studied Trista during the performance, all the while developing further envy and near hatred for the girl. There was something outstanding of the way she carried herself, her mannerisms and behavior. It was impossible not to see that Trista was highly intelligent and most-likely a couple years more mature than her peers. She played her solo so exquisitely with such vigor and passion. How proud Amber must have been of this girl. Why couldn't Kimberly's own daughter, April, be more like her?

After the solo, the audience applauded like they had done with previous performances. But interestingly enough, the claps were a bit louder with a hint of more energy from the crowd. And to further boil Kimberly's already seething jealousy, hatred and envy; Amber turned her face towards Jim for another deep setting of eyes into his and an expression that was as-if to say something.

Kimberly screamed an extension of harsh fornication to Amber in her mind.

But that witch heard it and turned her face back towards Kimberly. And you would think that the fire in Kimberly's eyes would have intimidated Amber. But this was not the case. Instead, Amber provided her smile of wicked persistence that suggested Kimberly should have everything to worry about.

"He's mine." the smile said. "It's only a matter of time before he surrenders to me."

Yes, Kimberly was jealous and full of envy. It was exactly what Amber wanted.

Chapter 19

Not every late night visit from Ms. Lutrova was made in person. Hours after the concert, she toyed with her victim through an opened dream portal. Tonight's game started off as a reassurance that all was well; just a simple conversation between voices carried across the dark of night.

"Awe... I'm sorry I didn't look at you. Yes, you are right. I was preoccupied with the students."

"And I wished I knew your first name so that I could call out to you."

"My first name? Oh, you only know me as Ms. Lutrova? Well now you can call me by my first name."

Jim informed her that he had yet to learn her first name. "I still don't know your name."

"Ah, but I would feel so special if you called me by my first name."

"But I don't know it."

"It would make me feel so special if you would say my name. Please say my name!"

There were a few minutes of silence as the mood changed. Suddenly, things didn't feel so warm and fuzzy between Jim and Ms. Lutrova. She broke the silence. "I'm starting to get my doubts about you."

"What? Why?"

"You haven't really proven anything to me. I call out to you at the carnival when you're with your little girlfriend. I put on a special performance for you at the Halloween concert. I visit you every night. But you don't even know my name?"

Jim suggested, "Well could you tell me?"

"I'm afraid it doesn't work that way. I need to see commitment. I want you to take some initiative to learn my name. I want you to do some research of me."

With that, Jim woke up. Ms. Lutrova was right. It was time to show how serious and dedicated he was of the woman. Jim was going to learn of her first name. He was so serious, that he was going to learn of her name right now. That handout left in the car would surely have the name of the orchestra teacher.

And so Jim crept out of bed and sneaked outside.

Chapter 20

Something cryptic and alarming was happening in her husband's life. This is what Kimberly concluded upon making the bed on the morning of Thanksgiving. It was suspicious enough to be awoken to the sound of Jim stepping outside at two o'clock in the morning. Startled and sharply awoken at the sound, Kimberly tiptoed over to the side bedroom window which provided a clear view of the driveway. From what she could see, Jim retrieved the solo and duet program handout from his car.

Kimberly had no need to question this. The strange act of stepping out to his car at this time of the night only verified a recent suspicion of Kimberly's that her husband had an attraction towards "that woman". He behaved so strangely while in her presence. It was too ironic that Jim reached for the handout while "that woman's" daughter played. Apparently, he wished to know her name.

Kimberly sighed to help cope with the sudden anxiety and outrage. How was she going to handle this? So Jim was intrigued with "that woman". Kimberly should have only been disgusted, but not concerned. Men will always look; and there was no way to prevent Jim from doing this—as long as he remembered who he was married to.

But this was the attitude Kimberly adopted *before* making the bed that Thanksgiving morning. She was startled to discover a strange item beneath Jim's pillow. It looked to be some sort of quartz crystal, an item that Kimberly immediately associated with magick and mystical things. Kimberly always knew "that woman" was a witch! She was probably instructing Jim in the use of sex magick and using his energy for her own gain. Suddenly, Kimberly was irate.

Kimberly wasn't going to inform her husband of the discovery at that moment. She needed more evidence and more discoveries that pointed to the terrible suspicion. She simply left the crystal under his pillow, made the bed and went about the morning.

And just as Kimberly expected, Jim apparently retrieved the mystical object from under his pillow at some point after the morning shower. He probably brought it with him on his sudden field service call, a small outage reported on the other side of town. In all her doubts, suspicions and hidden outrage; Kimberly blew her suspicions way out of proportion and believed that Jim was lying and actually visiting "that woman".

And this is why Jim left the house on Thanksgiving morning. For you see, although clumsy, Jim was already a step ahead of Kimberly. She could not be aware of online searches that included the last name of Lutrova in Mapleview. (The handout did not list the orchestra teacher with her first name, only Ms. Lutrova.) The computer in the den was to be used for Jim's work, but Kimberly often used it when the kids monopolized the laptops. There was no reason to prevent her from doing this. And being the case, she could have had full access to Jim's web browsing history.

Jim was even more careful than this. As he saw it, a wife was perfectly capable of accessing the modem or router for purposes of displaying other computer use in the home. Surely, it was possible for Jim to simply delete his cookies and web browsing history. But Kimberly could have easily sat with the laptop in the family room, and remotely watched what Jim was doing on his PC. As far as conducting web searches with his phone, a wife was also fully capable of snooping while her husband soundly slept or showered.

The same could be said of work. If obsessed with a certain someone, searches should not be performed at the office. Coworkers can access the routers and have other ways of remotely viewing computer use at work.

Jim had perfect solution. Being the lineman technician of Mapleview Cable, Jim had the ability to directly access a main utility box that fed Internet to hundreds of homes in one neighborhood. Just one chassis with a couple dozen circuit cards had the ability to send and receive 40,000 channels of data in one split second! Considering the vastness of one of these boxes, Jim's identity was a needle in the haystack as he connected an Ethernet cable to one of the communication ports. The other end was run to a modem in the utility truck that ultimately fed his laptop. A search performed of a mysterious woman with the last name of Lutrova could have been made by any number of people throughout several subdivisions of Mapleview. No possibility of Kimberly viewing his web history, and no possibility of people at the office remotely viewing his computer use; Jim was safe to browse as he wished, and freely search any names or information desired.

Thanksgiving morning was cold and windy in Mapleview with flurries and drifts of snow that blew across the roads. Because of the holiday, the roads and highways were virtually empty. Alone at the edge of town, off some isolated road, Jim sat in the safety of his warm Mapleview Cable truck and typed the phrase in the search engine, "Lutrova Mapleview".

It only resulted in the most frustrating result.

"Your search - lutrova mapleview - did not match any documents.

Suggestions:

Make sure all words are spelled correctly.
Try different keywords.
Try more general keywords.
Try fewer keywords."

Suddenly Jim's outdated palm-pilot styled phone buzzed. He reached for it, but discovered the screen was going through a reboot sequence. For whatever reason, the phone was momentarily powered down. Maybe the carrier pushed a software update.

Jim entered another search phrase. "Lutrova Mapleview Road"

"Your search - lutrova mapleview road - did not match any documents.

Suggestions:

Make sure all words are spelled correctly.
Try different keywords.
Try more general keywords.
Try fewer keywords."

"What the heck? She's got to be somewhere. I guess this woman really wants me to stalk her."

A highly powerful tool that any professional stalker uses is ZabaSearch. Once described as "Google on steroids", ZabaSearch scours multiple databases of public information for any individual provided. Results are often mixed in with other individuals who have similar names of the one in interest. If a stalker wishes for a complete report; credit history, marriage records, criminal background, email addresses, etc; there is a charge. But free listings include current and past residences and possibly telephone numbers—even sometimes the birth date and current age.

But even Google on steroids provided no results for Jim. ZabaSearch had no one in their records listed with the last name of Lutrova in Mapleview.

The phone in Jim's pocket buzzed again. "What's going on, here?" He pulled it out to see who or what it was.

It was a text message, nothing more than spam. "The Witch Connection: Need money? Love? Success? Answer to burning question? All spells proven to work! First spell is free!" There was an SMS code to allow texting needs to the Witch Connection.

Although certainly tempting considering Ms. Lutrova's game of Rumplestilt-skin, Jim wasn't ready to try it. It was, after all, spam.

Desperate, Jim entered the search phrase, "Arecibo Lutrova"

The only result was something completely unrelated,

"Iono!!

wn.com/IONO!!

... by luciella Lutrova THE BOHEMIAN GHOST PRIZE SLICE OF TRAN-QUILITY ... The Arecibo radio telescope located in Puerto Rico, was originally intended ..."

When clicked, the web page froze; equally frustrating as getting no results at all.

"Well that didn't help." Obviously it was a stupid search engine phrase. Who names their child after a radio telescope in Puerto Rico?

What Jim needed was an oracle like a Ouija board. Perhaps there was a web-site that offered an interactive Ouija board online that could provide him some answers. After a few seconds of searching, Jim found one:

http://www.museumoftalkingboards.com/WebOuija.html

It was so easy to use; simply type your question in the box and then hover the mouse cursor over the plachette. Within several seconds the answer is given.

Jim entered, "Lutrova Mapleview".

The Ouija board glided through a series of letters to spell out, "Maybe later."

"Oh come on! Is this the game they play?" Jim then entered, "Ms. Lutrova."

The Ouija answered, "Someone never seen. Someone never met."

"Well of course I've seen her! Let's try again!" This time Jim typed in an actual sentence in the form of a question. "Who is Ms. Lutrova of Mapleview?"

"Yourself..."

Himself? Was this an indicator that Jim was experiencing a fantasy that had spiraled out of control? Did he use imagination to breathe life into Ms. Lutrova so that he experienced her in fantasy and dreams? Maybe there was truth in the previous answer, "Someone never seen. Someone never met." Perhaps the Ms. Lutrova that Jim saw was really just an illusion of some woman who taught orchestra at the high school—nothing more.

But Jim wouldn't give up! Everything felt so real to him. There was no way that he could have fabricated an entire relationship like this in his mind. Jim was getting desperate. Ms. Lutrova expected him to find his name. Perhaps if he succeeded then she would reward Jim with finally meeting her.

Jim looked at the recent text message.

"The Witch Connection: Need money? Love? Success? Answer to burning question? All spells proven to work! First spell is free!"

"Well, what have I got to lose?" With the outdated smart phone's keypad, Jim typed in his simple question, "Who is Ms. Lutrova of Mapleview?" It was sent to the provided SMS code.

Jim waited in silence for several minutes while watching the snow drift across the highway. He imagined the ghostly apparition of Ms. Lutrova slowly walking towards the Mapleview Cable utility truck. Dressed so simple yet beautifully, her appearance would have been best suited for a springtime garden of late May where she might carefully approach and beckon a lost lover.

"Come to me... We are meant to be together... We belong together."

The calling beckoned from across the snow-drifted, isolated highway and carried across the cold, November gusts of wind. Perhaps by now her face peeked through the driver side window.

Just then a series of text messages came through.

(msg 1/4) Thank you for accepting your initial, free spell from the Witch Connection. Your request was categorized as... QUESTION IN NEED OF PSYCHIC READING...

(msg 2/4) and was delivered to a witch who specializes in this. Here is your comment/answer: "Warning! Ms. Lutrova is a 631 year old witch who practices

(msg 3/4) dark, evil magick. She resides in the afterlife in an alternate dimension, but can project herself into our world. She needs to regenerate herself and plans on

(msg 4/4) stealing your energy to do this. Do not trust Ms. Lutrova! Stay away!"

It was the most ridiculous thing Jim had ever heard. It was a good thing that his first reading was for free.

Chapter 21

To say that Kimberly was a lonely woman would be wrong. She had a husband and two children. She had a couple of good friends and some neighbors who she visited throughout the week. But no one on her side of the family would attend Kimberly's Thanksgiving dinner. Father had passed away, and Mother moved out of state to live with Kimberly's brother, Frank. Along with being physically distanced from her side of the family, Kimberly was no longer on speaking terms with them. She hadn't heard from Mother, her brother or her sister-in-law in a few years. Thanksgiving dinner this year would, again, be made for Jim, her children and Jim's side of the family.

After Kimberly's father passed away, Mother was financially comfortable for the rest of her life. This is the way her husband had planned it. He worked his entire life and built up investments so that when he died, his beloved wife could have a comfortable life. The money would be used for living expenses, and then to fund a possible stay at a quality retirement home when requiring assisted living. And only when Mother joined Father in Heaven, a place that has no need for money, the remaining savings and investments would be split between children and grandchildren. These things were spelled out in the will.

As sad as it is to realize, money brings out the ugliest of evil in people. As for Kimberly, she was similar to Amber in that she valued those intangible things in life. She understood that Mother's money was for Mother—period! Her brother, Frank, however, sought of ways to collect his share of the will before Mother died.

What worked in Frank's favor was the fact that he lived out of state in Georgia. For you see, a mother develops a love-hate relationship towards her nearest child. Living in Mapleview and very much a part of Kimberly and Jim's life, she saw every bit of bad in her daughter, son-in-law and grandchildren. But Frank, his wife and children lived far away. In their absence, she missed them so terribly in those extended periods between holidays. They were so, much, more civilized than Kimberly and her husband.

Perhaps this is why Mother hadn't a second thought towards helping her son in a time of need. He called on a Sunday afternoon. "Mom, we are in such dire straits right now. I wasn't going to say anything, but I had to take a cut in pay at work. Our bills are stacking up and we've been living on credit cards. They're threatening to take the car away, and we're already a couple months behind on the mortgage. Could you spare a little to help out?" These were lies, of course. Frank hadn't received a cut in pay. And although the materialistic lifestyle led to maxed out credit cards and heavy bills for Frank and his wife, it was only necessary to cut back on spending to catch up. Frank simply engineered a foolproof way to get his share of the will, now.

When it came to the inheritance, we're not talking millions of dollars. Through savings and modest investments, Mother could live comfortably for the rest of her life if following a budget. She voiced this to her son. "Frank, I'm on a budget. I need that money to live on. It might seem like a lot of money to you, but it's supposed to carry me through the rest of my life."

"I understand that, Mom. Here's what I was thinking; and I'll definitely pay you back, don't worry. Isn't your house paid off?"

"Certainly! Your Father made the last mortgage payment over 20 years ago."

"Good! What you can do is take out a home equity loan. Give me that money, and I'll be able to pay off the bill collectors, keep my car and not lose the house. And like I said, I'll definitely pay you back."

Mother wasn't exactly easy with the suggestion. Who would be? Hesitantly, she asked, "Well how much do you need?"

Frank sighed, "$100,000 would really help out."

Mother nearly fell out of her chair while exclaiming, "$100,000? You've got to be kidding me! Frank, how could you have gotten yourself into so much debt?"

"I know; I know, Mom! It just hit us all at once." Frank's voice began to tremor as he sniffled and produced a voice with a note of heavier estrogen. "I just don't know what else to do. I'm afraid of losing everything. Some nights I can't even sleep. If you could do this for me, it would mean a lot. And please don't tell Kimberly. I'm already ashamed for asking you this."

As far as Mother was concerned, none of Frank's life was any of Kimberly's business. She and Jim were far from perfect. Mother reminded her son of this.

And then she continued to address Frank's prospect of borrowing money. "You know what your Father would have told you, right?"

"I know, Mom. He wouldn't have done this."

There was a long pause, and then Mother spoke. "I'm going to need some time to think about this."

Only 24 hours were needed to consider her son's needs. All people experience their darkest moments in life. Shouldn't it be that a Mother helps her son in such a moment? A reassuring phone call provided Frank some much needed light and a promise that help was on the way. Help arrived in the form of certified mail with a $100,000 check from Mom.

Frank knew Mother well. Intending only to make a couple halfhearted payments towards Mom's loan, he knew she wouldn't pursue once the installments suddenly ceased. That $100,000 was his early share of the will, taken against the house that was to be split between him and Kimberly. $100,000 worth of proceeds from the final sale of the house would simply go back to the bank once Mother died. And of course; any remaining amount after $100,000 of the sale was returned to the bank would then be split between him and Kimberly. Lucky for Frank, he received $100,000 some years before it was time to liquidate and collect inheritances. Think of it as his clever way of receiving much more money than Kimberly.

Ah, but he was even more of a careless, self-centered prick. Shortly after Frank received $100,000 of his early share, he wacked the slot machine even further and struck the jackpot! This came on the day that his concerned sister called to discuss Mother.

"Frank, have you noticed anything unusual about Mom when you talk to her?"

"No…"

"Nothing at all?"

"No… Why?"

Kimberly described some concerning behavior recently noticed of Mother. "Frank, I visited Mom last week and immediately noticed the overpowering smell of gas in the house. I went over to the stove and could see that the pilot was running without any flames. I was like, 'Mom, didn't you smell this?' She was completely oblivious. And she acted like it was no big deal, saying that she must have bumped into the stove around lunchtime. It was four o'clock in the afternoon. Who knows how long that pilot was running?"

Frank said as little as possible. Only commented with a simple, "Hmm..."

"And it's worse than that, Frank. Yesterday she told me she couldn't sleep the night before because the furnace man was working in the basement and banging away at the registers. I said, 'Furnace man? You let someone in your house at night and then went to bed?' She told me that he's been down there for a few weeks, sleeps in the closet during the day and works on the furnace at night. I'm really worried about her, Frank. I'm afraid she might be in the early stages of Alzheimer's or dementia. Should we start looking into getting her in a home? I mean that gas could have killed her, you know?"

Of course Frank sounded concerned about Mother while urging Kimberly to make regular checks. "Right; this is definitely something to think about. See if you can get an appraisal done on her house and look into some retirement homes. I want to come out there, soon, and visit Mom. Then you and I can talk some more."

Thank God Kimberly had a brother to share in the responsibility of an elderly mother. But as Kimberly would soon find out, Frank had a devious plan in the works. He called Mother only an hour later. "Mom, are you okay?"

"Well of course I'm okay, Frank."

"The reason I ask is because I got a suspicious phone call from Kimberly. I guess she went over to your house last week and noticed a gas leak on the stove. Apparently, she's blowing it way out of proportion, trying to say that you have dementia or something."

Mother was shocked, "What? No! You've got to be kidding me!"

"I'm not kidding. And get this, Mom. Kimberly was talking about putting you in a nursing home. She's trying to convince me that you can't take care of yourself, anymore."

Poor Mother grew increasingly outraged, "Why would she do that? That's terrible!"

"I know, Mom. I think there's something going on in their personal life and they need money. My guess is if they can get you declared mentally incompetent, then they can have control of your finances. Dad left you a lot of money. I'm sure they'd love to get their hands on it!"

The poor, old woman was terribly disturbed by the news and already in the early stages of some old-aged, mental illness. In a weakened condition, she fed on every lie of Frank's while trusting her son with any insight he might have.

Frank continued to drive more worry into his mother. "You don't want to go to a nursing home, Mom. You just can't. They give you all those medications which make you get worse. You know how it is. Doctors give you pills to treat one thing, but then it has a negative effect on something else. Why else do you think people walk around like zombies in those places? Is that how you want to be; all drugged up and staggering around, pointing at imaginary people and little elves on the walls? And the food they give you is awful. Plus they put you to bed at six o'clock at night and make you wear diapers so they can chain you to the beds."

Poor Mother was in tears, "Oh my God, that's awful!"

"And they make you sit in your diaper until around eight o'clock in the morning. And I'm sure they yell at you while changing it."

Mother couldn't even sit in her chair as she now paced the family room, trembling with tears rolling down her cheeks. How could Kimberly do such a thing to her? If she needed money, Kimberly could have simply asked. Well Kimberly's true colors showed, now! "Frank, I only bumped into the stove and it opened the pilot. It could happen to anyone."

"I know, Mom; I know. I've done that before, too. Like I said, Kimberly is trying to blow it way out of proportion so she can get you in a home. Here's what you can do. You need to get out of Mapleview. You need to come down to Georgia and live with us. A change will definitely do you some good."

Her son was so goodhearted, but she couldn't take advantage of him. "Oh, Frank; I couldn't. I might get in the way."

"You're not going to get in the way, Mom. Besides, we need to get you out of there as soon as possible. I'm leaving tonight. I should be there in the next day or so to pick you up."

"Frank, that's so soon!"

"Mom, do you want to end up in a nursing home? Kimberly is serious about this. The quicker we get you out of there, the better. Just start packing up some of your clothes and necessary belongings. And definitely be sure to have your investments, your bank account information, any money you have in the house, all those antique coins that Dad collected, your jewelry; all that stuff. Kimberly and her husband will be going through the house when you're gone. They want money and valuables. As far as selling your house, I know a good Realtor out there named Jack Swieley. He'll sell the house for you, and the money will be yours."

Kimberly was never aware that her brother was in town. She simply received a phone call one late afternoon from Frank's cell phone. But it was Mother's voice! "Kimberly?"

"Yeah, Mom…"

"Kimberly, I thought I should let you know that I'm heading back to Georgia with Frank."

Suddenly, a surge of panic streaked through Kimberly. Mother was being kidnapped! How else would she be calling from Frank's cell phone? "Mom, what are you talking about?"

"I know all about it, Kimberly; how you were trying to put me in a home. I think it's rotten of you. Don't worry about my money and investments or anything of value. I have it all. And don't worry about the house. I'm putting it up for sale."

Kimberly desperately tried with all her might to talk sense into her Mother. Time was running out and she needed to be rescued. But for a woman Mother's age, she instinctively trusts her most powerful emotions. That moment of terror brought on through Frank's lies was all too real for Mother. How could she have trusted Kimberly?

And when asking to talk to Frank, Kimberly's brother would simply hang up the phone.

Kimberly and her husband, Jim, could only assume that Frank would soon have full control of the money. After all, if Frank could convince Mother to move down to Georgia, it would only be a matter of time before she signed everything over to his care. And that was how Kimberly lost contact with Mother, her brother, her sister-in-law, along with niece and two nephews.

It's evil, that money! People are willing to purchase a one-way ticket to Hell just for a few, lousy years of the highlife.

Chapter 22

Although another holiday would come and go without Kimberly's side of the family, Kimberly remained mindful of all the things she had to be thankful for. For one, at least she and Jim were financially responsible. They weren't dependent on inherited money to pay off bills, only to irresponsibly fund an extravagant year, or so, until the money ran out. She and Jim lived modestly—comfortably modest. Kimberly had two beautiful children. She was every bit a part of their life, staying at home as a fulltime mom. She had a wonderful husband who… well… maybe there was something dark and suspicious going on behind Kimberly's back, but she had a husband who appeared very much a part of the family and appeared to love Kimberly. At least in this moment over Thanksgiving dinner there was laughter, gayety and talk of happy things. Although lurking somewhere in her subconscious, Kimberly wasn't terribly mindful of her own family's absence. But through all the discussions of what her kids were doing and what Jim's nieces and nephews were up to these days, Kimberly continued to watch her husband. He would certainly be tested that evening.

As for Amber, the day wasn't terribly lonely. Estranged from her family many years ago and divorced from Michael, the only option was to make a small turkey dinner for her and Trista. Trista's father chose to be with that other woman and kids for the day. But maybe she could manipulate the afternoon in her favor so that Jim made a cameo appearance.

In the meantime, Jim sat there with his own family, discussing the old days with his two brothers, drinking more beer and acting as though nothing out-of-the-ordinary with life. And no one was the least bit wise to the dirty filth that stuck to his body. Jim needed a bath, a shower; maybe even have a fire hose spray him down with harsh force. The dirty bastard left the house that morning and had sex with "that woman". But Kimberly would find out more after everyone had gone home and the kids were in their rooms for the night.

Suddenly, Jim's outdated palm-pilot-styled phone sounded an alert. Hopefully it wasn't a Thanksgiving outage.

Kimberly studied her husband from a distance, just knowing that the text message came from "that woman". She was probably asking him to come over for Thanksgiving dinner. Kimberly was acting every bit an overly-jealous wife with unfounded reasons for her suspicions. Why in the world would "that woman" text Jim and expect him to come over for dinner?

Jim opened the message.

It was from Amber. "HAPPY THANKSGIVING!"

Jim typed a reply while Kimberly watched from across the room, "Happy Thanksgiving! How's it going today?"

After pressing the send button, Jim's father suddenly asked, "So Jim, in your opinion, who do you think has the best plasma TV? I'm thinking of getting one."

"Not sure, Dad. I don't know much about them."

"No? Don't you set those up in people's houses?"

"No, Dad; I maintain the outside equipment, remember?"

Jim's phone sounded an alert as another text message came through. It was Amber. "Not bad. It's just me and Trista. You should stop over and have a bite to eat. It would be nice."

Jim typed a message in return, "No, I can't get out of the house. The whole family's here. Didn't we celebrate last Friday?"

While Jim pressed the send button, Kimberly asked, "Who are you texting?" As far as Kimberly knew, Jim didn't have any friends. And all his family was there for the holiday.

Of course Jim lied while quickly deleting the chat thread. "Oh just people at the office sending out Happy Thanksgiving text messages."

For some reason, Kimberly had a difficult time believing her husband.

Sometime later, Jim's brother asked, "I got the new Motorola Droid. They just pushed the new operating system on me, but there seems to be some bugs. Are they going to resolve that?"

"I don't know, Mike. I don't have a Droid."

Moments later, Jim's other brother asked, "Hey, do you know of any cheap, lossless compression formats for music files? I hear MP3 takes some of the quality out of music files."

"Don't know; and to tell you the truth, I've never noticed any difference with MP3s."

Jim didn't know. *He didn't know*! For some reason, everyone saw him as the technology guru who could answer any questions on the latest gadgets or electronic goods. Satisfied with his TV from the year 2001, his outdated MP3 player and obsolete palm-pilot-styled phone from 2007; he was quite happy staying disconnected from the "latest and greatest" society. Half the time he had no idea what the hell people were talking about. And quite frankly, the Thanksgiving discussion of the latest gizmos and technology was beginning to bore Jim.

How he wished to be a wealth of information when it came to Ms. Lutrova. Jim's morning of web stalking, Ouija session and psychic reading was all in vain. He should have learned all about Ms. Lutrova and family; who they were, where they lived, stories of their lives and the causes they stood for. Despite how fruitless the web searches were, the hour of secret browsing had turned Jim into nothing less than an obsessed-psycho-stalker. And he was the frustrated type of stalker who had yet to learn anything of his victim!

* * *

One thing was certain in Jim's marriage. When it came to holidays, sex was not to be had! As he sat on the sofa with an evening bottle of beer, quartz crystal in his pocket and sneaking a text or two to his mistress; Kimberly walked in the family room, wearing just an oversized nightshirt and carrying a beverage with ice. In earlier years, had Kimberly walked in with just a nightshirt, Jim's hands would have found their way underneath. A man should be so lucky to have a wife like Kimberly; a hot, cinnamon, curvy blond with large breasts. Laying hands on those silky, creamy, bare thighs would only lead to pulling off her nightshirt and seizing the woman for more. But Jim learned not to look at his wife in that light. Pursuing her for sex only led to frustration. Only when Kimberly was in the mood could Jim finally have his way.

At first, Jim ignored his wife as she sat down next to him. In Jim's perception, placing her luscious, bare thigh on his lap was only Kimberly's way of being rude. Hopefully she didn't feel the phone buzzing in his pocket—another message from Amber.

Actually sex wouldn't be such a bad idea for Thanksgiving night. Amber was relentless with her desire to have Jim sneak over. Maybe he could stage a Thanksgiving night cable outage and visit the mistress for a little romance. It didn't need to be sex. Even Amber was a prude when it came to sex, as she had yet to fully put out. But Jim would have taken anything at that moment; making out, some nudity, feeling Amber's small breasts. The more Jim thought of it, the more he realized his horniness. And how lucky Jim was! Why did he waste his time with Ms. Lutrova and her silly game of Rumplestiltskin? Jim had a beautiful wife beside him and a mistress down the street just begging for him to come over.

Pulling out of his thoughts, Jim took notice of the mysterious drink in Kimberly's hand. She convulsed and made a funny face while taking a sip. Apparently, Kimberly was getting drunk! And this practice was only done on evenings when in the mood for love. Was Kimberly attempting sex on a holiday?

"What do you have in your glass?" asked Jim.

"Vodka and lemonade, except I made it really strong. Go ahead, taste it."

Jim took a sip. It was more like lemonade-flavored vodka. "Jeez! What, are you getting drunk?"

"It's Thanksgiving; it's a holiday." Kimberly would never admit to desiring sex. Instead, she took another sip from the glass, already feeling heavily buzzed.

To test his suspicions, Jim gently placed his hand on Kimberly's thigh and began to sensually rub.

Kimberly smiled in return.

It was on! After a five week gap, Jim would finally be rewarded to something he needed so badly. He further reached his hand underneath Kimberly's nightshirt. "Are you wearing panties?"

Kimberly slightly opened her thighs so that Jim could fondle as he pleased. Being that she removed her panties before slipping into something more comfortable, it was easy for Jim's finger to find the right thing.

Kimberly crossed her arm over towards Jim and laid her hand on his crotch. "You're not hard."

But who was Kimberly fooling? The stiff bulge was already beginning to form.

Jim didn't pay much attention to Kimberly's silly comment. He continued to play as he wished. And there was no denying for Kimberly of how pleasurable that moment was. She leaned in close and kissed her husband, losing herself in a moment of total ecstasy before returning to Earth for the next build-up. And it was shortly after this first trip back that she pulled away from Jim and looked him in the eyes. "Why are you kissing differently?"

Jim's fondling ceased. "What are you talking about?"

"You're kissing differently. Who have you been kissing?"

"I'm not kissing anyone else. Maybe you just haven't kissed me in a while." Jim gave his wife a simple kiss to her lips. "See, this is what I'm talking about. We need to do this sort of thing more often. Doesn't it feel good?"

Kimberly nodded. But she didn't believe her husband. She would prove it once-and-for-all with a trip to the bedroom. "We better get in the room. The kids could come in here any minute."

Unlike other evenings of romance, the bedroom light stayed on while Kimberly stood before her husband, eagerly waiting for him to do more. With his shirt off, Kimberly glanced at Jim's neck and chest for any hickies or bite marks. She even glanced in the bedroom mirror behind him for scratches. There was nothing.

This was done just a second before Jim seized her. He aggressively pulled off Kimberly's nightshirt to expose her large, bulging breasts, curvy hips and brown bush covering that which would soon be assaulted. He kissed her so crazily with his hands firmly squeezing Kimberly's thick, full ass.

But then Kimberly went back to the same, silly game. "You're not hard."

"You think so, huh?" It was only a cue for Jim to pull down his pants and expose the item in question. It was hot and hard, looking just as dangerous as ever. "There it is, Baby. Any more questions?" With his left hand firmly squeezing Kimberly's ass cheek, Jim's right hand was used to attempt touching her with the thing.

But Kimberly wanted no part of that thing. STDs, HPV or even yeast infections; Kimberly couldn't allow Jim to touch her with it. She quickly pushed Jim away. "Okay, that's enough."

Kimberly didn't push her husband hard enough. He only pulled her back and took hold of his wife's face while whispering against her luscious lips. "You like playing that little game, huh? You in the mood for some rough stuff, tonight?"

"No, Jim!" Kimberly had to be careful not to talk too loudly. The kids couldn't be aware of what was going on in Mother and Father's room.

Jim's hand grasped the back of Kimberly's hair as he enjoyed another kiss from her luscious lips. In earlier years, Kimberly and Jim enjoyed beautiful sex as any young couple does. Then, shortly after April had been born, Jim began playing out his sexual frustrations with small hints of aggression during moments of making love. One night, he had one of the greatest, sexual experiences of his life. Somehow, he and Kimberly ended up playing the rape game in bed. She squirmed and fought her attacker, begged him to stop and resisted any unwanted touches while looking away whenever kissed. Just about every husband and wife has played this once or twice. It's a very, exciting game!

But for Jim and Kimberly, this turned into a regular occurrence. Kimberly was so good at it, making the sexual experience spicy and intense for Jim. And so on that Thanksgiving night under much suspicion and mistrust, Jim only interpreted the resistance as a sign to play.

"No, Jim! Stop it!"

Hair is meant to be grabbed and to make a woman understand that "no" is not an option. Of course it hurts when pulled hard enough and can turn a woman irate. Jim wanted that irateness as he aggressively held the sides of Kimberly's sexy, cinnamon-blond hair and continued kissing her. He wanted his wife to be angry in that moment. He desired to see the furious beast come out, slapping him and biting him with a distressed look in her face. Every vicious scratch and every slap to Jim's face was appreciated and enjoyed.

Jim momentarily stopped to take sight of his roughed-up wife, breathing heavily with red, ferocious face. Then he told her, "Baby, you are so, freaking sexy when you're mad."

"I'm not playing, Jim!"

"Shut up and get on the bed." Jim seized his wife and pushed her across the room.

But Kimberly was strong and would not go down without a fight. She stood up from the bed as Jim approached, only to be pushed down against the mattress. Of course Kimberly squirmed and resisted as Jim lay on top. Occasionally, his dangerous thing would make contact with her. But she was good! Kimberly desperately fought off her attacker, even slapped and bit when given a chance. In fact, the difficulty in finally having what he wanted created a crazed frustration for Jim. Oh, she was good! She was so, freaking good! She made it all so real!

As Jim saw it, some women are simply made to play rape—especially Kimberly. A thick, curvy frame and such a strong body made it easy to play rough. But the same wouldn't hold true for Amber. Jim thought of this while battling with his crazed wife in bed. Amber's body was fragile and thin in comparison to Kimberly's. With such a delicate, pretty face and beautiful, blond hair; a woman like Amber was to be handled with care. Making love would be gentle and tender with slow, passionate kisses. Amber probably enjoyed her sex soft and cuddly, not hard and rough like Kimberly. In fact, Amber didn't have sex! Amber made beautiful love, Jim assumed.

I suppose many men have looked in the mirror and rehearsed for the possible moment when a wife discovers the other woman. For Jim, he could rehearse a convincing argument. "She meant nothing to me! I made sweet and tender love to that bitch and then held her for a long time after that. But I screwed you rough and hard, and treated you like a crazy animal!"

That would work, wouldn't it?

Nearing exhaustion, Kimberly had no choice but to allow Jim to take what he wanted. But it wasn't enough for Jim. While deeply thrusting himself, he would take turns wildly kissing Kimberly's luscious, hot lips; then to squeeze and suck her large breasts. She was doing this to Jim, "that woman". All that sex magick was turning Kimberly's husband into a crazy sex maniac. It was the only explanation for Kimberly. And to make matters worse, Kimberly was beginning to enjoy the assault. In fact, at one point, she even exclaimed, "Why do we wait so long to have sex?"

"I don't know." said Jim. "We need to do this more often." He continued to thrust himself while admiring the view Kimberly's gorgeous breasts that bounced up and down. The sight of them, alone, was enough to cause a near climax. Towards the end, Jim squashed his chest against Kimberly's so that nipples touched nipples. He loved her beautiful breasts! And he nearly broke her shoulders while holding on for dear life. Jim was hard as ever and finally exploded with an almighty force; his heart racing like a jackrabbit.

Kimberly, too, climaxed in that moment. One might think that husband and wife were truly made for each other. Jim voiced this as the surge of endorphins provided the ultimate high. "Baby, you're freaking amazing."

Kimberly giggled in reply…

…And then it was back to reality. Disgusted with herself, she stood up as Jim rolled over to Kimberly's side and lovingly stroked her beautiful, naked body.

But Kimberly was in no mood to cuddle. How did she let this happen? "Well, there's your Thanksgiving present."

Jim lay there and watched as Kimberly put her nightshirt back on and stepped out of the room. Amber would have laid there with Jim. She would have lain up against his chest to have Jim comb his fingers through her pretty hair. There would have been no urgency to watch the blasted TV in the family room. Amber would surely lay in the dark with Jim, cuddling and enjoying idle conversation until falling asleep.

Now alone, the phone in Jim's pants pocket buzzed on the floor. It was probably another text message from Amber.

Chapter 23

Something happened in that tool room; Daren just knew it. Now his own, little room in the cellar; Daren had two private clubhouses to enjoy. But the tool room was a dark place that filled him with such mystery, while at the same time provoking overpowering emotions. In contrast to that dark place, the family mausoleum safely held his beloved Mary Trivelli. She was safe, now; safe from her rotten husband who had murdered her nearly two centuries ago.

How badly Daren needed to be with her in those final moments of terror. While his own wife worked at the flower shop during the day, Daren would consume too many beers with Grandma Trivelli until reaching a point of despair. Nearly drunk and in a need to rescue his long-distanced love, Daren would return to the tool room and intimately place his hands on the tool bench in some attempt to bleed through the fabric of time-space continuum. Nearly two centuries of damage were deeply explored by Daren's fingers, every strike from a hammer and every gash from an axe blade. Strangely, alcohol did this for Daren. It shifted his consciousness to another realm that he had yet to understand. Sometimes he felt he could literally reach out and affect the outcome of things by penetrating some imagined veil. Surely he could traverse the small obstacle of time and save Mary Trivelli.

In frustration and in sudden doubt of this imagined ability, Daren would return to the family mausoleum to regain his mystical power that was made possible by longing for the woman in the jar.

"Daren, you need to focus on your wife, not me. Your feelings and concerns are much appreciated, but my granddaughter needs her husband."

Daren didn't actually hear Grandma Trivelli speaking through the jar, but he felt her wishes. She was right, of course. And Mary would be home in another couple hours. It was best to seal Grandma Trivelli back up in her crypt and lock up the mausoleum for the afternoon.

* * *

It was a late, Wednesday afternoon; two Wednesdays that followed Thanksgiving—already December. With Daren airing out in the family room from his afternoon, beer-induced stupor; Mary broiled some homemade hamburgers and potato wedges for dinner. Other than the taste of beer on Daren's breath when kissing him, Mary wasn't the least-bit aware of how badly he had drunk that afternoon. And Daren presented no reason to be concerned of this. Being a salesman was his livelihood, and he could create any personality he wished. Daren could act cheery for his wife and disguise the ugliness for that moment.

Over Dinner, Mary spoke of a recent, daily phenomenon at the flower shop. Perhaps Grandma Trivelli had done some intercession through her granddaughter. The story would emphasize just how much Mary needed those simple acts of affection.

Mary squirted some ketchup on her hamburger bun while introducing the story. "So, for the past few days we have this guy who comes in the flower shop and asks for a rose. He comes in about three o'clock and demands that the petals aren't wilted or dried."

Daren took a bite of his double burger with cheddar cheese. "Hmm…"

"But then I noticed that he wears a wedding band. Shelly and I are like, 'That's so sweet. Here the guy is buying a rose for his wife every day.' She's so lucky."

Daren took a sip of water before commenting. "He probably has a girlfriend. Or maybe he got in a really bad fight with his wife and he's trying to make up."

Mary sighed, "There you go, again! You always have to see something negative. Can't the guy just be really sweet and buy his wife a rose before going home?"

Daren understood that women appreciate candy and flowers, having the door held open for them or holding hands in public. But he also believed that too much of a good thing made it all-the-less special. "Look, I just know that men don't over-do it, and for a good reason. Okay, maybe your customer is a sweet guy and decided to start buying a rose for his wife every day. The first day is a surprise. The second day, 'Awe, isn't that nice.' By the third day, his wife is getting sick of finding vases for the roses. You know what I mean? That's why I concluded that either he has a girlfriend, or maybe he's trying to make up with his wife."

Again, Mary sighed; this time shaking her head in disbelief. "Oh, never mind! Just eat your hamburger."

"Alright, alright; we got off on the wrong foot. You were just trying to tell me a little romantic story over dinner. That's cool." Then Daren affectionately placed his hand on Mary's. "Is that all you need; some roses every now and then or little gifts and things."

Mary nodded with her cute, pouty face.

The story certainly did bring things back into focus for Daren. For a while, the results took his mind off Grandma Trivelli. But through a remotely connected series of events, Amber had been inadvertently placed in danger. And it was all Jim's fault!

* * *

There's an interesting phenomenon of Ms. Lutrova and her control of Jim. Only a day after Thanksgiving, he had already begun thinking about her. Recall that during the holiday, Jim had gotten frustrated with her little game of Rumplestiltskin. With such a gorgeous wife who offers spicy sex and a beautiful mistress down the street, what need did Jim have with some old woman orchestra teacher who offered nothing more than nightly fantasies?

But it's not so easy to get rid of Ms. Lutrova! That algae-green sex potion in the glass vials was causing prolonged nightly erections accompanied by intense, erotic dreams. Ms. Lutrova used this as a portal to continue tormenting her victim so that by the Monday after Thanksgiving weekend, Jim awoke in the predawn hours to go down in the basement and sit in the center of a six-pointed-star that was formed with quartz crystals at the points. In his hand was the outdated palm pilot. The screen was a Google Earth satellite image of what he believed to be Ms. Lutrova's home—near the place where Jim saw her walking on the morning of All Saints Day. Aware of flurries now outside, Jim imagined his consciousness to be broken into millions of pieces scattering along Ms. Lutrova's house with the falling snow. Through this technique, Jim used the palm pilot as a crystal ball to remotely view the activities of Ms. Lutrova and possibly connect with her.

Inside the house, the orchestra teacher lay in her bed in a half-dreamy state. She spoke to Jim, "Do you know what comes to mind when I think of snow?"

"What's that?" Jim lay beside her, under the blankets and cuddling.

"It reminds me of when I was a little girl and would get all bundled up to go outside and play. Maybe I'd go sledding or build a snowman; get cold after a while and then come in the house for some hot cocoa with marshmallows."

Jim smiled, "I remember that as a kid, too."

Jim clicked the palm pilot screen off and set it on the floor. There was too much of the supposed telepathic communication between him and Ms. Lutrova. How much of what Jim experienced was nothing more than fantasy? That fantastic world where he and the orchestra teacher were at the brink of making real contact began to crumble. They might have had a mutual attraction, Jim gave his theory that much. But the intensity of attraction was surely more on Jim's part. Any normal woman wouldn't bother with a man with such obsession, not to mention a married man.

What Jim really should have been doing at that moment was holding a flower and plucking out the petals while chanting, "She loves me; she loves me not." For no sooner after his sobering moment of reality, Jim was pulled into a different picture frame where he and Ms. Lutrova shared mutual concerns. Their thought processes and moods were in tune with one another's. As Jim questioned and doubted the reality of what he believed, Ms. Lutrova did the same. The two stood just inches from one another, yet separated by a wall. It was only necessary to walk some feet to get around this wall and finally be together. And yet they remained trapped, touching the wall, calculating what he or she might be thinking and feeling.

Throughout the week, Jim noticed a peculiar habit in which he would pay attention to little scraps of paper or small items on the ground. He would most often zoom in on these items in his driveway or near the house. Smiley-face or heart stickers that probably came from the kids, little folded up pieces of paper, even a nearly deflated balloon which had somehow blown in his driveway; these items gave hope to a possible calling, a test to see if Jim was connected. And might there be a message on one of these pieces of paper?

It could have been any simple, vague message such as, "Ms. L"—the orchestra teacher's initials.

Maybe it would be a smiley face and the word, "Hi".

Or perhaps, "Do you feel the same way?"

Or even, "Call me!" followed by Ms. Lutrova's number.

Only a person in tune with this world would be looking for messages like these. The recipient would hear it loud and clear and finally have the bravery to act.

But this was silly. No woman would ever go so far as to leave little, subliminal notes to be found. A woman hides in dark corners, hoping to be discovered, sometimes coming out to shake her tail in a man's face, only to run away with, "I wasn't giving you any signs!"

It was the man who needed to drop little hints and finally take charge. How foolish Jim felt! He should have simply walked up to her door and knocked. "Hi, I'm Jim." But then what? Hopefully Ms. Lutrova understood the complexity. Surely she realized that a married man had much to think about before making his move, if he ever made his move.

But the scraps of paper were an excellent idea. Why couldn't Jim have written sweet nothings and let them blow out his window while driving past Ms. Lutrova's house on the highway?

"Thinking of you."

"Wishing to hold you."

"Is it mutual?"

Like kisses that blow across the wind, the messages would somehow carry to Ms. Lutrova's doorstep so that when stepping outside for the mail, she would discover them. It might buy Jim some time; let her know that he wasn't a lost cause. And surely Ms. Lutrova would make her awareness of these sweet nothings known through some sign. It might even give Jim the confidence needed to finally initiate contact.

Ah, but Jim couldn't do this. What if the orchestra teacher had a family member living with her who might discover these notes? Then what? Sweet nothings were out of the question!

So Jim went back to despair, realizing that time was running out and that he was falling short from meeting obligation. All this silly nonsense of letting sweet nothings blow out the window; if a real man was going to play that game he would leave a rose at a woman's doorstep or lay it on the windshield of her car. But again, Jim couldn't do this. There might be a family member who recognized it.

Then it hit Jim like a flash of light! If Ms. Lutrova was truly in tune with whatever world Jim believed they shared, she would recognize the peculiar presence of rose petals scattered along her lawn. He could walk past her house in the predawn hours and let the petals scatter, perhaps along the driveway. When backing her car from the driveway or looking out the window, she would see the petals and suspect that Jim had left them there.

This brilliant idea took place on a Friday afternoon, one week after Black Friday. And Jim nearly drove his cable utility truck to the Mapleview flower shop. But the orchestra teacher wouldn't work on Saturdays and the petals would surely blow away by the time she would get out to her car and hopefully see them. It was better to do it on a Monday.

But having rose petals on Ms. Lutrova's driveway Monday morning presented a problem. The Mapleview flower shop was closed on Sunday. It would be necessary to purchase a rose on Saturday then leave it sit in the truck for nearly 48 hours. This would introduce the possibility of the rose petals wilting, and Ms. Lutrova did not deserve wilted roses! There could be only the best for her!

So Jim walked into the Mapleview flower shop on Monday afternoon where Mary had greeted him at the front counter. As usual, Mary was pleasant and friendly. "Hi, welcome to Mapleview Flowers. What can I do for you?"

"Yeah, um, do you sell roses, like a single rose?"

Mary seemed delighted. "Sure we do! Come on back to our cooler. We have a wide assortment of fresh flowers."

Jim followed behind until reaching the glass, refrigerated case that contained roses of various colors.

Mary had such a comforting, trustful way in asking, "Now can I ask, who are you buying the rose for? Is she a friend of yours; maybe someone you are interested in; a first date; or perhaps that special someone?"

Jim knew what Mary was asking. The color of a rose signified certain things or matched a particular occasion. From what he remembered, yellow stated a friendship where-as red stated more of a romantic attraction. Unsure of what Ms. Lutrova was to him, Jim realized that the relationship they shared was very special. It was much deeper than a friendship and much deeper than a thoughtless, extramarital affair. There certainly could be romance between them, but so pure and innocent. For that matter, Jim decided red would be the appropriate color. "I'm going with red. I need a red rose."

"Red? Okay, she's really special."

"Absolutely!" Jim agreed.

Jim paid cash for the rose, of course, and then threw away the receipt. Carrying the flower out of the store and into his truck was extremely awkward. What if Kimberly or Amber happened to be driving through town and saw him? He could appear disappointed and mention that the rose was a little "just because" surprise.

Finally safe in the truck with the rose in the passenger seat, Jim drove to the wayside parking lot of Hidden Lake Forest Preserve and parked. He felt so sorry for the delicate creature. Its destiny was to be delivered to the hands of a very, special lady; perhaps a first date or even a loving wife whose husband wished to surprise her on a Monday night. Instead, the petals were delicately pulled so carefully in such a way that there would be no tearing or what might appear to be scraps. Again, only the best for Ms. Lutrova! The rose shouldn't have felt so abused. It was, after all, being offered as a testament and sign to Jim's feelings for a special woman. And the same could be said of tomorrow's rose and the day after, and the day after that. Petals would be sprinkled along Ms. Lutrova's front lawn every Tuesday through Friday morning, to be blown and scattered in places where Ms. Lutrova might find them. Perhaps nothing would be recognized on the first morning or two. But after a week, Jim envisioned her entire front lawn would be littered with the petals of red roses.

While collecting the petals into a plastic bag for the following morning, Jim had the sudden concern that perhaps sprinkling rose petals on someone's front lawn might have been considered a magick spell. After all, Ms. Lutrova was a witch, and she might identify the act as some strange spell. What if the activity suggested something other than symbolizing love and attraction?

Fortunately for Jim he had his crystal ball for acquiring such knowledge. The outdated palm-pilot-styled phone provided immediate access to the Internet. The search phrase "sprinkling rose petals on someone's lawn" didn't provide much information. The results were mostly articles on improving landscaping. There were a couple articles on increasing romance in the bedroom with rose petals.

"Sprinkling rose petals love spell" provided better results. As Jim found out, there were countless love spells on the Internet that used rose petals. Many of them involved strange activities such as plucking out your hair and burning various colored candles while writing the desired person's name on paper and sprinkling it with roses. There was even a spell that involved burying the rose petals in a jar of honey and tasting the honey every day while repeating the desired person's name. They were such silly spells in Jim's opinion. The best spell, as he believed, was to sprinkle rose petals along Ms. Lutrova's front lawn every morning. There was nothing held secret from the person of his desire. And the true magick would come from Ms. Lutrova's reaction.

Feeling that rose petals were associated with love when it came to magick, Jim felt safe following through with his plan. Again, Ms. Lutrova was a witch, and she would certainly recognize the rose petal invasion as merely an act of love.

Chapter 24

Recall the morning of All Saints Day when Jim passed Ms. Lutrova on the high-way. The house she stood in front of and apparently hers has approximately two hundred feet of front yard that extends to the highway. Her actual home and property is really quite interesting. As you already know, the north section of Mapleview contains historic homes that are buried within the surrounding woods along the highway such as the historic Trivelli house.

But Ms. Lutrova or previous owners of that section of property must have had whatever home torn down. In its place is a beautiful, two-story log cabin with balcony running along the second level of both the front and back. The two hundred foot asphalt driveway slightly curves north while approaching the home and is outlined in a combination of pine and white oak trees. Needless to say, the property is absolutely beautiful in the winter with snow!

Had Ms. Lutrova lived on one of the neighboring streets in Maple Sap like Amber did, Jim's rose petal assault would have been easy to do. Just casually walk down the sidewalk in the predawn hours and inconspicuously drop the rose petals in the driveway or front lawn. But a property off the highway with two hundred feet of driveway posed a bit of challenge when considering incon-spicuousness. He certainly couldn't leave the petals at the edge of the highway. They needed to be somewhere near the house to be discovered.

None of Ms. Lutrova's driveway was illuminated. At night or in the predawn hours, the two hundred feet before her house was pretty much pitch black. Of course Ms. Lutrova did have security lights perimeter her home.

With the presence of darkness, Jim found it convenient to park his Maple-view Cable bucket truck on the shoulder of the highway a short distance from Ms. Lutrova's house. Then he would walk towards her property and ascend the area of grass that outlines the driveway and is furthest from the house.

Although surrounded in darkness, Jim felt as though his very presence was under a spotlight. Just like Kimberly and Amber, surely Ms. Lutrova slept in the predawn hours. But on this morning, the orchestra teacher was probably aware of Jim's plan. They shared a telepathic connection. She probably even broadcasted the idea for him to follow through with the daring act.

Finally very near Ms. Lutrova's house, Jim opened the plastic bag and allowed the petals to drift and scatter along the driveway near her garage. He couldn't run away from her house fast enough! Jim could see in his mind Ms. Lutrova standing some distance from a darkened window and noticing what was left behind; noticing that it was Jim who did this. So touched by his simple act she softly smiled. Jim did just as Ms. Lutrova wished.

But he wouldn't let this telepathic control of the orchestra teacher get the best of him. Walking towards her house on that first morning nearly resulted in cardiac arrest. The following morning, and every morning of the rose petal assault thereafter, Jim used a new technique. But you must first know about an unusual acquisition that Jim and his family received a couple years prior.

* * *

Two years ago while answering a customer's complaint for loss of Internet service at one of the stores in a strip mall of downtown Mapleview, Jim took notice of some intriguing merchandise from a shop being discarded into the dumpster. It was from the failed business, Mapleview Costumes. Offering a large collection of full body costumes of animals, Disney creatures and cartoon characters for rent; the shop mysteriously closed its doors and the owners disappeared. The phenomenon offered some interesting gossip throughout town for a couple of weeks. It appeared to be a shady business that was really used as a front for drug dealing, illegal gambling or any other Mafia related activities. Some say that drugs were smuggled in the area through shipments of the costumes. Whatever the case, there was something quite odd about the shop from the beginning. Who would have placed so much investment into the costume rental business?

The owner of the strip mall did the only right thing after seeing the storefront had been abandoned. All the lifelike costumes were discarded into the trash; giant gorilla suits, rabbits, Winnie the Pooh, horses, dragons—you name it, it was there for anyone to pick. And the lucky winner of that bizarre lottery was Jim, lineman technician of Mapleview Cable.

Kimberly was dumbfounded that her husband brought home all those costumes in his utility cable truck. What wife wants to find room for such useless items in her home that already was short of storage space?

But Jim insisted, "Oh come-on, Honey! It'll be fun! Just think; the kids will have the best Halloween costumes in the neighborhood each year. We can go to parties dressed up in this two-man polar bear suit, just me and you. Wouldn't you like that?"

Kimberly sighed, "It's up to you to find room for this stuff. It's not coming in the house! Put it in your garage."

And that's what Jim did. He made special shelving for his collection of life-like, full body costumes; and stored three, each, in large bins.

* * *

On Wednesday morning, the morning after the first rose petal assault of Ms. Lutrova's home, Jim dressed up in full body gorilla suit. Hopefully no one took notice of the beast exiting the Mapleview Cable bucket truck and prowling the highway in the predawn hours. But Ms. Lutrova surely took notice, Jim assumed. Tracking him through telepathic means and directing him to follow through with a daring activity; she probably stood some distance from a darkened window, waiting for another rose petal visit from Jim. But what was this? It was a gorilla that appeared in front of her house! The animal stepped onto her front lawn and threw the rose petals in the air so that they scattered along the light blanket of December snow. The gorilla beat its chest while facing Ms. Lutrova's house and then turned to walk away. But before getting too far, the gorilla turned towards the house, again, waved and then blew a kiss towards the window of Ms. Lutrova's imagined presence.

He did this activity every Tuesday through Friday morning from the 8th to the 18th of December. Dressed in a different costume each morning, his performances increased on Ms. Lutrova's front lawn; sometimes running along the center with streaks of rose petals flying from both hands, maybe dancing a jig or perhaps doing the Macarena (it was the only dance Jim remembered from earlier years). In disguise and unrecognizable, Jim had all the courage he needed to perform this way. After all, it wasn't Jim delivering the roses and the silly dances on Ms. Lutrova's front lawn. Maybe it was the 6-foot rabbit, the green lizard, the orange tabby cat, Winnie the Pooh or the adorable grizzly bear with bow around its neck. Any number of these individuals could have left rose petals in the front lawn.

And this is the sort of man who gives the woman he loves a rose every day. He does so out of maddening obsession, out of a painful yearning in wishing that he could have her. The feelings manifest themselves and lead to these desperate acts. You really have to love a woman so terribly to give her a rose each day, and to deliver it in such an unusual way.

Chapter 25

Throughout those two weeks there was a cute, little story forming between Jim and Mary—Daren's Mary. Jim would enter the Mapleview Flower Shop at around the same time every Tuesday through Friday. With each encounter Mary adored him more and more. Sometimes Mary was in the backroom, perhaps working on some floral arrangement. The shop's owner, Shelly (also Mary's best friend), would peak her head in the backroom and whisper, "Mary, your boyfriend is here."

Mary would answer back, "Oh, shut up!"

Both women softly giggled.

Mary would come out to the front desk alone while softly blushing. "Hey there! Another red rose for you?"

"Yeah, just make sure it's not wilted."

Believing the flower to be for a special lady, Mary took extra care in selecting the perfect rose for Jim, as she wished Daren would have gotten that very rose for her. Daren had yet to surprise his wife with any "just because" gifts or flowers.

And Jim was developing a slight attraction to his new friend, Mary. She was so beautiful and definitely the sort of woman he could fall in love with. (*Anyone could fall in love with Mary!*) Being an expert in flowers and appearing to be a well-grounded, down-to-Earth woman with an infinite wisdom of true love, Jim often wished he could talk to Mary about his recent experiences. He loved his wife, dearly; but had fallen so terribly in love with Ms. Lutrova. That's what happens when an ordinary person who knows nothing of magick attempts to cast a love spell on another person. As he or she may or may not realize, the spell comes back threefold! But as far as Jim knew, it was true love—he just knew it. There was no other explanation for his behavior in recent months. What would Mary say of this? Would she be enchanted by Jim's story of being hopelessly in love with a strange woman? Or would she be outraged to hear of Jim's betrayal to his wife?

Although a beautiful woman and someone Jim would have liked to confess his secrets to, Mary just didn't have the same effect as Ms. Lutrova did. In fact, no woman in recent times (including poor Amber!) appeared all that alluring and attractive to Jim. For so many years he viewed women as little pieces of candy that walked the streets, each one causing a rise in adrenaline and circulation. But that pleasure had vanished in recent weeks. The only woman who created such a stir in Jim's heart was Ms. Lutrova. Yes, Jim was actually that much in love with the old woman!

Although a good looking man and quite fond of him, Mary wouldn't even think of having something to do with Jim beyond the Mapleview Flower Shop. Mary loved Daren and pledged to be forever faithful on the day of her wedding.

But the same couldn't be said of Daren! Originally planning to get his wife a new LCD screen TV for Christmas, or a notebook computer with wireless router so she could browse the web comfortably; Daren considered Mary's recent indication of needing little, emotional gifts that symbolized his love for her. With Daren's salary, he could surprise his wife with both the pricey toys and something small and symbolic. What Mary needed was one of those beautiful love pendants that were advertised on TV during the holidays. The commercial featured a young, desperate, terribly-jealous and overly-possessive man who carefully observed the woman he loved from the other room. She appeared to be talking quietly on the phone, almost whispering as-if not to allow her jealous boyfriend to hear of the conversation details. Maybe this disturbed him. And seeing his girlfriend hang up the phone upon noticing being watched, he quickly approached and presented her the love pendant that was a series of joined hearts that were adorned with diamonds.

She looked so terrified with tears in her eyes. "Oh, it's beautiful! You really shouldn't have!"

But the young man reassured his girlfriend, "I'll always love you and will never let you go. And when you feel alone, I'm actually watching you; following some distance behind, making sure that you continue to wear my love pendant so that strange men know that you belong to me."

The commercial would end with a romantic jingle and a reminder to reward that special lady with a symbol of undying love.

Mary would love to receive such a beautiful pendant from Daren. And on the last Friday of Jim's rose petal assault (December 18th), Daren visited the Mapleview Department Store to shop for one of those pendants. And who do you suppose was the manager of the jewelry department? Amber worked the floor that morning while her two employees went on break. And what do you suppose Daren did as he approached the jewelry case where Amber worked? That's right, you guessed it; Daren counted an enormous wad of cash that was pulled from his front pocket. Amber was just as beautiful as ever, and Daren needed to put on his charm.

Amber was no stranger to money. For several years she had more money than she knew what to do with. And although certainly a nice thing to have in abundance, her marriage of those days-long-past lacked some important ingredients; mainly a husband who was present throughout the week.

"Hi, can I help you?" Amber greeted the customer.

Daren smiled while placing his money back in the pocket. "I'm looking for love pendants. Do you have any of those?"

"Yes, we do. Are you looking for something for your wife or girlfriend; maybe a mother pendant?"

"It's for my girlfriend."

Amber led Daren over to the area of love pendants and pulled out the very piece of jewelry that had been advertised on TV for the holidays. "This is a popular item." She handed it to Daren.

Daren examined the pendant and returned a peculiar look to Amber. "Can I ask you a favor?"

"Sure."

"I hope this doesn't sound weird or anything; but you look *exactly* like my girlfriend, and I want to see what this looks like on you. Can you put it on?"

"Sir I can't do…"

Daren interrupted her, "Come-on, just put it on. At least hold it up so I can see."

Amber reluctantly did as the customer asked. Policy prevented her from putting jewelry on, but simply holding it against herself didn't seem like such a violation.

Daren was impressed. "Oh, that's beautiful. You would look so good wearing that."

Amber immediately lowered the pendant. What was the customer doing?

Daren sighed, "I'm sorry, it's just… Well, I'm going through a difficult time with my girlfriend. You know how you can totally feel that you're about to break up and you want to make one, last effort to hopefully change things?"

Amber remained silent.

"Well, we're going through that now. I'm just wondering if this would work."

From what Amber could determine, the customer was either a poor liar or stupid. With a wedding band on, he should have been shopping for his wife. Obviously hitting on Amber, his offer for her to be the next "other woman" wasn't all that appealing or flattering. Amber maintained her professionalism and was apologetic. "I'm really sorry to hear that, sir. We have a 30 day, full money return policy. As long as the jewelry isn't damaged, we'll take it back. Did you want to make a purchase?"

"Yeah, why don't we go ahead and ring me up. I'll let you know how things work out between me and my girlfriend."

This wouldn't be Daren's last visit to the jewelry department of the Mapleview Department Store. He was definitely interested in Amber. And if you've taken the time to get better acquainted with Daren in The Tree Goddess, you certainly know that his obsession with a woman is never a good thing. In fact, it can be quite dangerous.

* * *

The morning of Friday, December 18th was to be the last morning of Jim's rose petal assault. Up until that day, there was only a thin, nearly-melted blanket of snow that covered the grounds throughout Mapleview. And on that morning of December 18th, Ms. Lutrova's front yard was clearly littered by red rose petals. They lay scattered in patches of dormant grass and frozen in the remaining snow of her front lawn. But Friday night brought with it a terrible snow storm that heavily blanketed the town of Mapleview. This, of course, covered any evidence of Jim's rose petal assaults. Jim took it as a sign to cease his predawn performances at Ms. Lutrova's house. Although rose petals would look beautiful in the midst of a blanket of snow; Jim imagined a deeper picture, one in which the arrival of snow had announced some mystical change in the world of magick.

Oh, it should be mentioned that there was another perceived factor that contributed to his decision to cease the rose petal assault. It was a sensation of overwhelming paranoia that was felt on the night of Monday, December 21st–the first night of winter in Mapleview of that year. On this night, there was an event at the Mapleview Community High School, the holiday orchestra concert. April was to perform, of course. But the very thought of being in the presence of Ms. Lutrova had Jim on edge. Was she aware of the mastermind and operative of the rose petal assault?

Just like the solo and duet performances, Jim bottled his anxiety while entering the main door of the school. But it was to get even worse! Paranoia, as Jim would soon find out, greeted him as he walked down the main corridor.

"*Good evening, Sir!*" There was such emphasis in the concierge's voice who was probably a volunteer parent of an orchestra student or maybe a teacher or some other staff member of the school. No explanation was needed. The intent look on his face and his voice told Jim everything. Somehow, the man greeting families and offering program handouts knew all about Jim and his obsession with Ms. Lutrova. She was probably friends with the concierge and told him everything; told him all about the rose petals. "*Thanks for joining us tonight, Sir. Enjoy the show.*" He smiled in such a way to hint of his awareness.

Why such betrayal from Ms. Lutrova? Couldn't she have kept her predawn surprises a secret? And if one person was knowledgeable of what Jim had done, how many others would soon find out through gossip?

Fortunately, Kimberly hadn't noticed the unusual behavior of the concierge. But while approaching the gymnasium, Jim suddenly considered that perhaps the man wasn't aware of anything at all. What really happened, Jim speculated, was a greeting made by Ms. Lutrova. She was capable of these things; certainly capable of telepathically hijacking a stranger's mind and speaking her intentions through his words and expressions.

And then there was Amber seated at one of the bleachers. Of course she would attend the performance. It was to be expected, and the usual protocols of secrecy would be followed. But while approaching the bleachers, Jim took notice of another person who joined Amber for the evening. It was a woman who appeared to be a family member of Amber's, perhaps her older sister. Jim didn't get much of a chance to look closely at this supposed sister of Amber's as he was careful not to call any attention of the connection shared between him and the mistress. Amber returned no eye contact as Jim passed as well. She was probably maintaining a low profile while in the presence of family.

It was understandable for Jim. At least Amber knew how to play the game of forbidden romance.

How could Jim have been so stupid in his two weeks of predawn rose petal assaults? That blasted Ms. Lutrova had to open her mouth and expose her secret admirer! The more Jim thought about it, the more he realized that the concierge probably wasn't under telepathic control by the woman. He was probably Ms. Lutrova's own boyfriend!

See what happens when an ordinary person who knows nothing of magick casts a love spell? As he or she may or may not realize, threefold karma returns as desperate thoughts and speculations racing along with the game of "loves me, loves me not". And it was about to get worse!

Not more than two minutes after finding a place to sit down and settle for the performance, Jim slightly glanced towards Amber's direction and was startled to see her sister carefully studying him. She made no effort to be inconspicuous. Apparently, this woman felt that if curious of anything, she should have every right to look and examine. Jim could do nothing but return a deer-in-the-headlights, confused look. In doing so, he was able to get a better look of the woman. With a face just as pale as Amber's, she had long, radiant-red hair with deep-brown eyes. There was almost something mesmerizing of her appearance, as-if she could place one's mind in a suspended state.

Oh no! Somehow Amber's sister had become aware of Jim's rose petal assault as well. Ms. Lutrova told her concierge boyfriend who told someone else, then another… then so on, and so on, and so on! By now, Amber probably knew of it as well. That's why she made no eye contact with him. She was angry and quite possibly finished with him. And how long would it be before Jim's precious Kimberly discovered the truth? How he wished not to have delivered those rose petals.

But then his thoughts shifted along with another swing of paranoia.

Jim could nearly hear Amber's, sister's thoughts. "So that's the man… the man Amber has been speaking of recently." In a psychic world, direct words really aren't received as some telepathic text message. Thoughts are somewhat felt with much interference and error. Jim wasn't sure of how much Amber told her sister, much less whether or not she did say something. But the woman seated next to Amber was aware of something.

Then again, maybe Amber told her nothing. Perhaps she merely shared the same intuitive gift as Amber and picked up Jim's interest in her sister. That was the most logical explanation. Such horror! Jim slightly failed in protecting Amber. He would have to make a greater effort in keeping his feelings secret.

With Amber and her sister seated together, Jim couldn't help but notice how strikingly odd the two were. There was almost something mystical of their presence. For a lack of better words, there was an eerie psycho-kinetic vibe emitted from both.

Appearing satisfied with her study, Amber's sister faced forward. Jim turned his attention to the orchestra, soon his precious daughter, April. The performance had yet to start for the evening. He waved at April and received a wave in return. And then from another area of the room, Jim could feel a presence carefully examining him. Who was it this time? Turning towards the direction, Jim soon realized that Amber's daughter, Trista, now had a fixed gaze on him. And she wasn't merely looking in Jim's direction. Trista's eyes had full contact on him with an expression of awe and wonder.

Oh no! Even Amber's daughter heard of the rose petal assault. Did April find out through indirect gossip from the kids? Trapped in some lonely fantasy brought on by his own love spell, everyone seemed to be against him that night.

Chapter 26

Christmas is a special time of year when wishes materialize and people finally come together. At least it's supposed to work this way in Amber's world. Although Amber would have preferred to awaken Christmas morning with Trista's father beside her, Christmas dinner that year was to be held on the evening of Tuesday, December 22. Hoping for miracles is a nice, but surely Jim would have to spend the holiday with that other woman he currently lived with.

As always, it was easy for Jim to leave the house. Simply announce some bogus cable outage, and he was a free man for the evening. Jim knocked on Amber's door, dressed in his Ivan Trovsksov attire—baggy, wool pants; double-breasted, black, wool coat; black, shiny boots and now a furry, Russian hat. This strange wardrobe of Jim's had much more of an effect on people than you might realize, and really shrouded his motives. For one; his wife, Kimberly, came to view this style of clothing as his work clothes. No one, after all, would wear that ridiculous attire for anything other than working outdoors. She certainly had no reason to fear of her husband going to see a possible mistress. Who would find him attractive dressed up as some goofy-looking polock?

As for Amber, Jim's strange wardrobe put her at ease as it reminded her that he deliberately dressed this way to rebel against the woman he lived with. It was a fashion statement that probably challenged Kimberly's wishes. She probably made all sorts of comments against Jim's style of clothing along with the simple things he enjoyed in life. And for all that it represented, Amber was developing a fondness for Jim's style.

She opened the front door to let Jim in, "Hey, Merry Christmas!"

Jim entered the house and then leaned in for a kiss. "Merry Christmas."

Amber pet the furry, Russian hat on Jim's head. "Nice hat! I love it! Where'd you get it?"

"At Walmart. They were a running a sale that day; only $5.99." While speaking, Jim removed his hat and coat.

Amber took the items and hung them in the guest closet. That's when she saw his unflattering Fruit-of-the-Loom, white undershirt with suspenders stretched across the front and back. For Christmas, maybe he could have worn something a little nicer. But hey, the other woman apparently did not like it. For now, Amber wasn't going to say anything.

The scent of toasted garlic hung in the air as Jim and Amber entered the kitchen. Apparently, garlic bread was one of the items for their Christmas dinner. Over the stove, a large pot of water was at a roaring boil. A sauce pan lowly simmered beside it. "Let's see if those noodles are done." Amber announced.

"So what's for dinner?" Jim was quite hungry after his long day out in the field.

"Spaghetti with meat sauce; and I have some garlic bread toasting in the oven." While answering, Amber pulled a couple noodles from the boiling water and blew on them before tasting. "We'll have salad before dinner." She chewed the noodles. "Al dente!"

What was this? Spaghetti and garlic bread for Christmas dinner? The salad was probably the cheap stuff that comes out of the bag! Apparently, Jim is high maintenance and hoped for a nice baked ham. Maybe he even wondered if there would be pumpkin pie for dessert. He was polite for the moment and commented, "Mmm... sounds yummy!" Then he asked, "Did you make some pie, too?"

Amber paused. "Pie? No, I have some cranberry sherbet in the freezer."

Cranberry sherbet for Christmas dessert? Jim was really disappointed! Kimberly would have had a nice, spiral baked ham with homemade, extra-cheesy au gratin potatoes along with candied yams and green bean casserole. Dessert would have been any number of things. But as a rule, she always had a freshly-baked pumpkin pie *and* pecan pie! Jim could have done one of two things at that moment. He could have been polite and shown respect for the modest dinner that Amber (who was on a limited budget) made for their Christmas (which they really weren't supposed to be celebrating). Or Jim could have used the moment to be more appreciative of his own wife and realized that losing her to Amber would mean having modest dinners every night. Between you and me, Kimberly was a much, better cook than Amber!

And Kimberly didn't speak white lies, either.

"So where's your daughter, tonight?" Jim asked.

"Trista, you mean?" Amber dumped the steamy spaghetti noodles in the strainer. "She's over at a friend's house; won't be home until around ten o'clock. Really it's not such a terrible thing for her to be around when you're here. Just something to think about."

Jim smiled in return, obviously uncomfortable with suggestion. Trista went to the same school as April and played in the orchestra as well. Kids talk, and…

"Here, why don't we pour the wine and get the party started?" Amber had a four liter bottle of Carlo Rossi Paisano and poured a glass for her and Jim.

"Do you have beer?" Ivan Trovskov was a real man and wasn't particularly fond of wine. Wine in his erroneous perception was for the ladies. But Jim was only an Ivan Trovsksov want-to-be. In those parts of the world that he secretly glorified, beer was drunk by children or maybe enjoyed by workers during lunch break as soda. A real Ivan Trovskov drinks vodka with dinner! But the true American man that he was, Jim preferred beer.

"Beer?" Amber set Jim's glass down. "Oh, I'm sorry; I got wine for us. What was I thinking? You don't like wine!"

"That's okay." reassured Jim. "I'll gladly drink wine for our Christmas dinner." He took the glass and raised it. "Merry Christmas!"

Amber clinked her glass to his. "Merry Christmas!"

They took a couple gulps and enjoyed a couple kisses afterwards.

"Go ahead and have a seat at the table. We'll have salad first." Amber gulped a little more wine and refilled her glass before setting it on the table. And she topped Jim's glass off as well. Was she trying to get Jim drunk for the evening? Maybe their Christmas celebration was going to be what Jim waited for all along!

"We have French, thousand island and Italian."

"Do you have blue cheese?" asked Jim.

"No, we're not fond of blue cheese around here."

"I guess I'll take thousand island." Ivan Trovskov didn't look happy and took a few gulps of his girly wine.

Amber was secretly growing impatient with Jim's rudeness. Why was it so difficult to make this man happy? She sat down and poured Italian dressing on her salad and then dumped croutons on top.

Jim softly cleared his throat. "So what are you and your daughter doing for Christmas?"

"Trista, you mean?"

Suddenly, the front door opened!

Jim nearly flew out of his seat and almost ran for the back room.

"Sit!" Amber ordered.

Jim stared in return.

"Sit! I will take care of this." Amber walked towards the family room. But it was too late. Trista already had full view of her suspected father seated at the kitchen table and appeared very surprised. All Jim could do was silently watch and wonder just how Amber was going to handle this.

All Amber said to her daughter: "We're having spaghetti, your favorite." And from what Jim could see by the expression of terror on Trista's face, Amber communicated something to her through eyes alone. It must have been a silent threat not to mess up the evening or tell anyone at school. Then she finally spoke. "You've seen Jim before. We're having him join us for dinner tonight."

Suddenly, Jim realized that Trista's surprise arrival home wasn't such a surprise. Amber planned it this way so that Trista would join the two of them for Christmas dinner.

Appearing confused and uncomfortable with the situation, Trista followed her mother over to the cupboard.

But Amber ordered, "Have a seat. I'll fix you a salad."

Then, as Trista cautiously walked to the table, Amber dropped—nearly threw—Trista's empty salad bowl onto the counter and turned towards her daughter.

The noise startled Trista, causing her to slightly jolt.

"You got into Nick's car and rode around with him, didn't you?"

"No I didn't! What are you talking about?"

Amber approached her daughter like a tiger about to pounce its prey. "Don't you lie to me. I told you that I do not like that boy one bit, and ordered you not to be around him. And you ride around in his car?"

"Mom, I was not with Nick tonight?

There was a foolproof test to determine if Trista was lying. "Let me see your palms."

"Mom, I was not with Nick. Why don't you believe me?"

"Your palms; let me see them!"

Trista held out her palms as Mother demanded.

Mother felt them. "Why are your palms sweaty? You're lying!"

"Mom, I'm not lying! I swear to God I was not with Nick!"

A woman like Amber knows not to swear to God unless one means it. Doing otherwise only asks for trouble. Amber screeched, "Blasphemy!" Then she hauled off and smacked her child across the face just like her own mother would have done years ago.

Jim was in shock at what he saw. "Hey, take it easy!" Kimberly never hit April or Collin, and neither did Jim.

"Stay out of this!" Amber snapped back. "Don't you tell me what I can and can't do with her!" In all the years of his absence, suddenly Jim was going to breeze in and know what was good for his daughter? Amber glared back at Trista who now sniffled and wiped away her tears. "You're grounded until Christmas morning! That'll give you something to think about. If I catch you with that Nick again, you'll be grounded the entire Christmas break and through Valentine's Day. Now sit down!"

With everyone seated and eating their salads, the first couple minutes of Christmas dinner was mostly silent. It was time for Amber to bring Father up to speed. "That boy, Nick, is no good. He was kicked off the football team because he was caught with marijuana. And from someone else's mother, I found out that it's not the first time he was caught with pot. Not only that, I saw his name last year in the police blotter for vandalism—lawn job. Is that someone you'd want your daughter being around?"

Needless to say, Jim was taken out of his comfort zone. He felt as though Amber was using him as some male reinforcement in her daughter's life. "Well…" Immediately, Jim began to think of his own daughter. What if this Nick tried dating April? "What's this kid's last name?"

"Bostas." answered Amber.

"Well, I wouldn't want my daughter around him. Kids like that attract the wrong crowd. Plus he could be stoned and get in a car accident with you riding."

Amber fully nodded. "Mm-hmm!"

Then Jim asked Trista, "Do you know my daughter, April?"

Trista was a bit hesitant before answering. "Just in orchestra. We're not friends, just acquaintances."

Jim could have asked a thousand other questions about April and whether or not the other kids know things—things about him and Amber… *things about Ms. Lutrova*! But it was best to leave it alone for the moment.

* * *

After dinner, Jim had a slight Carlo Rossi Paisano buzz going. It was time to slow down as he did need to return home to his wife.

Amber, Trista and Jim all went into the family room to sit around the tree. Immediately, Jim was given a stack of presents. Apparently he was very special to Amber.

"Oh, you shouldn't have! I didn't know we were… Gosh, I didn't even get you presents!"

"That's okay." reassured Amber.

Trista silently watched the scene play out. For being out of her life for so many years, one might think that Father would have had something for her. But Jim was still a bit flighty and not fully surrendered to his true destiny. It would take time.

Jim opened a package. "Oh, coffee beans from Starbucks! Hey, I love coffee…! A high-powered flashlight! This is better than the flashlight I use for the utility boxes late at night… Winter gloves with the breather hole to open and warm your hands… very nice… A twenty-dollar gift certificate for Big Boy's Beef and Ribs… Amber, this is too much! I actually feel guilty receiving all this stuff."

Amber reassured, "It's okay, Jim! There's next year." Deep down inside she felt a bit hurt for being forgotten for Christmas. And again, at the very least, Jim could have gotten Trista something. Why was this man so dismal and cold?"

Then out of nowhere, Jim suddenly announced that it was time to go. Trista continued to watch everything and was fully aware that he had a wife and kids at home. From what she could determine, Mother was having an affair with a married man who could also, very well, be Trista's own father.

Amber grabbed a small box from the kitchen and piled all of Jim's Christmas presents in it. Then she asked, "Do you want to take some food with you, maybe for your lunch at work tomorrow?"

"No, I'll probably use your gift certificate from Big Boy's. I love that place!"

Trista remained in the family room. Being the case it was not appropriate for Jim and Amber to smooch their good nights to one another. Instead, Amber pulled Jim's coat and hat from the closet. "Well, I guess you better go home."

"Yeah, thanks for having me tonight."

"You bet…"

"Merry Christmas…"

"Merry Christmas..."

Jim turned and walked out to the street to his Mapleview Cable bucket truck.

Chapter 27

Jim's penis was beginning to hurt. Since the initial dose of Ms. Lutrova's algae-green sex potion, Jim feared that he was having prolonged erections throughout the night in his sleep. Men typically experience an erection towards the end of a REM cycle, and then it goes away upon fully emerging. But Jim feared that perhaps his erections were had for the entire night. He wondered if this was a normal side effect of the medication and if whether or not he should tell the doctor. Even stranger, Ms. Lutrova's ghostly presence continued to haunt Jim in his dreams. The details fuzzy by morning, Jim was still aware that the woman was doing nothing short of raping him in his own bed throughout the night. Part of him enjoyed and welcomed the invasions, while another part of him feared that the sexual sorceress was damaging his penis.

But Wednesday morning was the last straw which fully motivated Jim to once-and-for-all find and approach Ms. Lutrova. Since the office of Mapleview Cable would be closed on Thursday and Friday for the Christmas holiday, the weekly staff meeting was held on Wednesday morning. As usual, Jim sat in the powwow circle, wearing his Ivan Trovskov attire. I suppose to be festive; Ivan Trovskov wore a pair of black and green checkered, baggy, wool pants with the legs tucked into his shiny, black, leather boots. And as he would soon find out; the baggy, wool pants had a noteworthy feature that would reveal embarrassing phenomenon at inopportune moments.

The plant manager made all sorts of boring announcements about stagnant sales in recent months. "We're not really seeing any growth in our customer base. We're not losing customers or any revenue, but the business is currently not at a growth like it has been in recent years."

Such boring discussions; Jim didn't care about any of that. As far as Jim believed, businesses go through ups and downs. Mapleview Cable should have felt lucky for all its continuing support from current customers. The meeting was so boring that Jim allowed himself to slip off into a little daydream. Mentally he was relaxed—enough that he could have fell asleep if allowed. And in this state, the unwelcome swelling of his penis could be felt within Jim's pants.

Ms. Lutrova was doing this to Jim! He just knew it! Raped all night, then teased and tortured throughout the day; the woman could not leave his penis alone. It was as-if she wanted it. Perhaps Ms. Lutrova had been so sex-starved for a number of years that her desires for Jim could be felt through his penis—as if it were a radio antenna.

Slowly it continued to inch its way up until it was quite apparent that Jim had a bad case of boner pants. He had no choice but to sit there so nonchalantly and act as-if nothing out-of-the-ordinary. But surely someone in that room would recognize it. It would only be a matter of time before the small, checkered black and green Christmas tree would be noticed at the crotch of Jim's pants.

The plant manager encouraged employees to finish the doughnuts brought in for the meeting and then wished everyone a Merry Christmas before adjourning. Now Jim had no choice but to stand up with a full, ninety-degree erection in his pants and sneak out into the hallway.

"Jimmy!" called out the plant manager. "Have another doughnut?"

"No, I've got to cut back. The doctor says I need to lose weight. Merry Christmas, by the way."

"Merry Christmas, Jimmy!"

Every second counted! With an annoying erection just throbbing in his pants, Jim briskly walked down the hall in an attempt to escape outside to the Mapleview Cable bucket truck. But wouldn't you know it? Someone else arrested Jim while halfway down the hall.

"Jim? Oh Jim!" It was Suzanne, the forty-something divorcee who may or may not have had a special someone to spend the holiday with.

"What's up, Suzanne?"

"I gave you a couple disconnects for your route today, but one of them is cancelled. The customer came in and paid the outstanding bill."

"Which one is it?" asked Jim.

"Umm… Want to come over to my desk so I can check? I forgot which one it is."

Jim had no choice but to follow Suzanne over to the front office where the dispatcher, administrator, and few other office girls worked. By now, his erection was softening and gradually lowering to idle position. But it had some distance to go.

"Okay…" Suzanne grabbed a stack of papers off her desk and flipped through them. "Woody!"

Jim nearly blushed, "Woody?"

"Yes, the customer's last name is Woody. Just write 'Cancelled' on your copy before turning in the paperwork. And be sure not to disconnect them!"

Originally a ninety-degree, stiff erection; Jim's penis was now extended at forty-five-degrees and bulging through the loose, baggy, wool crotch of his pants. Suzanne definitely saw it and certainly liked it! It was a special Christmas hard-on just for her.

But what was this? Soon other women approached Suzanne and Jim, seemingly in a means to surround the man who possessed a special Christmas surprise. What were they doing there? It was supposed to be Suzanne's. Kelly the radio dispatcher was eager to satisfy her curiosity. Wasn't Jim a little old for her? Jen and Laura had beaming smiles on their faces. Weren't they married?

There was just no pretending to ignore the reality for Jim. Four women surrounded him with much interest in what was happening down Jim's pants. And they didn't help matters, either. Pretending to make small talk, "So did you get all your Christmas shopping done…? Are you and the family going away for the holiday…?" they all maintained awareness on Jim's erection and caused it to rise and swell to a returned full ninety-degree capacity.

* * *

And it was all Ms. Lutrova's fault! Ms. Lutrova was being blamed for every unusual occurrence in recent weeks. Take for example; has the reader noticed Jim's peculiar belief that the doctor-prescribed ErexBoost is a sex potion created by Ms. Lutrova? You and I certainly realize that ErexBoost was created by a pharmaceutical company and tested for a few years on monkeys before administering it to humans for testing. But you see, Jim coexisted in a separate realm in which, somehow, Ms. Lutrova concocted a spell in a candlelit attic with results that manifested themselves sometime later as the experimental ErexBoost male performance drug. Through all her magick, Ms. Lutrova was the cause of all the bizarre perceptions, erotic dreams and now discomfort experienced with his penis. Jim probably even believed that Ms. Lutrova placed the office girls under her spell to influence the intensity of an erection. I suppose he imagined her seated before a crystal ball and observing Jim's events and surroundings throughout the day.

Ms. Lutrova was drastically affecting Jim's life in a negative way, probably for no other reason than to call out to him and demand sex. For this matter, Jim drove down Mapleview Road in the older section of Mapleview later that afternoon, en route to Ms. Lutrova's house. It was time to put an end to the woman's torment, maybe give in and provide what she was looking for.

And that's the only thing required for Jim to finally establish contact with the Mapleview Community High School orchestra teacher! She now stood at the very location where Jim originally saw her on the morning of All Saints Day, seemingly to wait for him!

Jim could hardly believe his eyes. He was so taken back by the woman's startling presence that he nearly drove away. But he reminded himself for his reason for coming while pulling into Ms. Lutrova's driveway and stopping with the back tire at the curb. Jim rolled down the driver side window and greeted Ms. Lutrova. "Good afternoon."

"Good afternoon." answered Ms. Lutrova.

There were a few seconds of silence. Exactly how was Jim going to break the ice and disclose his "schizophrenic" reasons for coming? To buy more time, he did what was natural and stepped out of the Mapleview Cable bucket truck to introduce himself. "I'm Jim. Nice to meet you." He offered his hand to shake.

Ms. Lutrova accepted the handshake. "Ekaterina, here at your service."

"Nice to meet you, Ekaterina." Finally, Jim learned of her name!

It was apparent to Ekaterina that she needed to take control of matters and wasted not a further second in suggesting, "Well, why don't we go to my house and we'll see how I can help you?"

"Sounds good to me!" From what Jim could see, Ekaterina's driveway was over a hundred feet in length. It wouldn't be right to drive up to her house and let the older woman walk alone. "Do you want me to give you a ride up to the house?"

Ekaterina returned a queer look. "No, maybe just park here on the shoulder. And why not pull up a little bit past the house?"

This was certainly an unusual demand for Ekaterina to make. Why couldn't Jim pull his truck up to the front door of the home? And why the apparent need to shroud the truck from the view of her house?

Jim parked where he was ordered, locked the doors after stepping out and met Ekaterina on the shoulder of the highway. And what was this? Rather than head towards the house, Ekaterina crossed the highway and motioned Jim to follow! From what Jim could see, there was nothing on the other side of the road other than untamed forest.

With Ekaterina already on the other side, Jim jogged across shouting. "Where are you going? Isn't that your house?"

"Noooooo! That house? I don't live there. What gave you that idea? Come, this way."

I suppose it's safe to conclude that all those predawn rose petal assaults were all done in vain! Ekaterina did not live where Jim originally suspected.

Jim followed the older woman over a guardrail, down a small ditch which led to an open patch of bushes. Passing through, Jim was now in Ekaterina's realm where he continued to follow through dense forest. Wherever Ekaterina was going, she apparently had the region memorized and hesitated not a moment in zigzagging around large trees, thorn bushes and crossing small streams. Where was she taking Jim? From what Jim could remember, there were no homes or subdivisions located near this section of forest.

It was a good thing that Jim wore his Ivan Trovskov attire that was complete with double-breasted wool coat, black boots and a furry, Russian hat if needed. It was cold in Mapleview. In studying Ekaterina as she led, Jim was reminded of an elderly person who is not so financially well off, and must walk the streets in the frigid cold for necessary trips to the store. She, too, wore a heavy, black, wool coat. In addition she wore a babushka to help keep her head warm.

They must have zigzagged and crossed the forest in a series of diagonal directions for about a mile until; at last, Jim could see a small building some distance away. As they neared closer, Jim could see that it was nothing more than a makeshift cabin that resembled more of a hut. It appeared to be crudely constructed with dead lumber from the forest, leaves and maybe held together with mud or clay. Somehow, Ekaterina managed to install two windows—as seen from the front of the building—and an entry door.

"This is your house?" Jim asked.

"Yes, this is where I live."

"Wow, you built this yourself?"

"All by myself…"

Ekaterina reached into her coat pocket and pulled out the keys needed to unlock the door. For being merely a hut-like cottage in the forest, the building was locked and secured quite well.

The inside of Ekaterina's home was warm and safe from the brutal, Mapleview winter. From what Jim could see while standing at the entrance, the cottage was nothing more than a large kitchen with a smaller room next to it that—as Jim speculated—might have been Ekaterina's bedroom.

At the center of the kitchen was a potbelly stove. This apparently radiated enough heat to be felt throughout the home. There was a kitchen table constructed with more lumber collected from the forest along with two chairs made with the same. Makeshift shelving that was nothing more than bound lumber was attached to the wall with pots, pans, dishes, glasses and necessary cookware resting on top. There was what appeared to be an antique ice box at the corner of the kitchen. Obviously the cottage had no electricity, and the ice box preserved any perishables of Ekaterina's. Finally, there was a third chair by a window with another forest lumber table at the side. On top were a few old books and an oil lamp.

The afternoon forest light glowed through one of the windows, but was not enough to illuminate the inside of the cottage. Because of this, Ekaterina lit two candles in the kitchen; one on the table and the other on her cupboard shelving. Then she bent down near the potbelly stove for a couple of logs and loaded them in the soon-to-die flames. Within a minute they caught fire; more heat to be enjoyed in the safe cottage on a winter's afternoon.

There's an interesting psychology with immigrants that come to America who never fully adapt to the culture. In fact, it can be seen to some degree with just about every immigrant. They seem to believe that our American society and culture is backwards and all wrong. Offering harsh criticism of our government, finances, education system, economy, job market and our overall modern culture; they can fix everything by comparing our country to the way things were back at the old country. It might lead one to ask, "So why don't they just move back home if things are so miserable here?"

Ekaterina was an extreme case. She saw much wrong with American culture and constantly lived up to her self-imposed expectations of being Russian, not American. Probably because she was older and isolated herself in the forest, she was under the assumption that all Russian people were exactly like her and believed the same things she did. While conversing with the woman, it wasn't uncommon to be educated of what Russian people do, think, believe and how they behave. These pointers were often used to reinforce how correct Ekaterina was in her actions and manners.

"Have a seat." Ekaterina invited Jim to sit at the kitchen table. "And take off your coat; stay a while."

Jim removed his heavy, black, wool Ivan Trovskov coat. The cottage was warm enough and there was no need for extra clothing.

Now we all know that Ekaterina was a Russian immigrant who spoke with broken English and a heavy accent. But it isn't necessary to emulate her manner of speaking. I'll spare the reader any of these poor attempts. She asked Jim, "So where are you from?"

"Oh I live here in Mapleview, just down Mapleview Road in the Maple Sap subdivision."

Ekaterina paused for a second, "Yes... but you're not originally from here. Where are you from? You look maybe Russian or from East Europe."

"No, I'm American. I was born in Mapleview and lived here all my life."

This intrigued Ekaterina as Jim didn't dress like most people in Mapleview. "Oh... You just don't look American. I'm Russian, and most Russian people dress the way you do." Again, Ekaterina was somewhat in her own world. Since when does the majority population of Russia dress like Jim's secret persona, Ivan Trovskov? Maybe his style reminded her of someone or perhaps an unusual era in her life.

Jim smiled and laughed nervously. "No, these are my clothes for working outdoors in winter."

"The cable company gives you these clothes to wear?" asked Ekaterina.

"No, I bought them."

"Well it looks Russian. I like it. You look Russian. Are you sure you are not from Russia or maybe East Europe?"

"Nope. I was born here in Mapleview." Jim was getting a bit annoyed with Ekaterina's insistence that he was Russian. But I suppose that one should be careful of what he or she wishes for. Wishes come true when you no longer want them.

Jim attempted to change the direction of conversation. "I really like your home. This is nice. Did you make this place all by yourself?"

Ekaterina was proud of her home. "Yes I did! I'm Russian and Russian people are accustomed to building their own homes. We are not like American people who take out mortgages and end up in debt. Think about it. If you lose your job and run out of unemployment, what is going to happen to your home? And what about your food? Well nothing will happen to me. I live out here in the wilderness and built my own home. I built all this furniture. Nobody owns it but me. Today I go to the store and buy the food I need and items needed for cooking. But if I have no more money, I can hunt for my food. Russian people know how to get the basics. We are not dependent on our jobs or the economy to survive."

Jim was impressed. "Wow! I wish I could do that! So does anyone know that you live out here in the woods? This is land owned by the government and preserved for wildlife."

Ekaterina laughed, "No one knows where I live! You see how hard it is to get here? Who is going to find this place?"

"Very true…" Jim agreed.

Ekaterina suddenly had the urge to show even more hospitality to her guest. "Can I get you something?—something to drink, perhaps?"

"No, I'm okay."

"You sure? I'll get you something. Russian people treat their houseguests really nice. You'll see."

"Well… coffee would be okay."

Ekaterina paused for a moment. "Oh, Russian people do not drink coffee. We drink tea. I have a pot of tea on the stove. Maybe you would like some?"

"Sure, tea would be fine." Jim was never much of a tea drinker, but he felt it best to accept Ekaterina's hospitality.

"I make my tea really strong and it sits out all day on the stove, brewing. I hope you like it this way." By now, Ekaterina poured the contents from an ordinary cooking pot into a cup. The pot was loaded with tea bags and the brew appeared terribly dark. And Ekaterina was sure to pour herself a cup so that she and her newfound friend could enjoy a late afternoon teatime, together.

Jim took a sip once the cup was set before him. The tea was Lukewarm and terribly bitter. It was so bitter, in fact, that the initial sip caused him to briefly convulse while swallowing.

Ekaterina nearly cackled hysterical laughter. "You Americans like things nice and sweet. Every morning it's coffee and doughnuts and then more coffee and doughnuts in the afternoon. Russian people do not like sugar like American people. We like a nice, strong cup of tea."

By now, Jim took a second sip and was already marveling at how refreshing the overpowering flavor was. "It's good! I like it. You make good tea."

"Why thank you." Then Ekaterina wasted not another moment in asking her burning question. "So who is the young lady always with you? Is she your girlfriend?"

"My wife?"

Ekaterina cackled some more. "No, not your wife. You don't have to lie to me. I know everything and can see everything. I'm talking about the young lady with you. She's your girlfriend, right?"

Jim was caught off guard. No one had ever mentioned the significance of Amber in Jim's life before. Now he needed to answer some questions. "She's just a friend."

"Oh, I think she's more than just a friend. I see the way you were smiling, laughing and looking at each other at the carnival. You remember me? I was operating the carousel."

"Yes, I remember you."

"I teach your daughter orchestra and see you sitting with your wife. But I can't help but wonder about this other woman whose daughter just so happens to be another one of my students. Ms. Dickly is a girlfriend, yes?"

Jim smiled sheepishly. "Yes, something like that." By now, Jim was more than halfway finished with his cup of overwhelmingly strong tea; probably drunk so fast in a means to cover his nervousness while being interrogated about Amber.

Finally, Ekaterina received the answer to her burning question and now did her best to cover the disappointment. Nearly shaking she took an angry sip of tea and then rested her elbow on the table to support her chin with the palm of her hand. Her mood shifted from trying to cover disappointment to that of implying that Jim was now in hot water and owing an explanation. Her dark, Russian eyes furiously burned into Jim's.

But things were not going well for Jim. Apparently he wasn't used to drinking tea of such strength. With lunch eaten a few hours ago, the food digested and his stomach was empty. The strong tea had been absorbed quickly and now caused havoc on Jim's body. His stomach quivered and turned. A sensation of weakness began to overcome him.

While fighting the uncomfortable feelings and increasing nausea, Jim struggled to defend his taboo relationship with Amber. "She moved down the street from me and I met her. I guess I really took a liking towards her. Hey, I never forget who my wife is."

Suddenly, the overabundance of warm, unpleasant saliva began to produce itself in Jim's mouth. This was typically a precursor to vomiting and made Jim all the more nauseous.

Ekaterina immediately sensed Jim's discomfort. "Oh, you're not used to strong tea!" She nearly jumped out of her seat and to the ice box where a roll of Old Wisconsin beef sausage was pulled out. Ekaterina quickly cut a few slices and handed them to Jim. "Here, eat this! The salt will help you feel better."

The last thing Jim wanted to do at the moment was eat something, especially salty sausage. He put his hand to his forehead and realized the inevitable. Jim was moments from vomiting.

"Eat it!" ordered Ekaterina. "You will feel better."

Jim did as ordered and oddly savored the salty flavor and spices of the beef sausage. It was like salami or summer sausage and ideal for making sandwiches. And just as Ekaterina promised, the nausea immediately subsided. Upon finishing his third piece, Jim was hungry and ready for more sausage. But he wasn't going to be rude and ask for more.

"Feel better?" asked Ekaterina.

"Oh yeah. That was weird. Does that happen to you, often?"

"No, you're just not used to drinking strong tea. Russian people have a stomach that can handle it because we drink strong tea all the time. The tea threw something off balance in your stomach and made you feel sick. The sausage gave you salt which made everything better."

Jim was impressed, "Hmm…"

Ekaterina walked over to her cupboard and grabbed a small, transparent, glass bowl. She carried it with her to a door that Jim originally thought was a closet. "If you need to use the bathroom, it's in here."

Ekaterina even had a small bathroom for herself?

Inside the dark room, the sound of a well hand pump could be heard extracting water. Apparently, Ekaterina even drilled her own well and had it feed directly to the bathroom. While alone and listening to the sound, Jim realized that it was getting late and he would soon have to leave.

Ekaterina entered the kitchen with the glass bowl filled with water. As she neared the table, Jim carefully announced, "It's getting late and I'm going to have to start heading home."

Ekaterina set the bowl at the center of the table and placed a candle before it so that from Jim's vantage point, the distorted flame and glow could be seen through the water and glass. "Leaving so soon?" asked Ekaterina. "You haven't had your questions answered."

"What questions?"

"You came here for something." insisted Ekaterina. "You're looking for answers, and I'm going to help you. Now, let me ask you something. Do you really think the young lady, Ms. Dickly, is the best thing for you?"

Jim remained silent.

"Look at the bowl." ordered Ekaterina. "Just think about your girlfriend. What is she doing to you? You know what she is and what she's trying to do to you."

Jim was no stranger to shifting his brain patterns for a brief moment. Recall his attempts of sex magick while sitting in the circle of quartz crystals. Perhaps this made his first session of scrying and seeking visions of Amber easy.

* * *

Trista had a secret; not a terrible one, but something she maintained from Mother's knowing. Sometimes at night Trista would hear walking around in the attic, upstairs. It was Mother; Trista knew this. But what could she have possibly been doing in that attic? Even, still, why would Mother have spent so much time up there?

In recent years, Amber discovered a God-given talent. Preluded by sketching with a pencil and paper, she wished to create images of some sought after reality. And with such a need to create these real-to-life pictures, Amber set up her own, private room in the attic with nothing more than some tables, soft lighting and an oil canvass. From that moment on, she spent many nights enslaved to some portrait, attempting to make it as real as possible. The art was more of a way to intensify her desires. The blood, sweat, tears and frustration all added to the energy that Amber felt was some magickal power.

Through time, Amber developed a trademarked style of creating mystical portraits. The landscapes were often fantastic places of nature with the subject appearing to be the object of Amber's desire. Amber often placed herself in the paintings so that the onlooker would be standing directly behind her. It can be assumed that Amber was the intended onlooker and she wanted to see herself interacting with whatever was in a portrait. And it wasn't uncommon for Amber to stand before creeks or small ponds where she would conjure up all sorts of things, real or abstract, even recognizable people. Would creating these images call into reality those things that Amber desperately desired?

Noises in the attic that often awoke Trista in the night created an overwhelming curiosity. On an afternoon while Mother worked, she ascended the unfinished stairwell into the attic. Once a crude place for storage, it was now a place where Mother existed in the late night hours. She was suddenly an artist, creating elaborate portraits on canvass, many of them quite beautiful. But there was something a bit frightening of the paintings, eerie undertones that suggested Mother to be under the delusion of possessing some mystical power. In her private realm of horror, the woman attempted to influence recognizable people while conjuring up forces of nature. Just who was Mother, and what was she doing?

Chapter 28

For Mary, Christmas Eve most often brought with it a mellow excitement that overshadowed the morning and throughout the day. Perhaps it was deeply rooted from her childhood days of anticipating the night's visit of Santa Clause. With the years passed, she most likely displaced that childhood excitement towards a more appropriate appreciation of the holiday. The two day celebration was a bit of Heaven touched onto Earth; peace and goodwill towards all.

And what better way to intensify those happy feelings on the morning of Christmas Eve with a fresh blanket of snow? Mary let Muffin the Yorkshire terrier excitedly run out the back door to do his morning business. The surrounding trees and forest preserves looked so beautiful dusted with snow.

"Good morning!" Daren entered the room and stood beside his wife. Both admired winter's fresh portrait, a little Christmas present to add to the cheer.

Then Daren suggested, "Hey, what do you say we go for a little drive this morning to Sillmac? We'll have breakfast and coffee over at the bakery; check out the snowy trees along the way."

It sounded like a great idea to Mary. "Sure!"

Sometime later, showered and groomed for the day, the couple loaded into Daren's car and descended the half-block, inclined driveway down to Mapleview Road. Daren turned left (north) and traveled along the wintery, forested highway, past the Hidden Lake Forest Preserve entrance and en route to where the road transitioned east.

Mary commented on the scenery. "The woods are so beautiful this morning." Steam and vapors hovered snaking streams that traveled through the snowy forest.

Daren agreed. "I know; it's gorgeous."

Then Mary harshly scratched the needle across the record that morning with some silly talk about her favorite customer at the Mapleview Flower Shop. "That guy doesn't come in the store anymore for his daily rose."

"No?" asked Daren.

"I haven't seen him since last Friday. I'm starting to miss him."

Daren briefly took his eyes off the road for a queer look at his wife.

Mary continued, "Shelly knew I liked him; knew that I admired the way he got a rose for his wife each day. Sometimes I'd be working in the backroom when he'd come in. Shelly would pop her head in the door, and say that my boyfriend is here."

Daren definitely had a jealous streak when it came to his wife, and it flared at that moment! "Whoa, whoa; wait a minute! So what's going on over there? You've got some boyfriend who visits you at the flower shop?"

"Daren, stop it! Shelly was joking with me. I can't tell you anything!"

Daren struggled and bit his tongue to keep the jealous feelings from further surfacing. This guy probably liked Mary and he knew how she adored his supposed romantic side. In fact, those roses were probably bought for Mary!

Now was the time for Daren to act! He needed Mary to understand how much he loved her. Daren pulled over onto the snowy shoulder of Mapleview Road, just where the road curved and transitioned east.

"Daren, what are you doing?" There was a note of worry to Mary's voice.

Daren had an intense look on his face as he reached inside the coat pocket and pulled out a small present. "I got something for you, just a small reminder of how special you are."

Mary smiled so adoringly while taking the package then tore into the wrapping like a little girl on Christmas morning. Whatever the item was, it was encased in a velvet jewelry gift box. Mary looked up at Daren with another smile. "What did you do?" She lifted the lid which immediately revealed the famous love pendant that had been advertised on TV throughout the holiday season—a series of joined hearts, adorned with diamonds. Its purpose was to remind a woman of her man's undying love for her.

It was beautiful for Mary, and received so well. She leaned in and gave her husband a kiss on the lips. "Thank you!"

Daren immediately took both ends of the pendant's necklace and motioned his desire to clasp it around Mary's neck. "Let's see what this looks like."

Mary pulled her beautiful hair from her neck while leaning forward. "You got it?"

"Almost... There, it's beautiful on you! Take a look!"

Mary pulled down the visor and glanced in the mirror while admiring the new addition to her jewelry collection. Then she leaned in to give Daren another kiss. "Thank you."

"Hey, like I said; just a little something to remind you of how special you are." Then Daren placed his hand on Mary's shoulder, "I want you to know that I'll always love you. I'll never let you go. And make sure you wear that at the flower shop so all those men know you belong to me." He wasn't joking, either. It was nearly an order.

It was a strange request for Mary. "Isn't that what my wedding ring is supposed to do?"

Daren reinforced his wish with a note of demand. "Just make sure you wear them both. And you never know; I might make a surprise visit one day to make sure you are wearing them."

Suddenly that beautiful, gleeful moment on the snow dusted morning of Christmas Eve lost its magick. Why Daren's transformation into Sleeping with the Enemy?

There were a few minutes of silence as Daren pulled back onto the highway and continued along Mapleview Road. Then he asked, "Christmas at your Aunt Loraine's house this year?"

"Yup." replied Mary.

"Are any of your relatives from out-of-town flying in?"

"Well of course, Daren. My Mom, Dad and two brothers will be there along with some friends and acquaintances of Aunt Loraine."

This was an unfavorable situation for Daren. Mary's family did not like him. For starters, Mary's side of the family urged her not to follow through with the wedding. And thanks to Aunt Loraine's need to talk of wild speculations, the family held a silent suspicion against Daren ever since Kelly had disappeared. Kelly was Mary's younger cousin and a temporary guest at the Trivelli house. For some reason, Mary's side of the family believed that Daren was responsible for her disappearance. Imagine that!

Mary offered the perfect solution. "You can fly out to Arizona and be with your side of the family if you want. I know you don't like my family."

This threw Daren into a fit of rage. "What are you talking about? Yeah, I'm just going to jump on a plane over Christmas and make it there in time to be with my family! Sometimes you talk out of your ass, you know that?"

Now the beautiful morning of Christmas Eve was definitely stained with some nasty spills of negativity and insults. Mary despised when Daren used profanity. Feelings hurt with a sudden, peculiar longing for her special customer at the flower shop, Mary exploded with the only logical argument she could think of. "Watch your mouth! Don't you swear at me!" Surely, Jim didn't treat his wife that way.

But Daren refused to be ordered by his wife. Using that horrible word of fornication, he told Mary to shut up. And then he reminded her that he'll talk however he wished, again, using that horrible word of fornication.

Mary and Daren were no longer on speaking terms, at least for Christmas Eve. She didn't deserve to be spoken to that way. Silence was Mary's way of controlling the situation. And besides, if Daren hadn't done those unmentionable things with Kelly while she stayed at the Trivelli house, Aunt Loraine wouldn't have held such suspicion against him. It was a dark reality that Mary and Daren never got to the bottom of.

Breakfast at the bakery was a miserable experience. After making his part of the order at the counter, Daren asked his lovely wife, "And what do you want?" He intended to relay Mary's request.

But Mary wasn't speaking to her husband. She was a grown woman and perfectly capable of ordering for herself. She spoke directly to the clerk. "Just a bagel and orange juice."

The clerk could see that Mary was angry with her husband.

Daren took notice of the clerk's realization which spiraled him into more anger and jealousy. The clerk had better stay out of it and not take sides if he knew what was best for him.

Eating in silence and receiving no eye contact from his wife, Daren finally asked, "So what's your problem?"

Was Daren for real? Since when was it acceptable to insult and use profanity at Mary? She returned a hostile and scornful look. It was going to be a long and miserable Christmas.

Chapter 29

I'm afraid I'm hardly qualified to fully understand and explain the strange, new perceptions of Jim. Since his initial encounter of Ekaterina on the carousel ride, it would appear that he was delving into a strange world of delusions that were becoming increasingly worse. To explain his condition, it might be best to seek the professional knowledge of Jim's own doctor, Dr. Millheimer.

When talking with the man, one can clearly see that Dr. Millheimer is a man of science with not only the credentials and years of experience as a physician, but a wealth of understanding into the human psyche. He once treated a patient whose wife was tragically killed in a car crash; but suffered the horrible hallucination of seeing her alive, conscious and well in the hospital room while signing the death papers.

To this, Dr. Millheimer advised the patient some days later, "The mind has been a mystery for countless ages, and it continues to baffle us. I'm afraid the more we try to understand the human psyche, the more we will realize how little we know of it."

And what answer does Dr. Millheimer give us with Jim's new perceptions? As he says, "There are many clinical papers written that address what is typically described as delusions of witchcraft. This phenomenon can be broken down into two classes: passive and active. Patients exhibiting symptoms of passive witchcraft delusions typically feel that some known or unknown, mystical force that was generated by a witch caused harm or even damaged the patient. In an active case, the patient is under the delusional belief to possess the abilities of performing witchcraft.

Now we need to be careful not to assume that everyone who speaks of or believes in witchcraft to be delusional. There's an entire religion, Wicca, that utilizes witchcraft, and these followers can be deemed normal. As far as believing in the imposed will of others (believing that harmful or beneficial spells are being casted onto one another): magick can be seen as an extension of the psyche. There is nothing wrong with believing in magick and using it as a vehicle to unlock the potential of the human mind—provided this is done in moderation.

So where do we draw the line? When should these so-called delusions of witchcraft concern the doctor? It's when the patient exhibits signs of paranoia and suddenly develops the strange perception of a surrounding population of witches who wish to inflict harm.

There's a clinical study currently in the works with results not yet published for it needs more clarification. There appears to be a correlation of young to middle-aged men who are so attracted to the opposite sex that they begin to believe that certain women are witches. Such men become confused from their overwhelming supply of the chemistry of attraction, and conclude that a particular woman casted some sort of love spell. As the delusional male further concludes; if his woman of desire causes such intense feelings simply by walking in the room, then surely she must be a witch who casted a spell for either causing him to fall in love, or simply as a means for telepathic tracking with purposes of consecrating her victim into magick.

We are also discovering that this delusion is extremely impacting by older women in their late forties and even beyond menopause. Naturally, older women do everything in their power to remain beautiful and young-looking. Are they not creating a slight illusion for the purpose of encouraging people to see them for who they wish to be?—young and beautiful. Could this be considered a mild form of witchcraft? Younger men are naturally attracted to older women as they represent the long-forgotten oedipal stage of being fascinated with Mother. Later in life, a man finds himself nearly mystified with the awe, beauty and allure of an older woman. An older woman is different than a younger woman. She possesses a certain 'sexiness' or charisma that a younger woman cannot emulate as an older woman has much more life experience.

It isn't uncommon for a man who suffers from delusions of witchcraft to place conscious emphasis on noticing items such as unique jewelry, application of makeup or unusual items of clothing. If a woman happens to wear, for example, a pendant of a geometric shape such as a circle or triangle; this is immediately interpreted to represent something mystical. Makeup is a complicated art—too complicated for a man to understand. When done properly, the application can place the woman in a certain framework that tends to draw out emotions or desires. Historic paintings of witches often portray these women painted with unusual designs of makeup. A man suffering from delusions of witchcraft immediately associate a suspected witch of applying her makeup in such a way to cast a spell.

Clothing worn by a suspected witch represents much more to such a delusional man than festive colors of the season or that sporty, new fashion. Jackets or sweaters of a particular color suggest that she is wearing these to enhance a spell or even subconsciously communicate an idea to her victim.

Through time, the patient develops the notion that his master witch is telepathically connected to him and can sense his thoughts or events throughout the day. He might imagine her seated before a crystal ball and watching all his activities. Through spells or magic, she can play a hand at influencing his day; either to inflict harm or to provide little magick lessons to further induct him into the art of witchcraft.

In the final stage of these delusions, the patient experiences momentary slips into psychosis in which his master witch can manifest herself in other people. Some report actually seeing her face or certain facets of her smile in another woman.

And then there are interesting accounts of what could be described as a telepathic network of cooperating witches. This, as perceived by a man under the delusion of witchcraft, is a network of witches who assist the master witch in passing on information or communicating with the patient. There could be thousands in this theoretical network who wait for the patient to arrive at work, school, the library, the grocery store or even in his own neighborhood for nothing more than to subconsciously communicate an idea or even give physical items needed to receive a spell. What's interesting is that the patient feels as though he were subconsciously programmed by his master witch and instructed to seek out these other women. He actually looks for witches! He becomes obsessed in finding them!

If a female coworker happens to have a quartz crystal on her office desk that is nothing more than a decorative centerpiece obtained on vacation, the patient immediately concludes this to be an item of witchcraft. He might try to befriend her, form a relationship or at the very least carefully study her behavior for subconscious clues to reveal mysterious truths.

If she collects seasonal items of nature for decoration such as autumn leaves, cat tails, stones from a creek to place in a jar; these items—under his delusion—

are used for spells. If she has a hobby or some activity involving the arts, this is actually her way invoking mystical powers to use in magick."

* * *

Mary made one correct assumption of Jim. He never used profanity towards his wife. He never called her a bitch or injected adjectives of fornication while arguing with her. This doesn't mean that Jim never used foul language at home. Kimberly was a bit more of a laid back sort of wife. She understood the importance of the nasty fornication word in the English language. Its use releases frustration; and if Jim needed to blow off steam while encountering trouble with a project at home, he should be able to use the F-word—within reason, of course.

Christmas Eve was different in Jim and Kimberly's home. For one, they were no longer newlyweds (relatively speaking). There was no overwhelming jealousy towards the young and beautiful wife. And there were two children that primarily set the stage in the home each day.

The Christmas tree and decorations glowed in the family room. The aroma of Mother's baking drifted throughout the house. While April and Collin dominated the notebook computers for the day, the TV Classics network aired an 8 hour marathon of the 1960s TV show, Bewitched. Talk about a programming glitch: what does Bewitched have to do with Christmas? But it surprisingly provided an easy-going, put-your-brain-on-cruise-control sort of afternoon. It might have also set the stage for an afternoon of warped fantasies and reasoning for Jim.

Jim gazed out the family room window at the fresh blanket of snow that had fallen overnight. All the little children in Mapleview were most likely at ease that Santa Clause could land on rooftops that evening.

Through each episode of Bewitched, Jim continued to study Samantha (the witch). She appeared to be outwardly normal and friendly to those around her. There was certainly nothing ugly of her appearance. Samantha was far from the classic wicked, old witch with ugly warts and green face. There was nothing evil of her nature. In fact, she appeared to be quite benevolent.

Through all of these observations, Jim supposed that real witches are probably very much like Samantha. Oh their personalities probably vary in much the same way that non-witches do. A certain percentage is most likely emotionally disturbed and mentally imbalanced, some that come from dysfunctional families, others that are simply delusional. But most witches who are truly in touch with magick as well as nature are surely nice people. And you would never know if ever encountering one. Witches, as Jim further supposed, do everything in their power to cover their identity.

Jim took occasional breaks from his afternoon marathon of Bewitched. While in the kitchen to sample some more of Kimberly's cookies, he commented, "Wow, you've been at it all morning and afternoon."

"Yup! Almost done!" Throughout the day, Kimberly created a vast array of Christmas cookies; from simple chocolate chip to sugar cookies to Russian tea cakes to gingerbread to kaleidoscopes, even brownies and fudge bars. She was proud of her yearly tradition. And besides, making cookies for Christmas gave her an excuse to indulge in sweets for the holidays. Winter gave her a chance to cover that accumulated jiggle while losing it in time for spring.

She was such a good wife and much appreciated. Jim wouldn't think of expecting her to cook for dinner that night. "What do you say we order a couple pizzas for dinner? You don't feel like cooking, tonight."

It sounded like a great idea to Kimberly. "Sure!"

Jim returned to the family room for more bombardment of Bewitched. But before sitting down, he looked out the family room window towards the direction of Ekaterina's shack in the woods and wondered how her Christmas Eve was playing out. Then he turned towards the direction of Amber's house and wondered the same. With Amber it was possible to simply pull out the outdated palm-pilot-styled cell phone, and type out a text message, "Hey, Merry Christmas! How's your day going?" This is what he did.

Then Jim sat down to continue watching the 8 hour marathon of Bewitched. He noticed that Samantha's presence brought with it all sorts of visits from fellow witches and warlocks. They communicated through quirky gestures and spoke charming incantations. And then there was Samantha's trademarked twitch of her nose. Witches, Jim imagined, probably have their own personalized technique of casting spells. As for Ekaterina, she did peculiar things with her eyes; such as the way she cast that love spell on Jim on the night before Halloween. But similar things were noticed from Amber; quirky facial expressions made on a number of occasions. By positioning her eye brows or gently twitching her pupils, Amber possessed the power to transform her face into something beautiful, sometimes awe-inspiring, other times frightening or psychotic. Each expression spoke volumes that placed Jim in a hypnotic trance of wonder and speculation. "What did she mean by that? What was she trying to say?" And just like a poison with an initial numbing and intoxicating effect, a deep cloud of some mystical feeling would suddenly overcome Jim as the numbness wore off. Was this Amber's way of tracking him, receiving his thoughts and watching him from a distance?

Jim finally flipped the channel. He had been watching a little, too much Bewitched for the day. In fact, he had been studying the show a little more than he should have. The speculations of Amber and Ekaterina were so far-fetched. Neither of the women were witches! Ekaterina was simply an eccentric, old woman that Jim had become mystified by. Perhaps if he spent some more time with her, a friendship might be developed between them which would eliminate those wild fantasies.

As for Amber… The phone buzzed in Jim's pocket. It was a reply to his text message sent to Amber from two minutes ago. "Hey, Merry Christmas. Do you think you might have a few minutes to stop over today?"

"I'll try, but it's not going to be easy." Jim was lying, of course. For all practical purposes, today and tomorrow was a holiday with the wife and kids. Jim already celebrated Christmas with Amber and Trista on Tuesday night. Hopefully Amber wouldn't sense Jim's dishonesty from several houses away

Kimberly's afternoon ended in the kitchen. She joined her husband and children in the family room with an assorted tray of Christmas cookies and already munching on sugar cookie. She seized the remote as she very much deserved to monopolize the TV. But what horror do you suppose she subjected Jim to?

"Cool! It's the Bewitched marathon!"

Jim tried to reason with his wife. "You really want to watch this?"

"Yes…"

Never before had a silly television show launched Jim into such a bad trip! Bewitched was terrifying him as it continued to educate Jim of the customs and ways of witchcraft. The secret society that walks among us has its own techniques of communicating and interacting with one another. And really, the television show was a bit of lie. Witches don't marry, Jim assumed! As he speculated, a witch would never subject herself to a submissive relationship with a male who felt it every bit his right to lead and dominate the woman in his life. Falling in love has a different purpose. It's a dreamy illusion that offers energy to enhance magickal spells. And if done correctly, falling in love with the right man could produce a beautiful, female offspring that would continue the lineage.

Nonsense! Silliness! From where did these wild thoughts originate? After two more episodes of bewitched, Jim asked his wife, "Are you still watching this?"

Just then, another text message buzzed in Jim's pocket. It was probably Amber.

Kimberly was losing her patience with Jim."Yes I'm watching this. It's either Bewitched or Little People, Big World. It's up to you."

Jim remained silent, desperately trying to cover his anxiety. How could he explain the terror that Bewitched provoked? It caused him to realize that he was associating himself with witches and worried of their intentions. In a further attempt to calm down, he quickly checked the text message that just came in.

It was Amber with a short and cryptic text. "Well, I guess if you don't want to see me today…"

Amber knew! She knew that Jim had no intention of visiting. Through Jim's exaggerated anxiety, only a witch would be capable of such insight. Of course he forgot that all women are intuitive by nature. Perhaps it was his momentary delusions that caused him to stir a little more in his seat and appear anxious. Through Jim's distorted perception at the moment, Amber and probably even Ekaterina watched him through a crystal ball.

Kimberly sensed Jim's discomfort and finally announced, "Well, it's Little People, Big World. I know you don't want to watch this."

At least the show about "little people" who swear they can do things like normal people took Jim's mind off witches.

* * *

Pizza was delivered; the Christmas Eve feast came and went. To finish the first day of their Christmas celebration, the family sat before the TV; digesting their overindulgence and watching the classic black & white Christmas Carol.

Chapter 30

Christmas Eve was definitely a long and miserable day for Mary and Daren. There was simply no communication throughout the afternoon and early evening as Daren received the silent treatment. How much longer would he have to endure the punishment? Was Mary being stubborn and maintaining her silence for a personal, angry promise made to herself earlier that day? She sat there on the sofa, eating cookies while watching TV. And it was suddenly noticeable that she no longer wore the love pendant.

Daren had some additional Christmas surprises for his wife, and he hoped it would pull her out of the angry stupor. On the night before Christmas as Muffin sat at Mary's feet in hopes for some cookie crumbs, the classic black & white Christmas Carol played on the large TV.

Daren finally spoke, "So are you ever going to start talking to me, again?"

Mary returned a pouty and scornful look.

Daren injected adjectives of fornication while asking, "What is your problem? You've been such a bitch all day! Merry freaking Christmas to you, too, bitch!"

That's when Mary finally exploded, "Don't talk to me like that! What the hell is wrong with you, lately?"

"Nothing! There's nothing wrong with me! It's just that you're such a bitch today! Why do you have to be such a freaking bitch if things don't go your way? You think you have it so bad around here? I'll show you something!"

Daren stormed over to the stairwell that led to the cellar. Muffin angrily barked behind him. Some time earlier that evening, Daren pulled the antique axe off the tool room wall—the same axe that Grandpa Trivelli used to murder his wife's stove back in the 1830s! It now sat at the top step, hiding from Mary, waiting for another evening of assault that was to take place nearly 200 years later!

"You want to see something?" He now approached Mary while yielding the axe like some sort of crazed murderer.

Mary shouted and jumped from the sofa. "Daren, what are you doing?"

"I'll show you something!" As if batting for an out-of-the-ballpark homerun, Daren swung the axe at the large TV screen, just as the Ghost of Christmas Past entered Scrooge's bedroom. There was a loud explosion, a flash of light and a cloud of smoke. "I'll show you something!" Daren continued to chop away at the insides of the TV. Sparks and snaps of light bounced as further destruction was administered by the crazed axe murderer.

Mary was well over the edge as she screamed in terror and outrage, "Daren, what's happening to you? What the hell is wrong with you? Stop it!"

Muffin joined in with a traumatized, nervous bark.

"I'll show you something… I'll show you something!" With every swing of the axe, Daren continued to let out maniacal, crazed laughter. Then he stopped and looked towards Mary. "I'm not done, yet!"

Mary ran out of her husband's way as he approached with the axe. No, he wasn't about to chop up his wife. Instead, Daren made his way over to den where the obsolete computer and monitor from 2001 sat at the desk. "You want to see something?"

Mary screamed out, "Daren, no!"

But it was too late; the axe blade smashed into the CRT monitor, producing a horrific explosion and flash of light. Then he swung at the aluminum PC tower. Knocked over, it was brutally murdered as Daren repeatedly raised the axe and smashed it through to the internal circuit boards like a psychotic railroad construction worker that laughed and laughed.

Poor Mary was terrified and had nothing left to do but run up the stairs, crying, and into her bedroom. Muffin remained downstairs, barking at Daren.

"Shut up before I chop your head off! Go upstairs!"

Muffin did as Daren ordered.

Huffing and puffing with beads of sweat pouring off his forehead, Daren examined the destruction while continuing to laugh. But don't be so quick to conclude that Daren was the hole of an ass. It was all in good fun for him. For you see, in addition to the love pendant, Daren purchased a brand, new, high-resolution, plasma TV for his wife; along with a high-powered notebook computer—wireless router installed in the house so that Mary could comfortably sit on the sofa and browse the internet.

Can you see how much Daren truly loved his wife? Demanding that Mary wear a love pendant out of jealousy, and purchasing her pricy toys for Christmas; a woman should only wish for a husband like Daren. Don't you wish you were married to him?

With his wife upstairs, Daren cleaned up the mess. The old computer was discarded into the garbage can outside. The smashed up TV and broken pieces that had been projected throughout the family room were hauled out to the trash. And once the area was clean, Daren pulled the high-resolution, plasma-screen TV from the cellar into the family room where it was set up. A red bow was attached on top.

The high-powered notebook computer was removed from the guest closet, flipped open and turned on. In less than 5 seconds it fully booted so that the LCD screen glowed as Daren ascended the stairs into the bedroom.

"Mary, I got you a little surprise."

"Go away!"

"Oh, honey; I was just joking with you. If you come downstairs, you'll see I got a brand, new TV. And look; check out the laptop computer. And there's a wireless router so you can sit wherever and surf the web."

Chapter 31

Christmas morning; despite the religious purpose of celebrating Christ's birthday on this holiday, the morning of Christmas continues to place significance in finally opening up all the presents. Jim, Kimberly and their two kids took turns unwrapping gifts from Santa Clause, each other or from Mom and Dad. And when the last present was opened, there was that sense of sadness in the air that Christmas was over.

Fortunately for Jim and his family, the unwrapping of presents did not mean the end of Christmas. Christmas morning also meant attending mass and properly celebrating the birth of Christ. Later that day the family would have a nice Christmas dinner. And as we've all come to understand, children play with their new toys throughout the day. Christmas is all day long! But you already know that!

As for Mary and Daren, Christmas came to the rescue and restored some much needed peace at the Trivelli house. Christmas morning started off on the uneasy side for Mary and Daren. As Mary opened her eyes, she could smell fresh coffee brewing downstairs. This disappointed her because Mary felt that only she could brew the perfect pot of coffee. And how she needed the perfect cup after a bizarre night at the Trivelli house.

"Good morning! Merry Christmas!" Daren was friendly and cheerful, acting as though the previous night never happened. Then he approached his wife to give an unwelcome hug. "Awe, I'm sorry Honey. I guess maybe I got a little carried away with a joke. It won't happen again; I promise. But I hope you like your Christmas presents."

Tears began to fall from Mary's eyes. And then she slapped her husband on the arm a few times while scolding him. "Don't ever do that, again! You really scared me last night. You don't know how close I was to calling the police."

Daren resumed his embrace while patting Mary on the back. "I'm so sorry. I didn't even think of that."

Feeling that she was on the road to reconciliation with Daren, Mary put her arms around her husband so that the two now held one another.

Daren continued with his apologies. "And I'm so sorry about the car ride to Sillmac. You know how I am. I get so jealous when it comes to other men. You're so beautiful and it just burns me up to know that other men might try to take you from me."

"No one's going to take me from you, Daren."

Daren acknowledged, "I know... I know..." Then he loosened his embrace and looked at Mary's chest. She wasn't wearing her love pendant. It would only require a simple request. "Put your love pendant back on for me. It looked so pretty on you."

Mary informed him, "It's upstairs on the dresser. I'll put it on once I take my shower."

But Daren insisted. "Why don't you make yourself a cup of coffee? I'll go upstairs and get that love pendant for you." And with that he dashed up into the bedroom and found it on the dresser. Daren returned to the kitchen with his arms held out in a motion to clasp it around Mary's neck.

Mary put the cup of coffee down and pulled her beautiful hair up so Daren could put the love pendant around her neck.

"There! Let's see it!"

It looked so beautiful to Daren. It barely rested on the top of Mary's cleavage which caused him the sudden desire to make Christmas morning love to his wife. "Wanna have make up sex?"

But Mary wasn't ready to fully give in to her husband. "We've got to be ready for church in an hour."

"Oh, come-on! Just a little 5 minute quickie?"

Mary offered an alternative. "How about tonight?"

It was a good enough answer for Daren; but how he missed the days before being married when sex was spontaneous and had freely.

Christmas mass was terribly crowded as Heathens dared to enter the doors that were only walked through twice a year—Christmas and Easter. Mary and Daren attended church regularly, but were inconvenienced on this day with having to sit way in the back as much of the church was already crowded by those noisy Heathens. Kids played with their electronic games or texted their friends with their nifty, new smart phones. Adults nosily chatted as-if seated at a reception hall. Every Sunday (except Easter) those moments before the start of mass were observed in silence and in prayer or reflection. Today it was a carnival!

At the middle of mass when "Peace be with you" greetings were given, Mary fully forgave Daren for the previous day's performance. It was Christmas and she had much to be grateful for. Surely marriage offers those dark moments that try the love of husband and wife.

* * *

As all of Mapleview enjoyed Christmas morning, Jim sat in the family room upon returning from church and thought of poor, lonely Ekaterina who would probably remain shut in throughout the weekend. Did she have family? Did she have people to celebrate Christmas with? It wasn't right for her to be so lonely on a holiday. With Christmas dinner some hours away, Jim decided to fabricate a cable outage; lie to his wife on Christmas Day and sneak off to the forest to visit some other woman.

Skeeters convenient store remains open on holidays. As a little Christmas gift for Ekaterina—nothing fancy—Jim purchased a small box of cheap, off-brand chocolate candies and was sure to toss the receipt away. Kimberly certainly could be aware of mysterious chocolates purchased on Christmas Day at around the time he left for the fabricated cable outage.

After driving up Mapleview Road and entering the old, wooded section of town; Jim pulled into the driveway of Ekaterina's originally believed house—the same house that received a couple week's worth of rose petal assault—and backed out to park off the highway. He was sure to inch his van up past the house as Ekaterina ordered two days prior.

Crossing the highway and venturing over the guardrail on the other side of the road, Jim entered the forest and followed with near, precise accuracy the way to Ekaterina's house. Recall how it was necessary to zigzag and cross untamed, forested wilderness to reach Ekaterina's cottage. How Jim remembered this route is nothing short of phenomenal!

"Knock-knock-knock-knock!" Jim rapped upon Ekaterina's door.

A moment later the old woman answered, appearing half asleep and somewhat annoyed to have been disturbed from whatever she was doing. Upon recognizing Jim a second later, her facial expression softened. "Oh, hi!" Ekaterina opened the door wider and let Jim in. What could he have possibly been doing there?

"Merry Christmas!" Jim greeted while stepping in.

"Merry Christmas?" asked Ekaterina with a queer facial expression. Her agitated mood returned. "Oh, Russian people do not celebrate Christmas today. We celebrate Christmas on January 7th." Of course! Being from Russia, Ekaterina was most-likely an Orthodox Christian. For them, Christmas day is on the seventh of January.

Jim apologized, "Oh, I'm sorry! I got you a little present."

"Let me see!" Ekaterina snatched the box of cheap, off-brand chocolates out of Jim's hand and tore into the plastic wrapping. The box could not be opened fast enough! Ekaterina nearly shook as she placed a piece of chocolate candy in her mouth. "Mmmmmmm!" With only a few chews, the candy was swallowed and Ekaterina reached for another piece. Apparently this was her breakfast!

"Sit down!" ordered Ekaterina as she motioned Jim over to the kitchen table. She slapped the box of candy at the center and then walked over to the cupboard for small glass. As Jim sat down, he noticed Ekaterina had additionally reached for what appeared to be a bottle of some authentic, imported Russian vodka. The writing was unrecognizable, and most-likely comprised of the Russian alphabet. The glass was set on the table and Ekaterina filled it three-quarters full. "This is my Christmas present to you. You like vodka, yes?"

Jim stared at the juice glass filled with three-quarters of clear liquid. It was certainly a lot of vodka! Assuming the glass had the potential of holding eight ounces, there were quite possibly 3 shots of vodka in it—being that the glass was three-quarters full and the average shot glass holds two ounces.

While Jim considered this and stared at his drink, Ekaterina reached for an identical glass and poured herself some vodka. But what was this? As she sat down, Ekaterina noticed that her guest hadn't touched his. "Go ahead! Drink it! It's good vodka. I am Russian. I know good vodka and would not give you something cheap."

"That's a lot of vodka." answered Jim.

"Nonsense! Drink it! It's Christmas, time to celebrate and enjoy."

At not even noon on Christmas Day, Jim raised the glass of vodka and took a sip. Immediately he coughed and exhaled burning heat through his lips. "Wow!"

Ekaterina laughed. By now, half of her glass was empty. "American people are not used to vodka. You like to mix it with your drinks and add sugar. But not Russian people! Russian people drink just vodka!" She pushed the box of candy over towards Jim. "Go ahead, have a piece."

"Oh, I couldn't..."

Ekaterina laughed some more, nearly cackling."What? You think this is all the chocolate I have?" She stood up and walked over to a small cabinet against the wall near the cupboards. Upon opening it, some couple dozen bags of chocolate candies were seen. "See, I have lots of chocolate."

With that, Jim helped himself to a random piece from the box before him. The inner filling was strawberry. He took another sip from the glass of vodka. This time the burn wasn't so bad and not such a shock to swallow.

Ekaterina reached for another piece of candy while asking, "So how is your Christmas at home? Everything nice? Are your wife and kids happy today?"

"Oh yeah..." Jim took another sip of vodka. "We opened our presents this morning and then went to church. We're going to have Christmas dinner later this afternoon."

"Well that sounds nice. How about your girlfriend? Is everything nice with her today?"

Jim was at a loss of words. He wasn't exactly comfortable talking about Amber, much less admitting to Ekaterina that Amber was a girlfriend or mistress. "Well, we had a little dinner a few nights ago. I won't be seeing her today. It's Christmas."

"No?" asked Ekaterina. "Not even a phone call or a Merry Christmas? Do you even know what she is doing today or who she is with?"

"No, I never asked her about that." Apparently Amber wasn't too important to Jim.

Ekaterina gulped the remains of her vodka and then walked over to the cupboard for a glass bowl. "We should find out what your girlfriend is doing today."

Jim took another large sip from his glass of vodka while watching Ekaterina carry the bowl into the bathroom. He knew what was in store for him, another hypnotic session of scrying; sort of a crystal ball approach to viewing Amber's activities. Perhaps this is how Ekaterina had been watching Jim's activities in recent months.

Sure enough, the sound of the hand pump could be heard. A moment later, Ekaterina returned and set the clear, glass bowl of water on the table before

Jim. From the moment he entered the kitchen and sat down, a small candle burned on the table for light. This could now be seen through the transparent, glass bowl of water.

Ekaterina poured another glass of vodka for herself and additionally topped off Jim's. Was Jim going to be drunk for Christmas Day?

"You should learn some things about your girlfriend." said Ekaterina. "What do you think she is doing today?"

Jim took a hearty sip from the glass, "I don't know. I suppose she and her daughter are celebrating Christmas."

"Well does she live with family?"

"No, she lives in a house down the street from me. It's just her and Trista."

"It sounds like a lonely Christmas with just the two of them."

"Yeah... Maybe they have family out of the area and they will be spending the day with them." suggested Jim.

"Maybe..."

As Jim and Ekaterina continued to discuss Amber and her possible activities for Christmas Day, Jim imagined with such clarity a car traveling the wintery highways, en route to a family Christmas dinner.

* * *

In addition to her knowledge of Mother's mystical artwork in the attic, Trista held another secret. Often when visiting Grandma and Grandpa, Trista would sometimes overhear Grandma speaking to Mother and make mention of "your mother" or "your father". It lead Trista to realize that her mother (Amber) had estranged her own parents—or vice versa.

Trista asked Mother of this strange observation one time. "Mom, why does Grandma sometimes talk about your mother or father? Isn't Grandma and Grandpa your real mom and dad?"

Mother returned a cold and frightening stare. "That's your Grandma and Grandpa, understand? You mind your own business when you hear adults talking." The cold and frightening stare chilled deeper into Trista. She truly feared that look in Mother's eyes. It had such an unexplained power over her, and she dare not challenge any further while witnessing it.

But don't think that because Trista had been spellbound with fear she wouldn't remain curious. She developed a longing for people that were fantasized as her real grandparents, real aunts, real uncles, and maybe even real cousins her own age—anyone besides those strange people that Trista was forced to visit and associate herself with from time-to-time.

As-is the case on Christmas Day when Trista accompanied Mother and her aunt on another hour drive from Mapleview to Grandma and Grandpa's house: sitting alone in the backseat, she drunk in the beauty of winter's painted forests of Mapleview while Mother drove north on Mapleview Road, followed the curve so that they transitioned east, then made a left onto Creek Highway where they soon connected to the Interstate highway.

Following the Interstate east, until connecting with Route 92 (runs north and south); one must continue traveling north to reach River County where Grandma and Grandpa live. At some point, the familiar Mapleview and Sillmac terrain loses its woodland appearance and exhibits landscapes of prairie and grassland. In this time of year, however, it was simply miles of wide-open, snowy fields.

Then there's a sudden change of terrain with the appearance of towering, northern pines. It begins near an almost mountainous section of Route 92 where the road inclines for about a mile and travelers can observe magnificent scenery as they gaze at forested valleys, below. Then the road declines for another mile where travelers now find themselves following a highway that is outlined by dense, pine forests.

"It's so beautiful in this section." commented Amber's sister.

"I know, with all the snow!" agreed Amber.

Amber's sister turned to the backseat towards Trista. "Do you need a Christmas tree?"

Trista smiled in return, covering her sudden disgust and apprehensions. Unlike Mother and her aunt, Trista didn't find this sudden change of scenery beautiful at all. Oh, she loved snowy, pine forests just like you and me. But this particular region only announced that Grandma and Grandpa's house was about fifteen minutes away. They lived out here in isolation from people and civilization. Trista wished to be anywhere but here; far away from those strange people.

Trista didn't have any resentment towards her aunt. In fact, she developed a fondness of her. Trista couldn't recall a time when her aunt was in a bad mood. There were even times when her mood was obnoxious in comparison to a humdrum Saturday afternoon that Mother and Trista had. Still, Trista had a strong suspicion that her aunt wasn't really Mother's sister. And although she lived only a few minutes away back in Mapleview, her aunt was one of them; those strange people who lived with Grandma and Grandpa.

One cannot see Grandma and Grandpa's house from Route 92. It was necessary for Mother to turn right onto Needle Road and follow it a good mile before reaching a decline in land elevation. Imagine a natural basin of pine forests with breathtaking acreage of wide open country at the bottom. In the center is Grandma and Grandpa's mansion. On this Christmas day it was lavishly decorated with holiday figurines, nativity scene, forest creatures and countless lights that were already illuminated.

There was stillness and quietness in the air as Trista, Mother and her aunt exited the vehicle. The bottom of the basin was usually sheltered from strong winds while allowing a gentle breeze to flow through. Today, the only sound was the crunching of boots into icy snow. Its sound only brought with it a need to quickly enter the warm house.

The décor of Grandma and Grandpa's mansion was rustic and Earth-toned. Trista could recall younger years of living in the Dickly castle and viewing brilliant, marble tile that paved a grand foyer. In contrast, Grandma and Grandpa's mansion immediately greeted a visitor with natural, stone tiled flooring—each piece with its own unique shape and natural design. The gigantic chandelier appeared to be wooden with decorative lighting that emulated candles. The bulbs even flickered like real candle flame. Furniture was either green or brown, sometimes a cranberry red. All tables, shelving units, countertops and cabinets revealed a hint of aged, country wood. And although Trista was never a fan of rustic decor, Grandma presented it in such a way so that it looked elegant and beautiful.

"You're getting to be such fine, young lady!" Grandma placed both hands on the sides of Trista's face, gazing deeply into her eyes and adoring everything about her appearance. "Just look at you!" She pulled Trista's hands forward so that her arms were extended while continuing to admire her granddaughter. It all made Trista feel as-if Grandma had big plans for her in the future.

"She took first place in her Violin solo." announced Mother.

"Yes, I know! I heard that! Congratulations Honey!"

Trista smiled in return. "Thank you!"

While this happened, Grandpa entered and made his greetings with hugs and kisses to Mother, Mother's sister and then finished with his lovely Granddaughter, Trista. Then he urged, "Let's go in the family room where everyone else is waiting."

And seated comfortably in the family room everyone was. They were the usual crowd of people, over a dozen who were encountered during a visit. These weren't guests; they were people who lived with Grandma and Grandpa for one mysterious reason or another. Originally introduced to Trista as her aunts, uncles or cousins, many of them often exhibited bizarre behavior and appeared to be quite crazy—maybe even out of touch with reality. They looked so peaceful and content while seated around the Christmas tree, enjoying their beverages and listening to orchestra Christmas music.

Suddenly, in walked another member of the house—a male named George who was once introduced to Trista as her Uncle. For that matter, Trista referred to him as Uncle George.

Uncle George immediately approached Grandma and knelt down before her while shaking out of apparent nervousness. Then he kissed her feet, "Blessed be thy feet that have brought thee in these ways." Then he kissed her knees, "Blessed be thy knees that shall kneel at the sacred altar." Then he kissed her womb, "Blessed be thy womb, without which we would not be."

Grandpa rushed over and interrupted Uncle George. "Easy George! This is just a Christmas get-together. You needn't greet my wife that way all the time!"

"Sorry, I was just... well, I thought..."

Grandpa put the words in George's mouth, "You thought it would be a clever way to inch your way up and bless my wife's breasts by kissing them, right?"

Grandma was shocked. "Herbert!"

Uncle George, too, was shocked and at a loss of words. "I'm sorry..."

"It's okay." answered Grandpa. "I mean with the way my wife flaunts her smooth bosom, it's enough to tempt anyone."

Again, Grandma was shocked "Herbert! What's gotten into you?"

Grandpa apparently felt that the situation was over, and immediately changed the topic. "So how are your paintings coming along, Amber? Oh, and how rude of me! Would you like something to drink?" He motioned to the bar while offering.

"What's everyone else having?" asked Amber.

A few raised their glasses.

"Egg nog..."

"Egg nog..."

"Egg nog..."

"We're all pretty much having the egg nog." said another to speak for the rest of them.

Amber made her selection, "I guess I'll have the egg nog, too."

"Me too." said Amber's sister. "It's heavy with rum, right?"

"As usual!" reassured Grandpa. "And how about you, Trista? You're a young lady, now. Egg nog?"

Amber spoke for her daughter. "I think not! No daughter of mine will walk around with liquor on her breath!"

Amber's sister put her arm around Trista's shoulder while whispering, "You need to come over to your Aunt's house more often. I'm more fun than your mother."

Amber appeared to see the humor in her sister's comment, but maintained her strict guidance as a mother of a teenage daughter. "Stop it! She's not drinking!"

"Oh, like you never drank in high school!" answered Amber's sister.

Amber finally gave in. "Fine, just one; and only one!"

Grandpa fixed egg nogs for Amber, Amber's sister and Trista. "Very good! It's Christmas and we should all have fun. Anyone else want a refill?"

"Me!"

"Me!"

"I'll have another."

Now the Christmas bar tender, Grandpa maintained conversation with Mother while preparing even more drinks. "So about those paintings; how are they coming along?"

It was in this moment when Trista suspected that Grandpa was the motivator behind Mother's sudden hobby.

Mother answered, "They're getting more detailed. I find that atmospheric color is one of the key effects."

"Very good!" commented Grandpa. "I've been doing my paintings for years and find that each one becomes all the more powerful." He approached Amber, her sister and Trista and handed them their drinks. Then he walked back to the bar to pour himself another Scotch whiskey. It was his beverage of choice. Grandpa appeared to be the retired businessman who continued to wear suits with neckties. Drinking Scotch whiskey added to the wild and entrepreneurial sophistication. Trista was never sure as to what Grandpa did, exactly, to make himself wealthy. It was something to do with real estate investments, or possibly sales.

Grandpa continued, "I think the most dramatic painting I ever made is hung in my study." He walked to the stairs to ascend the second level.

"Herbert, it's Christmas. No one wants to see that stuff." said Grandma.

But Grandpa insisted, "No, no; let me bring it down! Amber needs to see this one!"

Grandma shook her head and sighed, then spoke to Amber's sister. "So how are things back in Mapleview? How's the house?"

"Oh, it's great! I just did some re-decorating throughout the main level. You should come out some time and check it out."

Moments later Grandpa returned with a large, framed portrait and held it up for everyone to see. "Now here's one of my favorites." The subject of the painting looked to be some business colleague of Grandpa's who might have done him wrong at one time or another. Trista assumed this because the man in a suit sat in the driver's seat of a car that was engulfed by a raging fire. Not only did the expression on his face exhibit terror in his final moments alive, but Grandpa also exaggerated some greedy, backstabbing characteristics around the business colleague's mouth and eyes.

One could nearly hear the man screaming as he was trapped in that burning car. Outside of the car's interior, the man and the raging flames; everything else was pitch black which added to the eeriness.

Grandpa began to comment, "The amazing thing about this portrait is the fact that Dale Jensen..."

Grandma immediately cleared her throat and interrupted. "Herbert, put your gallery of horror away. It's Christmas!" She motioned her eyes towards Trista.

"Oh, very well. I suppose you're right." But then before bringing the portrait back upstairs, Grandpa mentioned a new work of art that was still in the stage of conception. "I've been dreaming up a sculpture. We could do it so well. All I need is..."

Again, Grandma quickly interrupted. "Herbert! You really need to bring that back upstairs, and I don't want to say anything else about it!" She motioned her eyes towards Trista.

Just like all intelligent girls her age, Trista was highly observant of her surroundings and knew there was some God-awful horror behind Grandpa's artwork that she could not be aware of. Grandma did her best to maintain some sense of normalcy in that house, and cover who and what the residents really were.

Grandma stood up from her seat. "Well, who wants to help me finish some things up in the kitchen? I bet that ham is almost done."

Chapter 32

Although just about everyone in Mapleview were having a lovely Christmas celebration, the same could not be said of the family get together at Loraine Trivelli's house. Daren brought with him an unusual style of Christmas cheer. Upon its display, one might expect the Trivelli family to exclude him from next year's celebration.

* * *

While driving to Aunt Loraine's house later that afternoon, Mary witnessed a dramatic change in her husband—a return to the monster he was on Christmas Eve. It was as-if he had become possessed by some ugly spirit while turning into Aunt Loraine's subdivision.

"Do me a favor?" asked Daren. "Don't be a bitch while you're with your family. Try acting like my wife for a change."

Mary was flabbergasted. "Daren, what are you talking about? What's wrong with you?"

"You heard me!" Daren whipped around the corner onto Aunt Loraine's street which caused the tires to screech. The sound of Mary's Italian cream cake and her seven-layer taco dip could be heard thudding in the back trunk. Two days of labor were spent on Mary's precious cake. Surely it was now smashed on one of the sides.

"Daren, I have a cake back there! What's wrong with you?"

Daren exploded. "Shut the hell up! You better not ruin the afternoon for me!" It was as-if Daren needed to project his negative emotions onto Mary so that she acted just like him while entering Aunt Loraine's house.

Daren stopped at the driveway of Loraine Trivelli's house and exclaimed, "What the hell is this?" Apparently, one of the children of the family brought a new sled to Aunt Loraine's house. Or maybe this child received it from Aunt Loraine as a Christmas present. Whatever the reality, it now lay in the driveway, blocking Daren's ability to enter and park. He lay on the horn to summon the attention of the sled's owner.

Mary was becoming embarrassed. "Daren, what are you doing?"

"Shut up! They should know better than to leave a sled in the driveway."

No one seemed to be running out for the sled. Being the case, Daren saw it fit to just drive over the sled, smashing into several pieces as the tires rolled over. "That's the way we do it around here! No courtesy for me, no courtesy for you!"

Now Mary was outraged! "Daren, you are such a jackass! You didn't want me to ruin Christmas? More like you're ruining the afternoon for everyone else!"

Daren retorted, "You haven't seen anything, yet!"

While both Mary and Daren exited the vehicle; little Courtney, Mary's niece, ran out of Aunt Loraine's house, crying. Apparently the sled belonged to her.

Daren soon informed the little girl, "Sorry about the sled. That's just what happens in life. You get in someone's way, they run you over!"

And if the asinine statement to a child didn't flabbergast Mary enough, Daren's next act did!

Daren turned to his wife, "Here, get your cake and dip out of the trunk." Then he threw the keys at her.

Mary isn't the greatest when it comes to catching. Instead of grabbing the keys in midair, they fell onto the wet, salty driveway. And she soon figured out that both her Italian cream cake and seven-layer taco dip would have to be carried into the house by herself. Daren wasn't going to help. He strolled up to the house with attitude, clicking his boots onto the sidewalk. And then he stuck his tongue out at little Courtney's brother who ran outside to witness the disaster to the sled.

Aunt Loraine greeted Daren at the door. "Well hello, Daren. Merry Christmas. You're welcome to join us for dinner."

"You're damn right I'm welcome! Now look out!" He nearly trampled over Aunt Loraine while entering the house. And while wiping off his boots in the foyer, Mary's brother angrily approached.

"Hey, you gonna pay for that sled? Huh?"

Daren wasn't concerned about Mary's brother. He had his trusty wad of cash in the front pocket. He simply pulled it out in front of Mary's, brother's face. "You want me to buy you a new sled? Here! Here's a couple hundred bucks!

Go buy your kids a real sled for Christmas!" Then he slapped the money onto Mary's, brother's chest; nearly pushing the man into the wall.

In the family room, everyone stood around the hors d'oeuvres table with their cocktails and small plates. The room grew silent as Daren entered.

"Hey, it's the happy Trivelli family! Merry Christmas to you all!"

A couple people halfheartedly acknowledged Daren's greeting. "Merry Christmas…" No one on Mary's side of the family liked Daren. Not only did he make this day very sad for little Courtney and her brother, but the family held a dark suspicion over Daren.

"So what do we have for appetizers?" Daren walked over to the hors d'oeuvres table and checked out the items on display. While everyone else politely loaded items on their small plates to snack on; Daren simply grabbed a few jumbo shrimp, dipped them in the cocktail sauce and took a bite. For more of an offensive display, he merely leaned over the cocktail sauce while doing this. It's not so bad to allow crumbs and dribble to land back into the food that everyone else wishes to eat.

Then he spotted two open bottles of wine at the end of the table. One of them was a bottle of imported Argentina Malbec. Rather than use one of the wine glasses provided, Daren helped himself to one of Aunt Loraine's 16 ounce tumbler glasses at the dry bar.

Paying no mind to possibly bruising the precious Argentina Malbec, he emptied the contents of the bottle so lively, making that harsh "glub, glub, glub" noise. By the time the tumbler had been filled, only a half glass worth of Malbec remained. No problem for Daren! He simply tipped the bottle to his mouth and drunk the remains. Then he tossed the empty bottle into the garbage can. Its noise drew brief attention from everyone else.

Just then, Mary entered the family room. Of course everyone loves sweet Mary. Mother, Father and siblings were so happy to see her.

"Hi Mary…!"

"Mary…!"

"Alright, what did Mary bring us…?"

"Merry Christmas…!"

Additional family members surrounded her and offered loving embraces and kisses to her rosy cheeks. Through all this, she briefly glanced over to Daren with eyes of fire. He was on her garbage list for the rest of the day. And there would no sex later that night!

Mary brought her Italian cream cake and seven-layer taco dip over to the table as Daren bit into a cracker that was topped with cheese and deer meat sausage. Just like before, he leaned in so that all his crumbs would fall back into the tray.

Then he looked over at his wife in surprise. "What's wrong with you? Why the face?"

Mary softly growled, "Use a plate!"

Daren took a few gulps of his 16 ounce tumbler of wine. It was going to be a long afternoon with the Trivelli family. And already his wife was being a bitch!

Moments later, Mary called from in the hallway while standing next to Aunt Loraine. "Daren?" She signaled him over once he looked up.

Reluctantly, Daren approached with his nearly finished 16 ounce tumbler of Argentina Malbec. Aunt Loraine had a bitter expression on her face. He was soon motioned to follow into the kitchen for a private chat with Aunt Loraine.

She was blunt and direct with Daren. "Listen, if you're not going to act right, today, I'm going to ask you to leave. I can always take my niece home at the end of the day. No one wants you here to ruin the afternoon."

Daren finished the remains of his 16 ounce tumbler and then spoke while pointing his finger at Aunt Loraine. "Now you listen here. Don't you start with me. You've had a problem with me ever since I got here. In fact, you've had a problem with me ever since I married your niece."

Aunt Loraine had plenty of ammunition and started with only the recent fifteen minutes. "Well why wouldn't I have a problem with you? You ran over the kids' sled with your car; you're insulting people and throwing money at them; you're acting rude and obnoxious at the hors d'oeuvres table; and now you're getting drunk! Does that sound like the sort of person I want at my Christmas party?"

How Daren hated Aunt Loraine! His rage grew with every word spoken by the woman. "Loraine, I'm telling you; don't you start with me! You don't want to start with me. You start with me, and I'll tell you something you're not going to believe!"

What possibly could the family jerk have to say that would disturb Loraine so badly? She dared him. "Really? Like what?"

That's when Daren responded with the most illogical, lowest and uneducated assault of words. It's difficult to describe the offensive verve in which he said it. But he rudely pointed his finger in Aunt Loraine's face and voiced a harsh wish of fornication.

It was such a silly and immature thing to tell someone. And really the only reason Aunt Loraine was so angered at that moment was the fact that Daren truly believed his profanity made a harsh impact on her. He proudly walked away as if victory was had. How else would you expect a drunk to behave?

In need to bring his nerves down, Daren returned to the end of the hors d'oeuvres table and picked up a half drunk bottle of Charles Shaw Merlot. Again, he paid no mind to bruising the wine as the nasty, "glub, glub, glub" sound could be heard while filling his 16 ounce glass tumbler. But this time there were no remains in the bottle. He simply tossed it in the garbage can which clinked against the empty bottle of Malbec.

One of the family members who grew tired of Daren's presence and behavior sharply announced, "I guess I'll open up another bottle for us all."

Daren took a few gulps from the glass and then helped himself to more hors d'oeuvres. Mary's seven-layer taco dip was assaulted by Daren's aggressive nacho chips. And he was sure to lean over it while taking a bite.

Several minutes passed as Daren stood in the corner, finishing his second 16 ounce tumbler of wine. He watched everyone in disgust and resented their animosity towards him. With an empty stomach that had been hit with a flood of 32 ounces of wine (two different types, mind you!), Daren was pretty much drunk. In this state, his dark emotions emerged. And there was no holding back!

"You know what I just realized?"

The chatter of people lowered as Daren's loud voice broke through. Mary buried her face in her hands. "What is he going to do, now?"

"I just realized that all you people think that I had something to do with Kelly's disappearance!"

Mary yelled out, "Daren! Stop it! You're drunk!"

"No, no; it's fine, Babe. This needs to come out in the open. You all think that I fooled around with her when she was living with us, don't you?"

The expressions on people's faces ranged from anger to disbelief. How dare he mention poor Kelly during a family gathering on Christmas Day?

"In fact, you all think that I did something to her—killed her to cover up what happened!"

Mary's face was flustered with tears. "Daren, you are *such a jerk*! Why did I even marry you?" She stormed out of the family room while controlling her sobs. As usual, Daren wrecked another family get-together.

Chapter 33

I suppose women secretly fancy themselves as the hero in a discordant marriage or some other harmful relationship with an overly-temperamental man. Behind all his sudden transformations into an ugly monster, the woman knows that a compassionate and loving man is trapped. One day she can rescue him.

After a display such as Daren's on Christmas Day, one would expect Mary to have divorced him. But she simply went home with him that night, merely exhibiting a bitter attitude and then serving the proper three days' silent treatment. And rest assured, by New Years Eve at the stroke of midnight, she and Daren welcomed the New Year with a loving kiss.

But what was this? In less than a week later, Daren paid a visit to the Mapleview department store; in particular, the jewelry department. He did this on a Tuesday morning, assuming that holiday help had been laid off and Amber worked the counter alone.

Unfortunately, Amber recognized Daren as he approached the counter while flipping through his ridiculous wad of cash. Recalling the strange customer forced Amber to greet him as-if he had made an impact on his last visit.

"Hi!" said Amber.

"Good morning!" announced Daren in return.

"What can I do for you?"

Daren sighed, "Well, do you remember the last time I was here and I told you about my girlfriend, and I told you that I thought we'd be breaking up?"

"Vaguely…" Amber lied. Unfortunately, Amber remembered all too well. She remembered everything in her daily life as she had a habit of intensely studying her surroundings and then drawing inferences with a mental note to check later. Those who habitually make inferences of other people without sound evidence are often considered crazy. But Amber wasn't crazy. In her world, Daren was that married guy who made up a sad story of being close to breaking up with his girlfriend. For some strange reason he thought it would entice Amber and open the door for some further, imagined seduction. She knew he would return for more. Why the hell else would Daren be standing at the counter without his purchased jewelry and receipt for a return?

Daren attempted to refresh Amber's memory. "I got her that love pendant and hoped it would help things. She still has it, but I really don't think it means much to her."

Amber remained silent.

Then Daren sighed. "Look, I know this sounds really weird. But you're the only person I told this to. It's just that you really remind me of my girlfriend, and I think I could use some of your advice. Maybe you would be willing to talk for a few minutes? Did they let you go on morning break yet? I'll treat you to a coffee and pastry over at the cafeteria."

Amber smiled and shook her head in disbelief. Then she momentarily glanced at Daren's wedding band while speaking. "I'm sorry, but I don't make it habit in having dates with married men."

"Date? I wasn't asking you out on a date. I just thought you could talk with me over a cup of coffee on your break."

Again, Amber glanced at Daren's wedding band. "You're married."

Daren took hold of his wedding band. "What? This? Does this bother you? Here, let me put this in my pocket for you. See, it doesn't mean anything." Now, Daren was naked of his wedding band.

It didn't change things for Amber. "You're still married, Sir. And I think I know the perfect person for you to talk about your girlfriend with. You should tell your wife all about her. See what advice your wife has for you."

And with that, Amber turned and walked away; not just to another area of the counter or the cash register, but to some door that led to an off-limits hallway—the back offices or stock room for all Daren knew. The conversation was over and there appeared to be no invitation for further pursuit.

So beautiful and sexy, causing extreme frustration for a man who cannot have her; do women have any idea as to how cruel they can be?

* * *

Alone in all his frustrations, Daren paid a visit to his secret clubhouse; the family mausoleum where the late and murdered Mary Trivelli resided. She had beer for Daren in one of the crypts. And being that it was January, the beer was ice cold.

Ah, that was better! Halfway through his first beer, Daren convinced himself that all the frustration felt from the woman at the jewelry store would be erased by the end of a second beer. With this thought in mind, he continued to take hearty guzzles.

The mausoleum was so cold in this time of year. With the iron door closed, Daren hoped that the illuminated sconces affixed to the rear wall would provide some warmth. He had air conditioning installed for the summer months. Maybe heat wouldn't be so bad for winter.

Really, Daren had no need to be frustrated with Amber. He had Mary Trivelli locked up in one of the crypts. She was all his and going nowhere. Speaking of which; when was the last time Daren had a personal visit with Mary?

He carefully unlocked and opened the crypt. There rested the oversized Mason jar with Mary Trivelli's beautiful head that floated in the dark, oily liquid. But so sad; the January cold created a layer of ice above Mary. Perhaps her soft, beautiful face had become hardened by the frigid temperature as well. And maybe this is why she appeared so cold and bitter towards Daren as he held the jar so lovingly in his lap.

Then again, maybe it wasn't that at all. Maybe Mary was truly disappointed in Daren for his behavior in recent weeks. He mocked her murder on Christmas Eve while terrifying Mary's granddaughter. He created a nasty scene at the Trivelli Christmas party. And what was this recent interest Daren had in the woman who worked in the jewelry department? Daren had much explaining to do.

Daren guzzled the remains of his second beer. A wave of sadness suddenly overcame him. "Don't be mad at me. You're the only person who seems to understand me."

The fool Daren was; didn't he understand that a friendship required care and consideration from both sides? Did he really believe that his harmful actions could be ignored while continuing to receive love from the deceased Mary Trivelli? Daren hurt her, and gave no reason to believe that he cared of anything important to the late Mary Trivelli.

Sadly, the world is full of people like Daren. Well, maybe not to his dramatic extent; but sadly, many people go about love and relationships with the mindset of what's-in-it-for-me. In Daren's world, Mary Trivelli was misbehaving, acting as though she forgot life before Daren came around. The magick between them had gone stale, almost like a favorite song that is played too many times. The oversized Mason jar was set back in the crypt. Mary was going nowhere. Daren was the master of this relationship. It would only be a matter of time before she changed her ways and showed more respect towards Daren.

And then a sickening light bulb flashed in Daren's head. Such a thought required that he crack open a third beer and mull over the possibilities. There were several crypts in that mausoleum. And a simple search online would surely lead to a vendor that could provide oversized mason jars.

It was a bad idea; a very, very bad idea! Daren quickly locked up Mary Trivelli's crypt and left the mausoleum for the day.

Chapter 34

Friendly conversation, good times, plenty of vodka and hypnotic sessions of scrying; there were many reasons why Jim enjoyed the company of Ekaterina Lutrova. And he was secretly growing fond of those mysterious sessions of scrying. With each one he realized himself to be opening up more and more to the woman. Ekaterina was Jim's psychotherapist and rapidly becoming someone to turn to for all sorts of advice. She was more than a psychotherapist. In Jim's understanding, Ekaterina was some sort of gypsy woman or perhaps a witch. She could read right through Jim; read every one of his thoughts from the deepest caverns of the subconscious. That might not have been a good thing, for at some point Ekaterina might not have liked Jim's thoughts at all!

"You have the gift; I see it." said Ekaterina one afternoon.

"Excuse me?"

"You whispered out to a woman once, and she heard it."

"Ekaterina, what are you talking about?"

"Now there's no reason to lie and pretend around this place. I know you, and I know that you have the gift. You did it once, and this is what started everything."

Jim remained motionless and at a loss for words. What on Earth could Ekaterina have been referring to? And what was this mention of "having the gift".

"You hurt someone as a result." continued Ekaterina. "You developed this gift and abused it. And someone ended up getting hurt."

Jim sat facing Ekaterina at the kitchen table and slowly shook his head out of confusion.

"Maybe I should help you remember." With that, Ekaterina stood up and went over to the cupboard for the recognizable glass bowl to be filled with water. It was time for another moment of scrying; triggered by a peculiar, old, Russian, witchy sort of woman who lived in the forest. Everyone should learn to trust this sort of person and be subjected to hypnotic trances, especially after being fed massive quantities of vodka. Was there ever a time that Jim considered what the old woman was doing to him?

Stepping away into the bathroom for a moment, Ekaterina returned with the glass bowl filled with water and set it in such a way that Jim could see the candle flame through the bowl. "Now, I want you to think long and hard. You have the gift. You discovered it many years ago and used it to your advantage."

* * *

Starting off an unintended, lifelong career at the cable company; Jim was a very, young man in 1993—the same age as Amber. In those days, he was nothing more than a sloppy installer who received much harassment from older workers. Jim had the poor reputation of "messing up" installs, drilling unnecessary holes through customers' walls, or being unable to locate the tap to feed a customer's home.

In those days, if Amber took the time to look out beyond Dickly Mountain one morning; she might have seen Jim drive by in his cable van, on his way to another disastrous install.

But before Amber was even aware of the Dickly castle; there was a cold, mid-morning in December of 1993 when Jim finished two Cable TV installs back in Mapleview. He drove the final stretch of Route 4, nearing the prestigious town of Sillmac. His next work order was to add a second cable outlet. If fortunate enough, the customer's residence would have been prewired for cable, making it possible to simply connect the right cable to the incoming line.

Jim had broken up with his girlfriend in May, a not-so-wise decision as he now spent many months alone and single. But he didn't care. In the two years of dating Becky, she remained locked at the knees while quoting some unheard-of 1950s catch-phrase, "Necking is for the neck up." Becky was beautiful and well endowed. Still a virgin, himself, Jim longed to finally touch anything that was naked and below Becky's neck. But she was a proper, old-fashioned girl who maintained strict celibacy before marriage. Aside from that, Becky was becoming increasingly critical of Jim's life. Along with the stressful, new job; his girlfriend was causing much frustration. There were plenty of other girls out there who appeared to flirt and call out for Jim's attention. There was no reason maintain his relationship with Becky.

But as Jim would soon find out, life doesn't work that way. From the moment he broke up with Becky, Jim lost that magick, the "pixie dust" that is sprinkled over an "owned" man. For some reason, young ladies throw themselves at a guy who is seriously involved with his girlfriend. But once he is single, they scatter and run like mice; hide away in holes and under rocks. Every person must endure that period of time in life of being single and unlucky in love. But on this morning, Jim's luck would change—at least for a brief moment.

Sillmac has a large collection of lonely, unhappy housewives who must endure an overworked husband that is often away on business. This was certainly the type of woman who brightly smiled and greeted Jim on his midmorning install. "Hi, I'm Julie! Come in!" Was her hair simply ultra-light blond, or had age transformed Julie's hair white? To this very day, Jim can't remember. But Julie was definitely an older woman, appearing to be in her early 50s; but still very, much attractive.

Jim returned the greeting. "Good morning; Mapleview Cable. I've got a work order for an additional outlet."

Julie didn't care about the install at that moment. "Yes, and I didn't catch your name."

"Jim…"

Julie took hold of Jim's hand and slowly shook while drawing her face near. "Very nice to meet you, Jim. Why don't you take your coat off and stay a while?" Her eyes burned into Jim's. There was something that radiated and beckoned from the woman, but Jim was too young to understand.

He hesitated and removed his coat. Underneath, Jim's tool belt was strapped to his waist.

"Would you like some coffee? I just made a fresh pot."

"No thank you ma'am. Why don't we get started on that additional outlet?"

*"Oh please, call me Julie." She led Jim up the stairs and into her master bedroom. "My husband's away on business, as usual. I figured maybe having **cable fed into my outlet** might keep me company."*

Jim looked near the area of the TV and could see that a cable outlet was conveniently mounted to the wall. This meant that the house was prewired for cable. But was it of the right quality? Sometimes construction crews used cheap cable that only caused poor picture quality. It was part of Jim's job to inspect the pre-wiring if opting to use it.

He informed the customer, "Well, I can see your house is prewired. Let me just double check if it's the right thickness."

Julie was excited, "The right thickness? Prewired? What do you mean?" She firmly took hold of Jim's arm. "Tell me, **exactly**, what you're about to do."

"Well, whoever built your house already ran cable through the walls. I know this because I can see an outlet near the TV. But I have to make sure it's the right type of cable."

Julie interrupted, "How are you going to do that?"

"I'm going to take the cover off and look underneath."

Again, Julie became excited. "You're going to **take it off**?"

"Yes, just to see if it's okay to use."

Soon, Jim knelt down near the wall and Julie was sure to join him. She watched carefully as Jim reached for his tool belt and pulled out a screwdriver. After both screws had been removed, Julie moved her face close to Jim's and seductively asked, "So you're going take it off and see what's underneath?"

But Jim was too involved in his work to hear what Julie was saying. "Yeah..."

Jim pulled the cover off, but discovered that there was no cable underneath! Such a disappointment. Now he would have to spend a good hour running cable through the house.

But Julie had some additional news for Jim. "In the attic is some coiled up cable that I think the builder never dropped down the wall. Is that what you're looking for?"

It was promising news for Jim. Julie pulled down the attic ladder in the hallway so Jim could go up, check out the cable and hopefully drop it down the interior of the wall. And sure enough, it appeared that every room had coiled up cables that waited to be fed between the drywall. There was even a hole drilled through the top of the 2x4 frame obviously intended for the cable. Jim fed the cable through Julie's wall and then returned to the outlet. Now he could connect it to the plate and fasten it back to the wall.

But what about the main, incoming cable? Surely all those upstairs lines led to a common place. "Okay; now I need to know where your cable comes in at."

Julie smirked, "Downstairs, of course. Isn't that were cable is fed, **from downstairs**?" She nearly winked.

Suddenly, a light went on for Jim. Was Julie hitting on him? He wasn't sure how to react to her behavior or answer to the subliminal references to sex. Instead, he reached into the tool belt and pulled out two small, electronic devices. This is a toner. I'll put this on your outlet, and we'll sniff out the line downstairs."

Julie sighed, "Oh, it sounds exciting. Let's go into the basement and sniff out that line."

Walking from behind provided Jim a chance to check out Julie's body. There is something appealing of a woman Julie's age who has a thick, robust and curvy body. It maintains smooth and youthful skin along with attractive hips and luscious bottom. Julie wore a pair of light, denim jeans and a thick white t-shirt. It soon became apparent to Jim that there was no outline of a bra strap beneath the t-shirt. Nearing the basement, Jim couldn't wait to face Julie again and sneak a peak of her chest.

Julie walked over to where the circuit breaker was mounted along with a collection of coiled cables that were draped down the wall. "Okay, here's where all the cables are."

Julie's white t-shirt was thick so that nothing could be seen underneath. But a closer look revealed that she had a mammoth pair of breasts withheld only by the shirt that was worn. Why did Jim miss this before? What was wrong with him? A gorgeous, curvy, older woman with large breasts was throwing herself at Jim. But still a virgin and lacking confidence, he was unsure of how to answer Julie's call.

Instead, he reached for the receiver match of the toner, took hold of a cable and connected it. The receiver made a loud squeal, indicating that the right cable had been found.

Julie was impressed. "Did that noise mean you found the right one?"

"Yeah…"

"You did it on the first try?"

"Yeah…"

Then Julie's face drew close to Jim's as she seductively whispered, "Maybe you just got lucky."

How Jim wished he knew how to get lucky with Julie! She seemed to find every opportunity to drop innuendo and suggest that if Jim took a chance, he could have her. But instead, he simply connected the bedroom cable to the TV, verified clear picture quality, and ended his midmorning job at Julie's house.

* * *

Still living at home with Mother and Father, Jim retired that night around 10:30. Although he had forgotten about Julie by lunch; a burning desire returned in those hours between dinner and bedtime. There was only one solution for the lonely, twenty-two-year-old virgin. With his bedroom door closed and the lights out, Jim crept into the closet and removed his dirty, secret toy from behind a collection of old books. It was purchased one weekend at the adult entertainment store, and was to be used to practice for that magickal first time.

As was often the case, Jim secured the thing by wedging it between two pillows. It isn't necessary to describe how the session was started. All Jim knew was that the darkness enabled him to close his eyes and return to Julie's basement.

"Maybe you just got lucky."

Jim immediately kissed Julie's warm and inviting lips; her silky tongue soon united with his. He lifted her t-shirt and finally exposed those gorgeous, mammoth breasts. Like a starved animal he frantically kissed them, not sure of which one to attack next.

Back in his own bedroom, Jim lay straddled on top of the pillows with the thing being the only pleasurable connection to Julie. But with his eyes closed Jim lay in Julie's bed; kissing, caressing and deeply penetrating her. It wasn't enough to simply discharge those desires and feelings in a brief moment of privacy. No; Jim had become skilled at controlling himself so that he could nearly exist in some fantasy that was made possible by orgasmic-altered-consciousness.

He called out her name in a whisper, "Julie... Julie..." The soft voice could carry outside Jim's bedroom window, across the town of Mapleview, along Route 4 and to the very doorstep of Julie's house. "Julie... Julie..." As if they shared some psychic connection brought on by intense, sexual feelings; Julie could hear every word whispered by Jim. "Julie... I want you... Please come back to me... Please give me another chance..."

Jim laid his forearm under his face and then softly kissed it. But it wasn't Jim's arm that was receiving the kisses. Across the miles it was Julie's very lips that received love.

* * *

The following morning, Jim left the cable yard with his van freshly stocked with equipment of the trade. Today's route was another collection of installs, and a few disconnects for some unfortunate customers who couldn't afford the bill. But halfway to his first install, the office dispatcher yelled over the radio. "Jim! Where are you?"

The dispatcher sounded irate, almost as-if she could reach her hands through the radio and strangle Jim. He was quick to reply, "Yeah, go ahead base."

"Jim, you get back over to that job you did, yesterday; 420 Crescent Lane in Sillmac..."

It was Julie's address! Did Jim's wish come true?

"The customer says you broke a light bulb in the attack, and wants you to clean it up. And I don't appreciate being yelled at over the phone by a customer!"

Oh no! Jim messed up another install! Nervously, he replied over the radio, "10-4, base! I'll get right over there!"

A second later, one of the older installers laughed over the radio. "Way to go, Jim!"

And so it was back to reality for poor Jim. He made sweet love to his precious Julie the previous night, only to learn of how she hated him. Why did it always turn out this way? Why couldn't Jim do anything right?

Twenty minutes later, the Mapleview Cable van pulled into Julie's driveway. Disgusted with himself, Jim quickly walked up to the customer's door; prepared to receive every bit of scolding, insults and any other punishment that he truly deserved. He was such a stupid guy who couldn't do anything right. No wonder Jim was lonely. No wonder people hated him so.

But then Julie warmly greeted him at the door with a friendly smile, and wearing nothing but a white bathrobe.

Confused and still disgusted in himself, Jim immediately apologized to Julie. "I'm so sorry. I didn't know I broke the light bulb."

But then Julie apologized as well! "Oh, honey; I'm sorry. Did your office yell at you? I hope they weren't too hard on you. I didn't know what else to say." With her fingertips, she lightly brushed the side of Jim's tousled, brown hair back into place."

Jim asked, "Do you have a broom and dust pan?"

"Sure, do you want to go up in the attic and see?"

Moments later, Jim ascended the pull-down ladder and carefully entered the attic. Looking around, he could see that every light bulb shined from its fixture. Walking the plywood floors, there was no evidence of shattered glass. From what Jim could see, nothing was broken.

Ah, but there was one very, delicate thing that had been broken; Julie's heart. Aware of her husband's affair with his young and beautiful secretary, Julie felt abandoned, old and unappreciated. But then along came Jim with his sweet baby-face, wind-tousled brown hair and youthful, toned body that rippled behind the cotton polo with Mapleview Cable logo. His voice was so young, and his mannerisms so innocent. How Julie longed for those days when she had such a guy. She was reaching him, she just knew it. It would only take time.

Further confused, Jim turned back towards the entrance of the attic and was startled to see Julie carefully approaching. Her white robe was fully untied; revealing the thick, untamed bush that lay between her luscious, silky thighs. Julie's round tummy only enhanced the sexiness as her enormous, left breast was fully exposed. So full and bursting with desire to be fondled, Julie's breast was adorned with a beautiful, wide areola and pink nipple.

Jim couldn't wait to fully open Julie's robe and explore both her treasures. But then senses returned as he nearly backed away.

Now very near, Julie had just the remedy to put the young man at ease. "Oh, Honey; don't be nervous. Everything is going to be okay." As Julie was learning, such a young and innocent guy needs to be carefully "groomed" before winning his heart. Speak kindly and use sweet names such as "Baby" or "Honey". It brings him back to the days of being in Mother's arms. How he yearns for a tender voice to reassure him that all is well. And be sure to look deeply and lovingly in his eyes while gently touching him.

If the young man still appears unsure, then place your lips to his. Once Jim could feel Julie's soft, warm lips; he could no longer control himself. Broken up with Becky for seven months, it had been so long since he kissed a girl... or woman, as Julie certainly was. In fact, Jim had never received kisses like these before. So hot and dripping with an invitation for so much more, Becky was never capable of this!

Jim's hand reached for the sides of Julie's naked hips and then caressed his way up to her breasts.

And then the doorbell rang! It caused Julie to immediately pull away. "I wonder who that is." She walked over to the small, octagon, attic window that overlooked her driveway. "I think one of your buddies is here."

With still a swollen triangle in his pants, Jim's anxiety suddenly spiked. "Oh no! Are you sure?" He looked out the window, and sure enough, the foreman's van was parked on the street. Certainly older and wiser, the foreman overheard the morning's conversation on the radio and rushed over to Julie's house in a mission to save Jim from doing anything stupid.

Both Julie and Jim greeted him at the door.

The foreman immediately cocked his thumb over his shoulder and towards the driveway while harshly ordering, "Get in the truck!"

With his head low and to the ground, Jim did as ordered and listened carefully to the brief conversation between his foreman and Julie.

"So the attic's all cleaned up?"

"Yes, everything is fine now."

And before walking away, the foreman made the unusual remark, "Yeah, we don't allow our installers to do that sort of thing."

Moments later he signaled Jim to roll down his window while approaching.

"Jimmy; what are you doing in there, huh? What are you doing?"

"I was just..."

Jim was interrupted, "Just getting yourself in trouble! Meet me back at the office. Let's figure out how we're going to handle this."

* * *

Poor Jim would have to endure two hours of already-viewed training videos on sexual harassment and aggressive housewives. The videos were made, specifically, for young men like Jim; who might have been the target of lonely housewives. The videos explained that women sometimes do things that are later regretted. It even provided a real-life case of an installer who fulfilled a housewife's dreams, only to be picked up by police some hours later for rape. Guilt had overtaken the woman. Claiming she was raped helped it all go away.

Chapter 35

Jim pulled out of the flashback and sat back in his chair. Then he looked over to Ekaterina who only smiled in anticipation of what he would say, next. "I forgot about that." Jim chuckled and took another sip of vodka. "That could have been my lucky day—my first time."

"Right!" answered Ekaterina. "But I'm more interested in the way you caused this to happen. You made a subconscious connection with her. You made her call the cable company and demand that you come over."

Jim smiled and nodded. "I guess I did. I never looked at it that way before." He was seriously buzzed, nearly drunk. With inhibitions down, the vodka sparked his arrogance to the point of being proud of his ability.

But within a split second, Ekaterina's smiling face turned fierce. "And you did it again some years later. You used this gift to get something you weren't supposed to."

Jim laughed, "What?"

"I'm not laughing! This is serious! You reached out and hurt someone. You caused someone to become gravely ill and nearly pulled all the life out of her. Is that something to laugh about?"

"Ekaterina, I have no idea of what you're talking about."

Ekaterina moved her body closer to the table and pointed to her head. "Think, Jim! Think! It was a dark time in your life. Things weren't going your way. You were younger, and had gotten selfish. You fell into some bad habits, remember?"

Jim's facial expression relaxed and eyes sparked with a sudden memory. He knew, exactly, what Ekaterina spoke of.

* * *

It was a New Year's Eve party in 1994, a significant moment because it was the night that Jim met his future wife, Kimberly. By early spring; both were very, much in love. And yes, Jim's magickal moment of finally losing his virginity had come!

Now a happy and content man with consistent romance, Jim would soon find more reason for happiness. In May, Kimberly announced that she was pregnant. Although a little sooner than expected, Jim simply proposed to Kimberly so that by January of 1995, he and his now wife enjoyed their new daughter, April.

After living in an apartment for the first four years of marriage, it might have been Kimberly's second pregnancy that prompted their search for a single family home. By the spring of 2000, the family had settled down in a nice ranch in the tree-lined subdivision of Maple Sap.

There wasn't anything unusual, at all, of Jim's lifestyle; blossoming family life, new home, raises and promotions at work. He was definitely living the dream! But despite how normal Jim may have appeared on the outside, there was something dark and foreboding stirring within. It might have been a combination of a couple things. For one, Kimberly was certainly taxed with the responsibilities of housewife and mother, not to mention the fact that one of her children had recently been born. When it came to romance, Jim certainly heard his share of, "Not tonight; I'm tired... My head is just throbbing... Can we take a rain check...?"

Jim was understanding and expected Kimberly to be cold in the department of romance. He was patient and realized that those nights of passion would eventually return. But don't take this to mean that Jim didn't paw at the ground and exhale steam from his nostrils while waiting.

Fortunately for Jim, there was a new appliance in the house called a computer. And being that he worked for Mapleview Cable, Internet service was 100% free. As Jim soon discovered, he had access to millions of images of naked women; many of them offered for free! For so many years he would look upon women in curiosity and wondered what was underneath their clothes. Now he could satisfy every bit of curiosity while switching from one fetish to the next. Red heads, brunettes and blondes; fat women, old women and pregnant women; Hispanic, African American or Asian: they were all at his fingertips to be used at his disposal.

"Not tonight, Jim; I've had a rough day."

That was okay. Perhaps in the predawn hours, Jim could carefully roll over in bed and slightly pull back Kimberly's covers. For a minute or two he might be able to carefully fondle his wife's breasts while she slept; followed by a trip to the computer for some great sex with stationary images. They fed his imagination so well. As Jim was discovering, the mind is the greatest sex organ of all and possesses the ability to pull one into a separate reality. Those moments alone with the images were so real; even better than the dirty, secret toy in his bedroom closet from years ago.

While driving the neighborhood streets of Mapleview in the summer months, Jim would look upon women from his cable van as-if they were nothing more than little pieces of candy that walked around. Dressed so promiscuous in their tight shorts with freshly-shaven legs; it was difficult for Jim not to imagine bouncing one of those women off his lap. Aware of his obsession, Jim only reassured himself that Kimberly would come around soon. Then he could forget about those crazy days of drooling over women.

The end of August had come for that year which meant that Jim and Kimberly's daughter, April, had started kindergarten. Being that Jim's job allowed him some flexibility, it was easy to join Kimberly in walking April to school on her first day. And what a spectacular day it was! There were women all over the school ground, young moms of the Maple Sap subdivision that Jim recognized from driving the neighborhood in his cable van. He could see them up close, now! And how delicious-looking each and every one of them was!

"Jim, aren't you going to say goodbye to your daughter?"

Of course! How silly of Daddy! One might have thought that his mind was somewhere else. Jim quickly knelt down and gave little April a hug and kiss. "Have a good day, Honey."

* * *

April attended full-day kindergarten which gave Kimberly plenty of quality time with her 5-month-old son, Collin. But there was a slight inconvenience for Kimberly when it came to picking up April from school. Little Collin would be in the middle of his much-needed afternoon nap. Kimberly actually used this time for a small nap, herself. Was there any way that Jim could pick up April from school?

Sure enough, Jim often had downtime in the mid-afternoon hours. This made it convenient for him to park the cable van in the school lot and then wait for April.

There was a rule for parents who picked up kindergartners. It was necessary for the parent to physically wait near the designated exit door for the child. No student could run out to the drive or parking lot to meet his or her parent. And it was on Jim's first day of picking up April that he stood near this door, drooling over the pieces of candy that chattered amongst one another.

Suddenly, the exit door opened and Jim's heart nearly stopped. There, before him, was a fine woman who immediately locked eyes with Jim and smiled all the more. Time froze for the two as Jim battered his way through the excited children that rushed to their parents. Only the voice of April that rang out, "Daddy!" broke him from the trance. By then, Jim was as close to April's teacher as possible while his daughter embraced him.

"Hi, Honey!" Jim rubbed the back of April's hair. Then he looked back at the woman who had nearly stopped his heart. "Hi, this is my daughter."

April's teacher smiled in return and then looked back down at April. "We'll see you tomorrow." Then she looked back up at Jim, soon with a worried expression brought on by the possibility that maybe she was subliminally asking April's father to return the following afternoon.

There's a serious rule that any parent should follow. In fact, along with "Thou shall not commit adultery"; there should be another commandment that says, "Thou definitely shall not have funny business with your child's kindergarten or grammar school teacher." It makes perfect sense! Would you want your child's educational experience to be based on the status of some romantic relationship between you and the teacher? Any decent parent inherently knows this. But Jim didn't care about some silly, unheard-of rule of morality. Once he and April drove off in the cable van, Jim was sure to ask his daughter, "So what's your teacher's name?"

April replied, "Ms. Haldman."

The prefix perked Jim's curiosity. "Miss? Is she married?"

"I don't know."

"What's her first name?"

"I don't know."

Mommy usually asked how April's day went, or what she learned in class. Daddy was more interested in the teacher's name and whether or not she was married.

* * *

"So did you find out your teacher's first name?"
"No."

It was the following afternoon as Jim picked up April from school. And it proved to be another heart-stopping moment as Jim and Ms. Haldman locked eyes. Being closer to the exit door this time, Jim did have an opportunity to glance at Ms. Haldman's left, ring finger. Sure enough, there was no wedding or engagement ring.

"No? You didn't find out?" Although disappointed, Jim did have to go easy on April. After all, he didn't specifically request that April ask of her teacher's first name. But maybe that wasn't such a bad idea. "Tell you what, Honey; tomorrow, why don't you ask your teacher. Say, 'Ms. Haldman? What's your first name?' Could you do that for me?"

April agreed, "Okay…"

The following afternoon, April certainly came through for Daddy. She ran right out the exit door with Ms. Haldman nearby and excitedly shouted, "My teacher's first name is Jan!" It wasn't exactly the timing that Jim preferred. Couldn't April have waited until they drove off in the cable van? And hearing April inform her father of the teacher's first name certainly resulted in an astounded look from Ms. Haldman.

But Ms. Haldman would learn even more from little April! The following day, just before lunch, April approached her teacher and asked, "Are you married?" Daddy hadn't asked little April to find this out. April was only being proactive, recalling Daddy's initial questions from a few days ago. Since he wanted to know Ms. Haldman's first name, maybe he wanted to know if she was married as well.

Ms. Haldman briefly paused and then answered, "No; why do you ask?"

"My Daddy wants to know!"

Now you would think that the recent activities and revelations surrounding April's father would have made Ms. Haldman uneasy. And initially these things probably didn't sit well with her for obvious reasons. But people react in the most peculiar ways. Married for only two years, and then divorced because of her spouse's sudden drug addiction; Ms. Haldman had remained single for many years thereafter, experiencing a few promising relationships that only flopped for one reason or another. Now in her late 40s and nearly given up on love, there was a man suddenly showing interest and inquiring about her. Although still so beautiful and young, the air can be terribly thin in the department of love for a woman that age—especially in Mapleview. It was only natural that she lay in bed at night, burning in curiosity of what could possibly be between her and April's father.

* * *

By the second week of the new school year, Jim's short-lived escapade of having sex with stationary images of nude women had finally ended. If your husband is suddenly obsessed and seemingly addicted to nude images of women, don't worry. It dies as he will surely grow sick of the repeated bombardment of naked women. That can only go on for so long! And Jim certainly was tired of searching for the next gorgeous, nude model along with seeing women as nothing more than little pieces of candy that walked the streets. Jim was all better, now. That dark chapter in his life had finally ended.

When was the last time Jim enjoyed the simple pleasure of just laying in bed while imagining and fantasizing of some beautiful woman he had encountered at an install or at some point in his daily travels? With his nudey-pic addiction over, Jim laid in the dark while pleasuring himself under the covers, allowing his imagination to let go.

And get this! Jim attempted to establish some telepathic link with Ms. Haldman in hopes that she could sense his feelings for her. Of course if alone with her, Jim wouldn't call her, Ms. Haldman. The woman's name was Jan.

How intimate it felt in that moment to know her first name. And how easy it was to create his own loving image of Jan, a cherished portrait that revealed her need to be loved and receive affection. To see the truth of her beautiful, naked body; her full buttocks that might have been revealed upon briefly standing up from bed; or her naked breasts that lay upon Jim's chest after making love: these thoughts and mental images had brought Jim to climax.

* * *

In contrast to the heart-stopping moments experienced during those afternoons of picking up April from school, there was soon a heart-racing moment of dreadful anxiety. Anyone who has ever gone to grammar school is fully aware of what open house is. After the first few weeks of school, parents are invited to an evening gathering at school to finally meet the teacher and observe their child's classroom. It's an exciting time for a child and most often includes the showcasing of a special project made just for Mommy and Daddy for the night of open house.

Jim was definitely excited—a little overexcited while entering the door of the school with his wife and two kids. Part of him was eager to finally meet Jan Haldman. But another part of him realized that he had ventured into forbidden territory. Jim should have done like any decent parent and maintained any encounter with Ms. Haldman as professionally as possible. Now they were aware of one another, burning in curiosity of what could be and shouldn't be.

Jim's anxiety spiked upon entering Ms. Haldman's classroom. She looked as beautiful as ever; smiling and so friendly with the room full of parents. As April's parents approached, Ms. Haldman's friendly face changed to that of dread. April's father was near; a moment she had worried over the entire day!

Kimberly extended her arm in friendly greeting. "Hi, I'm Kimberly; and this is my husband, Jim."

As she reached for Jim's hand, Ms. Haldman's face turned flush and her voice cracked from a sudden dryness. "Nice to meet you." Poor Ms. Haldman; she never meant any harm. Jim was such a nice, good-looking man. Why is life so cruel?

But she was sure to have herself covered for parent/teacher conference—a lengthier, one-on-one meeting with parents before the first quarter ended. These are held to convey performance of the child to parents. April was a bright girl who learned quickly, was neat and mostly well-mannered. There wasn't much for Ms. Haldman to discuss with Jim and Kimberly during this meeting. But in an attempt to break the ice and bring the dreaded encounter back to Earth, Ms. Haldman offered an interesting tidbit of information. She smiled and nearly blushed while speaking to Jim, "I dated a guy back in college that looked just like you." So bold, the palm of Ms. Haldman's hand lightly patted Jim's forearm while saying this.

Then again, maybe that wasn't such a great idea! It certainly would have provided an excuse for her behavior during the open house. But the other side of the cryptic message, intended exclusively as a desperate S.O.S to Jim, might have been heard by Kimberly as well. Let's just say that it made for some interesting conversation on the ride home.

* * *

There wasn't much left to fuel Jim's fantasy romance with Ms. Haldman, as there were no further significant encounters. The holidays came and went. The early spring months arrived. Occasionally, Jim would think of Jan in the darkened room while lying in bed. There might have been a moment when he pondered of how to initiate an actual romance with her. Might there be a time when Jim would go to her house to install a cable outlet? Such an install could provide an opportunity for lengthier conversation, maybe even be invited over to Jan's house for dinner later that night. But this opportunity never came. He and Jan were *simply not destined to be together. Besides that, there were new fantasy romances on the horizon.*

Now it isn't necessary to bore you of how these pointless games began with other women. There was Kelly (Not Mary's cousin!), who started at Mapleview Cable as an office administrator. This was around the time that Jim received his grand promotion of lineman technician. During this time, both he and Kelly learned through rumor of their mutual attraction. Needless to say, the games of locking eyes and occasionally encountering one another in the hallway only to barely provide a greeting had commenced. There was definitely an infatuation between the two of them. And while spending 3 weeks out of state to train for his new position at Mapleview Cable, Jim had the most intense fantasy romance.

Kelly dined with Jim in the evening. They sat out by the hotel pool and drank wine. Afterwards, he and Kelly would retire for the evening to make love until exhaustion; then to lie cuddled, sleeping. By morning, Jim would wake up with his arms wrapped tightly around the pillow. He couldn't wait for his hours of job training to end for the day so that he and Kelly could enjoy more time together. It's amazing how dangerous the imagination can be!

But there was no harm done. Kelly was soon replaced by an IT associate at the bank. Having trouble with his online account, Jim briefly met with Tina, who... well, let's just say another senseless game had been started! This time, through all the crazy fantasies, Jim desperately found any reason to contact her. Any petty thing noticed with his online account, Jim would email Tina; even make unrelated, small talk that sadly appeared to be diffused by Tina.

Somewhere in the middle of these pointless, fantasy romances of Jim; his son, Collin, turned 5 years old and had started kindergarten. Sadly, he didn't have that nice Ms. Haldman who Kimberly really liked. Collin had another kindergarten teacher. But while bringing her boy to school one morning, Kimberly had an opportunity to see and briefly greet Ms. Haldman. How nice it was to see an old friend.

But later that night, Kimberly had some interesting gossip for her husband, Jim. "I think there's something wrong with Ms. Haldman."

"Really? Why do you say that?"

"She looks sick. I think she has some kind of disease. She's gained a little weight; she's looking stressed; her hair is a mess and turning gray in some places."

Oh no! That was bad news for Jim! Surely he would be on a lookout for Jan on the night of open house.

On that night while on the way to Collins' classroom, the family passed Ms. Haldman's room. Sure enough, Jim took sight of April's kindergarten teacher. But she wasn't sick as Kimberly suggested. Instead, Jim could see that poor Ms. Haldman had been struck by a sudden, bad case of menopause.

At that very moment of taking sight of Jan Haldman, Jim was at such an angle that his view of her was through a large, plate-glass window at the side of the entry door. As the two faces recognized one another, Jim provided a friendly smile.

But Jan's face revealed such desperation, leaving Jim to feel that she was a split second from diving through the plate glass to attack him. He could almost hear her crying out, "Please don't leave me! Don't abandon me! There's still time!"

* * *

Some years later, just before April started high school, Jim made a quick trip to the Mapleview grocery store with both kids. And there in the produce aisle stood Ms. Haldman. Both Jim and April greeted the kindergarten teacher, who had remarkably aged with cracked face and hair mostly turned gray. It was quite a shocking contrast for Jim, recalling the first time he had laid eyes on Jan Haldman. Did Jim do this to her? It was a nagging thought that secretly haunted him for many weeks. If his fears were correct, then surely he deserved punishment.

Chapter 36

Jim and Ekaterina sat in silence for some time. Then Jim shrugged his shoulders, "I mean you can't tell me that I caused her to go into menopause. It happens to every woman. She probably didn't take care of herself when it started. And hey; it takes two to tango, right?"

"You did it to her." reassured Ekaterina. "You made her suddenly age. She was so much in love with you..."

Jim interrupted with a laugh, "In love with me?" It was the stupidest thing he ever heard.

Ekaterina exploded, "Damn you! You fool! Damn you! Why are you so stupid? What the hell do you think all those looks and all that interest told this woman? She was older. She was lonely. And suddenly a young man showed interest. You made her feel like you had something for her. She truly believed this. And through all her hopes and dreams, she fell in love with you. And you left her all alone. The heartbreak drained the very life out of her and caused her to turn old."

Jim stared at the table in silence. With everything he had experienced in recent months, Ekaterina's interpretation did have some validity. What if he really did cause some acceleration factor in Jan's aging process? And what about bad karma?

It was as-if Ekaterina read Jim's mind. "All the strange things that are happening to you and about to happen is the punishment you deserve. It's the Law of Return. You affected someone in a negative way, and there is punishment for this."

Jim was definitely spell-bounded and believed every word. "But I didn't mean to hurt her." he rebutted. "What can I do?"

"Ah!" exclaimed Ekaterina. "Now you understand why you've come to see me. You are aware that I can help you with something. Finally, we've gotten to the bottom of it. Yes, I can help you. I can help you pay this debt much sooner."

"What do I have to do?" asked Jim.

Ekaterina remained silent, smiling from ear-to-ear and gazing, deeply, into Jim's eyes.

"What...? What do you want from me, Ekaterina?"

Ekaterina's voice rang and echoed through the small cottage with one, simple word. "Sex!"

"Excuse me?"

"You heard me! I want you to give me sex. For forty-nine consecutive days, you must come here to have sex with me. You will be all mine each day for a little while."

Sex with Ekaterina; sex with a crazy old, Russian immigrant-woman with patchy hair—nearly bald—mostly gray. And it appeared to be never washed. Her hair was only the tip of the iceberg. Ekaterina's eyes were dull and unattractive from the discoloration around the whites. And when was the last time that she brushed her teeth? Gangly and discolored; surely she suffered from old lady gum disease. And who knows what that breath might have smelled like? Of all the fantasies that Jim had of the woman, he was now face-to-face with her and being demanded of sex. Suddenly she didn't look so appealing. She looked exactly like an ugly, old woman.

Jim had to think of something fast. "Ekaterina, I'm married."

"And what about your girlfriend? Do you think of your wife when with your girlfriend and lying in bed? Did you think of your wife while destroying the other lady, Jan, with all your flirty looks and interest? Your time is up. There is a price for everything, and I will help you pay this debt. Besides, I'm not so bad. You will see. You just need to get an acquired taste for me; that's all."

With that, Ekaterina swigged the remains of vodka in her glass and stood up from her seat. "We'll start today."

"Huh...?" Only minutes ago, Jim was drunk and numb from the vodka. But now he was one hundred percent sober and terrified for his life. All the bad things that Jim ever did had finally caught up with him. There was a karma deficit, and it was time to pay the piper before his life was ruined. The only way to satisfy this debt was to have sex with an unattractive, old woman.

"Now!" ordered Ekaterina. "I want sex, now! This will make for one day out of forty-nine." She walked towards her bedroom and then turned around to signal Jim to follow. Ekaterina made the most disturbing "come here" signal by slowly motioning her index finger. It resembled the wiggle of a worm and had the power to bring Jim to his feet and walk in the direction of Ekaterina's bedroom. Even more baffling was Jim's willingness to remove his suspenders and Fruit-of-the-Loom undershirt while making his way into Ekaterina's bedroom. It was as-if he were under some mental control.

Inside the bedroom, Ekaterina was already undressing. She slowly unbuttoned her old lady dress in a seductive manner, apparently under the impression that Jim enjoyed the sight. He wanted her—as far as Ekaterina knew; wanted to see her naked and finally take her down. The delusion was so disgusting and far from reality. But this is one of the many powers of a witch. She begins her spell by firmly believing in the web of perception that she creates.

Ekaterina wore no bra! Russian torpedo tits hung down towards the navel as her dress widely opened and the strands of long, gray hair were brushed behind her shoulders. It was all followed with a look of desire that said, "Come get me!"

Having no choice, Jim did as ordered. He figured the safest way to start would be to cup his hand over one of Ekaterina's large, old breasts. But it was cold and stiff, just as you would expect a witch's tit to feel.

A look of delight stretched across the old woman's face as she seized Jim's free hand and placed it on her other breast. "Squeeze…" Ekaterina whispered with demand. "Squeeze them both. I want you to squeeze the hell out them like there's no tomorrow!"

Jim squashed those cold and stiff tits that were feeling more and more like they belonged to something lying in the coffin. And as-if a corpse being risen from the dead, Ekaterina briefly returned to younger years and cocked her back while making disgusting moans of sickening ecstasy. She loved every minute of Jim's reluctant foreplay!

Wild, psychotic eyes returned their stare onto Jim's and begged for more; something with more passion and feeling; something like a kiss that would reveal Jim's true feelings.

There was no escape! As Jim massaged the life back into those old, Russian torpedo tits; Ekaterina's lips met Jim's. Gangly, discolored teeth and diseased gums were now a part of Jim's mouth. The only thing that disguised Ekaterina's foul breath was the purification of vodka. Perhaps this even killed the strong and likely presence of fungal bacteria as old lady slime found its way into Jim's mouth with the deep unification of tongues.

And while French kissing the victim, Ekaterina inched her hand down her old granny panties to feel her dried-up pussy. So maniacally she frigged her clit while enjoying the assault to her breasts. The young man kissed her and surely wished to further invade and assault Ekaterina by sticking his hands down those panties. To reassure that this was okay, Ekaterina seized one of Jim's hands and quickly tucked it down her panties.

Immediately Jim fondled and explored the old, battered treasure.

And wouldn't you know it? This still wasn't enough for the old witch. Ekaterina unbuttoned and unzipped Jim's jeans and then pulled his underwear down to expose his penis. But what was this? Jim was not erect! Maybe it was his age and he simply needed help.

Ekaterina fondled, squeezed and slowly stroked Jim's cock to life. There seemed to be a lot of raising the dead in that bedroom. And after a moment or two, it began to grow in size and stiffness so that, finally, Ekaterina held a nice, hard cock in her hand.

When was the last time that Ekaterina felt such a thing against herself? She pulled Jim's stiffness towards her crotch and assisted the invasion under her granny panties by pushing the swollen head of Jim's cock against herself.

Finally, Ekaterina led the foreplay to her dirty bed, and lay down on her back with legs spread to be taken in missionary position. Jim had no choice but to pull down those granny panties and pile drive his manliness home. But Ekaterina wanted more! She wanted dirty, kinky sex. With Jim between her thighs, Ekaterina toed her panties back on from the floor, briefly raised her legs and let the panties slide back to her thighs. Jim was now locked in with old lady thighs and smelly, granny panties.

And so was Jim's initial exposure to sex magick; his first installment to the bad karma deficit which was thoroughly enjoyed by a dirty, horny, old woman.

Chapter 37

What, exactly, defines cheating?—in particular, cheating on a spouse? It's a question I'm afraid we'll never be able to accurately answer—at least for men. Here in America, some men keep a secret girlfriend or two and often observe the famous philosophy of former president Bill Clinton. For them, cheating is a matter of sex. And according to their hero, Bill Clinton, sex isn't sex unless a penis penetrates a vagina. In this mindset, it's perfectly okay to make out with another woman and even receive oral sex.

A husband rationalizing with himself over an attraction to a new secretary might say, "Bah! Receiving oral sex from my secretary isn't cheating! There's nothing intimate."

But ask this man how he would feel about another man giving oral sex to his own wife and it would provoke outrage. How dare you suggest such a thing? He won't admit, however, that the act would be considered cheating in his eyes. No one should be able to look upon or touch his naked wife.

In some parts of South America, men of high status are expected to have a mistress along with a wife. But this presents a problem if the man happens to be Catholic—which is usually the case. To defeat this obstacle, such men find it acceptable to merely engage in oral and even anal sex with a mistress. Vaginal penetration is to be reserved for marriage. What's more, this practice protects the virgin status of a mistress who is yet to be married.

But then there are those at the other extreme who would declare that Jim had been cheating ever since he found a sexual outlet in masturbating before naked images of women. He cheated on his wife while driving around in the cable van and lustfully looking upon other women. He was definitely unfaithful while playing the hurtful game between him and Jan Haldman. And even though Jim had yet to engage in sexual intercourse with Amber, he did kiss her, cuddle and often lay in bed—activities that are certainly considered intimate. And lying to his own wife, Kimberly, to escape the house and be with another woman is certainly another element of cheating.

There is no denying the fact that Jim had been a lying, cheating husband for nearly ten years. But this new activity with Ekaterina (in Jim's mind) took him to new territory.

* * *

Feeling cheap, dirty and violated; Jim staggered through the woods back to his cable van on Mapleview Road in a near, drunken, vodka-induced stupor following his first encounter of sex magick with Ekaterina. It was the middle of January, Friday the 15th. His first of forty-nine days of sex with Ekaterina had been fulfilled, but already Jim was feeling guilty. For starters, while enjoying sex magick at Ekaterina's cottage, he missed a series of text messages from the office dispatcher that asked where he was. It was best to get back to the van before answering. At least that way he wouldn't be lying about disclosing his whereabouts on Mapleview Road.

What's more, this was the first time that Jim had sex outside his marriage. Kissing and cuddling with Amber wasn't considered cheating in his world. But screwing some old witch in the forest was definitely grounds for divorce (in his mind). It might even get Jim fired if not reaching the cable van fast enough.

And to any man who ever decides to engage in extramarital activity; don't ever be fooled into believing your taboo relationship to be a secret from the wife. She knows; she knows from the moment that you call or as you walk through the door. She also knows that a husband would never answer truthfully of where he's been. Accusing him simply out of that guilty look in his eyes or the vague tone of his voice would only provoke defensive behavior.

As is the case for Amber; things had gotten terribly out of control with her husband. For so long Amber maintained the patience of a saint while Jim lived with that other woman down the street, hoping that through time he would come back to his senses and move back home. At least he and Amber were talking throughout this difficult separation period. And at times Amber believed that his heart was nearly won back. But now there was some new and foreign element that suddenly distanced Amber's husband further away.

It was eight o'clock pm on Friday; the same Friday that Jim experienced his initial encounter of sex magick with Ekaterina. Amber had yet to hear from Jim for the day. She sent him a text message. "Hi! Haven't heard from you today. Everything ok? Can I see you?"

His reply was short and to the point. "Sorry. Busy day. Really tired and not feeling good. Not tonight."

What was this? What if Amber hadn't texted Jim? Would she have heard from him at all? Amber answered back. "Okay... maybe see you tomorrow?"

"Yeah it depends on how I feel."

Amber knew better. Jim wasn't sick! Instead, somehow that other woman had gotten into Jim's mind and convinced him that his heart should remain in her home with those other children! And this was causing Amber to run out of patience. What power did this other woman have over Amber's husband? With as gifted as Amber had been through her life in wishing for things to come true, Amber now felt so powerless.

Maybe it was time to play dirty. Maybe it was time to win her man the old-fashioned way with a game of jealousy. For so many months Amber presented herself as available and accessible to Jim, nearly begged for him to come home. But maybe the trick was to play the opposite game. It's when we are about to lose someone we love to another person that those overwhelming feelings of intense desire suddenly return. Perhaps pushing Jim away and causing him to feel jealous would be the motivation he needed to finally come home.

And this is why Amber suddenly had a change in heart towards that annoying and persistent customer who regularly visited her in the jewelry department, Daren. Actually, she hadn't seen Daren since that Tuesday morning shortly after the holidays.

But it was on a late, Monday evening; only three evenings after Amber decided to play the new game of jealousy with Jim that Daren resurfaced with perfect timing. On this particular evening, Amber stayed late for store inventory which means she didn't leave until 10:30 pm. Many of the employees had finally gone home for the evening which left her, the manager of electronics and two other employees to be the only remaining people in that store. The two employees were soon allowed to leave so that only Amber and fellow manager, Tim, remained.

The last person(s) out of the building must activate the alarm for the evening. As Tim did this, he asked Amber, "Are you going to be okay walking out to your car? I parked some distance away from yours."

"No, I'll be fine. Maybe just watch me walk over to my car."

"No problem." answered Tim. "Good night."

"Good night." returned Amber.

The Mapleview Department Store leaves its parking lot lights on all evening for security purposes. With the parking lot nearly cleared of all vehicles, Amber quickly walked towards her black Grand Prix. It was a typical, cold January night in Mapleview with the season's accumulated snowfalls plowed into frozen piles at the centers of the parking lot.

While near her car, Amber noticed something vaguely unusual. The car sat there, alone, and looked exactly as she had parked it earlier that day. But something about it looked tampered with. Now close enough to open the door, Amber slowly circled her car to examine anything that stood out of the ordinary. Nothing physical could be seen. It was more of a residual energy, something in the surrounding air that warned Amber that her car had been tampered with. Maybe someone tried to break in but gave up.

Now shivering from the cold, Amber unlocked her door, quickly entered and then started the engine. She huddled her body for about a moment while allowing the engine to warm. Freezing and wishing so badly just to get home, Amber backed out of her lonely spot and took off for the main street in town.

Although a well established town with plenty of businesses and restaurants, most of Mapleview shuts down in the evening. Not only that, it was only January and the middle of winter. Because of this, the roads were nearly desolate—not a car in sight throughout downtown Mapleview.

Suddenly, Amber's engine began to stall and jerk.

"What? What's wrong?" It sounded as-if her car was running out of gas. Amber immediately looked over to the fuel gauge and discovered the tank was on empty. "That's impossible!" yelled out Amber. Earlier that day she had just over half a tank. With no choice, Amber pulled over to the shoulder before her car stalled in the middle of the road.

Just as the transmission was slipped into "park", the sputtering engine of the Grand Prix finally died.

"No!" cried out Amber. "Come-on! I just want to get home!" Poor Amber! Who could she call for help? Jim would have been her first choice, but he was to be alienated in this new game of jealousy. And where was this sudden, new man who would play jealousy with Amber?

Frustrated, Amber stepped out of the vehicle. The cold January winds of Mapleview howled through the empty, main road in town. The gas station was about a block away. It was going to be a long walk in the cold! Maybe a police car would pass and spot Amber.

As Amber was no more than six feet away from the trunk of her car, a pair of spotlights seemed to have appeared out of nowhere, then pulled over to the shoulder about 20 feet behind Amber's Grand Prix. From what Amber could see through the flood of headlights, it was a red pickup truck. Apparently a good Samaritan was about to offer help.

The driver stuck his head out the window. "Are you okay? Do you need help?"

Amber froze for a couple of seconds. She heard that voice before, and detected a bit of danger from it. Who was that in the red pickup truck?

The driver emerged and stepped out onto the highway. It was Daren; that annoying, married customer who tried so hard to have a coffee break with Amber and discuss his so-called "girlfriend problems". And he looked so surprised, soon delighted to see Amber. "Oh, hi! You work in jewelry over at the Mapleview Department Store!"

Amber nodded her head and then sighed. Really she had no choice. Daren was the person who was going to help her. "It looks like I ran out of gas." informed Amber.

"Ran out of gas? Yeah, that happens to everyone at least once or twice in their life. It's why I keep a couple containers of gas with me during the winter months. I see a lot of people like you stalled on the roads. Don't worry. I'll fill you up."

Of course Amber still wasn't sure. But then what choice did she have? Would she actually be so stupid as to turn down Daren's help and then walk in the cold to the nearest gas station? "Okay..." answered Amber. "If you've got some gas, I'll take some."

"No problem..." Daren paused upon realizing he didn't know Amber's name. "What's your name?"

"Amber."

"Amber; that's a pretty name! I'm Daren. Nice to meet you." He extended his hand and shook Amber's. "Go ahead and sit in my nice, warm truck. This'll only take a couple of minutes. Then you can get going."

Less than two weeks ago, Amber couldn't stand the man. Now she was accepting his offer for help and sitting in the passenger seat of his nice, warm pickup truck. Although she hated to admit it, the warmth felt so good.

Two gas containers that held five gallons each sat in the back of the truck, right next to a large box of extra-jumbo-sized mason jars that were about the same size and diameter of Mary Trivelli's jar back at the mausoleum. Daren seemed to be developing an obsession with jars of that size in recent days.

Amber watched from inside the pickup truck as Daren carried the two containers of gas over to her Grand Prix. He opened the tank and began to re-fill it with Amber's gas that had been siphoned out some hours earlier. It was then that it suddenly dawned upon Amber of what was happening. So that was Daren's little technique? The man was so persistent that he actually took the time to siphon out Amber's gas and then meet her on the highway to play hero?

All Amber could do in that moment was shake her head in disbelief. Too bad Jim wasn't here to see this and understand that another man tried so desperately to have Amber. That's when Amber reached another realization. Why was she playing so hard to get? Daren was the answer to her wish. Another man wanted her. Jim wasn't around and certainly in need of a good, hard lesson. Maybe it was time to lighten up a bit with the annoying, married customer and accept an invitation for coffee or even go out for dinner.

One five gallon container of gas was filled into Amber's tank, then another. As the minutes passed, Amber further convinced herself that Daren was the answer to all her wishes. And she felt so wanted, so sexy and flattered to have man desire her so badly that he took the time to siphon the gas from her tank.

Daren returned and placed the empty gas containers in the back of the truck. It was then that Amber emerged into the cold to greet Daren with a warm smile.

"All done?" Amber asked with plenty of ladled friendliness.

"Yup! That should give you plenty of gas to take you home or even to the nearest gas station."

Amber and Daren stood facing one another for a brief moment. Amber broke the silence. "So…"

"Yeah, why don't you go see if you can get your car started." suggested Daren.

"Sure!" Amber walked towards her car and then momentarily turned to face Daren. "So will I see you around, soon?"

"Excuse me?"

"I haven't seen you in while in the jewelry department. I trust everything is going well with your girlfriend?"

"Eh… we're kind of seeing each other right now. It's not that serious like it was before. How have sales been since the holidays?"

Amber shrugged her shoulders, "It's kind of slowed down a bit. We've got Valentine's Day coming up."

"Right…"

Amber couldn't believe that she was now the one doing the chase. She suddenly wanted Daren so badly. Why wasn't he getting the hint? Was he going to make a move and ask her out for coffee? Maybe he needed a hint. "Gosh, it's so cold out here."

"It is!" agreed Daren. "Now go see if your car starts! I want to get home."

What was this? Daren was pushing Amber away and rejecting her? Dumbfounded, Amber returned to her driver's seat and started the Grand Prix right up. She looked out towards the direction of Daren's pickup truck and gave him the thumb up.

But Daren was already climbing into his truck. He merely nodded and smiled. Then he closed the door and drove off, leaving Amber all alone on the highway! With nothing left to do, she simply slipped the transmission into "drive" and made her way home.

Men were always so confusing for Amber!

Chapter 38

Amber woke up the following morning; a Tuesday when she had to report to work for store opening. It was during awkward scheduling like this that Amber truly hated the Mapleview Department Store. She worked from store opening, yesterday, until late in the evening past store closing. And now Amber had to be there bright and early this morning? Was there no end to this never-ending cycle of work, work, work?

Still not fully awake and not quite motivated to start her day, Amber sat down on the sofa and opened up the laptop. Maybe she would check out the social world of Facebook before stepping into the shower. The notifications ticker showed that her small group of friends and coworkers had recently posted pictures of their own private family gatherings, or functions at their kids' schools. A couple people posted some You Tube videos of some head-banging hair bands of the 1980s.

Oh, and Amber loved when people shared their personal problems for the whole world to read in an update status. "Sometimes life can be so hard for a mother. You try and try so hard to show your love, but then your son breaks your heart. Some days I don't think I can go on. Lord, give me the strength! Maybe someone else out there can take my son. I think I'm done being a mother."

The best part: nine people actually "liked" this status update!

Then Amber glanced back over to the notifications ticker and noticed that someone had sent her a private message. She clicked the notification which opened up a direct message from Daren! Yes, it was actually the annoying, married customer who had been trying to ask Amber out, and even siphoned gas out of her tank to come along and play hero!

Needless to say, the message took Amber by surprise. So dumbfounded by last night's episode, she truly thought that Daren was a lost cause.

"Amber,

I'm sorry for writing you out of the clear blue like this, but last night left me feeling like there was supposed to be more. I felt like maybe I was supposed to ask you to join me for coffee or something. I know that maybe you and I got off on a bad start. It was the holidays and I was sort of clumsy in the way that I approached you in the jewelry department. But you know, deep down inside, I think that there is something between us. Do you feel it? Is this mutual?

I guess I'm just continuing where I left off from last night. Maybe we can have coffee some time and get better acquainted.

Daren"

Amber shook her head in disbelief. "What the hell is this? How did he even get my last name?" She read the message a second time and then a third. This Daren was truly out of his mind! Amber clicked Daren's profile page which contained his general information. The man worked at a biomedical equipment company with headquarters out in Arizona. Daren's hometown was in Arizona. He now lived in Mapleview and was certainly married, as evidenced by the freely-shared photos of him and his wife. As for Mary, she was quite a beautiful wife. She was so young and beautiful, in fact, that Amber had a split-second of envy. And if Amber didn't know any better, there was something in the photos of Daren and Mary that suggested a beautiful daughter was maybe a year away from being born.

For some unknown reason, Amber suddenly felt an urge to hurt Daren and Mary. She hated them for nothing more than being a happy, young couple and wished to destroy them.

Just then, Trista scuffed past the family room and on her way into the kitchen to make coffee.

"Trista, come here." Amber nearly ordered. "Look at this." Amber really had no one else to share this new phenomenon with. At times like this, Trista was Amber's best friend.

Trista overlooked her mother's shoulder and struggled to understand what was being shared. Apparently, some stranger messaged Mother.

"This guy has been visiting me in the jewelry department and wants to take me out on a date."

"He's not bad looking…" commented Trista.

"I know; he's actually a really, good-looking guy. But he's married. And get this. Last night he actually siphoned the gas from my tank to come rescue me on the highway when my car stalled."

"Whoa! That's creepy, Mom!"

"I guess he's trying to ask me out over Facebook?"

Trista sighed. Mother was an older, single woman who apparently hadn't been on the dating scene since, perhaps, before Trista was born. She needed to be brought up to speed. "Okay, Mom, you need to know this. When a guy tries to hit on you or ask you out on Facebook, you're supposed to ignore him. Pretend that you never got the message."

Amber returned a queer look to her daughter.

"I'm serious, Mom. Trust me; this is what losers do. This Daren guy is pretty much saying, 'Okay, I really like you but I'm afraid to ask you out in person. So I'm doing it on Facebook in hopes to maybe break the ice a little.' You can't let that happen, Mom. If you're really interested, you need him to work a little. Let him approach you in person like a real man. You deserve it, right?"

Amber nodded in agreement. She was truly blessed to have a teenage daughter who was up on things. Not only was Trista knowledgeable on fashion and the right music to listen to, but she was also the best source of dating advice.

"Besides, Mom, the guy sounds creepy. He siphoned the gas out of your tank?"

Amber shrugged her shoulders, "I guess…"

Trista made her way back into the kitchen to make coffee.

Amber snapped the notebook computer shut and made her way to bathroom for her daily shower. It all came back to Amber; those younger days of when she dated guys. Amber was and always will be the queen of sex magick. She knows how to absolutely drive a guy nuts by totally wanting him with all her heart and then simply ignoring him. A guy breaks down and finally snaps so that he's head-over-heels in love with Amber. And that pretty, young wife of Daren's was going to get what's coming to her. Amber can win any man!—even the ones who are married to beautiful, young, wholesome women. It was about time that Amber destroyed a marriage and made people miserable. Why should that Mary be fortunate enough to have Daren?

Amber turned on the steamy, hot water and stepped into the shower, naked. Daren only wished he could have a piece of that. There are women out there, like Amber, who are just too good for Daren. As the narrator, I can tell you from what I see that Amber definitely has a gorgeous body. Small, perky tits that freely hang in the spray of the shower and a perky ass with soap bubbles that run down towards her sexy, shapely thighs; too bad I can't enter the fictional world and attack Amber myself!

Amber fondled and squeezed her naked breasts while imagining Daren's thick and strong hands touching them. He wanted those, and wished to do all sorts of things to them. But Daren couldn't have them!

Amber massaged and stimulated her clitoris and then inserted two fingers through the entrance of her vagina while imagining it to be Daren's desperate, hard cock of desire. It would feel so good for Amber! She even whispered his name, "Daren... Daren... What's wrong with you? I want you... Please come get me... Please..."

Daren wished to screw Amber so bad. But again, he couldn't have her! Daren was married. Aside from that, Amber was much, too good for him.

After her shower, Amber blow-dried her pretty, shoulder-length, blond hair and then styled it so that her hair hung wild and free. Daren probably liked blond women, especially sexy ones with gorgeous brown eyes and a hint of perfume sprayed on their naked breasts and pubic area. Amber stepped into a pair of silky, sexy thong panties and then turned her back towards the mirror to admire the reflection of a perky ass. She rubbed her hand on one of the cheeks of her ass while thinking of Daren. For a moment, it was his hand that felt that ass. But too bad Amber was too good for him. He could never touch it!

Next she strapped on a sexy, pushup bra so that breasts squashed together to form delicious cleavage. To make it even more delicious, she touched them up with a light spray of perfume. Only in Daren's wildest dreams would he be so fortunate to unlatch Amber's bra and watch her breasts burst forth.

January was too cold for a sexy dress. But a pair of dress slacks that snuggly hugged Amber's perky thong-covered ass would have been enough to drive a man wild. If close enough, an onlooker would notice the outline of a thong.

Finally, she put on a flimsy, button-down blouse so that her creamy push-up bra cleavage could be seen. Because it was January and cold, it was necessary for Amber to wear an open single-button sweater—open enough to display beckoning cleavage.

Trista was taken by surprise as Mother walked into the kitchen for breakfast and coffee. "Wow, Mom! Big meeting today or maybe a date later tonight?"

"No, I'm just the manager of the Jewelry department and need to look nice."

"Yeah, right! Maybe that guy will come and see you today."

"Oh, please!" answered Amber. "I'm not going to waste my time with that loser! You're right; if he can't be man enough to ask me out in person, then I'm not going to give him the time of day."

Trista smiled to herself. It appeared that Mother learned quickly.

* * *

Oh, but Amber's thoughts and behavior didn't suggest any of this while at work. All morning and afternoon, she worked behind the counter of the Jewelry department and imagined Daren watching her from a distance like a hungry wolf that drooled at a piece of luscious meat. But he could have drooled all he wanted. Despite how badly Amber wanted him, Daren could never have her. Daren was married—for one—and definitely below Amber's league. The only type of women available to Daren were those average, frumpy women; not someone as elite as Amber.

But it was difficult not for her to fantasize. Occasionally when she had a moment, Amber traveled in her imagination to one of the back rooms where Daren took her by surprise and stripped her naked to ravish her body. Although a very, bad thing and something Daren had no right to do; some part of Amber might have actually enjoyed this. And this is how the crazy, stewing energy of sex magick builds up. Although Amber had those overwhelming, primal urges to be taken down and raped by a desperate man who couldn't help himself; Amber maintained her prudence while reminding herself that there were men much, more worthy to have her. Patience, after all, is a virtue.

This doesn't mean to say, of course, that Amber didn't release those urges in the late night hours. With the bedroom door closed so that Trista wouldn't hear her, Amber lay in bed—naked—while fondling all her private treasures. She whispered and called out for the man who so desired her, "Daren... Daren... Why can't you be here with me? Why do you have to be married? Why can't you be man enough to force yourself in this house... in this bedroom and take me in this bed?"

Amber squeezed her naked breasts while imagining that it was Daren's hands that did this. It was wrong to let him touch her, but felt so good. He even pinched her nipples. And to emulate his warm tongue, Amber moistened her fingers with plenty of saliva and circled her nipples with fingertips.

Perhaps in need of a kiss, she opened her mouth so that her thumb and tongue danced and played with each other. The index finger lightly stroked Amber's lips. It was Daren who kissed her; again, so wrong and yet feeling so good.

Oh no! Daren's hands made their way down towards Amber's crotch as she made both hands wrestle with each other. One hand wished to touch Amber's pussy while the other fought to hold it back.

"Daren, no! You can't do that! Please, nooooooo…" She whispered it so seductively to intensify her pleasure in fantasizing the act of being seduced.

Daren's fingers finally touched Amber's clitoris which sent waves of excitement through her body. But he wanted more!

"No, Daren! You can't!"

Amber wiggled and squirmed her crotch around while two of her fingers tried to penetrate the entrance of her vagina. "No! No!"

But his hard cock found its way inside.

Amber whispered out long and hard. "Noooooooooooooooo!" In her mind she screamed and yelled out with a voice that was drenched with adrenaline and sorts of sex hormones. Amber's heart raced and she shook with excitement as Daren's big, hard cock slipped in and out.

"Can't you see how much I want you?" Amber whispered. "Don't you want to do this to me? Where are you? Hurry, Daren! Hurry and get in this bedroom before I cum!"

But it was too late. Amber exploded while releasing all her wishes and desires into the night. For now it was another night, alone, without Daren in her bed. But if you've come to know Amber, then you know that all of her wishes come true!—all of them! And if you've come to know Daren—particularly in **The Tree Goddess**—then you know that playing sex magick with such a man is very dangerous, and a bad idea.

Chapter 39

Kimberly brushed her teeth every morning and night. But on this particular evening, she was a bit hurt at Jim's sudden announcement of her offensive breath.

"Pew! I'm sorry, but you've got bad breath!"

Kimberly refused to let his verbal assault go unanswered. "Oh, like your breath smells nice all the time?"

"I just thought you wanted to know. It smells like doggy breath—even worse than that! It smells like there is something wrong."

"Something wrong?" Kimberly asked.

"Yeah, like you're sick or something."

Again, Kimberly would not allow her husband to have the last word. "Oh, whatever! You should smell yours after eating cheese. Now that's nasty!"

Sometime later in the quiet bathroom while preparing to brush her teeth, Kimberly noticed the peculiar need to take rapid breaths. It was almost as-if she had completed an afternoon jog or had just come in from doing yard work. It was now in the evening hours, a time of day when she vegged out in front of the TV. Kimberly's respiration and heart rate should have been slow and relaxed. Why the alarming need to take deep and quick breaths?

The following afternoon, Kimberly noticed the increasing need to cough which was followed by that infected taste that is exhaled from the chest when sick. That's when Kimberly concluded that a lower respiratory infection was developing. It certainly explained the need to take deep and quick breaths the previous evening. And it certainly explained Jim's observation of Kimberly's bad breath. But Jim didn't need to know this.

"Great! I don't have time to be sick! Now the kids are going to catch it and might have to stay home from school!" Kimberly reached for her first line of defense; an Airborne effervescent tablet to be quickly dissolved in water. Has the reader ever used this miracle? Many people swear that taking one of these before or after being in a crowded area with sick people prevents the common cold. Many, still, are probably skeptical. But I'll tell you first hand that Airborne has an even greater effect than what is believed.

Consider that moment when you first realize that you are coming down with a cold. Maybe you have a slight tickle in your throat. Maybe you feel your blood pressure or circulation is not right. Whatever your early warning light is, be sure to dissolve an Airborne effervescent tablet into water and then drink it down. It's loaded with vitamins, supplements and herbs that boost the immune system. And whatever that initial symptom is that you might feel, it will be gone in a few hours.

I don't think that Airborne serves as a cure to the common cold. I believe the user still has the cold, but never actually "comes down with it". Personally, I can live with that!

Unfortunately for Kimberly, she would soon find out that she had more than a common cold. Airborne doesn't work for more serious illnesses. As a couple days passed, her throat and lower respiratory passages developed an uncomfortable, hacked and dried sensation which resulted in uncontrollable coughing. No secretions could be produced; only a need to cough all the more. Kimberly's voice turned low and cracked. And then whatever infection invaded her lower respiratory passages, it moved its way up to the back of her throat which resulted in a raging sore throat; the kind that makes eating and drinking a miserable experience. Kimberly's lymph nodes were painfully swollen. Then her inner ears began to tickle. Finally, the infection invaded her nasal passages which initially caused a stinging pain while exhaling. Only the over-production of mucus brought relief to this discomfort.

Now, on an evening in early February, Kimberly lay on the sofa in a long-overdue realization that she was terribly sick. Bundled up in a blanket and shivering from the chills, Kimberly was deeply concerned over the battle to keep her temperature down. The fevers would attack at night. Could she die from some strange flu or virus?

Jim was concerned of his wife. "Honey, do you want me to take you to urgent aid? You can't go on like this."

"No, I made an appointment with the doctor. I see her tomorrow."

"Are you sure?"

"I'll be alright, Jim."

Jim studied his sickly wife on the sofa and then placed his hand on her forehead. "How's your temperature?"

"It's at 100. I just took another Motrin." It wasn't uncommon for Kimberly's temperature to reach 103 and even 104 degrees in the evening hours. That's serious for an adult!

For over a week, Kimberly had been sleeping on the sofa. Jim assumed she was being considerate. But on that night, he felt the need to offer the bed. "Honey, why don't you sleep in bed tonight? I'll sleep on the sofa. You should get a good night rest. It might do you good."

"No, Jim; that's fine. I won't be able to sleep. The TV kind of keeps me going through the night." If you live in a modern, well-to-do society; then you might take the TV for granted. With a terribly high fever and pain throughout respiratory passages, the TV nearly keeps one alive. As one dozes off, only to be startled awake from bad dreams, those late night infomercials or cooking shows seem to restore a sense of comfort.

* * *

Zpak is a modern-day, antibiotic wonder. A brand name for Azithromycin, it is often sold in a packet that contains five days worth of antibiotic therapy. The user takes two initial tablets, followed by one tablet per day for the remaining four days.

Zpak is highly effective in treating respiratory infections. After taking note of Kimberly's night fevers, swollen lymph node glands and the fact that other patients throughout Mapleview had visited with similar complaints; the doctor felt it best to prescribe her patient with a treatment of Zpak.

But it additionally included a dose of scolding from Dr. Klause, who was somewhat unhappy with Kimberly's weight. Not obese, Kimberly had always leaned towards being full sized. "I see you haven't had a doctor visit in over a year. What's going on?"

Kimberly apologized, "I know. I've just been busy and time goes by quick, you know?"

"It's understandable." reassured Dr. Klause. "But I see you've gained over 20 pounds since your last visit. That's not healthy. You're almost 40 years old and you have things like cholesterol, diabetes and hypertension to consider. Your blood pressure is fine, but you haven't had blood work done in over a year. How do we know something isn't going on?"

Kimberly further apologized, "I'm sorry..."

Dr. Klause handed Kimberly the five day Zpak along with an order for blood work. "Promise me that when you feel better you'll get some lab work done. I'm having them screen your cholesterol, check your blood sugar and some of the other basics. You fast for twelve hours before going, understand?"

Kimberly understood that Dr. Klause was right, so she reassured her physician, "I promise; I'll do it." She'd say anything to experience the relief from those antibiotics.

* * *

In a miraculous turnaround, after only three days of antibiotic treatment, Kimberly no longer felt ill. The fevers had subsided; the raging, sore throat and dry, unproductive, cough was gone. That overall feeling of things being infected inside was gone. As a result, Kimberly resumed night-full rests in her own bed while sleeping next to her husband. She was inconvenienced on her first night, however, with a nasty attack of post nasal drip in the midnight hours. It awakened her as she had the uncontrollable urge to cough. The tickle in her throat was maddening.

"Have I been coughing long?" Sitting up in bed, Kimberly was aware that Jim was awake.

"Yeah, ever since you fell asleep."

"Oh, I'm sorry! Why didn't you wake me up? I would have taken some Robitusson."

"Eh... it's not so bad..."

Jim was only being nice. Kimberly knew this. She scuffed over to the medicine cabinet for a shot of Robitusson cough syrup. Nyquil probably would have done equally as well, but Kimberly wasn't about to load up on narcotics for the night. Outside of some midnight post nasal drip, she was feeling much better thanks to the Zpak.

After slipping under the blankets, it didn't take Kimberly long to fall back to sleep. And it didn't take long for the Robitusson to ease her urge to cough.

But Jim lay awake in the dead of night. It wasn't the disturbance from Kimberly's coughing that made it difficult to fall asleep. Rather it was the mixed feeling he had towards the recent activity of sex magick with Ekaterina. Although it violated every moral and belief that Jim could think of, he knew it was necessary for correcting his incurment of bad karma. If only Ekaterina could have had been more appealing and attractive. Once upon a time, she might have had heart-stopping, beautiful torpedo breasts. But now they were saggy and hung down past her navel. Such a shame; Jim loved breasts.

Jim really loved breasts! Amber had a nice pair, but she never allowed Jim to touch them. Why would such a beautiful woman prevent her man from enjoying such gorgeous breasts?

Kimberly, too, had a beautiful rack. In younger years, Jim would play with Kimberly's breasts as often as he liked. But sexual activity seems to be far and few between after some years of marriage. For now, all Jim could do was watch his wife's breast-covered chest rise and fall under the blanket. He listened as Kimberly took deep, full breaths and was convinced that she was sound asleep.

In earlier years of their marriage, Jim enjoyed stealing a late night fondle of Kimberly's sexy, oversized breasts while she slept. When Jim dated her, she possessed a very, nice c-cup rack. Through the years, her breasts actually grew in size so that Kimberly now possesses an astonishing, triple-d rack! This was probably due to Kimberly's gradual gain in weight.

Jim certainly didn't mind Kimberly's chunkiness. After all, chunky women typically have bigger tits than normal-sized women. He carefully rolled over towards his wife and slowly pulled the covers down. There lay the two luscious mounds that protruded through Kimberly's flannel night shirt. Jim delicately cupped his hand over the nearest breast. It felt so good to touch a young woman's breast with his hand.

One time in the earlier part of their marriage, Jim managed to successfully pull Kimberly's nightshirt above her breasts. This presented an opportunity to gently fondle as he pleased. As Jim recalled, Kimberly's naked breasts were so warm to the touch as she soundly slept that night. Tonight she wore a flannel, button-down night shirt. What an exciting challenge it would be to carefully unbutton and expose Kimberly's naked breasts. And so one-by-one, Jim undid each button, requiring nearly 10 minutes of careful diligence. Kimberly would occasionally change her breathing which signaled a possible awareness of her surroundings. At one point, she turned her head slightly while jolting her arm. But Jim couldn't give up! He was so close to seeing what he so strongly desired.

With sufficient buttons undone, Jim pulled apart Kimberly's flannel nightshirt. And there they rested; Kimberly's gorgeous, oversized, naked breasts! They resembled two gigantic cupcakes with perhaps a jellybean at the center of each one for decoration. And like a child who drools in anticipation of a pastry, Jim wanted Kimberly's breasts.

He delicately laid his hand over the nearest breast. And just as anticipated, the feel of Kimberly was warm, silky and sexy. Jim's arousal returned as he carefully took hold of Kimberly's breast with his thumb on one side and fingers on the other. He thought of everything he was going to do to those luscious breasts the next time he and Kimberly had sex. And while doing so, his other hand managed to wedge under the covers and under his boxers to stroke his erect penis to orgasm.

Apparently, Jim had gotten a little too excited. Maybe he was beginning to squeeze Kimberly's breast; for she suddenly woke up and slapped Jim's hand away. "Excuse me, do you mind?"

Jim apologized, "Oh, I'm sorry. I thought you were sleeping."

Did that really excuse Jim for his invasion of Kimberly's privacy?

Kimberly quickly buttoned her nightgown and then turned on her side, facing away from Jim. It looked like the only breasts that Jim would get to play with were the ones that belonged to Ekaterina!

Chapter 40

Actually, Ekaterina wasn't all that bad. Through all the daily encounters of sex magick, something was happening to her. And if Jim didn't know any better, Ekaterina was beginning to care for her appearance. She apparently adopted the new practice of bathing every day. Ekaterina's lifeless, split, gray and terribly thin hair was seemingly coming back to life. She wore makeup. Her dull, bloodshot eyes were suddenly clear and bright with an extra sparkle when looking at Jim. Ekaterina was beginning to wear colorful clothing, and might have even burned those old, black, faded dresses. Her new outfits suggested a cute, curvy figure—something to captivate a man's attention. Sex can apparently do amazing things for an older woman!

But it was more than simply an old lady who washed, put on makeup and wore new clothes. To illustrate this mysterious phenomenon of Ekaterina's transformation, the reader would have to consider those times in life when a man begins to look at older women. Perhaps you're a man and can recall these moments quite well. In college years, you might have allowed your attention to escape your group of friends and your young girlfriend, to gaze over at a table and notice an attractive woman in her thirties. In those days, a woman that age would have been considered an older woman. She was sexy, alluring and very intriguing. How you wished and fantasized to be with a woman like this.

One day, you reach thirty years old. Attracted to the pretty, young girls and women your own age; you might allow your attention to momentarily escape the wife and kids to notice a woman in her early forties, sitting at a nearby table in a restaurant. There is something undeniable in her appearance; something that suggests this woman to be powerful and sexy with a perfected beauty that a younger woman could never have. How you wish to get to know this woman, become her friend, experience the moment when you boldly give her kiss. And sex with her would be out of this world!

How about that woman in her late forties? Sure, you'd have no problem being with her. Women are learning to take care of themselves and remain youthful in their appearance as they get older. Early-to-mid-fifties? Women at that age begin to change. Although at times sensitive, a bit emotional and moody; she can be very friendly and outgoing. She does everything in her power to remain youthful and attractive. She comes to the office on a summer morning in a short-sleeve blouse, boasting skin that—although has slightly aged—is still inviting the onlooker to touch. An hour or so later, a shawl or sweater covers this up for she gets cold. As a man gets older, he realizes that menopause isn't the end of attractiveness for a woman. She's aged, but how you'd love to take her to bed with you!

Then comes a day that you walk through the store, and notice a woman in her sixties staring at you with bedroom eyes. Just like a younger woman, she is dressed in nice clothing and does her best to remain attractive. But she's old enough to be your mother—quite possibly a granny! Yet she's inviting you, nearly asking out loud to give her one, last moment of romance and sex. Once-upon-a-time you would have gagged at such a thought or suggestion. And you might even do this, initially, now. Then you take a second look and notice something appealing. Yes, you could be easily convinced. In fact you are already convinced, doing your best to refrain from pawing at the ground with erotic fantasies of an afternoon in bed with a woman who is old enough to be a grandmother to your children.

This is the state of appearance that Ekaterina suddenly reached. She went from a sloppy, dirty, stinky old witch; to a sexy and alluring old lady. Jim was beginning to look forward to the daily sexual encounters with her.

* * *

Today, Ekaterina stood before the window in the small area of her cottage that would be considered the family room. Even Ekaterina's home was coming back to life! It was neat and clean with no used dishes lying around. It was decorated with pictures along with the sudden appearance of small statues and knickknacks on tables or shelves. There was also the undeniable aroma of sweet, scented candles and the glow of candle flame. Ekaterina's home was now a place that made visitors feel good.

"I want to ask you something." informed Ekaterina while standing before the window. She wore a serious expression while looking at Jim. "Are you still with your girlfriend?"

"Amber?" asked Jim. "To tell you the truth, I haven't seen or heard from Amber in a few weeks. I think it's over. Do you want me to totally forget about her?"

Ekaterina nodded, yes. "You cannot have someone else while doing this with me. You must be all mine. Your wife I don't mind... sort of. But you must definitely leave your girlfriend!"

In the small amount of time that Jim had spent with Ekaterina since late December, he couldn't help but realize that they shared a relationship far deeper than the silly affair with Amber. Ekaterina immediately became a friend to Jim, taught him how to enjoy vodka, gave insight into his life through guided scrying, and even exhibited some positive changes after having sex with him. If that weren't enough, Jim was developing some strong feelings for Ekaterina. Being asked to leave Amber for good was certainly no problem.

"Sure, no problem!" reassured Jim. "Is that all that's bothering you? I don't care about her anymore. My life has become so much better since becoming your friend." He approached Ekaterina and embraced her. He caressed her back so tenderly and lovingly while deeply breathing in the smell of Ekaterina's perfume. Then he pulled back enough to see her face up close. Although still aged, there was something about Ekaterina; something in her eyes that Jim desired to deeply drink in. The only way to satisfy this sort of feeling and attraction is to kiss the lips of a lover. This is what Jim did; savoring every bit of softness and warmth as well as the way Ekaterina received his kisses. He tasted her breath and couldn't wait to slip his tongue in her mouth.

And then it all just went crazy after that. Clothes suddenly come off in these early moments of falling in love. Jim couldn't strip Ekaterina of her blouse fast enough. When finally removed and tossed on the chair, he nearly shook while taking hold of her bra. Those large, Russian torpedo breasts needed to be seen right then and there. Had Ekaterina fought Jim's hands, her bra would have been torn off. But she was eager to be fondled and sucked. Her breasts bulged out to be naked and free. Even they had gone through a transformation. What were once the cold and stiff tits that belong to a witch were now soft and warm with luscious nipples that called out to be played with.

Kissing, sucking, biting and fondling, then to return to Ekaterina's lips; Jim soon removed the remainder of her clothes. He couldn't wait to glide those silk panties down Ekaterina's freshly-shaven legs. And of course his throbbing erection couldn't wait to be inside of her.

Ekaterina pulled her lover into the bedroom where they enjoyed some of the hottest sex one could ever dream up in one afternoon.

So if ever there comes a time when you encounter an old woman out in public who cannot take her eyes off of you, remember that you could easily be convinced! The two of you could do amazing things for one another!

Chapter 41

A couple days passed after Kimberly completed her Zpak antibiotic therapy. From what she could determine, that nasty bug had been defeated. But then she woke up on the third morning with some disappointing news for her husband. "I think I'm sick, again. My throat's all sore like before and..." Kimberly suddenly coughed, making that dry, hacking sound.

Jim felt sorry for his wife, "Oh, you don't sound good."

Kimberly shook her head while swallowing. Just the sound was indicator enough of a throat that was terribly swollen and sore.

"Oh, honey; why don't you call the doctor? Maybe you need more antibiotics."

Kimberly coughed some more and then replied with a raspy voice, "I'm going to do that later this morning."

* * *

It was only necessary for Kimberly to call Dr. Krause and inform her that she was sick, again.

"Okay, I'm going to give you another five day dose of Zpak. I'll have the office call it in to your pharmacy. Pick it up ASAP! And be sure to take the initial dose ASAP!"

Kimberly did exactly as instructed, and by the second day she was feeling much better. And of course she was sure to complete the five day treatment, this time including extra doses of vitamin C and getting plenty of rest.

But alas, by the third morning after Kimberly had completed her second five-day therapy of antibiotics, the blasted sore throat returned along with the dry, hacking sensation in her bronchial tubes. What sort of super bug invaded poor Kimberly's body?

It just so happened that Kimberly received a telephone call that morning from one of the moms of another orchestra student at Mapleview Community High School. Anna was acting director of the orchestra program for the school year and had set out to inform parents that morning of the annual bakery sale fund raiser.

"We've had much success with this in recent years, Kimberly. Families bake pastries, cookies, cakes, brownies—anything sweet—and then we sell them at the arts and crafts fair. But if contributing, expect to make tons of whatever you supply. If you make cookies, bring a couple dozen batches! A special cake; make about a half dozen cakes! The craft show brings in crowds of people and we always run out before the day is over. $11,000 we made last year!"

Kimberly coughed over the phone and spoke with her cracked voice. "Wow! You do that well?"

"Absolutely!" replied Anna.

Kimberly had a knack for baking and wished to contribute. But her words were so painfully spoken over the phone with a low, raspy voice and coughing in between. "I can make this (cough, cough) toffee and (cough, cough, cough...) Excuse me! I can make a toffee and chocolate chip cookie. How would 15 or 20 dozen sound?"

Anna immediately noticed of how ill Kimberly sounded over the phone. "Honey, you sound horrible! Are you okay? Do you have that nasty bug that's been going around?"

Kimberly coughed some more, "I'm sick as a dog. I've taken 2 rounds of antibiotics, but it keeps coming back."

That's when Anna informed Kimberly of the super bug that would plague her for many weeks. "Oh, I had that same bug back in October. I was sick all through the holidays; fevers, infected bronchial passages, nasty sore throats, runny nose..."

Kimberly gave more information, "I've taken two rounds of Zpak already..."

Anna interrupted, "Yup! The bug is immune to it! The Zpak will only put it on ice, but it comes back. For me, it seemed to travel up the bronchial passages and to my nose and throat. I had wicked cold symptoms for a few days and then it would work its way back down to my chest. I figured my body was getting rid of it, but then it traveled back up to my nose and throat, making me terribly sick for a few days. It'll actually bounce back and forth a bunch of times before your body finally defeats it. It's some kind of super bug!"

Kimberly coughed some more, "I'm so sick! I don't know what to do!"

"It'll be about 3 months before you feel better. There's nothing you can do to treat this. Just let it run its course. I totally feel for you!" Then Anna changed the topic back to the fund raiser. "The bake sale will be in April." It was currently February. "Do you think you'll be alright by then to make those cookies?"

"I should be okay." replied Kimberly

"Okay, I'll put you down for 20 dozen cookies."

Chapter 42

It was towards the end of the week, but not quite Friday—only Thursday. As usual, that annoying alarm clock woke Amber up for the day, announcing it was time to get ready for work. And just like many mornings, Amber scuffed over to the computer to wake up over Facebook before hitting the shower.

Much to Amber's surprise she received another message as indicated in the counter at the top of the screen. That familiar surge of adrenaline and excitement could be felt. Was it Daren?

Yes, it certainly was Daren! After many days he finally messaged her again. Maybe he was going to confess to how badly he wanted Amber. Every woman, after all, secretly wishes for a man to strongly desire her to the point of no longer holding back.

But what was this? This time he sent her a letter of apology.

"Amber,

I think I might have done something that I shouldn't have. I am really sorry for sending you that previous message. I guess I was overtired on that Monday night when traveling all those hours, and it carried over to the following morning. For a few weeks I've been in panic mode and thinking, 'What have I done?' I feel so stupid, and again, I want to apologize. It won't happen again.

Daren"

Amber clicked her tongue in disappointment while shaking her head in disbelief. What the hell was this? What in the world made Daren think that he did something wrong? Ever since Amber received the message from Daren, she had been eagerly waiting for another one. But now it seemed that he was no longer interested.

Just then, Trista scuffed her way across the family room and on her way into the kitchen.

"Trista, come here." ordered Amber.

Trista did as Mother asked and felt an equal amount of excitement in anticipation of another message from Daren. "Is it that guy?" she asked. "Did he send you another message?"

Now standing over Mother's shoulder, Trista read what Daren had sent. Then she commented, "Huh? What's this guy's problem? One minute he wants you, and then he changes his mind?"

"I know!" agreed Amber. She continued to slowly shake her head in disbelief and then looked up to her daughter, "I don't know; maybe I was being rude in not replying back? Maybe this message reveals some truth. Maybe my silence caused him to freak out for a few weeks, and made him second guess himself?"

"No!" answered Trista. "He knows better. He should know how to play the game. If a guy is interested, he is not supposed to be hitting on you or asking you out on Facebook. Only a loser does this. He is supposed to go up to you in person. When he finally does approach you in person, you are supposed to totally reject him. Let the guy work for you. Never appear interested." Trista was a teenager and definitely an expert in dating—even in the adult world.

Mother stared at her daughter and remained speechless. Where did these new rules come from? From what Amber remembered, a girl wasn't supposed to appear desperate like she'd take anyone. But to totally reject a guy that she wanted just to see him work sounded so cold and heartless. Is this what guys wanted now days?

Amber sighed and closed the Facebook screen. "I suppose you're right." It's a good thing that she had Trista to guide her. Amber would have replied back, apologizing for her delayed response, and reassuring that Daren had done nothing wrong. But it's a different world now. Despite how badly Amber wanted Daren, she was supposed to push the man away and reject him.

While walking to the bathroom, Amber suddenly stopped and turned towards her daughter to ask a burning question. But Trista already made her way into the kitchen. This was a good thing! Amber was about to ask when it was appropriate for a woman to finally give in. But that would have made Amber seem clueless to the dating scene.

For so long Amber had walked on cloud nine at work with the feeling of being so wanted. She was so powerful; a sex goddess with the ability to push Daren over the edge to the point of unleashing and attacking her. But now the game had grown cold. He apologized for the previous message and was done chasing Amber.

What about those weeks over the holidays when Daren visited Amber at the jewelry counter? He tried so hard to have coffee with her and made up some silly story about a troubled relationship with a girlfriend. At least Amber did the right thing at that moment. She rejected Daren just as Trista would have advised. If a man were truly serious, Amber speculated, he would invite a woman out to be wined and dined and then taken to the opera or someplace fancy. Expecting to have coffee with a woman is probably for losers.

So when was Daren going to return? And would he ever send another message on Facebook?

* * *

Meanwhile at the historic Trivelli house...

For Mary; clothes and jewelry were always nice gifts to receive. But after being married for a couple of years, she saw nothing wrong with receiving a new dishwasher for Valentine's Day. Besides, this sort of practical gift could be given in addition to a sentimental gift from Daren.

It was Saturday morning, a week away from Valentine's weekend when Mary so nonchalantly suggested to her husband the possibility of purchasing a new dishwasher. Daren seemed on edge that week, and Mary was careful to approach him about the dishwasher over breakfast.

But much to Mary's surprise, Daren seemed receptive to the idea, even suggested shopping for one that morning. "What do you say we hop in the car and cruise over to Best Buy or Walmart for one?" he asked.

But Mary already had her dishwasher picked out. She saw it in a recent advertisement and was impressed. All she needed to do was check it out in person; make sure it was roomy and ultra-silent while washing. "There's a nice one over at the Mapleview Department Store. Let's go over there."

Oh no! Not the Mapleview Department Store! This was the same place where Amber worked. What if Mary wanted to briefly look at the jewelry while passing through to the appliance department? "The Mapleview Department Store?" Daren asked. "You don't want to go there. I've heard nothing but bad things about appliances from there. Rumor is they will no longer be carrying appliances in a year or two. How will that affect your service contract and warranty?"

"What are you talking about?" retorted Mary. "The Mapleview Department Store is privately owned. They've carried appliances ever since I can remember. In fact, Grandpa Trivelli bought Grandma Trivelli her new stove from there back in the 1830s. As for the warranty, it's covered by the manufacturer."

"No!" exploded Daren. "Absolutely not! I will not buy a dishwasher from the Mapleview Department Store. The service is bad over there, and all their products are made in Pakistan by women and children under slave labor. End of discussion!"

Mary clicked her tongue in disappointment while shaking her head in disbelief. It was just like Amber would have done earlier that week. It seemed a lot of women were confused with Daren's behavior recently. Then Mary asked, "Daren, what is happening to you? You've been like this all week. I can't believe you made up some story about women and children in Pakistan so that we don't go to the Mapleview Department Store. What do you have against the place?"

"Nothing! I'm just saying! Appliances are low quality over there!"

"Daren, this is the dishwasher I want. I want it for Valentine's Day. It's a good price and the colors seem to match our kitchen."

"Colors… big deal! Most dishwashers come with interchangeable housings so you can get any color you want."

"Please, Daren! I've had my heart set on this dishwasher for about a week. Can we go? Please!"

Daren sighed. Maybe Amber wouldn't be working on Saturday. If she was, maybe the store would be too busy for her to raise a scene if encountering Daren with his wife. "Fine!" answered Daren. "Let's check it out."

"Yay!" cheered Mary with a happy face. Then she moved close to her husband and gave him a gentle kiss. "Are you okay?"

"Yeah, I'm fine."

"You just seem different lately, like something is really bothering you."

"No…" reassured Daren. "It's just February—cabin fever."

* * *

By midmorning, Daren and Mary walked through the main entrance of the Mapleview Department Store. Daren was sure to park near this entrance so that he and Mary would walk right to the appliance department—no need to pass through women's clothing, children's… *or jewelry*!

Mary found her dishwasher and immediately opened it up. She marveled at the ultra-slick racks that smoothly glided out and offered plenty of room for dishes, glasses and silverware. The color was perfect. The noise rating was at 41dB—ultra quiet!

Mary pulled at the tag and pointed to some print at the bottom. "Look, Daren; it says that it's made in the U.S.A!"

"That doesn't mean anything!" snapped Daren. "They ship the dishwashers with the knobs, buttons and stickers not attached. An assembly plant here in the states puts these on so that they can claim them to be made in the U.S.A"

Mary rolled her eyes at another ridiculous story.

Just then, a sales associate approached. "Can I help you folks?"

"Yes!" answered Mary. "Do you have any of these left in stock?"

"I have four left. Are you ready to make a purchase?"

Of course Mary was a smart woman like any woman is. Although she had her heart set on that particular dishwasher, she was sure to have the friendly sales associate (named Bernard) follow while she checked out a few others. Any smart woman is sure to shop around and explore all her options.

But as far as Daren was concerned, Mary should have quit "*shopping around*" once she met Daren—definitely once becoming married. Daren didn't like Bernard. He didn't like the way that the kid was looking at his wife. Bernard was being a little too friendly with Mary.

And while at the cash register upon taking her sales receipt with the scheduled delivery and install date, Mary inquired of the future of the appliance department. "Will the appliance department be closing down in the near future?"

Bernard returned a queer facial expression. "Absolutely not! Where did you hear that from?" Then Bernard turned towards Daren while smiling. "Whoever told you that obviously doesn't know what he's talking about!"

Mary patted Daren on the back. "See, it was just a silly rumor. You can't believe everything you hear."

By now you certainly know Daren and realize how prone he is to outrage and jealousy. In his world, Bernard stole Mary and turned her against Daren. Had he not been out in public, Daren would have pummeled Bernard's face with an explosion of punches. It's what the kid deserved!

Oh, but his silent jealousy and outrage was immediately put on ice while Mary walked towards the opposite direction of the parking lot. "Where are you going?" Daren nearly shouted while asking.

"I thought we'd check out some jewelry."

"Jewelry? What for?"

Mary returned her cute, pouty face. "Daren, it's almost Valentine's Day." Practical gifts are always nice, but every woman likes a little jewelry for Valentine's Day.

Had Daren been thirty years older, he would have surely dropped of a heart attack. Such a clash of strong emotions; he was now overwhelmed with rage and jealousy while at the same time fearing an encounter with Amber. "Oh that's right! Silly me! Let's browse the jewelry and see if there is something you like."

Daren's throat turned dry, and adrenaline spiked through every nerve of his body. All he could do to calm his fears was hope that maybe Amber wouldn't be working that day. Oh, how stupid Daren felt! How he wished to have never become obsessed with Amber. Amber was different from the other women. Amber was stronger than they were and had some sort of control over Daren. And to make matters worse, she never responded to any of his Facebook messages.

Daren could have sworn that every hair fell out of his head while discovering the terrible certainty of Amber working on Saturday. She stood behind the counter while waiting on a customer and looking just as beautiful and radiant as ever with her ultra-blond, shoulder-length hair and fair skin. Amber's body was simply divine in a knee-length dress that snuggly fit over her gorgeous figure. Why was she looking so sexy today? Did Amber have a date? Did she have a boyfriend or husband?

Mary now stood at the glass counter and pointed at a few items. "That's cute... Oh I love that..."

Just then, Amber looked up and towards the direction of Daren and Mary. Her face turned bitter and cold with eyes that could have set Daren on fire— and not in a good way! Amber exhibited such resentment and hatred towards Daren. She shook her head in disapproval and then called out to one of the sales girls, "Marla! Do you want to help these people out?"

Amber was sure to glance back at Daren and give one, final bitter look that left him feeling stupid, undesirable and immature. She wouldn't waste her time with such a pathetic excuse for a man—that is if Daren could be considered a man.

Chapter 43

Amber was turning into nothing short of an emotional wreck. She wanted Daren so badly and knew the feeling was mutual. But would he not send another Facebook message or make a surprise visit in the jewelry department? How about siphoning the gas from her tank and then playing hero to rescue her on the cold and dark road? Men are so confusing and frustrating. They like to play mind games and waste so much time in teasing the women they desire. Who teaches men to do this? Why do they feel that women like this sort of thing?

Amber lay awake in bed on Monday morning for about an hour before the alarm was set to go off. Round and round her thoughts spun as she could feel herself going increasingly insane. Sometimes Amber would softly cry and wonder why Daren couldn't just be a man and come out with the truth. Why couldn't he clearly state that he wanted her? She would give anything to hear from him—anything, even a simple Facebook message to indicate he was still thinking of her.

Five minutes before she was supposed to get up for the day, Amber switched off the alarm and made her way into the family room. Was there a message for her on Facebook? Would today be the day that Daren finally broke his silence and resumed communication? Perhaps this is how the young Paulette felt many years ago when that nerd engineer dumped her on the dating website. She, too, might have been delirious with hope just as Amber was at this very moment.

As Amber flipped open the laptop computer and clicked the web browser; that moment of years ago with Paulette played out in her in mind with such crystal clear memory. Amber desperately tried to bring Paulette back down to Earth on that sad, sad morning.

"Alright, fine! You want to see if maybe he has thought things over and is crawling back to you? I'll login, but you have to promise me something. You have to be

realistic. Chances are there isn't an email from him. And if you don't see an email, I don't want you to fall apart. Can you promise me that?"

But Amber was now the fool in love with blind hope to have received a Facebook message from Daren. And much to her surprise, there was a message in her Facebook inbox, and it was from Daren! Unlike poor Paulette, all of Amber's wishes really do come true!

"Amber,

I'm really sorry, but late last night I did something strange. I don't know if you discovered it yet, but I left you a rose at the front door. Actually, I quietly opened the screen door and set the rose inside so that it rests against your entry door. I'm so sorry!

I think the reason I did that was to find some way to patch things up between us. I know you saw me in the jewelry department on Saturday, and you gave me such a bitter look! I mean if looks could kill! I can tell that you really hate me.

It shouldn't be like that. I feel so bad that you and I have come to this. I've been trying to make contact with you and bring things to a more friendly state. All I want now is your forgiveness and maybe to be on speaking terms. Please accept the rose as a sign of my need to be forgiven. I am so sorry. It's been nearly a month of hell for me.

Daren"

Amber sighed and then walked over to the front door. Sure enough, upon opening the door, a long-stemmed rose that was complete with thorns had fallen inside on the foyer floor. Amber picked it up and held it close to her chest. Her eyes flooded with tears upon realizing that Daren came back. He was still interested and willing to patch things up with her.

Just then Trista scuffed into the room and on her way into the kitchen to make coffee. But she stopped dead in her tracks at the sight of the rose. "Did he leave you a rose?"

Amber nodded, "Yes, at the front door."

"Oh... my... gosh! He is such a creepy stalker! What a loser!"

"He sent me another Facebook message, too."

"Oh, now this I have to see!" Trista sat down before the laptop and quickly read the message. "Oh my gosh! That is so pathetic! Mom, you're not falling for that, are you?"

It's a good thing Amber had her daughter. For a brief moment Amber really did fall for the new Facebook message and the rose left at the door. "No!" answered Amber. "Of course not!"

Trista continued, "Yeah, this is the sort of thing that a nerdy loser does when he has run out of options. He actually thinks that this little stunt demonstrates a sweet, sensitive, romantic side to him. He thinks it might help you appreciate how desperate he is. That's what he is. He's desperate, Mom. He's turning into nothing more than a psycho-obsessed stalker."

Such a disappointment. Amber never considered these things. Why did Daren have to be this way? To cover her ignorance of modern-day dating, Amber agreed with everything Trista said. "Oh, I know! This Daren obviously has some psychological issues. I don't want someone like that in my life."

But Trista was proactive and offered even more useful information for Amber. "Okay Mom, it's time you understand how the world has changed a little since when you were younger. You know how in reality shows like American Idol how people get voted for which decides whether or not they can stay on the show?"

Amber nodded.

"Okay, that's pretty much how the real world works, now. See, this Daren guy is cheating and not playing by the rules. He is not supposed to be approaching you in private and trying to start a relationship with you. When a guy sends you a private message on Facebook or through personal email, it's a bad thing. He does it because he knows that other people will not approve. He's hoping that you will disregard the advice from your personal council—your friends on Facebook.

This is how it's supposed to work: Once he gets past all of your rejection and somehow figures out how to finally get you to go out with him—*and he is supposed to do this in person, not over Facebook messaging*—you go onto Facebook and request him as a friend. Once he accepts your friend request, you make a post that says something like, 'Looking forward to going out with Daren on Friday night.' Then you tag him in the post.

Of course Daren is going to like it. But he doesn't count! He can't vote for himself! And the same goes for all of his friends. They don't count! You only care about the votes from your own friends. You want to see how many of your own friends actually like your post about going out with Daren. If you get enough people to like it, then you know that people approve of you going out with Daren. If you don't get many likes and a bunch of negative comments, then you might want to reconsider going out with him."

Throughout the lesson of modern-day dating, Amber's facial expression grew increasingly baffled to the point of hardly believing what was being said.

"Mom, this is how it works! I'm telling you! It's just like reality TV. This Daren guy believes that he stands a chance with you. He's auditioning in front of you and it's best to be like Simon on American Idol. Eventually if Simon (you) gives him a yes, it'll be time for America (your Facebook friends) to vote. That's what's so great about Facebook. You have an entire audience that can make serious decisions for you and tell you how to live your life. I mean if you don't understand the rules of TV shows like American Idol and Dancing with the Stars along with social websites like Facebook and Twitter, then you're pretty much a social failure by today's standards."

Poor Amber must have appeared as though her mind had been scrambled. Where did all of these strange rules come from? Did Facebook really play such a crucial role in society, enough to allow strangers to make private decisions for other people?

"It's not a total waste, though." reassured Trista.

Was there still some hope for Amber?

"I guess if you have fantasies of some guy being obsessed with you then it's not so bad. Some women learn to make the most of a stalker. They actually think of an obsessed guy as a trophy and use him to help boost the ego. Think about it: You have a guy who is crazy in love with you to the point of maddening obsession. The best part: he can never have you, despite how badly he wants you. Doesn't that totally elevate your ego and make you feel good?"

Amber thought about it and then laughed. "Trista! That's not nice!"

"Well it's true!" With that, Trista scuffed off to the kitchen. She was a gold mine of knowledge and wisdom pertaining to dating, love and romance. It was most fortunate that Amber had Trista as a daughter. At least someone had it together in the home.

Still, some hidden place within Amber felt won over with the long-stemmed rose and honest Facebook message that asked for her forgiveness. Despite what an obsessed-psycho stalker Daren had become, Amber brought the rose into the bedroom and put it in a small container full of water on her dresser.

* * *

Later that morning in the Jewelry department, Amber sorted through some advertising banners that were to be displayed for the Valentine's holiday. Is this all Amber's life was?—rising early each day to report to a less-than-thrilling management job at the local department store, then to return home in the evening to be alone while pining for Daren's presence? Life was becoming depressing some years after the divorce. Amber was turning older and forced to chase men who did nothing more than play mind games. How she needed someone close; someone real who could restore her sense of pride as well as belief in herself. The only thing Amber had now to boost her ego was some stalker fantasy. There was certainly an obsessed psycho that was madly in love with Amber. But when would it start to feel good?

It can be depressing for a woman to be alone on Valentine's Day, especially when managing the jewelry department and being surrounded by reminders of love and romance. How difficult it suddenly became to hold back the tears. Where was Daren? Why didn't he come to see her? How she longed for the days to return when Daren would visit her at the counter and look for any excuse to just talk to her. Such a good looking man; he would approach the glass while flipping through a massive wad of bills. Apparently he was trying to impress her.

Just then, a fair-skinned, blond, handsome stranger approached the counter. "Excuse me?"

Amber was pulled out of her sad trance of speculations. "Oh, I'm sorry. I was deep in thought. Can I help you with something?"

"Yes I'm looking for a tennis bracelet for my wife." He was dressed in business clothes.

With as lonely as Amber felt in that moment, the stranger's visit was most welcome. "Well, come over to this area. We have a nice assortment. What price range are you looking in?" Now it just so happens that from where the stranger and Amber stood, there was a small swing door that allowed Amber to step out from behind the counter and next to the stranger. This is what Amber did as the stranger explained what he needed.

"I really don't want to go over $500. I mean she's definitely worth it, but it's only Valentine's Day."

Amber returned a questionable look. "Are you sure? *Only Valentine's Day?*"

"Yeah…? Unless you suggest maybe jumping up in price?"

Amber gently placed her hand on the stranger's shoulder. "Let me tell you a mistake men make while shopping for Valentine's Day. They think it's nothing more than a Hallmark holiday and give cheap gifts. Is that what your wife is?—cheap?"

"No, certainly not!"

"Well, then choose your tennis bracelet accordingly."

Both Amber and the stranger now leaned over the glass counter. Amber's arms and shoulders were pressed against his and enjoying every bit of masculine body heat.

"Hmm…" exclaimed the customer. "Maybe I should go with the $1100 dollar bracelet?"

With her face close to the customer's, Amber giggled while displaying her white teeth. She looked so sexy and flirtatious in that moment.

The timing was perfect! As Amber looked up with beaming face, she spotted Daren nervously approaching down the aisle. What the hell was he doing there? Amber was sure to change her happy face to provide a wicked, scornful look. Daren had best stay away! Amber had no need for such a pathetic loser who was nothing more than a silly, psycho-obsessed stalker. Daren was childish, immature, insecure and a complete waste of Amber's time. She was much, too good for him. It was men like the stranger next to her that Amber wished to associate herself with.

Seeing the reality before him, Daren quickly turned around and walked the other direction. Maybe now he would finally get it.

* * *

Later that night was a different story. Obviously the handsome stranger made his purchase early that afternoon, and would probably never be seen again. Another day had come and gone, and Amber found herself—once again—alone in bed without the man she so desperately desired. Why was Daren doing this to her? Why did he continue to play such frustrating mind games? The only thing tangible Amber had at that moment was the long-stemmed rose that Daren left at the door.

Amber briefly got out of bed and reached for her rose on the dresser. After laying back down she brushed the petals against her lips. It certainly smelled like a rose which reminded her of love—deep, red, passionate love. Soon, with eyes closed and in some other place, Amber began to give delicate kisses to the rose petals while imagining that it was Daren's lips receiving them. Could Daren feel the kisses from across town? Would they remind him of how badly Amber wanted him?

Amber lifted her nightshirt and began to tickle her breasts and abdomen with the rose. This is how she wanted Daren to touch her. She wanted him to drive her insane with gentle tickling. And it didn't take long for the tickling to find its way down to Amber's vagina. His delicate touch drove her all the more wild! It was so crazy that she soon needed to reach with her other hand and rub her clitoris.

That's when Amber turned angry and violent. She was tired of experiencing love and sex with Daren this way. She wanted the real thing, but he was only into playing mind games. With the thorns of the stem, Amber began to scratch her inner-thigh while imagining that Daren could feel it some miles away. She raked and raked, allowing the stinging sensation to represent the frustration she felt. While rubbing her clitoris, Amber pulled the thorny stem close to her vagina and allowed it circumnavigate her most delicate and secret treasure. She wanted blood. She wanted the very rose that Daren had given her to shed the crimson of angry passion and frustration from the very place on her body that wanted him most.

The thorns scratched their way up towards Amber's navel. Nearing climax, she pressed harder to ensure that the scratches broke skin.

"You bastard!" Amber loudly whispered. "I hate you, you bastard! I hate you! Why don't you get in this bed right now and be a man and finally take me. I'm sick of the games, you bastard! I hate you! Why can't you be a man and take me?"

Amber's wishes were amplified through the night with peak orgasmic energy and climax. The very sheets where Daren would ultimately grant this wish for Amber had been lightly spotted with her own blood. Just as blood stains are impossible to remove; when shed during sex magick, there is no reversing the wish. And everyone knows that all of Amber's wishes come true.

Chapter 44

It was Valentine's Day, Sunday morning in Mapleview. Just as many Sunday mornings, Loraine Trivelli attended early mass at the Infant of Prague Catholic Church. Like many parishioners, Loraine felt so strongly about the Eucharist and wished to distribute it during communion. This is why she is a Eucharistic minister.

Every Sunday, Loraine Trivelli would greet each parishioner as he or she approached with hands in praying position and prepared to receive the body of Christ. She would announce, "Body of Christ."

The parishioner would acknowledge by replying, "Amen" before taking the host. Many of them, however, had little reverence for this ritual and walked some feet away from the altar before popping the host in his or her mouth. To make matters worse, these people often chewed and chewed as-if the host were nothing more than a Ritz cracker! That's no way to take the body of Christ!

But then what could be said of Loraine's rare form on Valentine's Sunday? It wasn't bad that she was dolled up in a red dress with a silk, red scarf around her neck that had rose print. It was unusual, however, in the way she greeted parishioners who approached for a host. Rather than announce, "Body of Christ"; Loraine simply smiled and wished, "Happy Saint Valentine's Day!" and then presented the host!

It definitely threw parishioners for a loop! How does one say, "Amen" to that?

After mass, Loraine Trivelli stopped at the Sillmac bakery to pick up some Valentine's pastries and a nice poppy seed cake. Then she visited her lovely niece at the historic Trivelli house.

Daren was upstairs taking a shower.

"Happy Valentine's Day!" greeted Aunt Loraine as Mary opened the door. The two hugged, and then Mary was given a poppy seed cake for her and her husband to enjoy.

"So are you and Daren going to church this morning?"

"As always, Aunt Loraine. We go to the nine o'clock mass every Sunday."

"So did you go out last night for dinner?" asked Aunt Loraine.

"No, we're going out tonight, instead."

"Oh, you'll probably get your Valentine present later today."

That's when Mary decided to show off her early present. "I got my first one yesterday afternoon. Check it out." She signaled Aunt Loraine to follow into the kitchen.

Aunt Loraine gasped at the new appliance. "You got a new dishwasher?"

"Yup, it's the practical gift. The sentimental gift is later today."

Aunt Loraine shook her head, "Well, aren't you Mrs. RB?"

"Mrs. RB?" inquired Mary. "Who's Mrs. RB?"

Aunt Loraine was quick to answer, "Mrs. Rich-Bitch!"

Mary was flabbergasted "What? Over a dishwasher?"

Aunt Loraine chuckled as-if her name-calling meant nothing.

* * *

Later that evening, Daren and Mary sat at the Mapleview Supper Club in downtown Mapleview. It was originally Daren's intention to treat Mary to dinner at the elegant Perry's Seafood in Sillmac. Unfortunately it slipped his mind to make reservations. He had other things on his mind that week, mostly Amber. And of course, because it was Valentine's Day, many of the restaurants in the area were packed with people. The Mapleview Supper Club was the only decent place that could accommodate Mary and Daren for the evening.

Mary didn't seem to mind. Enjoying a family style dinner of fried chicken, mashed potatoes and green beans at long tables suitable for a wedding at the VFW hall while seated next to other strangers in town wasn't so bad. Besides, she sported her new diamond bracelet—the sentimental gift from Daren. (Of course he didn't purchase the bracelet from the jewelry department where Amber worked!)

What did bother Mary was Daren's behavior. Although he talked to her and exhibited his usual caring, loving self; Daren was a bit distant in recent days. There was something wrong. Mary could sense this. There was something going on in the background of Daren's life.

"Daren, what's wrong?" Mary finally asked. "You're just not yourself. Something is really bothering you."

"Nothing! Why do you keep asking me that?"

"I don't know; you're just distant from me. I mean you talk and interact with me, but it feels like something is going on in your life that I'm not aware of."

Daren sighed, "No, everything is okay. I guess I'm just a little disappointed that I overlooked reservations. I really wanted to treat you to Perry's in Sillmac."

"Oh, don't worry about that! It just slipped your mind, that's all. Besides, you know I like fried chicken. I like the Mapleview Supper Club. You got me a new dishwasher and this nice tennis bracelet. Are you sure that's all that's bothering you?"

Daren nodded, "Yeah, plus I'm just a little tired. It's February and I want spring to come."

But this was a lie! Daren knew why he was so distant. The current situation between him and Amber was terribly nerve-racking. What was it about her? Amber was so much different than the other women. She was strong. She possessed a certain power. The other women were uneasy and a bit fearful of Daren which made everything easy for him. But Amber had a mysterious control over Daren. And as the time went on, Daren couldn't help but believe he was falling in love with her.

The truth: Daren was so spell-bounded with Amber's magick that he was beginning to question his marriage. He was beginning to consider that perhaps he no longer loved Mary. For now, Daren was merely going through the motions.

* * *

It was all caused by Amber's personal brand of sex magick. Even Amber didn't understand the full spectrum of her will that was being imposed on Daren. You see, from the very, first time that Amber saw Daren's Facebook page; she hated the happiness that he and Mary appeared to share. She wished so strongly to ruin them. Amber wished to hurt young and beautiful Mary and steal her husband. After all, why should a woman like Mary have a husband and not Amber?

Later that night, Trista awoke from some very strange and disturbing noises in the attic. What in the world was Mother doing, now? Trista pulled the pillows over her head and struggled to go back to sleep, for she wished not to know the truth. Mother had truly gone crazy! It sounded as-if she walked around on the hardwood floors with high heels. There were popping sounds that one would immediately conclude to be the sounds of balloons bursting. Whatever Mother was doing, Trista wanted no part of it! And she suspected that the activity had something to do with that creepy guy who was after Mother.

And right Trista was! She would have been frightened to know how precise and accurate her visions were. Upstairs, Amber walked the hardwood floors in a slow and sexy gate that swayed her bare ass. She was completely naked with the exception of stiletto high heels. The electric lighting was off and replaced by several candles throughout the attic. There were six mirrors positioned at various places so that Amber could observe her reflection while walking. And on the floor were a few dozen inflated, elongated balloons.

Amber was sure to telepathically link herself to Daren while performing this strange ritual. In observing her naked, sexy reflection in the mirrors; Daren was permitted to receive the telepathic images. And each time a balloon had been popped under the sharp point of high heel, Amber imagined it to be Daren's excited penis.

"Pop… pop… pop…" Although Daren might have gotten aroused with all the sexual tension between them, Amber was sure to mutilate and diffuse a possible erection from Daren. He couldn't have Amber, no matter how badly he wanted her. She had the ability overpower Daren in such a way that erections were impossible.

Just down the street and up Mapleview Road; through the historic section of Mapleview, and inside the legendary Trivelli house; Daren sat naked on the side of the bed with head buried in his hands. Mary lay naked under the bed sheets with a very concerned and disappointed look on her face. Tonight was the first night that Daren had been unable to perform in bed.

"Daren, is there someone else?" Mary whispered.

Daren nearly shouted in return, "No! I just can't get it up tonight! I'm tired or something."

"Well maybe you need to go to the doctor."

"Mary, I'm fine! It's just late, I'm tired, and I'm kind of at a low right now with things being slow at work."

Mary sighed, "Why do I think there is someone else? Are you sure you're not cheating on me?"

"I wish you would stop thinking that, Mary!"

Chapter 45

Guardians, guides, messengers and gurus; in the spirit realm there are councils in place that oversee the numerous, daily affairs of magick in the physical realm. You can think of them as saints who once devoted their lives on Earth to the art of magick, and continue to provide positive guidance to those who now grow within this art. One of their functions is to ensure that danger does not happen to people who expose themselves to magick. And they communicate with us in all sorts of ways. If needed, they sometimes manifest themselves in the faces of other people and transmit their information through facial expressions while using telepathy. They don't actually possess the living person that they borrow. Think of this phenomenon as casting a reflection of one's self onto another's. The person serving as the mirror is none the wiser. He or she might smile or produce an intense facial expression towards the intended recipient, but never realize that this was done.

Could this phenomenon be used to describe what appeared to be Jim's meaningful encounter with Amber's sister? She certainly appeared to have something important to tell Jim. Or did she really? Perhaps she merely recognized him as one of the friendly faces in town; and beyond that wanted nothing to do with him.

What if a guide from the spirit realm were assigned to Jim to steer him out of danger? What might this person be experiencing throughout this assignment?

She probably sits outside his home and watches him get into the cable van each day while shaking her head and sighing. "He's just not getting it! What am I going to do?"

Maybe she favors Amber's supposed sister. She might like this woman's overall appearance and style. Perhaps Amber's sister even reminds the guide of herself when alive on Earth.

Doesn't this theory make sense? What, after all, could Amber's sister want of Jim?

Chapter 46

Is there really a difference between a violin that costs—say—$75 and one that costs around $300? If your child were serious about school orchestra, you would certainly consider this.

Mapleview isn't as prestigious as the neighboring town, Sillmac. The average population in Mapleview consists of the working middle class. But this doesn't mean that parents of an orchestra student couldn't afford a $300 violin. Some actually do purchase a violin at this price. And some see nothing wrong in giving their child a $75 violin for school orchestra. Many other parents simply opt to lease the musical instruments through the school for a reasonable cost. This means that the lease agreements are renewed each year.

Now you would think that a lease form would simply be sent home to be filled out, check enclosed and returned for the following school year—provided the student wants to resume orchestra. But those in charge of high school orchestra saw this as an opportunity to discuss and encourage parents to participate in the upcoming fund raiser, ask for personal donations to help offset the operating costs of next year's orchestra and even request volunteers for various functions. The grueling evening included Power Point slides with graphs and pie charts that were seriously unnecessary and created by people who were simply proud of the fact that they could make nifty graphs and charts. It could be considered one of the most boring meetings that a parent would have to attend. And to make matters worse, it was mandatory!

Kimberly was aware of this mandatory meeting to be held on the Tuesday evening of February 23, 2010. But she knew all too well that her body would be under attack by a terrible fever. Her only option was to plead with Jim that he attend.

Kimberly asked her husband, "I know you need to go to bed early. I know you've been working all day in the cold and are probably tired. But I can't make it, Jim. Could you go tonight?" Kimberly asked her husband this over dinner. Tonight she gathered as much strength as possible to simply make Hamburger Helper for her family. For years she prided herself in creating only the finest home-cooked meals for her family; pot roasts, homemade chili, stuffed cabbage rolls, pork chops and steaks—a real modern day Donna Reed. But in recent times, she found it convenient to throw together the ingredients from a box. Kimberly just didn't have the strength to cook as she normally did.

Jim was understanding, of course. And he was more than happy to attend the orchestra meeting that Tuesday night. "Of course I'll go, Honey. You've been working and slaving all day and you're sick. You need to rest on the sofa and get better. I'll go; no problem!"

Kimberly was so fortunate to have a wonderful husband like Jim. She vowed to make it up to him when finally better.

But little did Kimberly know that Jim had extra motivation for attending the meeting. You see, Jim was in the middle of his spicy sex magick love affair with Ekaterina. And if you recall, Ekaterina was the orchestra teacher at Mapleview Community High School. Jim couldn't imagine her doing anything that would reveal the taboo relationship to Kimberly. But what if? What if through purely unintentional means, Jim's wife discovered the terrible secret through nothing more than intuition? Women can do this. Women know everything!

You can understand why Jim was so eager to attend the boring meeting that night! He did, however, fear a slight "catch 22". He hadn't seen Amber in many weeks. Being that Trista was in the orchestra, Amber would surely be there. This would be a most-awkward encounter. How does one deal with a mistress that was simply abandoned with no offered explanation?

The meeting that night was to be held in the high school gymnasium. Upon entering, Jim noticed that Amber had yet to arrive. He sat some distance away from his usual location and waited nervously for Amber to enter the gymnasium. It was going to be an interesting evening, indeed! For tonight, the dumped mistress would quite possibly learn of her replacement—Ekaterina.

But what was this? Some moments after Jim sat down; Amber's sister entered and chose a seat. And if Jim didn't know any better, it would appear that she developed a recent fascination with him. She removed her jacket; combed her fingers through the side of her long, radiant-red hair and then shook her head ever so slightly before turning to face Jim.

Jim was stunned! What in the world was this woman doing? Her tight blouse and dress slacks revealed that Amber's sister had quite a nice body. She certainly was attractive with her deep-brown eyes and radiant-red hair. And now she flaunted a wave of sexiness towards Jim?

"You've got to be kidding me!" Jim thought to himself. "Was she really just doing that? That had to be my imagination." Jim speculated that perhaps Amber sent her sister that night as a scout or a messenger. Maybe Amber was desperate for Jim to come back, but hesitant in contacting Jim directly. Being that sisters can be very close; Amber's heart might have been visually and undeniably broken which left her no choice but to disclose to her sister her dark secret. Aware of Amber's sad heartbreak, Amber's sister might have offered to attend the meeting to be the messenger and encourage Jim to come back.

It's funny how men develop such over-swollen egos. Too bad he didn't know the real truth about Amber!

Twenty minutes later, the meeting finally started and the master of ceremonies approached the podium. "Ladies and gentlemen; I want to thank everyone for taking time out of your busy work week and joining us this evening. I'd like to begin the evening by introducing you to someone that we all certainly know; the very talented Mapleview Community High School orchestra teacher, Ms. Ekaterina Lutrova."

The audience applauded. But then it seemed to prematurely diffuse as Ekaterina stood and faced the podium. Of course applauds always diffuse as a speaker stands before the microphone. But there was something eerie, almost frightening in that moment. Where was Ms. Lutrova? The woman standing before the audience did not look like the Ms. Lutrova that people remembered.

"Good evening!" Ekaterina greeted her audience. "I just want to mention what a joy your young men and women have been to teach this year."

There was something youthful and beautiful about Ms. Ekaterina; a far cry from the crazy, old woman who usually wore faded, black dresses and appeared to bathe but once a week. What happened to her? Did she recently have cosmetic surgery? Was she receiving some radical hormone therapy?

Ms. Lutrova continued, "In a moment we are going to pass out the forms for instrument lease renewal. But we also want to use this time as an opportunity to discuss the financial state of our Mapleview Community High School orchestra."

Instead of deathly strands of split gray hair, Ekaterina had a full head of long, beautiful, black hair. It was shiny and healthy; shimmering under the flood of overhead lights. And once old, weathered and wrinkled; Ekaterina now had a smooth, collagen-enriched face with only a few lines to reveal a bit of age. She even dressed like a younger woman.

Her shocking, new appearance was enough to startle even Jim. What was happening to Ekaterina? Was Jim seeing things correctly?

And that's when Amber's sister turned her head towards Jim. Is this why she came, tonight?—to warn Jim that he was in danger. Jim was engaging in an activity with dramatic consequences, and Ekaterina's new appearance was proof. He helped her reach this new state of existence by being tricked into participating in sex magick!

Unfortunately, Jim did not understand this. Instead he interpreted the facial expression from Amber's sister as a desperate call to return to Amber. It's tragic how a man's over-swollen ego can distort some much-needed truth.

Chapter 47

Sex magick was about to finally pay off for Amber. It was Wednesday evening, her scheduled night that week to work late as the acting manager of the Mapleview Department Store. Now 9:37pm, she let the last employees out of the building and then set the alarm so she could lock up.

For being only the middle of the week, Amber was exhausted and couldn't wait to go home. It was as-if some mysterious energy drain was sucking the very life out of her. Maybe it was all those nights of strange, sexual rituals in the attic while desperately pining for Daren. Tonight, however, she only wished to change into her comfy pajamas and slip into bed.

Ah, but wishes are granted in the order they are made. And in recent times there were some serious wishes being made that were driven by strong emotions. What was that little wish that Amber had made; to mysteriously run out of gas and then be rescued by Daren? Well guess what? Shortly upon exiting the parking lot of the Mapleview Department Store, there is block of desolate terrace that isn't well lit at night. It's hidden by a berm on one side with businesses on the other side that shut down early in the evening. For all practical purposes, Amber was hidden and alone. It was in this moment and in this place that her engine abruptly died in the middle of the road.

"No! Come-on! Not now!" Amber pounded her open hand on the steering wheel. But this is how wishing and magick usually works. It's when we no longer want them that our desires come true.

Amber pulled out her cell phone for help. But what was this? There was no battery life! She attempted to boot the device, but the screen displayed the empty battery symbol before going dead. There must have been a loss of signal at some point in the evening which caused the phone to continuously search for a network. This, of course, drains the life of the battery. Now what was Amber going to do?

Just as wished in her little "run out of gas on the road" fantasy, a pair of headlights appeared from behind. It was a red pickup truck that quickly pulled up and parked near Amber's Grand Prix.

Amber sighed. It was Daren. He was the last person Amber wanted to see. Apparently the psycho-obsessed stalker had, once again, siphoned the gas out of her tank to play hero. To make matters worse, on a freezing-cold night, Amber was on a dark terrace stretch of road with no one in sight. Without a cell phone, she would have no choice but to accept Daren's act of heroism.

Amber partially opened her driver side window. With the key in the ignition she still had electric.

"Good evening!" Daren greeted with a smile.

"Hi…" returned Amber."I'm stalled again…" Just having to answer Daren made her skin crawl.

"Stalled again? What happened?"

"I don't know. Maybe I ran out of gas?"

"Ran out of gas? Are you sure?"

"I think so."

"It doesn't sound like you are so sure. Why don't let me sit down in the driver's seat? I'll check it out for you."

What was Amber to do? She had been transported in a new reality framework so that she was now stranded out in the middle of nowhere on a cold, winter night. Daren was the only person to help. Reluctantly, Amber hopped over to the passenger seat and allowed Daren to get in.

He cranked the ignition a few times. "Hmm… It looks like you might be out of gas. But how do we know for sure?" Then he looked over to Amber, "I've got a trick I want to show you." Daren opened the driver door and stepped back out onto the road.

Amber imperceptibly shook her head in disbelief. What sort of trick was Daren going to show her? Couldn't he just fill the tank up with the siphoned gas so that Amber could go home?

There was a knock at the glass of the passenger window. It was Daren, signaling Amber to come out.

Once again, she had no choice. Amber was under complete control at this moment and reluctantly did as ordered.

Daren stood near the gas tank with what appeared to be a long length of wire. "It's a little invention of mine that I call the tank-snake. Let me show you how it works." Daren opened the fuel door and unscrewed the gas cap. Then he began to unravel the length of wire while sticking it in the tank. Several minutes passed as Amber stood in the freezing cold and shivering while watching Daren struggle with wire.

"Almost… almost… I think I've got it… Ugh, that's not right."

Freezing beyond belief; very tired and wishing to just go home for the night; Amber finally asked with a slight note of irritation, "Can I ask what it is you're trying to do?"

Daren returned a look of surprise. "Well I'm trying to get this wire in your gas tank."

"Why?"

"Well, once I get it in there I'll be able to see if it's dry. Think of the wire as a dip stick for gasoline."

Amber had enough! "You know, I'm pretty sure I'm out of gas! Don't you have some in the back of your pickup truck that you can refill in my tank?"

Daren continued to futz with the wire. "No, this time I don't have any gas. If your tank is empty, I'll have to get some for you. Sorry!"

This was unbelievable! What sort of stunt was this psycho-obsessed stalker trying to pull, now? If Amber didn't know any better, Daren was deliberately taking a long time to play with the wire in the gas tank just to watch her shiver in the cold.

"There we go! I reached the bottom!" Daren next pulled the wire out of the tank. When fully removed he exclaimed, "Ah-ha! See that?" He showed the point of the wire to Amber. "Look at that!"

Unfortunately, it was necessary for Amber to play this little game of Daren's. She looked at the wire as Daren ordered and knew his experiment demonstrated an empty gas tank.

"See, the wire is dry. Now if I pulled it out and it was wet with gasoline, this would have meant that you had gas in your tank. But it's not. It's dry. This means your tank is empty. Did you forget to fill your tank?"

Amber returned a dirty look. This little game of Daren's had gone far enough. He was the one who siphoned the gas from her tank. How dare he suggest that Amber was too dimwitted to prevent running out of gas?

But Daren didn't care. He was playing hero for the night and courageously suggested, "Well, I guess we better get some gas for you. Come on, my pickup truck is warm inside."

Despite how Amber's fingers and toes were numb while shivering from the freezing, February air; the last thing she wanted to do was get into the Daren's pickup truck!

It didn't take long for Daren to realize this. Immediately he argued, "Uh-uh! No way am I leaving you alone on a dark road in the cold. Get in the truck!"

Amber stood motionless. Was this really happening?

"Come-on!" he nearly yelled. "I don't have all night. Let's get you some gasoline."

And so Amber reluctantly walked over to Daren's pick-up truck and climbed into the passenger side. Just as promised, the inside was toasty warm and felt so good! Maybe this was symbolic of their current relationship. Amber insisted on keeping her distance from Daren and remained in the unbearable cold. But maybe finally surrendering to Daren would prove to feel good—warm in a metaphoric sense.

Daren drove off and head towards Mapleview Road. The ride was mostly silent between the two of them until he passed up a gas station. Why didn't he stop? That's when Amber asked, "Where are you going?"

"I've got three containers of gas back at my place." answered Daren. "I usually drive around with them, but I left them at home tonight."

It sounded like a reasonable answer. But then Amber knew Daren had siphoned the gas, nearly a full tank from her car. Why did he bring them back to his house? What did he have in store for his victim while playing hero?

Soon they reached the edge of town and entered the old forested section of Mapleview. This was not good! What woman wants to get into a stranger's vehicle late at night and take a drive into the woods? Of course Amber was only experiencing unreasonable anxiety. Daren, as you certainly know, lives in the historic, wooded section of Mapleview.

Daren slowed down and clicked the blinker to turn onto the half-block driveway.

Amber exclaimed, "You live at the Trivelli house?"

"Yup, the one and only legendary Trivelli house! This is where good-ole Grandpa Trivelli murdered his wife back in the 1830s. But don't worry. The house is clean."

Now let's step back for a moment and consider what Daren was doing. He was actually taking Amber to his house where Mary lives! You have to admit;

Daren possessed an incredibly bold side to him. Either that or he was stupid! What man brings a woman of obsession home where his wife happens to live?

Amber couldn't help but notice that Daren pulled the truck only slightly past the halfway point of the driveway. She understood at that moment that Daren's wife was home. He probably wished not to make Amber's presence known.

"I've got three containers of gas." began Daren. "Could you help me carry one of them while I carry the other two?"

Amber nodded, "Sure…"

"But you have to be quiet. Try not making any noise, okay?"

Again, Amber nodded. She assumed herself to be safe with Daren's wife in the house.

The two of them slowly walked across the backyard (as-if not to make crunching noises in the frozen snow) and towards a small building that Amber assumed to be a storage shed. At the door, Daren removed the keys from his pocket and unlocked his mausoleum. Inside were two electric space heaters working to ensure that the building was nice and toasty warm.

Both Daren and Amber entered the building. Much to Amber's surprise and concern, Daren closed the door so the two were now alone. It didn't take long for Amber to realize what the building is.

"Is this a mausoleum?"

"Yup! It was a little weekend project."

"So there's no one dead in here, right?"

Daren paused, "Well, I wouldn't say that. That crypt over there is where the late Mary Trivelli… excuse me… Grandma Trivelli has been put to rest. As for her husband; let's just say that he doesn't belong here."

Needless to say, Amber wasn't exactly thrilled with standing in a family mausoleum late at night with a deceased occupant. She strongly urged, "Okay, let's get the gas cans and get out of here!"

But Daren had other plans. "Wait! Let me show you my favorite crypt." He proceeded to unlock the crypt nearest the entry door.

"What the hell are you doing?" Amber had enough for one evening and was falling deeper and deeper into anxiety. She was locked in a mausoleum with her psycho-obsessed stalker, and he was unlocking one of the crypts.

"Don't worry! Relax! This won't hurt one bit."

Amber had to get out of there! If she could just get past the door and out into the backyard she could scream and wake up Daren's wife. This is what she tried to do while dashing over to the door.

But Daren stopped her. He was bigger, much stronger and had no intention of allowing Amber to escape.

"I'm leaving! Let me go!"

Daren shoved her towards the rear wall. "We're not going anywhere, yet. Let me just show you this." With the crypt open, he reached inside and pulled out two bottles of beer. Then he handed one to Amber. It was ice cold and probably just the thing that Amber needed.

But Amber put the beer down on the bench. "No! I'm not drinking with you! And let's go! I want to get out of here and get home."

With his thick and muscular body standing before Amber's, Daren picked up the beer and opened it. Then he handed it back to Amber. "Drink! And sit down!" He forced Amber onto the bench with the ice-cold beer in her hand. And there was worse. Daren immediately sat next to her—not side by side, but straddled so that he faced her and stared at her.

In this moment, Amber shut down. She didn't like Daren, and didn't appreciate being ordered around by him. Now she was trapped with nowhere to go.

"We're not going anywhere." Daren took a swig of his beer. "This is my little club house, and I guess this is the only way that I can meet a beautiful woman like you for a drink. You put up quite a fight, you know?"

Amber remained motionless, nearly in a catatonic state. Where was her power? Where was her ability to wish for things to come true? Would no one come to Amber's rescue?

Daren took another swig of his beer. "So, I don't know if you've checked your Facebook inbox, but I've been sending you messages. Have you gotten any of them?"

For the first time in over a minute, Amber turned to face Daren with a bitter expression, enough to cause one to immediately combust. What was Daren thinking? Of course Amber had been receiving the messages! But Amber didn't need to reveal this. It should have gone without saying.

"Oh, I see. You got them, but you weren't going to reply to me. You're one of those types of women."

Daren removed his coat and then lifted off his sweater so that his thick and bare chest, shoulders and arms were exposed. "Man, it's getting warm in here."

Then he stood up. "I have something for you." He reached into the open crypt and pulled out a long-stemmed, red rose—the same type of rose that had been left at Amber's door. Bare chested, he carefully approached Amber and held it out. "I left one of these at your door one morning. I assume you got it, but never bothered to thank me."

Amber remained motionless, holding her unwanted beer with eyes fixed to the floor.

Daren set the rose on Amber's lap. "It would be nice if you thanked me for that; maybe say it was sweet of me."

In defiance, Amber gently knocked the back of her knuckles against the rose so that it fell to the floor.

Daren didn't care. He simply took Amber's beer and set it on the bench. "Man, it's getting warm in here." He proceeded to remove Amber's coat while suggesting, "Why don't you take off your coat and stay a while?"

Amber sprung up from her catatonic state. In that moment she had enough strength to pull away from Daren and jump over to the corner. Then she cautioned, "Stop it! Leave me alone! That's enough! I want out of here!" Amber was serious! She was so serious that she now shouted.

Daren simply met her in the corner and nearly tore the coat off. It was thrown on the floor, and then Amber was pushed back over to the bench. "Have a seat, Amber!" Once again, she was forced to sit down. Oh, she tried to stand back up, but Daren was too, damned strong. He made her sit there. Then he handed the beer back to Amber and sat down, facing her.

"You haven't touched your beer. Why don't you drink it?"

Amber returned to her catatonic state, this time with a face of rage that indicated her to be a split-second from unleashing her violent, wicked side.

"Tell me thank you." Daren ordered. He picked up the rose and placed it back on Amber's lap. "Say, 'Thank you, Daren. Thank you for the rose.' And why aren't you drinking your beer? Drink it!" Daren had enough of Amber's rudeness and lifted the bottle to her face. "Drink! I'm going to pour it on your face if you don't open your mouth."

He wouldn't dare! This is what Amber thought. But much to her unpleasant surprise, cold beer had been dumped on Amber's face. She violently shook her head, did the spit-take and then knocked the bottle out of Daren's hand while exploding with a primordial scream, "Stop it!" She jumped out of her seat and stood up. "You son of a bitch! Stop it! I hate you!"

Daren calmly took a sip from his bottle. "That was cute. I like that side of you. Oh, but look; you've got beer on your blouse." He took another swig of beer. "Take off your blouse."

The evening was turning into nothing less than a sexual assault. Amber's face was red and her eyes equally matched. The nerve of Daren to demand this!

"Take off your blouse! Let's go! Take off your blouse and your bra!"

Of course Amber stood there, hating Daren with all of her heart.

"Come-on! I want to see some tits! I want to see what Amber's tits look like! Take off your blouse and bra." It appeared to Daren that he would need to help Amber. And that's when the violence for the evening began.

Before Amber knew what happened, Daren lunged over and tore her pretty blouse open. He was so strong and it happened seemingly in the blink of an eye. Daren didn't have time to waste playing with unclasping Amber's bra. Like a piece of paper, he tore open the front and then whipped both the bra and blouse off and onto the floor. In equally amazing time, Amber's skirt had been yanked down along with her panties. All-in-all, in less than seven seconds, Amber was completely naked.

"Look at those gorgeous tits!" Daren stepped back and admired Amber's body. "You're beautiful. No wonder I want you!" But rather than take Amber right then and there, Daren walked over to the opened crypt and pulled out another beer. He finished his first and then opened up the second. Then he sat back down on the bench. "I want to check you out for a while."

This wasn't Amber's idea of fun. Feeling humiliated and unfairly exposed, she immediately bent over to pick up her clothes.

"Uh-uh! Leave those alone! Put those clothes down! You are not to put your clothes back on. We are far from done.

Amber covered her breasts and vagina with the bundles of clothing.

"Did you hear me? We're not done!"

But Amber would continue to disobey.

"Actually, I've got a better idea." Daren set down his beer. "I don't think we've established the rules around here." Daren bent down and picked up the rose from the ground. Then he approached naked Amber. "Tell me thank you!"

Amber stared at the ground. He could strip her of her clothes and even rape her. But she would never thank him for the stupid rose!

"Tell me thank you! Let's hear it!"

Amber remained silent.

And just like before, with brute strength and speed, Daren secured both of Amber's thin arms above her head with one hand and then pinched her naked nipple with the other. He pinched and squeezed; enough to make Amber scream out in pain. "Tell me thank you!"

All Daren could hear were blood curdling screams from Amber.

"Come-on! Thank you! Let's hear it! I'll pull it off. I'll pull this freaking nipple right off your tit! It's either 'thank you' or you lose your nipple. Now what's it going to be?" And that's what Daren started to do. He pulled Amber's nipple so hard that her beautiful breast turned into a cone. The very flesh attached to the chest nearly felt like it would rip. He was so crazy, demanding to simply hear "thank you" from Amber's lips.

Even Amber's powers couldn't save her in that moment. She had been dominated, belittled and brainwashed in that moment to the point of truly fearing that she would lose her breast. And that's why she finally gave in. She actually thanked Daren for the rose. "Thank you!" she screamed out.

Daren eased up on the pulling, but maintained the painful hold on Amber's nipple. "What?"

"Thank you!"

"Thank you for what?"

"Thank you for the rose!"

"Who gave you the rose?"

"You did!"

"So who are you going to thank?"

"Thank you, Daren! Thank you for the rose! It was wonderful of you!"

And with that, Daren released his aggressive hold on Amber's nipple and then wrapped his arm around her back. The two of them eagerly kissed like they were starved to be kissed. Soon, Daren released Amber's wrists. But to make sure she understood his control, Daren firmly pressed the thorny rose against Amber's breast while engaging in one of the hottest, steamiest make out sessions ever had in that mausoleum.

It didn't take long for Daren's pants to come off and for Amber's naked body to be thrown on the mausoleum floor. Convulsing and being whipped around like a rag doll that mopped the floor, Amber had the living hell screwed out of her. And when I say screwing, I mean Daren slammed himself in and out like he was angry and severely punishing Amber for being a naughty, cock-teasing, little bitch. That's what she was, a little cock teaser. And that's what you do to a cock teaser! You rip her clothes off, dominate her and then screw the living hell out of her.

Amber could only lie there, screaming and creaming. It's what she needed!

So let this be a lesson to all the young women who consider attracting a man with sex magick, or casting one of those silly love spells. The problem is most women run away and lose interest once a man has been affected. But the spell can never be reversed. He turns crazy and won't stop until he finally has you, even if he has to violate you in a mausoleum late at night.

* * *

About an hour later, Daren and Amber stood on the road near her Grand Prix that had "run out of gas". The two giggled as Daren poured the remaining gas into her tank. And before departing for the evening and going their own separate ways, Daren informed Amber, "Next time we'll do it in your bed, okay?" Then he slapped Amber's ass.

Daren was such a gentleman that he made sure Amber's car started and then watched her drive off. His work was done. Amber had been satisfied. Finally, Daren would have the ability to make love to his beautiful wife.

Chapter 48

It seems everyone was enjoying rough sex in Mapleview! The following afternoon, Jim kneeled in Ekaterina's bed, straddled over her Russian ass while engaging in aggressive doggy-style sex. In recent days, Ekaterina seemed to enjoy rough sex. And she was beginning to cry out unusual poetry in between her vocal expressions of being dominated.

"You the dog! I the bitch!
You the helve! I the axe!
You the cock! I the hen!
That, that I desire!"

It was all beginning to alarm Jim. Only weeks ago, Ekaterina was a crazy, old lady. But from what Jim could see now, Ekaterina was the same age as him. Her sexual emotions were complex. And lately it seemed she was in need of rough sex. Some afternoons she would put up a fight and refuse to become submissive. She wished to be manhandled and dominated, then to have her clothes torn off and coerced into sex. At the moment of submission, Ekaterina appeared to slip into an erotic trance in which she would slowly caress herself while finally being taken by Jim. She would kneel or lay in whatever position Jim had wrestled her into and act as though her aggressor had forced a taboo pleasure onto her. At some point during the sexual encounter—usually before climaxing—Ekaterina would cry out what could have been described as pseudo-poetry, citing that the she and Jim had metamorphosized into savage animals and then cried out for her desires to finally manifest into reality.

If you were a man who observed such bizarre, ritualistic behavior during sex with an older woman, and then witnessed her radical and undeniable transformation into a young woman; would you be alarmed? Jim certainly was! These days of Ekaterina's sex rituals and her undeniable transformation were a turning point for Jim. Since December, Ekaterina had exposed him to an alternate reality in which Vodka could place one into a dreamy trance and make for hypnotic sessions of scrying. There was talk of Jim having a severe deficit in his Karma that could only be repaired by allowing the old, witchy Ekaterina to have sex with him. And now she had changed into someone younger and un-recognizable. Magick happened; Jim participated and he worried that perhaps there were consequences. Was he tricked into all of this?

Chapter 49

It just popped out of nowhere! At least this is how it happened in Jim's perception. Oh, he knew since the before-Christmas office staff meeting that Mapleview Cable was experiencing a lack in customer growth. There were rumors floating around of a possible company buyout and even layoffs. In fact, even the name of the company that would purchase Mapleview Cable was known by some of the people throughout the office. It was a German company by the name of Fernsehen Comm. For weeks the inevitable was unofficially made known to the staff of Mapleview Cable, but only in the "rumor stage". But Jim did everything in his power to ignore the warning signs. It wasn't his focus. No worries for the future and no concerns of what he would do for money if laid off later that year; it was almost as-if Jim didn't care. Of course we all know what was really on his mind. Jim's was preoccupied with things like Amber and Ekaterina. Some people just don't have their priorities right.

It was Friday morning; the time that is reserved for the weekly staff meetings at Mapleview Cable. The entire staff now sat in the circle of chairs in the large conference room. This was nothing new. Ryan the plant manager preferred this seating arrangement as it encouraged everyone in the room to participate. But this morning's meeting officially confirmed everyone's fears of a recent rumor of company takeover in the near future along with possible layoffs. The experienced shock and sudden anxiety by everyone suddenly converted the room into a place for people to hash out their feelings.

The plant manager was of no help. It should first be worth mentioning that outside of the younger cable installers, Ryan was younger than everyone in Mapleview Cable. With only a business degree and no life experience (outside of 1 year of marriage with no children), he still found his way in a high-paying, upper management career. In his mind, Ryan experienced success so quickly because he was so awesome with God-given wisdom that other's around him lacked. In reality, Daddy knew some people who pulled strings to get the job for his son.

Ryan stood in the center of the circle that Friday morning, addressing the staff of Mapleview Cable. "Well, the big day should be July 1st. The Mapleview Cable Company sign will come down. In its place will be the Fernsehen Comm sign. *Fernsehen...* Does anyone know what the word *fernsehen* means?"

One of the installers jokingly suggested, "Beer?"

Another one added, "Yeah, I hear that in Germany, workers are entitled to one beer for every 4 hours worked."

The worried faces throughout the room momentarily lit up while cautiously giggling. Wouldn't it be cool if the German company brought with it such traditions?

Apparently the installers were not so hard hit by the company takeover. It was Ryan's job to make sure that people understood the gravity of the situation. "Beer? Funny! Gentlemen, do you think this is funny? Is this something to joke around about?"

The installers suddenly forced serious expressions on their faces while shaking their heads, no.

Ryan continued, "I mean more than half of the people, if not all of us, are in jeopardy of losing our jobs in a few months. You think this is a situation to joke around about? Come-on, Gentlemen! Grow up!" Then Ryan looked around the room. "Anyone else want to take a shot at it? Anyone know what the word fernsehen means?"

Martha, one of the customer service reps suggested, "Cable?"

"Not quite, Martha. Anyone else?" Ryan looked around the room at the silent faces then softly whistled. "Are we all awake this morning? How about you, Jim? I bet you know what fernsehen means. You look German."

"I don't have a clue." said Jim.

"By the way, Jim; see me after the meeting. I need to talk to you."

Jim nodded.

Ryan continued his discussion of the German word, fernsehen. "Come on, people! Someone might be able to tell me what fernsehen means. No?" Then Ryan shouted, "**It means *television*!**"

The room remained silent, people most likely wondering why they were suddenly being yelled at.

"See, people, this is what I'm talking about! There's a company by the name of Fernsehen Comm taking over in July, and nobody bothered to look the word up. Are we so dismal and apathetic that we don't care anymore? Martha, did you do some research into the company?"

"No…"

"It looks like you've had a bad week, Martha. Did you have a bad week?"

"A little…"

"What was so bad about it?"

"I don't know. The weather is bad out there and angry customers keep calling and yelling about outages. Plus I guess maybe I was a little worried about the company takeover… Now I guess it's true." Poor Martha did everything in her power to hold back the tears.

And that's exactly where Ryan wanted his employee, admitting to being affected by stressful situations. "Shame on you, Martha! You need to remove emotions from business. When you come in those doors each day, you need to put your personal interests aside and think for the team. How would you like it if I came in a little affected by the weather and couldn't run this company? I sacrifice myself each day to come in here and run Mapleview Cable. I put my personal interests aside." Ryan looked around the room. "And the same goes for each and every one of you. Don't let the Fernsehen Comm takeover affect the way you interact with customers and ultimately do your jobs."

After the bizarre staff meeting of officially announcing a company takeover, insulting everyone's intelligence and nearly scolding the employees for being affected, Ryan adjourned the meeting with, "Everyone have a great day!" But today he included, "Jimmy, let's talk in my office."

Jim hadn't a clue as to what Ryan needed to discuss. If costly infrastructure was ever damaged in storms or wear and tear, Ryan would briefly meet with Jim to go over the details for a report. But in recent times, nothing serious had happened with Mapleview Cable infrastructure. Only a couple PC cards were changed in utility boxes or some filters near customers' homes—standard business operations throughout the week.

"Have a seat, Jim. And you're not in trouble. I just need to go over something with you." Sitting on Ryan's desk was a defective 12" x 15" control circuit card that had been replaced from one of the main utility boxes in town. It was to be delivered to the manufacturer's warranty service center for diagnosis and repair. Ryan picked up the paperwork and read Jim's note, "Defective unit.

Powers up but will not boot." Then he looked up at Jim, "Did you swap this card out?"

"Yes, on Monday."

"Did you bother to analyze the card any further and see what might have been wrong with it?"

Being that the control card was under warranty, Jim was not to analyze or troubleshoot any of the components on the card. His job could only go so far as to identify the card being defective and send it off for diagnosis. Jim reminded Ryan of this. "Well all that equipment is under warranty. We're not supposed to do that. Plus we don't have the diagnostic equipment to do that."

Ryan was quick to reply, "You don't need to make up some excuse. Surely you could have done some troubleshooting without altering anything major on this card. Did you do that?"

"No…"

"Let me ask you, Jim; do you know what this card is?"

"Yeah, it's a CAM—a control access module."

"Good! At least you know that much! And did you know that if you go online and type in the model number of this CAM along with the manufacturer, you can find a specification sheet. It even explains how the card boots up and goes online with the main chassis! How about that? And look, I can tell you all about it: the synthesizer clock is delivered to the CPU which immediately boots up. The boot sequence goes through the memory controller, through master-in-serial-out, and then begins to run voltage checks of the digital to analog controllers. Do you even know what that stuff is, Jim?"

You might not know what these things are, but Jim certainly knew! Realizing his intelligence was being insulted, Jim was losing patience. Ryan had a business management degree, not a technical degree (not to mention background like Jim possessed). "Yes, Ryan; I know all about that. I have an electronics degree and had a do a thesis paper on computer hardware boot-up sequence."

"Well you sure could have fooled me! Seeing this report you filled out, it looks like you have no idea what you're doing. I'm thinking of letting one of the installers out there try out the job as lineman tech for a while. I'm going to email you this specification sheet. Read it! Start showing the warranty repair center that we know what we are doing. Try debugging and analyzing these cards!"

Ryan was not done. "So I guess on Wednesday our customer service desk received a call from a very, irate Mrs. Linden. She wanted to watch the Oprah

Show [this was 2010] but her signal had all kinds of grainy lines running through it. Do you remember that call? She said in the process of you being there, her screen went blank for about 10 minutes. She missed 10 minutes of the Oprah Show."

Jim recalled the morning. "Yeah, it was a defective tap. I replaced it and restored service for her."

"Defective tap? Where was this defective tap?"

"It was on the line. I had to replace it."

The answer was not good enough for Ryan. "No, I don't want you tell me that the tap was on the line. I want you to tell me where the tap was at."

Surely Ryan had to understand what this meant. But Jim provided more detail. "It was the tap on her telephone pole in the backyard."

"The tap on the telephone pole in her backyard... Who's backyard, Jim?"

"Mrs. Linden's..."

"And where is Mrs. Linden's backyard? I don't know where Mrs. Linden's backyard is. Do you?"

Jim nodded, "I know where Mrs. Linden's backyard is."

"Where's that, Jim?"

Unfortunately, Jim only knew from memory. He didn't have an exact address, but gave the best answer he could. "It's on the paperwork."

"On the paperwork... You see what I'm getting at? You don't know where that pole is. Is that how we refer to telephone poles around here? The pole behind Mrs. Linden's house... The pole at 123 Mapleview Road... The Pole at 456 Lint Road..."

Jim affirmed, "It's how we've been doing it for years."

"See, Jim; that's what's wrong with you. You've been accepting things for the way they are and just continue to do business that way. I'm not satisfied with calling a telephone pole the pole at 123 Mapleview Road. The other morning I was getting off the exit ramp for Creek Highway and noticed some lettering on the light poles. It said something like N41. I would bet that the highway department has an elaborate system for labeling their light poles and uses latitude and longitude coordinates. I would bet that N41 represents North, followed by some coordinate. Even further, some surveyor or land engineer used some GPS device to pinpoint the exact location of the light pole so that its full name on an infrastructure map is light pole N41.689060 E74.044636. We should do the same with our telephone poles."

Jim agreed, "We could do that. Do you want to hire some surveying company to do this?"

Ryan laughed. "Jim! Let me ask you something. Was there ever a time in your life that you took some initiative to make a difference? Probably not; but that's okay. Don't worry; I'm here to be your savior, your guide to help you grow in life and better yourself. I'm just disappointed that you never came in my office and suggested purchasing a GPS device and offered to hit every telephone pole in Mapleview and Sillmac for a better addressing system. Be a change driver! Do something big for the company! Go online and find a reasonable GPS device and I'll approve its purchase. Then get out there and start giving those telephone poles some real names! What do you say about that? Have your eyes finally been opened?"

Jim was silent in disbelief. Did Ryan really think that he had the time to play with a GPS device at several thousand telephone poles? All he could do was answer, "Sure…"

Chapter 50

Although leaving the plant manager's office, Jim had not seen the end of Ryan for that day. And Friday was only about to get worse.

Before heading into the field to do his Friday tasks, Jim sat down in his cubicle and opened the Google Earth desktop application on the PC. If Jim knew of a more efficient way to handle a detailed project, he would certainly do it.

Once Google Earth had been fully loaded, Jim typed in the town Mapleview. If the reader is going to try this, be sure to enter "Fictional Mapleview" for it doesn't exist, except in the fictional town of Mapleview!

What's nice about Google Earth is that maps are presented in detailed satellite imagery. It's possible to zoom in on streets and houses with crystal clear resolution. Being the case, Jim zoomed in on Mapleview Road, downtown, and located a telephone pole. There's another nice feature with the desktop application of Google Earth. While hovering the cursor directly over the telephone pole, Jim looked at the bottom of the screen and took note of the detailed latitude and longitude coordinates. Spending eight hours on a Saturday and Sunday, Jim could very easily follow each telephone pole on Google Earth and reference these coordinates throughout Mapleview and Sillmac. If done as Ryan directed, the project could take weeks.

* * *

A cruise through downtown Mapleview, Jim continued traveling to the southern tip of Mapleview to the very desolate road he had visited on Thanksgiving morning. But don't think he was there to simply connect anonymously to the Internet for purposes of stalking. He had no need for this anymore. Instead, Jim had some legitimate diagnostic tests to perform on that particular utility box.

A load-emulation test involves connecting an Ethernet cable to a debug port in the utility box. On that morning an Ethernet cable from the debug port fed a modem which ran to Jim's laptop in the Mapleview Cable truck. The actual test duplicated heavy customer traffic on the utility box and detected any possible errors or faults with a particular card. Performing this test could predict possible outages months in advance, giving Jim a chance to correct a problem before it appeared. Less than 3 minutes were required to initiate this automated test. Waiting 15 minutes for the test to complete gave Jim a chance to casually browse the Internet. Why not?

Suddenly, there was a loud rap on the driver window of the cable truck! It was Ryan the Plant Manager! What was he doing there?

Using Alt-F4, Jim quickly closed his web browsing page and then opened the truck window.

Ryan asked, "What are you doing?"

"Load-emulation test; I've got this utility box scheduled for today. What's up?"

Ryan wasn't there to answer any of Jim's questions. Instead he asked, "*Load-emulation test*? Why are you doing that?"

"Well all the utility boxes get it done at least twice a year. Friday mornings present the least amount of customer traffic so it's easier to perform."

Ryan walked around the front of the truck to the passenger side and opened the door. It was necessary for Jim to quickly lift his tool belt off the passenger seat for Ryan nearly sat on it!

Ryan next asked, "So show me this so-called load-emulation test of yours."

Jim turned the laptop towards Ryan and showed him the diagnostic screen. "The test takes about 15 minutes to complete. As you can see, there are no errors to report which is a good thing."

Ryan seemed uninterested and quickly changed the subject. "Do you have that specification sheet I sent you earlier?"

"No, it's in email back at the office."

Ryan sighed, "Let me see your laptop!" Once given, he opened a web browser screen and typed in the product and model number of the utility box outside. It provided a specification sheet which Ryan opened. A few minutes later, he turned the laptop over to Jim. "See here: It says you can gauge the general performance of a utility box by pressing the reset button. This will momentarily interrupt power, forcing the chassis to reboot."

A look of horror came across Jim's face. "I wouldn't recommend that!"

"Jim! Come-on! It says in the specification sheet that you should do this!"

Jim argued, "Yeah, but you're going to cause a severe outage and make customers mad. That utility box takes several minutes to fully boot. Even then, it needs to synchronize with all the feeds throughout the area and could take a good half-hour for service to be restored."

Ryan only smiled. "See Jim; this is what I'm talking about. You have to be so negative about everything. I'm going to hit that reset button and you're going to find out that it won't be as bad as you predict. I mean I can't justify wasting fifteen minutes of company time for your little load-emulation test." With that, Ryan opened the passenger door and stepped out to the exposed utility box.

Jim momentarily buried his face in his hands. "My God! What is wrong with that kid? Who gave him this job? I don't want to deal with an outage!"

Jim looked over to the utility box.

Ryan motioned, "come here" to Jim with his finger.

Jim had an urge to answer Ryan's order with a slightly different gesture that used the middle finger. Instead, he opened the driver door and stepped outside to join Ryan.

Once at the utility box, Ryan pointed out the reset button to Jim. "See that button?"

"Yeah…"

"Press it!"

Jim looked at Ryan in hesitation. Apparently the plan had changed. Jim was to be the person responsible for an outage that day!

"Come-on, press it!" Ryan ordered.

Jim did as Ryan ordered and watched in horror as all the lights on the cards blacked out, followed by an audible alarm at the side of the box.

Ryan asked, "What's that noise?"

"That's an alarm, Ryan. It's letting us know that the chassis lost power and all the cards are offline. They have to reboot now."

"Well can we turn it off?"

"Nope! I have to cut the wires to do that. The alarm won't stop until it senses the master control card is fully booted."

A few minutes later, the master control card fully booted which stopped the alarm from squealing.

But then Jim's phone began to sound alerts. "And those are automated text messages that let me know of an outage."

Clearly understanding of the mess he created, the only defense Ryan had at that moment was to act out the role of a business leader. "Automated text messages that let you know of an outage? How much money is the company wasting on that service?"

Jim began to raise his voice. "Well how do you think we handle outages late at night? Those alerts are our first line of defense!"

Ryan wasn't impressed. "I mean how do we know that there is really an outage? You actually trust those text messages?"

Losing patience, Jim finally shouted, "We interrupted power at the chassis! This utility box feeds several subdivisions along with businesses...!"

Ryan calmly interrupted, "Jim... *Jim*... Watch your voice around me. Don't shout at me, okay?"

Jim's cell phone rang. Before answering, he suggested to Ryan, "It's probably the customer service desk, letting me know of an outage." Then he answered, "Yeah...! Yeah I'm over here with Ryan. We had a little problem at the utility box... Give it about a half hour; everything should be back up... okay, bye."

Ryan stepped back and shook his head in disbelief. "So why are we doing this little load-emulation test of yours?"

"It's not supposed to be done like this, Ryan. The automated test isn't nearly as destructive."

Ryan quickly cut Jim off. "Not nearly as destructive? The point is we shouldn't be doing this. I see no reason to come out here and cause a serious outage and possibly lose money just because you're looking for something to do. Did you look into that GPS device?"

"Not yet."

"That's what I want you to do, Jim. You're number one project is to get all the telephone poles properly named and you're to use detailed latitude and longitude coordinates, understand?"

"Yes."

"And I don't want you to perform any more of your load-emulation tests. Are we clear?"

"Yes."

And with that, Ryan turned and walked back to his own vehicle, soon to pull away and look for another employee's day to ruin.

The rest of the day was spent handling a rash of customer service calls that, ironically, were in the area affected by what Jim secretly called, Ryan's outage. And at the peak of these service calls it was necessary for Jim to escape to the woods and join Ekaterina for another session of bizarre sex magick in which he had to play aggressive rape and then watch Ekaterina transform into an animal to recite poetry for all her desires to finally come true. Jim was so close to not fulfilling his daily obligation that Friday afternoon. He was growing increasingly fearful of these bizarre encounters and beginning to suspect that they were spiritually harming him. But then he realized there would be some serious consequence for skipping a day.

Of course after zipping his pants back up and throwing on the winter coat, he discovered a rash of text messages from the office dispatcher. "Could you go over to 1198 Circle Drive…? Jim…? Hello…? Where are you…?"

Friday was a very, bad day!

Chapter 51

Make no mistake about it; Kimberly is a strong woman, both physically and in spirit. Although Dr. Krause showed legitimate concern for Kimberly's chunkiness, the bulk of it was comprised of natural muscle. A fine, German woman's muscular build; God probably made Kimberly for a life on the farm. Strength, endurance and stamina; she wasn't some skinny, wimpy, little lady who falls apart over some trial or tribulation. Aside from an affliction of a super bug, the woman was quite healthy and strong.

But this doesn't mean that the super bug didn't beat her down each day and night. This was more than a virus! This was an illness which brought on some serious life change and stress for Kimberly. Every night her body was under attack by serious fevers. They could reach 104 degrees if not treated by large doses of ibuprofen and laying cold rags on her forehead and various extremities. The spells would begin sometime after six o'clock pm when Kimberly suddenly felt drowsy or as-if sleep walking.

Battling nightly fevers; drugged up throughout the day on a mixture of cold medicines; nearly drowning in her own mucus; wishing for the day when she could enjoy a simple glass of water without the agony of painful swallowing; Kimberly suffered so terribly from the relentless super bug. The muscular aches brought on by nightly fevers had surely taken a toll on Kimberly's strength.

And she was so tired of carrying baskets of laundry up the stairs, pausing half-way to gasp and wheeze, only to push her way up the remaining stairs and collapse. Shortly after lunch one afternoon, Kimberly lay collapsed on the floor with a clean basket of laundry scattered before her. Her heart raced as she desperately attempted to gain control of breathing. Panic-stricken, her difficulty with breathing created terrible thoughts of possibly dying at that moment. What did she do to deserve this illness? She cursed some imagined terrorist who may have bio-engineered the terrible bug that would remain with victims for weeks and weeks. She even cursed some imagined illegal immigrant who would have selfishly carried the super bug into the United States. These were the only things for Kimberly to do in that moment as she gained control of her breathing, converted anxiety to anger and then wiped the tears from her face.

That's when a savior entered Kimberly's life. As she lay there gaining control, Kimberly glanced up at the TV from across the room and immediately noticed that a cable TV talk show featured Samuel Crummings; quite possibly the wealthiest and most successful TV evangelist in American history. He owns three massive churches on the west coast—one in San Jose, one in Los Angeles, and a third in San Diego. Complete with interior, marble walls; dramatic three story cathedral ceilings; impressive stained glass art windows; numerous statues and astronomical fountains; each church takes up enough real estate to accommodate a jumbo shopping mall. And each church rakes in an average of 4.7 million dollars per week from combined donations from around the country. In addition, Samuel Crummings owns an equally impressive Positive Life Transformation commune in the wilderness of Colorado where those in need of spiritual healing can stay until they are all better. This, of course, is provided they have enough financing. But some people have turned to devoting their entire lives and careers to Samuel Crummings and his wonderful religion of Positive Life Transformation.

Along with spreading the word on television, Samuel Crummings' numerous books and seminar tours are another quick and inexpensive way of converting people to become dedicated followers of the Positive Life Transformation. The hope is one day it will be necessary to open several more communes throughout the United States as countless followers will choose to stay and live in spiritual, blissful, happiness and harmony, forevermore.

It was a tetractys on the TV screen that immediately caught Kimberly's attention. A tetractys, in case you are unaware, is a geometric symbol comprised of ten dots arranged in such a way to resemble the alignment of pins in a bowling alley. The number ten is a triangular number for you can stack ten objects in such a way to create a triangle. In addition, there is a believed ancient power with the tetractys for the simple reason that 4 dots, plus 3 dots, plus two dots, plus one dot equals ten. Ten is the only triangular number of this phenomenon.

Samuel Crummings was discussing his Positive Life Transformation model. "It's nothing new, and it's not my invention." he informed the world. "This tetractys has been used by the Pythagorean Society for ages. When done with devotion, following each point guides you through your personal journey of physical, mental and spiritual transformation. Every day you should pray to the forces of the tetractys with this ancient Pythagorean prayer: Bless us, divine number, you who have generated gods and men! Oh holy, holy Tetractys, you that contains the root and source of the eternally flowing creation! For the divine number begins with the profound, pure unity until it comes to the holy four; then it brings forth the mother of all, the all-comprising, all-bounding, the first-born, the never-swerving, the never-tiring holy ten, the key holder of all."

Suddenly, it all made sense to Kimberly. It was her mind and perception that turned the virus into a long-termed illness. By following the points on the tetractys she could develop her perception into ultimate transformation, and finally rid her body of the illness.

And this is why she had purchased one of Samuel Crummings' recent books, Transformation by Holy Ten. It was no easy task, mind you! She really wasn't supposed to leave the house and venture through the brutal Mapleview cold. What if Kimberly had another attack of difficult breathing? But she was in need of milk to mix in the powdered seasoning of Hamburger Helper. (Yes, Kimberly was now feeding her family this easy-to-make dinner at least twice a week.) And as long as Kimberly was out for milk, it wouldn't hurt to stop at the bookstore and head over to the special Samuel Crummings section for one of his books.

* * *

Jim returned home that Friday evening after battling what he called Ryan's Outage. There, sitting on the family room table, was a book with the name of Samuel Crummings in bold print at the top. The picture cover was nothing more than a tetractys, followed by the name of the book, Transformation by Holy Ten.

Jim picked up the book, "What's this?" he asked.

"It's a book I've been reading!" Immediately Kimberly snatched it out of her husband's hands and walked away, apparently with the intention of putting it away.

But Jim was curious. "Samuel Crummings? Isn't he that cult leader out in California who has three money-sucking churches and a brainwashing commune in Colorado for his cult member cadets?"

This threw Kimberly into outrage. "He's not a cult leader, Jim! He's a religious icon! He's cited as one of the most motivational, uplifting people in the world, today!"

Jim shook his head in disbelief. "Kimberly, this guy's church is not Christian. He doesn't even mention the vaguest thing about God. He says nothing in his sermons about the Ten Commandments..."

Kimberly immediately cut her husband off. "As if you have any right to preach about the Ten Commandments! See, this is what I hate about you! **I hate you** because you criticize everything I ever do! You don't understand me or care about me!"

Jim retorted in disbelief, "Kimberly, that's not true."

But Jim's wife stormed away into the bedroom with the book. The sound of the dresser drawer could be heard slamming shut. Then she returned with a furious warning. "Stay out of my private life and leave the things I value as sacred alone!"

Such alarming behavior; it was as-if Kimberly had suddenly gone insane. But, unfortunately, this would be all part of Kimberly's transformation. The writings of Samuel Crummings had anything but a positive effect on Jim's wife.

Friday was a very, very bad day for poor Jim.

Chapter 52

Outside of Kimberly, it seems everyone in Mapleview was enjoying great sex. Maybe it was the wintery cold and a need to snuggle up nice and warm under the blankets to exchange sexy body heat. Whatever the reason; later that night, Amber lay on her back and received what was probably the greatest screw of her life. She was in the very bed where she stimulated her clitoris some nights ago while scratching her delicate flesh with the thorns of Daren's rose—hard enough to draw blood and spot the sheets red—then to wish for Daren's presence under the intense energy of orgasm.

Well, all that masturbaic sex magick combined with blood caused Amber's wish to come true. It was Daren who now lay on top of her, holding her wrists against the pillow and driving himself deep within. Daren was such a strong, hard man and seemingly mesmerized in the moment while manhandling Amber. The experience was almost scary for Amber.

But then I guess he needed to be rough and aggressive with Amber in bed. Amber was certainly no easy catch, and Daren surely had some leftover frustration to take out on the new girlfriend. After the impossible Mexican Hat Dance played with Amber, it's surprising that he now lay in bed with her. What caused Amber to give in a second time, enough to invite Daren into her bedroom? Maybe she really enjoyed what happened at the mausoleum, and could no longer deny her desire for Daren.

As for Daren, Amber was unlike anything he ever had. None of the other women were like her. And Amber was certainly different than Mary; a little more spicy and intense. It was as-if Amber controlled Daren and made him act out such aggression in bed. In fact, Daren was beginning to fall in love with Amber. Who wouldn't?

But this effect and control over Daren would soon be forgotten the following morning as Amber lay sleeping soundly next her newfound lover. Both were naked and surely enjoying sweet dreams of sex after their night of passion.

"Mom?" Trista poked her head into Amber's bedroom. Then she saw the unbelievable sight of who Mother laid up against. "Mom?"

Startled, Amber quickly sat up. Apparently she forgot to set her alarm clock for work. "Oh no!"

"What are you doing?" asked Trista, now in total shock.

"I forgot to set my alarm clock."

But that's not what Trista was asking about. She studied Daren in complete disbelief as he lay there with his thick, muscular, bare chest and strong arms.

Daren stared back at her with an intense, crazy look in his eyes.

"I can't believe you, Mother!" Trista knew who this man was. Mother actually gave in and brought the creepy loser home with her. What was wrong with Mother? How could she have lost all self-respect?

Daren could feel Trista's attempted hex of negative perception. But he didn't care. This was Daren's world and he was much, too strong to be overcome by a young girl who allowed herself to be dictated by silly rules of dating followed in high school. Aside from that, Daren immediately fell in love with Trista and decided at that moment to alter her thoughts so that the feelings were mutual. Most men would understand that Amber's beautiful daughter was still a young girl, and would behave accordingly. But to Daren, Trista was a nubile, young woman who was hopefully still a virgin for purposes of serving the mere pleasure in defloration.

Do you see what horrible things can be welcomed into life with the misuse of sex magick?

Chapter 53

Martha de los Santos; television news anchor in the Mapleview region for over thirty years. In recent times she co-hosts the morning news, the mid-morning talk show and then makes a special guest appearance in the evening for the lottery drawing. People make a joke about Martha de los Santos being the co-host of the morning news. Oh, maybe jealous women throughout the Mapleview area that hate Martha might insist she is only the co-anchor. But everyone knows that Martha de los Santos is the star of the morning news. Martha de los Santos brings the ratings up because she is so, damned gorgeous! Nearing sixty-years-old, the woman has some God-given gift to freeze the aging clock and forever be in her late thirties. She has a curvy body, complete with bursting cleavage that nearly explodes in the camera. Her Hispanic face is pretty with voluptuous lips, perfect teeth, dark and sexy eyes and long, beautiful, black hair.

It was 9:30 in the evening on a Saturday as Jim and Kimberly sat in the family room watching the evening news. It should be mentioned that Jim goes to bed later on weekends, being that he doesn't have to report to the office the following day. If there are any winter outages on a Friday or Saturday night, he can take a nap if tired the following day.

Everything was going well that Saturday evening until the news aired the nightly lottery drawing. Martha de los Santos' smiling face appeared before the camera which slowly backed up so the world could finally see the woman's gorgeous body.

"Oh good!" exclaimed Jim. "It's Martha de los Santos doing the lottery."

Kimberly shook her head and sighed.

"Good evening, everyone, I'm the one and only Martha de los Santos, here to bring you the Saturday night drawing of Lottery. Hopefully you picked out your magick, lucky numbers." As Martha walked over to the Lottery wheel, she offered the Mapleview region a dose of her fortune cookie wisdom for the evening. "It's cold out there and the weather might be bringing you down. But you need to fight the depression. Maybe go for a walk tomorrow. Exercise is good for you... get some fresh air... why be fat, lazy and miserable?"

Kimberly shook her head in disbelief. "Is she serious?" Tonight's insulting advice was similar to Thanksgiving when Martha suggested to people, "I know you want to keep eating and eating and can't stop. The best thing you can do is just push yourself away from the table."

Jim watched under a seeming spell of hypnosis. He was fascinated with Martha de los Santos. As the Lottery wheel went into motion, Jim softly cried out, "Spin those balls, Martha!"

Kimberly returned a bitter glare at her husband.

"And your first number for tonight is 6..."

"Wow!" exclaimed Jim.

"And for your second number, 4..."

"Oh wow! Gimme more, Martha!" Jim nearly begged as-if in pain.

With that Kimberly flipped the channel. "Good bye!"

"Hey, what did you do that for?"

"I hate that woman! I can't stand her!"

"But that's the nightly Lottery drawing!"

"Did you play?"

"No..." Jim had to think of something quickly. "What about the news?"

"We'll go back to it in a moment." reassured Kimberly. "I just refuse to watch my pathetic husband have an orgasm over Martha de los Santos doing the Lottery drawing. I hate that Martha de los Santos!"

* * *

Hate: it's a curious word for Kimberly to use now that she's embarked on the path to spiritual greatness. She hates her husband because she suddenly believes him to be unsupportive of her new path in life. She hates Martha de los Santos for being the irresistible, sexy news anchor. She hates imagined, illegal immigrants who might have brought the super virus into the United States. Who knows what else she hates? In any case, Kimberly has turned into a bitter, angry, hateful woman.

But there was a cure for this negative energy. As far as Kimberly was concerned, Martha de los Santos was responsible for triggering this source of bitterness in her life. She received this realization from a statue outside in the backyard. While gazing outside the window the following Monday morning, she took notice of the weathered statue of Saint Francis near the birdbath and birdfeeder. The patron saint of animal caregivers, and the originator of the famous Prayer of Peace actually communicated to Kimberly of the evil surrounding Martha de los Santos.

Now Jim and Kimberly aren't Catholic, but it isn't uncommon for people to have small statues of this saint in the backyard to watch over the birds and small animals. Aside from that it's important to understand that Saint Francis would *never* communicate disturbing, untruthful information to people. If anything, a harmful spirit from the dark side might have wrongfully reflected itself off this statue to provide Kimberly a horrible course of action regarding Martha de los Santos.

Martha de los Santos was an evil witch-of-a-woman who had lived her reign of power long enough. There were countless housewives in the Mapleview area like Kimberly who had suffered enough because of this sexy news anchor. Being that Kimberly had knowledge of the ancient, Holy Tetractys, she was empowered and directed to destroy Martha de los Santos.

Kimberly was to create a metallic representation of the Holy Tetractys and use it against Martha de los Santos in a means to destroy her. The sooner, the better. And no one would be the wiser as the unseen Forces of Ten would ultimately lash out and put an end to Martha de los Santos.

The plan was easy for Kimberly. Shortly after her husband and kids left for the day, she reported to the kitchen to create a magick tetractys. It was nothing more than a sheet of aluminum foil which had been folded several times for thickness, and then further formed into a triangle. Afterwards she poked holes in precise locations where the ten points of the tetractys should be. And she was sure to trim and clear the holes as neatness certainly counted. Satisfied that a magick tetractys has been created, she placed the item on the coffee table in the family room next to a candle, a book of matches, and a pair of needle nose pliers.

By the time the necessary items were gathered for this magick ritual of retaliation, it was 9:07am and already time for the midmorning talk show that featured Martha de los Santos. She laughed and joked with the interviewed guest who just so happened to be a handsome gentleman. Being the case, Martha exhibited her well-known flirtiness as this was expected from her.

Seeing Martha de los Santos in full form sickened Kimberly. She hated the woman and wished to destroy her. Kimberly immediately lit the candle and then picked up her magick tetractys. While watching Martha de los Santos in action on the TV screen, Kimberly called to mind all the horrible things that the sexy news anchor ever caused. You see, as Jim watched Martha de los Santos night after night on TV, his desires had been broken down and finally released so that he attempted to start an affair with "that woman" down the street (Amber). And to some larger extent, it was even Martha's fault for Kimberly's recent sickness. All the anger, all the hate, all the jealousy and all the bad things that Martha had ever caused were transferred onto the magick tetractys. Riding along with it were the countless allegations of other women throughout the Mapleview region who had suffered because of Martha de los Santos. That tetractys was filled with so much energy!

When the item was fully charged with negativity towards the news anchor and very close to exploding in the family room, it was held in the flame of the candle with needle nose pliers. At that moment, Kimberly called upon the Spirit of Fire to reach out and deliver the justly-delivered retaliation to Martha de los Santos.

"Burn her! Burn that bitch! Destroy her! Give Martha de los Santos all that she deserves!" To amplify her wicked desires, Kimberly recited the ancient Pythagorean Prayer of the Tetractys, "Bless us, divine number, you who have generated gods and men! Oh holy, holy Tetractys, you that contains the root and source of the eternally flowing creation! For the divine number begins with the profound, pure unity until it comes to the holy four; then it brings forth the mother of all, the all-comprising, all-bounding, the first-born, the never-swerving, the never-tiring holy ten, the key holder of all."

The prayer further built up Kimberly's negativity towards Martha de los Santos. At that moment in time the family room nearly exploded from all the forces that Kimberly had conjured up. Then she spoke directly to the flame for her wishes against Martha de los Santos to finally be delivered. "I hate you! I hate you will all my heart and soul! Burn! Burn you bitch! **I... Hate... You!**"

The charred magick tetractys shook in the flame from Kimberly's convulsing hand. Samuel Crummings taught her well. The man was truly an inspiration with the power to change the lives of those in need. Samuel Crummings would certainly be proud of Kimberly.

Unfortunately, Martha de los Santos must have been wearing an amulet of protection that day. This is the only explanation Kimberly had for the unexpected reverse effect of her magick ritual of retaliation. But between you and me, those councils of spirits who oversee the affairs of magick might have been teaching Kimberly a lesson.

Just like every day, Collin was the first to come home that afternoon. But on this day he immediately complained that he was not feeling well. "Mom, I've got a stomach ache. It feels like I have to go diarrhea, but it's stuck."

This immediately alarmed Kimberly. "When did it start?"

"I don't know... early... about nine..."

That would have been around the time that Kimberly performed her ritual against Martha de los Santos. Did the energy somehow become misdirected and find its way onto poor, little Collin? Kimberly knelt down and placed her ear against Collin's belly. "Let me listen to your tummy..."

Inside Collin's belly the sound of churning and gurgling could be heard. Then it made a loud growl. The sound immediately sent a wave of panic through Kimberly. She knew from ancient knowledge that when the stomach makes unsettling noises, it's actually an evil spirit that somehow finds its way in. As Kimberly listened more, she further surmised that the spirit was the Devil and had manifested itself in the form of a snake. For all practical purposes, Kimberly's magick ritual of retaliation had impregnated little Collin's digestive tract with an evil serpent. That Martha de los Santos was an unstoppable bitch! Damn her! Damn that woman for causing such a terrible misfortune to a small child.

For now, however, Kimberly had to do something to rid little Collin of the Devil. She was, after all, partly responsible for it being there.

"Go sit on the toilet." Kimberly ordered. "I'm going to get you something to get rid of your stomach ache."

Now I'll spare the reader the unpleasant details. You really don't care to know them. But five minutes later, Collin had been given a rectal suppository to stimulate his digestive tract.

"Wait a few moments and try to go poopie, okay." softly ordered Mother. She rolled up a bath towel and wedged it between Collins abdomen and thighs. "Crunch down so that the pressure pushes your poopie out."

Little Collin grunted. Then he looked up with a pale face. "Mommy, I don't feel so good."

It was the Devil. The Devil was fighting the suppository and refusing to come out. While keeping calm, Kimberly ran a washrag under cold water and then used it to sponge down Collin. "Feel better?"

Collin nodded, "A little..." Then his tummy loudly gurgled.

The sound sent an intense wave of panic through Kimberly. "Collin, listen to me." She came close to her son's face. "You have to push, okay. The Devil is inside of you. Mommy did something early today to punish someone, but they somehow managed to give it to you." Kimberly broke down into tears and nearly shouted, "Please push, okay!"

Now frightened, little Collin joined his mother in crying. "Okay!" He grunted and pushed with all his might. "I can't, Mommy! It won't come out!"

"Keep trying! Don't you understand? There's an icky snake inside of your tummy! That's what the Devil is. It's an icky snake that wants to hurt you!"

Collin wasn't fond of snakes and imagined one slithering around inside of him. He nearly jumped off the toilet, screaming in terror. "I can't Mommy! Help me! Help me get rid of it!" While being forced to remain on the toilet seat by Mommy, he stamped both his feet to work off the anxiety.

Suddenly, massive flatulence could be heard from the toilet bowl. It was the Devil announcing a soon arrival. Kimberly screamed and wished to run out of the bathroom. But no mother abandons her child in such a dark moment. The ugly serpent birthed itself into this world in such an unmentionable mess. But it soon transformed into a lifeless, biological matter that is more commonly known as diarrhea. It was the only thing that now sat in the toilet bowl as Kimberly and little Collin cried. Thankful that the terrifying ordeal had ended, the matter was flushed down.

See what happens when you do evil magick and wish bad things against other people? It comes back to haunt you! For Kimberly, it impregnated her son with an evil serpent in his digestive tract to be born as lifeless diarrhea. So don't do evil magick!

Chapter 54

It was Monday afternoon—the first day of March—and nearing five o'clock as Daren sat on Amber's family room sofa. No one was home; it was only him. You see, Amber had fallen so much in love with Daren that she felt it appropriate to give him a house key. It wasn't necessary for her to be home if Daren wished to come over. Besides, in Amber's world, Daren was as good as her next husband which also meant that her house should also be his (emotionally speaking).

But it wasn't Amber who Daren waited for! In some twisted fantasy he now imagined himself as Amber's husband who also adopted her beautiful daughter. In all the filthy websites he visited, Daren often wondered what it was like to marry another woman who had a totally-hot teenage daughter. Such a circumstance would be likened to inheriting an additional sex partner to help spicen up the love life. For that matter, Daren suddenly fancied himself as Trista's stepfather, and had every intention of launching an illicit and underage affair with her.

Just then, the key could be heard opening the front door.

Daren remained seated with a calm face, perhaps smiling to himself on the inside.

Seconds later, Trista walked through the front door and was surprised; not exactly happy at Daren's presence.

"Hi there! Welcome home!" greeted Daren. He remained on the couch.

"Where's my mom?" asked Trista.

"Oh, she's not here. I assume she'll be home in a little bit."

Trista softly sighed and shook her head in disgust. What was Daren doing there? And just how safe could she feel being alone with someone so creepy? Trista would definitely have a word with Mother, later.

"So do you always get home from school this late?"

"Excuse me?"

"Well it's after five o'clock. That's kind of late for coming home from school."

Trista removed her coat and pulled off her boots. "I have orchestra practice plus I stopped at the library afterwards."

"The library? Why? And were you with anyone?"

That's when Trista decided it was time to draw the line and set some boundaries. "That's none of your business! And don't you have a wife waiting for you at home?"

Daren laughed and stood up. "Trista, Trista! What's the problem? Why get so defensive?" Then he approached Trista while continuing, "I was just concerned about you, that's all. Your mother and I are getting close, and naturally I see you as my daughter. Is that such a bad thing?" Now close to Trista, Daren rested his hand on her shoulder.

Trista jerked her shoulder away and walked around Daren to get to the kitchen. This was not good! Apparently Daren felt it every bit his right to invade Trista's personal life, even touch her.

Slowly and carefully Daren followed some distance behind and watched Amber's daughter with such vile lust in his heart. She was his, as far as Daren was concerned, and seconds from being taken right there!

But it was the sound of the garage door opening that put an end to a soon-to-be dangerous moment. Amber was home; Mother was now here to protect her girl from Daren. He had no choice but to walk back towards the family room and wait for his fantasy wife to enter the house. Sex with a fantasy stepdaughter must be done in secret for fantasy wives don't appreciate that sort of thing.

Moments later Amber finally entered the house and was delighted to see Daren standing there and waiting to see her. "Hi" Amber greeted.

"Hey, welcome home!" Daren approached and kissed Amber on the lips. "How was your day?"

"It's better now that you're here."

In the kitchen Trista privately stuck her finger in her mouth with tongue partially extended to mimic gagging. It was the most ridiculous thing she ever heard Mother say. It nearly nauseated her to observe Mother carry on the fantasy game of husband and wife with Daren.

The two could be heard approaching the kitchen. Not very far Mother finally announced, "Well, I suppose I better start dinner. I've got some pork chops thawing and can broil those up. What do you say? Sounds good?"

But Daren wasn't one hundred percent committed to the husband/wife and stepdaughter game. He had a real wife at home who would expect him to be there. "Actually, I've got to get going—get ready for an upcoming business trip." It was a lie, of course. The truth would be too harsh. "Maybe next time." And with that, he kissed Amber, grabbed his coat and walked out the door.

Amber sighed. Needless to say, she was not happy. Men were always so mysterious and seemed to play confusing games. The same thing happened with Trista's biological father, Jim (biological through a similar game of powerful fantasy now played with Daren). Recall that he came over for an early Christmas dinner, neglected to bring Christmas presents for her and Trista, and then abruptly left after opening the ones he received. A similar phenomenon was observed when coming home late at night. He'd come home at 2am, crawl into bed for a couple of hours, and then leave before the sun came up. But Amber wasn't stupid. She knew that it had to do with the other woman who lived down the street. And the same can be said about Daren. He had another woman who seemed to be under the impression that Daren was supposed to live with her, even eat dinner with her. Is that all Amber's love life was to be?—great guys who end up cheating on her?

* * *

Later that night during dinner; Trista and Amber ate in partial silence, only briefly exchanging updates about their days. Suddenly, Trista put her fork down. "You know, Mom, I need to talk to you about something—something important."

"Sure! What is it?"

"It's about this Daren guy. I don't appreciate having him here alone with me. I don't feel safe with him.—you know? Did you give him the house key?"

"Yes… is there a problem?"

"Mom, he's a stranger! You don't know who he is or what he's about."

Amber laughed, "Trista, he's a nice guy. You know, for so long you've made it seem like he's this bad person. And I'm tired of you telling me how to run my love life. I would have had him sooner had I ignored your silly rules of playing hard to get. I'm the adult around here, and I know when to trust someone."

"Mom, I don't trust him. He acts like he's my father; wanted to know where I was and who I was with."

"And that's a bad thing? He cares about me, and obviously cares about you as well. And maybe you need a fatherly role in your life, someone to keep you in line when I'm not around. If you ask me, I'm glad someone is here to give you the third degree when I'm not around."

"Mom, he touched me."

"Touched you?"

"Yes, and I don't like the way he looks at me!"

"How did he touch you? And when?"

"He touched me this afternoon when you were not here. While giving me your so-called third degree, he took it upon himself to put his hand on my shoulder. And then there's the way he looks at me."

Amber sighed. "Trista, that's the way he is. He's a compassionate man. I really don't think that he touched you out of lust. And how is he looking at you?"

"With lust, Mom."

Again, Amber sighed. "Honestly, Trista; don't you think you're a little out of touch? I mean you're certainly a beautiful, young lady; but do you really think that every guy who looks at you totally wants you? He seems like a classy gentleman and reasonable enough to understand that you are young enough to be his daughter. Maybe these lustful looks are taking place in your mind?"

Outraged at her mother's blind-in-love stupidity, Trista now shouted. "I can't believe you, Mother! I'm trying to warn you about something that is not right! I don't feel safe with a stranger coming in my house, but you won't listen! What is wrong with you?" With that, Trista picked up her plate and discarded the scraps into the garbage. "And one other thing, Mom—something you refuse to recognize about the men you date—Daren is married! Do you want to know where your supposed nice guy is? He's at home with his wife! It sounds like he's really committed and a nice, compassionate gentleman!" Then she stormed off into her bedroom for the night.

Chapter 55

The following afternoon, Trista walked home from the bus stop on lengths of sidewalk that were either partially shoveled, or containing permanent sheets of compacted ice. In a couple weeks they would hopefully thaw out as the vernal equinox occurs in March. She was used to this inconvenience year after year. Only when finally entering the house, dropping the school bag, and removing her coat and boots was the day finally over. The bus ride was anything but relaxing. And of course a lengthy walk through the Mapleview cold on hazardous sidewalks would be added. But now Trista wondered if there was a new variable that would further delay her time in finally relaxing for the day.

Would Daren be there? Would she have to put up with his unnecessary third-degree interrogations along with further attempts at touching her? Maybe she could track down Daren's wife and inform her of her husband's recent whereabouts. Then again, who knows where such a bold move might lead her. It was probably best to let the novelty of Mother's romance wear off so that she grew tired of Daren and finally break up. Or maybe count on the unpleasant certainty of extramarital affairs: It's not a matter of if you get caught; it's more a matter of when.

Trista reached the doorstep of her house and entered. Sure enough, Daren was sitting on the sofa and waiting for her.

"Hi!" greeted Daren. How was your school day?"

"Fine..." Daren was the last person Trista wanted to see.

"No orchestra practice this afternoon?"

Trista did not have to stay after school on Tuesdays, but she felt it was none of Daren's business. However, she remembered from yesterday that reminding him only invited Daren to approach her. Trista's safest option was to remain silent.

But Daren continued the conversation as-if Trista was part of it. "So Tuesdays are your early days. That's nice. It gives you a chance to relax a little before your mother comes home."

Trista remained silent.

Then Daren smiled, "I have a little surprise for you."

This mention worried Trista and it certainly showed as she glanced over to him.

"Oh, now it's nothing bad! Relax! Don't you trust me? You just need to warm up to me, that's all. Your surprise is in the kitchen—a little after school snack."

Trista wasn't interested, but felt obligated by some apparent mental control of Daren's to check out the surprise in the kitchen. She scuffed over to the kitchen where she noticed a bag from the Mapleview Cookie Shop. Curious, she opened it.

Inside was a jumbo chocolate chip cookie that had been folded over like a taco shell and filled with chocolate butter cream frosting. Two eyes were formed over the chocolate frosting with white and blue butter cream frosting.

"You like it?" Daren asked while entering the kitchen. "I got it at the Mapleview Cookie Shop. They call it a Peak-a-Boo. I guess they call it that because of the eyes."

All Trista could do was return a blank stare to the madman who was beginning to scare her. Daren was about to do something bad. Trista could feel it.

"Go ahead and take a bite."

"Umm... maybe later. Thank you, though. It was nice of you."

But this wasn't good enough for Daren. "Come-on! Take a bite! What are you afraid of?"

"I really don't want..."

Before Trista could say anything further, Daren snatched the cookie from her hand. "Come-on, take a bite!"

Unfortunately, Trista was backed into a corner and unable to escape. All she could do was look down at the cookie and appear stubborn. She was not going to take a bite of that cookie and hated the fact that Daren was forcing it upon her. She was just like Mother; putting up a fight and being quite a challenge for Daren.

"Take a bite!" ordered Daren. "I'm not going anywhere until you take a bite!"

Trista shook her head, no.

"We can stay here all day. Like I said, I'm going nowhere until you try some of this cookie!" He waved it towards Trista's mouth. "Come-on… you know you want to…"

Trista was losing patience. Apparently the only way to escape was to follow Daren's rule and take a bite of the cookie. So that's what she did. She opened her mouth and allowed Daren to stick the end of the cookie in. Trista bit off and then chewed. Needless to say, the pastry was absolutely delicious; but most-likely terribly fattening. The cookie itself tasted freshly baked, soft and moist. The butter cream was sweet and guaranteed to deliver a sugar high.

As Trista chewed, Daren broke off another small piece. Chocolate butter cream frosting pulled apart so that the broken mass of sandwiched frosting between cookie was held with his finger and thumb.

"Have some more." Daren held it before Trista's mouth.

But this wasn't fair. Trista believed she was playing according to Daren's rule and could finally escape by taking a bite of the cookie. Now there was more to be had. She looked up with an expression to suggest this.

"Come-on, have some more of the cookie. You like it."

With no choice, Trista took the broken piece from Daren's hand with her mouth and chewed it up. Just like before, the whole taste and experience of sugar was nearly euphoric. And there was even more! Yes, Daren continued to break off additional pieces and hand fed them to Amber's teenage daughter. Rest assured, he thoroughly enjoyed watching Trista's beautiful, sweet lips along with blue stained tongue and mouth from the butter cream eyes take more and more cookie from his hand. What would it be like to kiss those young and sweet lips? At one point, some frosting had accumulated on the side of Trista's lips. Daren wiped it off with his finger—enjoying the very touch of her lips—and then placed it in Trista's mouth. With no choice, she sucked the frosting off.

And that's when reality finally hit Trista. She was being trained and conditioned in that moment to obey and be submissive to Daren. She didn't like this, needless to say, and wished there was a way to escape. But more and more cookie stuffed with chocolate butter cream frosting was being handfed to Trista. The top of her head began to tingle from the overload of sugar. All the while Daren carefully watched with such pleasure in his eyes. At that moment, Trista was the most beautiful creature in the world.

Why didn't Mother listen to her? So frightened and overwhelmed by Daren's passive conquest, Trista began to shed tears. She was breaking down emotionally but had no choice but to continue accepting piece after piece of cookie from Daren. She sniffled and cried some.

"There, there…" answered Daren while placing more cookie to her lips."Everything is alright. There's no reason to get upset. She looked so beautiful with sweet, sugary lips and tears running down her cheeks. "Why are you crying, Honey? What's wrong?"

With mouth full Trista struggled to answer. "I can't eat anymore. I'm getting sick."

With that, Daren put down the cookie. "Getting sick? Well you don't have to eat anymore. I thought you liked it, and that's why I kept giving it to you. See, we just need to open the communication between us. I listen."

Just seconds away from receiving an unwanted hug from Daren, Trista did the only thing and turned to face the counter. Then she folded her arms in some strange need to protect herself.

But this was only an invitation for more touching. "You're so tense." With that, Daren began to massage Trista's shoulders. "You need to learn to relax."

He rubbed her arms and back so slowly and sensually. Really it felt good for her, but a little frightening. This man had no right to touch her! The entire massage lasted over ten minutes as Daren enjoyed breaking his fantasy stepdaughter in. Breaking in a young virgin is a careful matter. She's so fragile and delicate; easily frightened and overly emotional. You can't make the ultimate move too quickly. It takes time. She must be slowly trained and conditioned to be receptive to affection and sensual touch. Then again, for Daren, this pleasure was all part of the seduction.

Chapter 56

There was nothing too out of the ordinary to report for the remainder of the first week of March. Daren and Amber continued to play their game of pretend husband and wife while Daren continued to make progress with his fantasy adopted daughter, Trista. It should also be mentioned that as usual, Daren continued to successfully pull the wool over poor Mary's eyes. As for Jim and Ekaterina; their practice of afternoon sex magick in the forest remained in full swing. Kimberly remained an increasingly-neurotic follower of Samuel Crummings and his writings of the occult.

* * *

Welcome to Kimberly's ongoing journey into occult-driven madness...

It was the evening of Wednesday, March 10, 2010—the Ides of March only five days away. Should Jim have been warned of this? Maybe he should have been warned of the vernal equinox only ten days away. Or perhaps it was the full Moon to fall on March 30th and Easter shortly following. Whatever the reason, the danger wasn't very clear. Something wasn't right, and for now it manifested itself in the face of Kimberly.

Jim was beginning to notice a certain distance and even resistance coming from his wife. Was it because of Ekaterina? Did Kimberly sense the intense, extramarital, sexual affair taking place between her husband and some other woman (assumedly Amber down the street)? Or was it because of Samuel Crummings' writings which pulled Kimberly deeper and deeper into his brainwashing cult? Kimberly did, after all, attempt a destructive magick ritual against television news anchor, Martha de los Santos, which backfired and caused a traumatic afternoon for little Collin.

So what was the cause?—Jim's extramarital affair with Ekaterina, the writings of Samuel Crummings, or simply the physical strain placed on Kimberly's body from the illness? It's best to let the reader decide. Incidentally, this church of Samuel Crummings couldn't be all that bad. Since embracing his teachings, Kimberly noticed herself becoming increasingly well—nearly recovered from the horrible super virus.

But why the need for Kimberly to emasculate her husband? I suppose this is what women do in their 40s. They go through some sort of psychological change in which they feel it necessary to break down a husband's confidence and strength in the family.

Outside of exhibiting a plain-faced and not exactly thrilled expression, there wasn't anything in particular that Kimberly did during those initial moments of sitting around the dinner table that night. But for whatever reason, Kimberly's facial expressions, tone of voice and body language had an ability to drain the emotional energy from Jim.

Tonight's dinner was homemade beef stew, the sort of recipe that calls for dipping the chunks of beef in breading and then frying it in a pan before mixing it in the slow cooker with vegetables and potatoes. Kimberly certainly was feeling better, and quite finished making her family Hamburger Helper for dinner.

"Mmmmm!" exclaimed Jim. "Looks good!"

But Kimberly wasn't open to receiving compliments from her husband. "Whatever… you'll eat anything…"

Just as Jim reached for the ladle in the stew, Kimberly grabbed his hand. "Let me see your nails!"

"Huh?"

"Oh my!" exclaimed Kimberly. "Why don't you cut your nails? You look like a sissy girl! Are you trying to get in touch with your feminine side?"

April laughed at her Mother's suggestion. Apparently she was invited to emasculate Father.

No husband and father wishes to hear this at the dinner table from his wife and endure disrespect from the children. And really Jim's nails weren't bad. They simply looked like it was time to trim them. Kimberly was blowing their appearance out of proportion.

Only returning a blank expression that might subtly suggest not appreciating Kimberly's comment, Jim loaded his bowl with stew. Then he sat down.

"So how was school today, Collin?" Jim asked.

"Fine…" Collin's face remained down and facing his food. In recent times, both Collin and April remained distant from their father during meals, or any family time for that matter. They only answered Father when he asked a question and made minimal eye contact. Something was happening in an invisible world. Jim was suddenly the enemy in the family, and it seemed that Kimberly was responsible.

"Fine?" asked Jim. "Well that's good. Algebra not too hard for you?"

Kimberly cut in, "They don't learn algebra in his grade, Jim! Don't you think he's a little young for that?"

April laughed which possessed some strange and invisible ability to hurt Jim's feelings.

But Jim knew it wasn't about April. He simply retorted to his wife, "Well I'm just making small talk. Can't I lighten things up around here?"

Kimberly returned a wicked-cold stare and shook her head in disbelief before taking another bite of stew.

"What…? What's the problem?" As the seconds passed Jim fell deeper and deeper into a mysterious sadness. Why the animosity? Why was his family being so critical and attacking him? Jim could feel the very life being sucked out of him at that moment.

"So did you get the milk before coming home?" Kimberly asked.

Uh-oh! Jim was in hot water, now! "Awe jeez! I'm sorry! I forgot! I'll run over to the store after dinner."

Kimberly dropped her spoon into the bowl. "I knew it! I knew you'd forget! I ask one simple favor—*just one thing*—and you can't even do that!"

What could be described as cold, blue and diffused energy radiated around Jim's shoulders and head. It was that split-second before crying that is felt just before tears begin to pour. That split second had been frozen in time, indefinitely. Jim was now plunged into an eternal realm of sadness and depression. Kimberly had a remarkable power to drain the emotions and life from her husband. All Jim could do in that moment was plead for wife's mercy. "Honey, I'm sorry. It was a mistake. I said I'll go to the store after dinner."

"No, that's okay, Jim! Don't worry about it. I'll go to the store after dinner. It's dark outside. In your old and feeble mind, you might forget where you are along the way and get lost—sundowner syndrome."

Both April and Collin laughed.

Jim was getting impatient with his kids' disrespect. "Hey, watch it!" he yelled. "I'm your father! You don't laugh at me."

But Kimberly came to the defense. "Don't raise your voice to our children. They did nothing wrong. It was *you* who forgot to get the milk."

This was the moment that Jim had been waiting for. It was time to discuss a recent, troubling find. "Is that all this is about, Kimberly? Are you sure? Maybe you have something else you want to say to me?"

"No... Just eat your stew, Jim. I'll go to the store after dinner."

"Kimberly, I want to ask you something, and I want an honest answer."

"Sure, what is it?"

"Are you planning on running away to Samuel Crummings' brainwashing commune in Colorado?"

Kimberly took the defense, "No! Oh my gosh! What are you talking about? You are nuts, you know that?"

"Kimberly, I saw on the computer that you downloaded an application form to check in to the commune in Colorado. You even used the cost calculator to see how much money you would need, and how long it would take to save it up."

Not appreciating being put on the spot, Kimberly nearly exploded. "What business do you have stalking me on line? Now you're looking at the cookies and web browsing history?"

"Kimberly, no one does that anymore. No one looks at cookies and web history. That's a thing of the past. Most people use Google Chrome and open an incognito window to cover their traces. You left the screen open on the computer. I saw it—saw everything. There was no need to look for it."

At a loss of words, Kimberly merely shook her head in disbelief and resumed eating.

"So are you going? What are your intentions? What about the kids?"

Kimberly dropped her spoon in the bowl. "Jim, I was just curious, that's all! And what if I did want to spend some time at the Positive Life Transformation center? I think I need it. You need it, also, but you are too narrow-minded and could never qualify."

Jim interrupted, "That's great, Kimberly, but what about the kids? Are you leaving them to go find yourself? It would be nice to know these things."

"Jim, the Positive Life Transformation center is a highly-respected campus. People who visit are cured of depression, anxiety, drug and alcohol addictions, personality disorders—the list goes on. Doctors really want to know more about the patented Positive Life Transformation so that they can send their patients to Samuel Crummings. As for kids, they do have programs for them which usually results in young graduates who become high achievers in school and in their communities."

Jim sighed. Kimberly had become nothing more than a brainwashed walking advertisement for Samuel Crummings' church of Positive Life Transformation. "So it's safe to conclude that you are taking the kids with?"

Both Jim and April looked up.

Kimberly snapped back, "Alright, you know, this conversation has been blown way out of proportion! I was just curious about the Positive Life Center, that's all. Nobody is moving there! My gosh, you act like it's this bad place, like a brainwashing cult or something. And you know, ever since I started studying Samuel Crummings' writings, my life has turned around 180 degrees…"

Jim interrupted, "And what was wrong with your life?"

"I'm not sick anymore!" answered Kimberly. "I'm healed of whatever illness I had! And if you haven't noticed, I'm no longer under your control. You no longer bring me down. I can finally believe in myself. Our family finally has some sort of direction and structure. I'll never turn away from Samuel Crummings and his teachings!"

Jim was floored. "What? Kimberly, are you out of your mind? There was nothing wrong with our family! And just how have you gotten control of your life; by insulting and alienating me during dinner and throughout the day? What next? Divorce me?"

"No one's insulting and alienating you, Jim. And no one is serving you with divorce papers… yet. Once again, you like to see things the way you want to see them. You're delusional, Jim, and that can be very damaging to loved ones."

Jim finally exploded, "Oh, come-one! From the moment I sat down, you ripped into me because of my finger nails and because I forgot to pick up milk. All I ever get from you lately are dirty, cold looks. You've got the kids turning against me—won't even look at me when I talk to them. And now I hear that you finally have your life in control by doing these things! What the hell?"

Kimberly sighed. "Okay, okay… relax. I hear what you are saying. I believe you. I believe that these things are happening to you. But I believe that they are happening in your mind, and not necessarily in reality. There's a difference."

Jim couldn't believe what he was hearing. "What the hell is that cult leader teaching you?"

Just then, the sound of Jim's double-breasted, wool, black Ivan Trovskov coat could be heard falling on the floor. Rather than hanging it up in the coat closet upon coming home, he simply hung it on the doorknob after leaving his black work boots on the floor nearby.

"Your coat fell, Jim" informed Kimberly. "Why don't you go over there and put it away like a big boy instead of leaving it on the floor. It'll get dirty. Gosh, the kids know to hang up their coats and put their book bags away when coming home. Why are you any different? I feel like you're their little brother."

April and Collin laughed.

Jim's wife needed a good smack to the floor. And so did his kids. But instead of doing this, Jim held the rage in, stood up from the table and walked over to the coat on the floor. With every step, the anger and outrage felt as-if it exploded from the top of Jim's head. And while this happened, he could see Kimberly, April and Collin in the reflection of the window, silently laughing and whispering to one another with gestures.

But then again, maybe this only happened in Jim's mind.

Chapter 57

Sexually speaking, the thirties could quite possibly be the perfect age for a woman. Some people refer to it as the "dirty thirties" and believe that a woman reaches her sexual peak at this time. Oh, she's cute in her teens; beautiful at the nubile age and through her twenties. But a woman doesn't truly qualify as "sexy" until she reaches her thirties. It's somewhere smack-dab in the middle of youth and old age, where life has bestowed a certain wisdom and character to a woman. And yet she is still young. Her sex hormones remain in high gear, and her body is in phenomenal shape.

How lucky a man is to experience great sex with such a woman. Jim was definitely thankful for Ekaterina. She came into his life just in time. Although still baffled as to how the old woman was suddenly younger than him, Jim wasn't going to ask any questions. In recent times, Ekaterina was doing a fine job in filling in as a lover while Kimberly went through her strange and dark moment. Who knows; maybe Jim's wife was going through the early stages of menopause. Do women really go crazy at the initial change of life? At least for now Jim had a young, beautiful and sexy woman to make love to.

It was the following afternoon as Jim and Ekaterina lay under the covers of Ekaterina's bed. Unlike previous weeks, Ekaterina was no longer craving rough and aggressive sex. She was no longer metamorphorosizing into animals and expressing her desires through strange, erotic dances. She no longer called out pseudo poetry while asking for her desires to finally manifest into reality. Instead, she lay in bed with Jim and enjoyed simple, beautiful sex.

"I love having sex with you..." she whispered at some point in the middle of her climactic buildup. This just feels so good... I wish this could last forever..."

For Jim it had been several years since hearing words like these spoken. Now coming from Ekaterina, the words infused Jim's heart into hers so that he and Ekaterina became one spirit. In such a moment of heated, loving passion; Jim's sexual confidence and character had been strengthened. Whatever damage Kimberly had done the previous evening it was now repaired by Ekaterina's love. No drug in the world can ever replace an emotionally altered state of consciousness like this. In fact, the effect of great sex with a beautiful woman who truly loves and craves you lasts for many days thereafter. Any man who has experienced this can attest that he no longer looks at other women, for he is deeply satisfied. You see, women at their age of sexual peak know how to truly win and keep a man. She does it by loving him, and she does it by exchanging sexual energy in beautiful, private moments together.

Ekaterina's toes curled at that last moment before finally releasing. Then she laid there while allowing the orgasm to drift away.

Some moments later, Ekaterina broke the silence while rolling over to lie against Jim's naked body. "I've got some sad news for you."

"What? What is it? What's wrong?"

Ekaterina sighed, "Well… it's March 11th, and your obligation with me has been over since last Friday. There's no reason to keep coming here. You're done with me. Your debt is paid in full."

Jim looked over to his young, beautiful and sexy Ekaterina. He knew she was only joking. True, the forty-nine days had come and gone, but the two remained together. At some point it was mutually and silently understood that they had fallen in love. There was no way for them to separate. But Jim played Ekaterina's mischievous, little game. "Really? Are you serious? You mean we can't do this anymore?"

Ekaterina kissed Jim. "Sure you can. Everything after last Friday is extra credit. And you're definitely earning plenty!" Ekaterina kissed Jim a second time. It seems there was no quenching her sensual desires. "You've changed so much since I first saw you. Those forty-nine days not only paid your deficit of bad karma; but it's made you stronger, more confident and youthful. Jim, I can see that your spirit is stronger and that you are more in tune with the truth. Before you met me you were getting old with a cob-webbed mind and no moral conscience."

Then Ekaterina smiled, "And look what it's done for me."

"Oh, yeah!" Jim agreed. "You're so young and gorgeous. I even forgot what you used to look like. Where is that old lady that used to live here?"

Ekaterina laughed. "You're looking at her."

"So is this like witchcraft or something?"

Ekaterina paused for a few seconds. "Something like that."

"So can people do this forever?—turn back the hands of time by just having sex with each other?"

"Umm… well, there are those who would like to believe that this can be done forever. But forever is a long time, don't you think? I've heard of cases of people who lived and remained young for several centuries with this practice. But I don't think it's easy. For starters, what if something tragic were to happen to one of the partners? Would the other person be able to just find a new mate and continue? Even more, what's to guarantee that two people will always feel the same way about each other? What you and I experienced is nothing short of extraordinary. The intense love and sexual energy was made possible by those initial moments of getting to know one another. Will we ever be able to duplicate this moment, again? Think about it: you loved your wife so much when you first met her. Aren't things just a little different between the two of you?"

Jim sighed. "Don't remind me!"

This comment seemed to perk Ekaterina's interest. "Excuse me?"

"Yeah, she's definitely changed. I don't know if she's going through something right now, but there's a dark patch in our marriage."

"Sorry to hear that. It's not because of me, is it?"

"No, she's picked up some books from Samuel Crummings. You've heard of him, haven't you?"

"Yes…"

"Well, I think she's getting brainwashed. It's like she's being turned against me—like she wants to leave me and move to the commune in Colorado."

"Are you serious?"

"Yeah… and lately she's been turning the kids against me. I think she plans on taking them with."

Ekaterina was at a loss of words. "I'm so sorry." Then she set free those feelings which had been buried in her heart for so long. "Come live with me, Jim. I want you to be with me. Jim, I don't want to live for hundreds of years through the practice of elevating sexual energy. But I love you, and I want to spend the rest of my life with you. We can run away, together. We're young and strong enough to start a new life in some faraway land."

It was time for Jim to bring both him and Ekaterina down to Earth. "I'm married, Ekaterina. Unfortunately, I have to stick it out and see through this dark moment with my wife."

"But it's not going to last." warned Ekaterina. "...not like you remember it. She's changing. She's getting old and turning against you. Just think about it. Don't make a decision today. Just think about what's happening. Imagine a life of you and me living happily-ever-after."

Chapter 58

Trista and her mother, Amber, share a certain personality trait when it comes to aggressive men like Daren. They both fight tooth and nail and want no part of such a man. **No** means **no**!

Their rejecting body language and facial expressions should make this clear. But why won't a man like Daren understand this? It's because he knows that women like Amber and Trista really want something from him. Although they deny it, they secretly enjoy the aggressive seduction from a stalker while shamefully hiding this pleasure under a self-perceived reputation of wholesomeness and prestige.

This type of woman actually needs an aggressive, forceful man. You see, she prides herself in being complicated; takes her lonely heart and locks it up in a bulletproof, fire resistant cast-iron safe. She chooses a lengthy combination and never writes it down for purposes of forgetting it. Then she buries it hundreds of feet below the base of a mountain, and is sure to fill the hole with concrete before covering the rest with soil. All her days and nights, thereafter, she lives with the knowledge of desperately needing love, and longs for the day that her knight in shining armor comes along to rescue her heart. But you see; any man who attempts this is immediately rejected! No man is good enough for her.

So sickening to see a woman deny what she needs for the sake of appearing mysterious, complicated and much-too special for an ordinary man. But after finally being cornered by a man like Daren and forced to accept what she truly wants in her heart, women like Amber and Trista realize that a man like Daren isn't so bad. They come to understand this and crave him even more. He changes them. In their encounter, they finally come to terms with the truth and are emotionally healed from the experience.

You don't believe me? Consider young and beautiful Trista who despised Daren from the moment Mother began to receive harassing Facebook messages from him. She insisted that Daren was a creepy loser. She was disgusted to see Mother lying against his thick, muscular, naked body in bed. And when Daren surprise-greeted her in the afternoon, Trista was sure to remind him that he had no business being there. But then she was forcefully handfed that sweet and sugary cookie by the very man Trista hated. The cookie was so sweet, in fact, that it caused a numbing rush at the top of her head. The unpleasant incident was finished with an unwanted, lengthy, sensual backrub that felt oh-so-good. It felt so good, in fact, that tears silently rolled down her cheeks as confused emotions struggled to process why she disliked such a good-looking, muscular man touching her.

Rumor now has it at Mapleview Community High School that Trista receives a ride home from school by her totally-hot dad. Well… at least that's what onlookers initially believed Daren to be—Trista's father. But what teenage girl kisses her dad in front of classmates? And it wasn't just a simple daddy/daughter peck on the lips. This was several seconds of lip-locking, tongue-tangling, spit-swapping kisses. It didn't take long for some of the kids to conclude that beautiful Trista was going out with an older guy.

Surely these rumors were nothing more than rumors. Amber wouldn't allow such a thing. Daren did mention to Amber of making positive progress with Trista, and then suggested giving her rides home from school.

Amber's reaction: "Oh, that would be great! She'd like that!"

* * *

It was Thursday afternoon as Daren pulled out of the parking lot of Mapleview Community High school with his adopted teenage daughter, Trista. Not more than two blocks down Mapleview Road, he pulled into the parking lot of Starbucks.

"Are you in the mood for a little afterschool treat?" asked Daren.

"Starbucks!" Trista exclaimed.

"Of course! Only the best for you, baby!"

There used to be a nice coffee house in Mapleview owned by one of the locals called Mapleview Coffee. But thanks to Daren, it went out of business in the autumn of 2008.

Coffee beverages and pastries wouldn't be the only gifts that Daren offered to buy Trista's love. He was aware of how Trista was beginning to enjoy bathing in her high school reputation of dating a much older man. Receiving an expensive bling bling gift would not only fuel this reputation, but also bring Daren one step closer down Trista panties. "Hey!" Daren called out as Trista's grabbed the door handle. "Before we get our coffee, I've got something for you." He pulled out from his inner jacket pocked a small, gift-wrapped box.

Trista's face and eyes lit up! It was the sort of look that every man wishes to see on a young woman as she is falling in love. "What did you get me?"

"A little gift… go ahead, open it."

Trista carefully unwrapped the box and opened it. Inside was a diamond tennis bracelet. Her mouth opened as she quietly gasped. "Wow! How much was this! What would my mom…"

Daren quickly interrupted her, "Don't worry! I got you and your mom matching tennis bracelets—mother and daughter gift. She'll get hers later tonight." Then he winked at Trista. "Go ahead! Put it on."

Trista hesitated not another second and wrapped it around her wrist. Her hands trembled from the excitement which made fastening the bracelet impossible. "Could you help me clasp it on?"

"Of course!" Daren did so with pleasure and enjoyed touching her young, delicate wrist. He wanted to touch Trista in so many ways, but for now simply held her hand while walking through the parking lot and into Starbucks.

Chapter 59

It was such a contrast for Jim to spend wonderful time with Ekaterina in the afternoon, then to come home to his bitter wife after five o'clock. He was certainly living a double life. During the day and away from Kimberly, Jim was young, strong, full of life and deeply involved in a magickal love affair with his beautiful, sexy Ekaterina who lived in the forest. By night, however, he was a weakened, depressed, middle-aged man who was trapped in a marriage with a wife who seemed to hate him.

"Hey…" greeted Jim as he came home on Friday as Kimberly made dinner. He assumed the evening and weekend would bring more bitterness and animosity from the wife and kids.

Kimberly didn't return the greeting. Instead she immediately informed Jim, "You have an important message from Doctor Millheimer on the answering machine. You better check it out!"

Jim carefully walked over to the landline phone in the family room and pressed the message button on the answering machine.

"Hello, this is Doctor Millheimer calling for Jim. I would like to schedule an urgent visit from Jim for this coming Monday, March 15 at one o'clock in the afternoon. It's nothing serious. I just need to go over a few items and check some things. Also, I'm going to order that you no longer take the ErexBoost medication that was prescribed during your last visit. If you have been taking this medication and getting refills, you are hereby ordered from this moment on to no longer take it. There was a recent finding with this medication that can cause some potential health concerns.

Again, it's nothing serious—nothing to be alarmed about. I'm going to set this appointment as tentative; so unless you call to reschedule I will expect to see you on Monday.

Thank you and have a nice weekend."

As Jim listened to the final warning of potential health concerns, Kimberly walked in the family room and stood nearby. Then she added her input at the end of the message. "You're not going to take that stuff anymore, are you?"

"Well, no. The doctor said to stop taking it."

"That's probably what's been making you act so strange, lately. I mean ever since you bought those goofy clothes and shaved your head, you've been really acting weird." Yes, Jim was still wearing his wintery Ivan Trovskov wardrobe.

"Kimberly, what are you talking about? I bought my winter clothes before seeing the doctor, remember?"

Kimberly shook her head in disbelief. "See, Jim, this is what I'm talking about. Lately you've been argumentative, easily agitated and delusional. I looked up ErexBoost online and found out that it can cause psychological and behavioral disorders. I'm glad Doctor Millheimer called and ordered you to no longer take it. I really think that this medication made for 90% of the problems in our marriage. I mean I was actually thinking of serving you with divorce papers because you've been so intolerable."

Jim couldn't believe what he was hearing. "Kimberly, I was just saying that I bought the clothes before Doctor Millheimer prescribed the medication. I was just making a point, that's all! I wasn't here to fight and be argumentative. And you know, maybe it's the other way around. Maybe since you've been reading those books from Samuel Crummings, you're mind is becoming warped."

Kimberly threw her hands in the air in a motion of throwing a fit. "Here we go, again!"

"Kimberly, it's like you actually look for things that could be wrong so you can fight with me. Now I hear that you actually think of divorcing me?"

"We're done, here, Jim! I'm not going to fight anymore. Doctor Millheimer can take care of the rest. He'll be able to see the warning signs and get treatment for you. I'm just glad you're off that medicine." And with that, Kimberly walked away from her husband and resumed making dinner.

* * *

At least Jim had Ekaterina to see him through this difficult time. Jim entered the forest the following Saturday morning and embarked on his hike towards Ekaterina's cottage. Finding his way was certainly no challenge. He had been doing this every day for several weeks. Aside from that, both his and Ekaterina's hikes to and from the cottage formed a permanent, narrow path through the forest.

As Jim was halfway to the cottage, Ekaterina suddenly jumped out from behind a tree and made a loud noise to obviously scare him. "Blah!"

Of course it startled Jim which was immediately replaced by laughter. "You! I'll get you!" Then he playfully chased Ekaterina through the forest until catching her. She was grabbed and forced to the snowy ground to be attacked by kisses. In between a series of kisses Jim asked, "What are you doing out here, huh? Are you scaring people?"

Ekaterina giggled and laughed as more kisses were given.

After some moments the play died down. The two remained on the ground which soon called to mind a noteworthy observation that was quickly stated by Ekaterina. "Spring's obviously on the way." she said. "We wouldn't be laying here if it were December."

"Yeah, it's warming up." agreed Jim. "I think you're right. The smell of spring is in the air."

"Why don't we go for a little walk?" suggested Ekaterina. "I want to take you to a special place where I like to go sometimes."

"Sure!"

And with that, both nearly leapt from the ground and embarked on a journey in the forest that was led by Ekaterina.

Now Ekaterina was continuing to possess younger and younger features. But there was a cut-off point in this reverse aging phenomenon. Jim assumed it was due to the fact that Ekaterina was an adult. Ekaterina wasn't Benjamin Button's sister, of course! She wasn't regressing and shrinking in size through reverse adolescence, childhood and ultimately taken to the state of a helpless infant. Rather, looking at the fully-transformed Ekaterina was as-if looking at a young woman in her mid-twenties who exhibited the maturity of a woman in her thirties, along with something in the eyes that suggested being older. That's the best way to describe what had become of the young woman who had been old several weeks ago.

Ekaterina even talked and sounded like a young woman in her twenties. Have you ever paid attention to the voice of a woman at this age? You might agree that it's best described as though she partially holds her breath while speaking. You've noticed this, yes? Women that age also speak words and sentences quickly, and have a sort of musical tone to the voice. Sentences are jumbled together with a seeming intention to communicate multiple points at once. Along with this, there's an air of excitement and nervousness surrounding a woman this age with an indescribable scent of being at prime fertileness.

Ekaterina possessed all of these features. She was definitely a young woman in her twenties. She would remain like this until the sex magick wore off, and the slow process of aging would turn towards the undesirable direction.

After some time of hiking through the forest, both Jim and Ekaterina slowly climbed up a forested incline. Jim gasped some, "Are we almost there?"

Ekaterina laughed. "What, are you an old man all of the sudden? It's just up there. The view is amazing!"

About a minute later both Jim and Ekaterina reached the destination and stood some two hundred feet over a roaring stream. They had reached a massive ravine in the forest with a depression too treacherous to scale down towards the bottom. But what fun would climbing down have been? The whole point of making this journey was to stand above and admire the amazing scenery.

"Wow!" Jim exclaimed. "This is beautiful!"

"I come here sometimes. Feel that?"

"What? The wind?"

"Yes... Don't you find something wrong with it?" The wind was actually blowing against Jim and Ekaterina as they faced the bottom of the ravine. On the other side of the ravine was more forest. In a closed, forested environment; where could the wind have possibly been coming from?

Up until recently, Jim hadn't spent much quiet time in the deep forest, and hadn't a clue of what was considered normal. "I don't know... It's wind. It's a strong breeze... Wind, that's all."

"No..." answered Ekaterina. "Pay attention to the surroundings. There are miles of trees around us. A strong wind couldn't possibly be coming off the stream. It's not a wide-open lake. The wind is magickal. This is a magick place."

Jim still didn't understand the phenomenon, but certainly agreed in the presence of magick in that spot with the dramatic, surrounding beauty.

Ekaterina stood before Jim and took both of his hands while looking deeply into his eyes. "I have something to tell you."

"What? What is it?"

"We're having a baby. I'm pregnant."

"Pregnant? Wow! I had no idea..." He was about to say that he had no idea that an old lady could become pregnant. But Jim knew sex magick had made possible many things for the two of them in recent weeks—mainly the fact that Ekaterina was transformed into a young woman.

The wind continued to blow from across the ravine and seemed to originate from the unseen and infinite. There was a vast, invisible world before them. Ekaterina offered more insight of this mysterious wind and its origination from the unseen and infinite. "Come with me, Jim. At this very moment, the infinite is open to us and we can build our own world together; a place where we can live happily-ever-after."

Jim smiled and halfheartedly giggled through his nose. It was a nice thought. "You don't know how close I am to doing just that, Ekaterina. If only you knew." He was speaking of the recent condition of his family life at home. What Ekaterina suggested was far better; a fresh, new start with a young woman who loved Jim in a way he remembered from younger years. With a baby now on the way, Jim and Ekaterina had a family of their own—a life of their own.

Ah, but what about Kimberly, April and Colin? Despite how bitter things were at home with the constant animosity and rejection from the wife and kids, Jim believed that it would all soon pass, and that his promised obligation of husband and father would have to continue.

Speaking of which, Jim needed to get back home. It was Saturday and he lied about another outage to escape home and into the forest. But such an awkward moment to announce that it was time to leave. "That would be really nice, Ekaterina. And your news of being pregnant is very exciting!" Jim embraced his young lover, but could feel what she sensed. She sensed that he wasn't "there with her" at that moment. He didn't see it. He didn't understand. Instead, Jim filled in the awkwardness with a loving hug while reminding her, "I need to get back. It's getting late."

Ekaterina looked so sad. "Okay... You can go ahead. I just want to stay here for a while."

"Are you sure?"

"Yeah, I'm fine. I'm just not ready to leave, yet."

Jim kissed Ekaterina on the forehead. "Okay... sure... whatever you need..." Then he offered some words of hope; something for Ekaterina to look forward to in the near future that would reassure her of Jim's intended commitment. "We need to start working on a nursery for the cottage. We'll get everything we need."

Ekaterina halfheartedly smiled and giggled through her nose. It was a nice thought of Jim's.

Chapter 60

Sunday came and went without Jim visiting Ekaterina. Oh, rest assured he missed her and felt guilty for leaving his lover alone that Sunday. These were delicate times, and Ekaterina would surely need more and more of Jim as the months went by. But it was the nagging feeling of his obligated husband/father duty that caused an equal amount of guilt. Jim had been following the practice of lying to his wife for several weeks of a fabricated cable outage just to see Ekaterina. For that Sunday, Jim decided to stay with his family. Perhaps it was the previous day's realization that time continues to change everything, and that Kimberly's dark moment would pass. I suppose Jim was in the middle of a moral dilemma.

And what a difficult moral dilemma it was. Although Jim did what most of us would believe to be the right thing—stay with wife and kids on Sunday afternoon—the time spent with Kimberly was anything but pleasant. She mostly sat in the family room, engrossed in another book by Samuel Crummings.

At some point, Jim turned off the TV and went into the kitchen for a can of soda. He returned to the family room and looked out the window. "Spring is almost here." he announced.

"Yup…" Kimberly's eyes remained glued to the book.

"We'll have to think of some fun things to do this summer with the kids."

Kimberly sighed, "Yup…" It was almost as-if she were agitated with being interrupted.

Every now and then a spouse needs to be approached on a matter of concern. Lately it seemed to Jim that his wife valued the writings of Samuel Crummings over their marriage. "Kimberly?" Jim called out.

"Hmm…" She briefly looked up while turning the page.

"Kimberly, is there anything in those books that talk about the importance of maintaining healthy relationships and communication with a spouse? I mean do we even talk like a husband and wife anymore?"

Jim finally had his wife's attention, for Kimberly looked up with eyes of fire and growled, "Go to Hell! Don't you have an outage or something to take care of? Is this how our Sunday is going to be? I can't even sit here and read a book without you trying to start a fight with me?"

Jim interrupted, "Kimberly, we're not fighting! I'm trying to have a conversation with you. Ever since you started reading those books, you've been distant from me."

Kimberly sighed, "It's okay, Jim. You need to keep reminding yourself that this is something happening in your own mind, and not necessarily in reality. Tomorrow when you see the doctor, he'll make everything better for you. Okay?"

Frustrated, Jim had no choice but to walk away. He wasn't that out of touch with reality. He knew that Kimberly was playing a little mind game with him.

Walking down the hall, he came to April's bedroom where she sat on her floor, texting. "Hey there!" Jim greeted.

"Hey..."

"So when's the next concert?"

"In a few weeks."

"Oh yeah? How's your orchestra teacher been?"

"Fine..."

April was too busy texting her friend to have a conversation with Father at that moment. But the mention of April's orchestra teacher reminded Jim that Ekaterina might need to take time off work in the middle of the following school year. April would probably have a substitute orchestra teacher. Even more, little would April know that Ms. Lutrova's baby was actually her sister!

* * *

The Ides of March fell on Monday morning and was brought in with a surprise staff meeting at Mapleview Cable. Recall that weekly staff meetings are traditionally held on Fridays. Immediately, everyone noticed the presence of a young newcomer who appeared to be in his early twenties. The plant manager, Ryan, stood at the center of the circle and immediately motioned the new hire to stand next to him. "Everyone, this is our new employee, Cody. Be sure to welcome him and help with anything he needs. Cody is going to be assisting us with utility functions. He'll eventually be going out of state for some training and then come back enlightened to do his job."

Cody smiled and nervously giggled through his nose in response. Initially, the staff of installers assumed that they would be training him. But hearing Cody would be assisting in utility functions suggested greater plans.

It didn't take long for everyone at Mapleview Cable to consider how odd it was to have a new-hire. With the company takeover in July, there should have been a hiring freeze. People were worried of losing their jobs. Why a new-hire?

Ryan motioned Cody to return to his seat and then resumed the meeting. "Alright, one important thing I need to bring to everyone's attention: If you don't know what you are doing, don't do it! If you have questions, ask. If unsure, ask for guidance. We had a little incident a couple weeks ago…" Ryan looked over to the company's lineman technician, "*Jim*… I happened to see him parked on the road with the utility box open and messing things up. I guess he was looking for something to do? Well, Jim caused a serious outage." Again, Ryan looked over to the lineman technician. "I guess Jim learned a valuable lesson that morning. *Right Jim?*"

Jim couldn't believe what he was hearing. The plant manager was making up lies about him. Even still, there was the humiliation of now being at the mercy of this liar. Jim had been with Mapleview Cable since back when Ryan would have been in, say, 5th grade. By the time Jim trained for and held down the job as lineman technician, Ryan would have been some little shit in high school, or recently graduated at most. Jim was thoroughly trained to perform diagnostic tests and had been following a regular schedule for years. The entire network of Mapleview and Sillmac belonged to Jim, and he cared for it well. Now some pompous, little prick who knew nothing of cable infrastructure—much less how to operate a cable company—was declaring Jim's method of daily business to be wrong? Aside from that, it was Ryan who caused the outage from a couple weeks ago, not Jim!

Ryan continued to use Jim as the clown for his examples. "And another important thing you all should be following: If I tell you to do something, do it. Apparently some people in this room didn't get beat enough when they were growing up. It's like they need discipline or something. Not more than a half hour after meeting with Jim that Friday and asking him to do a little project for me, I discovered him playing around in the utility box. Had he done what I told him, that outage would have never happened. ***Right Jim?*** Jim has no idea how close he came to being written up for insubordination." Ryan turned to Jim, "As a side note, see me after the meeting."

Outside of officially introducing Cody to the staff at Mapleview Cable, bearing false witnesses against Jim and then humiliating him was the only purpose of the surprise Monday morning staff meeting. And with Ryan's order to join Jim in the office, afterwards, Jim assumed that a write-up was to follow. But there was no write-up. It was something worse.

Cody stood in the office with Ryan as Jim entered.

Ryan announced, "Jim, I'm going to have Cody share some of the responsibilities of lineman technician. In the future he'll be going out of state to get the same training you did. For now, I'll have him ride with you for a couple weeks so you can bring him up to speed. We'll probably turn the bucket truck over to him and let you have one of the installer vans out in the yard. That way you can concentrate all your efforts on that telephone pole project. Afterwards, you'll do miscellaneous projects for me; maybe help out the installers on a day with heavy loads. Think of it as being my right-hand man."

It all came clear to Jim at that moment. The company was being taken over by younger new-hires, and Cody was to be Jim's replacement. Many companies do this today in an attempt to scale back salaries. It was probably ordered by Fernsehen Comm to begin this phasing out early in the year. Surely, Jim would be among the employees to be terminated in July. The guy who handles small, miscellaneous projects is always pooled with others whose positions have been eliminated. In contrast to the overwhelming rage and anger from moments ago, Jim felt a wave of numbness. Life was soon to change!

Ryan continued, "Anyway, why don't you take Cody with you today. Show him around a bit; introduce him to our network and maybe have him assist you with the telephone pole project. And don't do any of your load-emulation tests!" Then Ryan advised Cody, "Keep an eye on this guy. Don't let him teach you any bad habits."

But before leaving, Jim informed Ryan, "Oh, I'll have to return Cody some time after lunch. I've got a doctor's appointment at one o'clock. I hope that's okay."

"Sure Jimmy. That shouldn't be a problem."

* * *

Realizing his inevitable destiny of being laid off in July was only half of the shocking news that morning. Jim would learn so much more while riding with Cody in the bucket truck.

For starters, the kid was a little, too excited with the arrangement. Clearly, he didn't understand what was about to happen to Jim. Or maybe he did and just lacked the empathy to trigger a guilty conscience. Whatever the reason, his motor mouth told quite a behind-the-scenes story.

"This is a sweet deal for me!" boasted Cody. "Ryan is my cousin and he told me about the job opening last week. I guess my dad and my uncle—his dad— were talking about my job situation (as in lack of having one). Thanks to Ryan, I've got a decent job. Connections; it's not what you know, it's who you know!"

Sudden anger that now pulled Jim out of numbness encouraged him to reply, "Oh yeah? Well there you go!" Either Daddy, his uncle or older brother must have educated Cody on the 90s catchphrase, "It's not what you know, it's who you know." Once upon a time these were words of wisdom that any career savvy or business professional used when seeking job opportunities. And they probably still do follow these words of wisdom. People lean towards hiring family, friends and past coworkers. I say, "Once on a time" because the majority of this country understands the overall consequences from religiously following this catchphrase. Certainly understandable that it's human nature to hire family, friends and past coworkers; this wisdom was soon abused so that career savvy people positioned themselves to simply ride the coattails to the top. They became chummy with bosses and those in high places. No longer necessary to develop skills and knowledge base, socializing proved to be the shortest route to promotion after promotion.

And what happened? Would you say that in America there are countless companies being driven—nearly kamikazeed—into the grave by those who don't know what they are doing?

Jim was curious as to how qualified Cody was. "So do you have a technical degree or some kind of engineering background?"

"Nope! It's all connections! I've only completed one semester over at Sillmac Community College. But you know I was surprised with the salary. I mean I would think someone your age would be at about 150, 200K. How do you even support your family on this salary? It's decent money for me, though."

Maybe Jim could take Cody to the edge of town and show him a utility box. When Cody isn't looking, Jim could slam the metal door shut on his head.

"Oops! Sorry about that, Cody!"

Unfortunately, Jim couldn't stoop that low.

Chapter 61

It was Monday afternoon and time for Jim's urgent visit to the doctor's office. He sat in the waiting room with three other people and hoped it wouldn't be too long. Then again, why the rush back to work? The earlier he returned to work, the more it would be necessary to spend quality time with his replacement, Cody.

The back office door opened, and the attractive Nurse Corrine appeared. "Jim!" she called out. "Right this way."

Jim stood up from his seat and followed the nurse into the hallway.

"Okay, let's first get your weight."

Jim stood on the scale as ordered.

"258 pounds... very good! It looks like you've lost some weight since your last visit. You went from 281 to 258."

Jim was surprised. "Wow!" He hadn't made an effort to lose the weight. Maybe it was the daily, wintery hikes in the woods to Ekaterina's cottage.

Jim followed Nurse Corrine into a vacant office where she ordered, "Okay, let's get your blood pressure checked."

Before sitting down; Jim removed his black, Ivan Trovskov, double-breasted, wool coat. Underneath, as you know, was simply his white, Fruit-of-the-Loom t-shirt with suspenders strapped across. Spring was on the way. Maybe he could change his wardrobe to something more appropriate for the season. What do people in Russia wear in the spring and summer months? Perhaps Jim could take Ekaterina with him shopping so that she could pick out some clothes for him.

While considering all of this, Nurse Corrine strapped the blood pressure cuff around Jim's arm. She pumped, released and waited for a reading. "122/70; perfect! You've definitely made some positive changes since your last visit. The doctor will be in momentarily to see you."

Jim waited alone for about five minutes. These positive health changes certainly were out-of-the-ordinary. He hadn't made an effort to lose weight or eat differently. Maybe the effects of sex magick transferred onto Jim so that he had gotten somewhat younger. The original purpose was to pay his debt of bad karma. But with all the extra work he had done with Ekaterina, maybe Jim received extra credit.

There was a soft knock at the door. "Hello?" In walked Doctor Millheimer. He seemed delighted to see Jim. "There you are! How are you feeling?"

"Never felt better, Doctor."

"Good! I see that you've taken my advice offered at the last visit and lost some weight. 258 pounds; that's a little over twenty pounds shed. And on the paperwork, I see that your blood pressure is excellent. So how did you do it? Exercise? Diet?"

Jim was unsure of what to say. "Well, a little of both. I've taken up hiking in the woods, and I guess I stayed away from sweets and junk food."

"Very good! Jim, could you lift up your shirt? I just want to do a quick exam." Jim did as asked.

Doctor Millheimer appeared satisfied. "It looks like the swelling has gone down around your breasts." He felt Jim's chest and softly squeezed the surrounding tissue and nipples as if fondling a woman's breast. "There is no longer the presence of excessive subcutaneous fat. Yes, it's safe to conclude that you've done your homework. If I didn't know any better, those man boobs from your last visit have been replaced with the emergence of pectoral muscle." Doctor Millheimer looked down towards Jim's abdomen. "And you've lost your love handles. You're like the model patient! I wish all of my patients followed my orders as well as you do. Go ahead; you can put your shirt back on."

As Jim stood up to put his shirt back on and tuck it in, Doctor Millheimer discussed the more pressing matter that yielded the scheduled visit.

"So Jim, I called on Friday of last week to order that you no longer take the ErexBoost medication. You did as I ordered, yes?"

"Yes, of course!"

"Very good! But just a few questions to ensure that no damage had been done: If at any time while taking the medication, did you notice any episodes of depression or anxiety?"

"No."

"Any compulsive thoughts such as a need to gamble, or maybe excessive sexual urges?"

"No, I don't gamble. As for sexual urges; not any more than I usually have."

"Good! And I trust you never contemplated suicide while taking the Erex-Boost?"

"Never!"

"How about false beliefs or strange delusions that suddenly appeared shortly after taking the medication? Delusions are most often characterized with fantastic ideas such as the notion that a stranger is in love with you, or that you have some great power above everyone else, or that you believe your wife is having an extra marital affair, or that you believe someone is out to hurt you, or even that you believe yourself to have some disease."

Jim shook his head in negation while listening to Doctor Millheimer. The only stranger who had fallen in love with Jim was Ekaterina. But she was certainly no longer a stranger.

As for a great power above everyone else; Jim was the lineman technician of Mapleview Cable, and definitively knew more about the business than the plant manager. And this was fact, not a false belief!

Jim seriously doubted that Kimberly was having an extramarital affair with anyone. Maybe she was a little preoccupied in those books by Samuel Crummings. But Samuel Crummings lived a considerable distance away. What, if any, contact would the two have?

Was someone out to hurt Jim? Well, his head was being positioned on the chopping block for possible layoffs at Mapleview Cable. But again, this notion was probably true and gained through years of wisdom and street-smarts. What else would someone conclude with the announcement of Jim being "promoted" to fulltime telephone pole addresser while a young kid took his current job?

Imagined illness? Jim hadn't felt this good in years. He certainly wasn't dreaming up any imaginary illnesses.

As Doctor Millheimer described delusional disorders, Jim continued to shake his head in negation.

"There is another delusion that seems to be a growing trend in society. Some people are under the impression that they are influenced by paranormal forces. For example they might feel that... oh I know this might sound silly; but some people believe that aliens from outer space are watching them and plan to abduct them."

Jim returned a queer expression at this suggestion.

Doctor Millheimer continued. "Some people experience what is called delusions of witchcraft. It's a peculiar belief that a witch can remotely view a victim from the distance and inflict harm through some magick power or a spell. Sometimes people who suffer from this delusion actually identify the suspected witch, and blame recent misfortunes by the meddling of this person in question. Other people believe that they, themselves, are a witch and can cause desired outcomes—whether good or bad—from a distance with the use of a certain magick power. Then again, this later example would qualify as delusions of grandeur.

How about you, Jim? Has a witch wronged you? Maybe you know of a witch who lives in the town of Mapleview? Or perhaps even you are a witch?"

Suddenly, the conversation was turning uncomfortable for Jim. Ekaterina was a witch, but this certainly was no delusion. Jim watched her transform from an old lady to a young and beautiful woman in a matter of weeks. She even healed Jim with the use of guided scrying and transferring the positive effects of sex magick onto him for purposes of correcting bad karma.

The more Jim thought of it, the more he realized that the two of them had procreated a child—probably a witch daughter, or maybe a son who would one day follow the path of magick and become a witch himself.

Just as a side note: If you really want to sound like you know what you are talking about; never, never refer to a male witch as a warlock! Warlocks were bad people. The word warlock is Scottish for "oath breaker". Historically, these people were nothing more than cheats, go-betweens or con-artists that negotiated money from the church for disclosing the whereabouts of witches to be tracked down and burned. No decent, male witch refers to himself as a warlock, or prefers to be called this.

Surprisingly, Jim knew of this. And he also knew to protect Ekaterina, even if it meant putting his own life before hers. Ekaterina was his "witch mother" who brought him up in only a matter of weeks in the ways and customs of magick. He would be forever indebted and in love with the woman. They made a child together. Jim, Ekaterina and the baby were now a family of witches; and Doctor Millheimer was suddenly a witch hunter who apparently caught wind of a witch in Mapleview.

All Jim could do was shake his head. "No, I can't say I've experienced anything like that."

"No? Are you sure, Jim? Sometimes when a sufferer of a delusion is challenged of the belief, he or she becomes defensive—sometimes even violent."

"Hmm… was I getting defensive, Doctor?"

"It appeared to be something. Maybe you are only tired and I misread your reaction. How about hallucinations? Have you noticed any instances of hallucinating? Hallucinations are different from delusions in that rather than simply believing in some fantastic notion, the sufferer actually sees or hears things that are not present in reality. Do you experience this?"

"No."

"You don't hear unexplained voices calling you, or witness questionable occurrences that other people, nearby, might insist they didn't see?"

There were all those nights of Ekaterina flying into Jim's bedroom window and disrobing herself to rape Jim as he lay defenseless in sleep paralysis. But again, this really happened. Ekaterina was a witch and capable of doing these things. Jim simply answered, "No."

"Very good! After my examination I will safely conclude that the ErexBoost caused no health issues or negative impact to your mental condition. For the time being, however, I'm not going to introduce any new medications such as Viagra or Cialis to improve the quality of your erections. Just take a break from sex for a while. Maybe some months down the road we will look at the more traditional medications if you are still experiencing erectile dysfunction."

Chapter 62

Jim had an important obligation; a seemingly new purpose in life. Why hadn't he seen this before? It took the probing of Doctor Millheimer for Jim to finally realize these things.

Jim had been called and inducted into magick by an old witch. Together they fell in love and created a witch child. The three were now a family, and Jim was their protector with an obligation to care for Ekaterina and the baby. And it should have been no problem doing this as Jim had fallen deeply in love with Ekaterina.

After leaving the doctor's office that Monday, Jim parked the Mapleview Cable bucket truck on the shoulder off Mapleview Road for some much needed time with Ekaterina. He was such a fool for leaving her on Saturday! Where did Jim ever get the idea that playing family man with Kimberly would have been the right thing to do? Ekaterina was his new wife and new purpose in life.

He climbed over the guardrail and descended into the forest. Immediately, the small trail created by Jim and Ekaterina could be spotted. Even with the snow melting, the ground had been worn so that the presence of the narrow, off-beaten path could be seen. It zigzagged and curved around large trees, bushes and streams. After traveling them since December, Jim knew these woods like the back of his hand. They were home. This was his neighborhood; the place where he, Ekaterina and their soon-to-be child would live.

Ekaterina was so right with her statement from several weeks ago. Being that her home had been built by herself and sat in the middle of wilderness, there would be no concerns if she ever lost her job. Ekaterina lived in nature. All food, water and shelter were found here. And if Jim did, in fact, lose his job at Mapleview Cable; he wouldn't have to worry about a thing. There was no mortgage, utilities or taxes on Ekaterina's cottage in the woods. Jim could simply get a job at Walmart or some small business in Mapleview to afford food and needed items for the baby.

As for Kimberly; let her run off and live with Samuel Crummings at his brain-washing commune. The kids? In recent times, even they had turned against Jim. Let them go with their mother to become super-achievers and leaders of the Samuel Crummings brainwashing cult.

Jim passed the tree where Ekaterina had jumped out from behind on Saturday afternoon. He continued to hike and passed the area where he finally tackled her and kissed her silly. How he loved the sound of Ekaterina's laughter. It filled Jim with such happiness. Although the snow in the area was nearly melted, Jim knew that the two had lain there only two days ago.

Now nearing Ekaterina's cottage, Jim called out, "Ekaterina!" He laughed before making a very, bold statement, "I'm home!" But of course she would want Jim to move in with her. That was the whole point of her suggestion on Saturday afternoon. "Ekaterina!" It was as-if he expected her to run out after Jim and meet him with a loving embrace and wild kisses.

But then something didn't look right. "Ekaterina?" Jim was now at the very place he had been many times before where he faced the cottage. He was still some distance away, but why was Ekaterina's home not visible? Did Jim make a wrong turn? Did he get confused with the melting snow and change of scenery and turn a different direction? It was the only explanation.

But, no! This was the place. This was the very place where Ekaterina's cottage was supposed to be. Jim recognized every tree—in particular the tree that made a perfect Y-shape. There was the circle of five pine trees off to the right that, had it not been for one of them misaligned and closer to the interior, would have made a perfect circle. There was no denying; this was the exact location in the forest of Ekaterina's cottage.

So where was it?

"Ekaterina!"

Rather than her cottage in the expected location, there was a thick, overgrown patch of bushes. It was as-if they had been there for decades. There was no foundation or impacted evidence of a home ever being there. As for Ekaterina's well that provided water to her cottage: from what Jim could see through the dense bushes, there was nothing—not even evidence of a hole once being there.

Jim placed his hands to his face out of panic. What was happening? Was he experiencing some sort of hallucination brought on by no longer taking the ErexBoost? Should he have returned to Doctor Millheimer and mentioned this incident? But then what would Jim say? Who was Ekaterina, and why did she live in the forest? The very situation described might cause alarm in itself. Confused and unable to deal with what was happening, Jim had no choice but to turn around and head back for the bucket truck.

Chapter 63

It had to be a hallucination, or maybe a moment of serious confusion brought on by the recent stress in Jim's life. This was the only reasonable explanation. Of course Ekaterina's home didn't suddenly vanish! Since December Jim had been visiting her on a daily basis. He saw it with his own, two eyes. He had been inside of the cottage time and time again. But the momentary incident of hallucination that afternoon had disturbed Jim. He sat down at the dinner table that Monday evening with the intention of working the conversation in the direction of April's orchestra teacher.

But before anything could be said, Kimberly seized control of dinner talk. "So did you go to the doctor this afternoon?"

"Yes."

"What did he say?"

"Well, he said I'm losing weight and that my blood pressure is under control. I think he also did some sort of evaluation on me to make sure the medicine didn't hurt me."

As little Collin reached for a piece of garlic bread he asked, "What medicine? Are you on medicine?"

"Nothing..." reassured Father to little Collin. "It was just some new medicine for my blood pressure. But the doctor realized it wasn't good for me and told me to no longer take it. I'm fine, though. Don't worry."

Kimberly stared at Jim and finally asked, "Well?"

"What?"

"Well, what did the doctor conclude? Did he notice anything wrong?"

"No! He says I'm fine. He said I passed his mini-psychological exam with flying colors. He just doesn't want me to take the medicine anymore."

Kimberly sighed, "Okay...?"

Jim would have liked to have argued and asked his wife, "What the hell is your problem? Did you want me to have something wrong?" But instead, he moved the conversation towards the direction of Ekaterina. He looked over to Collin, "So... how was school today?"

"Fine..." answered Collin.

Then he looked over to April, "How about you? How was your day?"

"Good..."

"How's orchestra coming along? When's that upcoming concert?"

"In a few weeks..."

"Yeah? How's your orchestra teacher... Ms. Lutrova, I think it is?"

April returned a queer expression, "Don't you mean Mrs. Linder?"

"No, I mean Ms. Lutrova; Ms. Ekaterina Lutrova."

By now Kimberly set down her fork. "Huh? Jim, what are you talking about? April's orchestra teacher is Mrs. Linder."

Jim did his best to cover his outrage. "Come-on! Ms. Lutrova, the Russian lady! I've seen her plenty of times. You have to know who I'm talking about!"

"Jim, are you sure you went to the doctor, today?" asked Kimberly.

"Yeah!" Then with every second, Jim's heart raced faster and faster. Adrenaline spiked through every nerve and every vein. He was on the verge of a serious breakdown. What was happening? It really appeared as though Ekaterina and her cottage in the woods never existed. And what about the lively, Russian orchestra teacher who placed Jim under a spell of fascination? Even she didn't exist? Now April suddenly had an orchestra teacher named Mrs. Linder, and she was the teacher all along?

It was Jim's pale face and bluish lips that suddenly alarmed Kimberly. "Jim, are you okay?"

"I... I... I just..."

"What? What is it Jim?"

"I'm just having trouble at work and under some stress?"

"Stress? What sort of stress?"

"The company is being sold. Things are kind of up in the air right now."

* * *

The following morning, Jim pulled out of his subdivision in the Mapleview Cable bucket truck. Perhaps a good night's sleep might have restored his sanity.

Jim knew that Ekaterina existed, and was bound and determined to prove this to himself. Jim saw her with his own, two eyes. He spent time in her house. He had sex with her and fell in love with her. There was no denying what his eyes had seen, what his lips had kissed and what his hands had touched. Still, the recent events were a little bothersome. Why was there a seeming conspiracy to cover up the existence of Ekaterina?

Perhaps Ekaterina was in trouble. Maybe Doctor Millheimer was a witch hunter and realized that Jim knew of a witch's whereabouts. Ekaterina might have sensed this and quickly performed a spell of non-existence for safety. She was probably somewhere in a magickal, invisible realm where she would eventually come out of hiding once the witch hunters had gone away.

Surely Ekaterina sensed Jim's alarm and frustration. Oh, and of course she could telepathically receive his desperate thoughts. She was a witch, after all. Jim called out through telepathy, "Ekaterina? I know you are there, somewhere. I know you are in hiding. Don't worry! I won't leave you. I'm still here and waiting for you. I'm sorry about Doctor Millheimer. I didn't know he was a witch hunter. You know I would never do anything to hurt you. I love you. I'm here to protect you. Don't be gone for too long." This is what Jim telepathically communicated to his witchy lover while pulling into the Mapleview gas station. His tank was nearly on empty and in need of a refill.

That's when he spotted a sight for sore eyes. No, it wasn't Ekaterina. It was Amber, filling the gas tank of her black Pontiac Grand Prix. She looked so beautiful which triggered a sudden longing for her.

She noticed Jim as he pulled into the gas pump next to hers. Then he stepped out of the bucket truck and approached her.

"Hi! Long time no see!" greeted Jim.

But Amber wasn't exactly thrilled in seeing Jim. "Hey…"

"So what have you been up to?" asked Jim.

"Same-old, same-old."

"Oh yeah? I've been alright." Suddenly, Jim realized how important Amber was in his life, and strangely wished for their friendship to resume. "Hey… you know… I guess maybe some months ago I had gotten a little overwhelmed and didn't know…"

Amber interrupted, "It's okay, Jim! I understand. I'm okay. I'm actually seeing someone right now. I'm over us."

"You are? Yeah?"

Amber nodded, "Mmm-hmm." Then she removed the hose from her tank and fastened it back to the pump. "Not to cut this short, but I'm running late for work. See you around." And with that, Amber walked over to the driver side door, entered her Grand Prix and drove off.

And I guess that's how life works. We really don't know what we have until it's gone. Only months ago, Amber wished for Jim to be closer. But he pushed her away. Now confused and heartbroken, he needed a friend; someone to confide in. But Amber wanted nothing of Jim. She found someone else who really cared about her.

Jim had to focus! He needed to forget about Amber! The important thing was to somehow find Ekaterina and ensure that she was alright. But there was a little matter of reporting to work that morning as well as training the kid who was obviously to replace him. At some point in the day, Jim planned on returning to the forest and finding Ekaterina. But that would have to take place later.

As Jim walked through the office hallway of Mapleview Cable, he glanced into Ryan's office where he spotted Ryan and Cody. Both young men had sickening smiles on their faces, as-if they were up to no good.

It was difficult for Jim not to hear the words of Doctor Millheimer in his mind at that moment, "*How about the delusion that people conspire against you, or set out to hurt you?*"

"Jimmy!" called out Ryan. "Here's your buddy for the day. Train him well!"

Jim nodded.

About 20 minutes later, Jim and Cody drove along Mapleview Road like two peas in a pod. Despite how Cody represented the Bearer/Bringer of Change, Jim had to be friendly, almost nurturing to the young cable cadet.

Jim demonstrated the signal leakage detector mounted on the dashboard. "This will probably be one of the most important tools in your job. Once a year, the FCC will do a flyover and measure any signal leakage coming from our system. In some places of the country, portions of cable systems have been shut down because of leakage. We cannot have that!"

Cody agreed, "Of course!"

Jim continued, "The detector is connected to a small antenna on the roof. When driving around, sometimes you might notice it squeal. That area could have leakage at one of the taps or utility boxes." Jim and Cody were about to pass a utility box that always caused Jim's detector to sound an alarm. "Now listen closely; once we get near that box, you'll hear the detector alarm.

Right at the intersection of Mapleview Road and 6th Avenue, the signal leakage detector loudly squealed.

"Hear that?" asked Jim.

"Yeah!" answered Cody. "Aren't you going to do anything about it?"

"Nope!" Every system is allotted a certain percentage of negligible leakage. That box contains an extra amp to feed an additional square mile of homes. The only way to fix it is to cut down on power by removing the amp. But then you would lose a square mile of service."

Suddenly, Cody was a seasoned veteran in the cable business as he argued, "It seems to me there should be a way to fix it. You can't have leakage like that."

Jim reassured the cadet, "Dude, relax! Our system has passed year after year with that box generating leakage. It's all under control."

"Still, you think we could install another utility box up the road. I'm surprised you never brought this to Ryan's attention and proposed a new box. Ryan likes proactiveness, you know."

It was time to put Cody back in his place. For now, he was the inexperienced cadet, and so was Ryan for that matter. "Well, when Ryan was in grammar school and high school, we had no problems with the signal leakage coming from that box. Aside from that, are you going to lobby a million dollars for additional infrastructure and construction crews to install the equipment? The leakage level from that box is acceptable."

Cody wouldn't be put in his place. There was a new generation taking over Mapleview Cable, soon to be Fernsehen Comm. It was best that Cody shove Jim out of the way by softly answering, nearly under his breath, "We'll just have to see about that..."

"What's that?" asked Jim.

"Huh?"

"You said something."

Cody remained silent.

"Look, you can drop the attitude with me!" declared Jim. "I get it. I pick up what you're doing. But don't forget that I'm the one who holds the key to your training, alright?"

Cody finally looked over, "Listen, it's no secret that Ryan and I are family. His dad comes over to our place a lot. I mean they're brothers—my dad and his. Over the weekend, Ryan was saying how he needs people who seem to know what they're doing, not people who screw things up or slack off on the job.

Maybe he just thinks I can do a better job than you because I'm younger, you know? It's nothing personal."

Jim sighed. When did life become so cruel? Is this what getting old meant? Ryan and Cody seemed like nothing more than a couple of little shits who didn't know what they were doing. But maybe Jim was just getting too old for his job, and Cody could do it better than him.

Jim pulled up to a utility box at the side of the highway. "Time to get you acquainted with the insides of these."

As the two stepped out of the bucket truck, Cody asked, "Hey, shouldn't you have a safety cone behind your truck?"

It was best that Jim play it by the book and provide a good example. "Good point, Cody. Yes, you should have a cone out. Although we do have the yellow, flashing light; it's still best to follow the rules for safety."

"Very good!!" answered Cody. "I'd hate to have to let Ryan know about safety violations on my first week with you."

Jim bit his tongue and remained silent. He walked over to the utility box, opened it up and began pointing out the various cards along with amps. But when turning towards Cody, he could not be found. "Cody?"

Cody was standing behind the truck with the rear door open and examining the safety inspection log. He turned towards Jim, "Hey Jim? It says your safety gloves are a month overdue for inspection and certification."

"Yeah, I know. The certified inspector is behind schedule. What can you do?"

"Well you should have said something to Ryan!"

Jim was losing patience. "Ryan knows about it, Cody. And did you want to see the insides of the boxes; get your training?"

Cody sighed, "Sure..."

He slowly walked up to the now flabbergasted Jim while further commenting, "I mean I just can't believe you're touching the inside of that box with safety gloves that are overdue for inspection."

Jim proceeded to demonstrate the inside of the box. "Okay, this is the Master Control Unit, Main Memory; these are your row of Control Access Modules..."

As Jim looked over at Cody, he had the sudden urge to beat the living shit out of him. Rather than actually get something out of his training, the young cadet stood with arms crossed and a goofy smirk on his face while staring at Jim's gloves and shaking his head in disbelief. How would you like to remain courteous and respectful in such a situation?

Bringing Cody with to service calls or to assist with routine maintenance provided more opportunities for verbal abuse by the young cadet. But Jim's darkest moment in life in which he felt no larger than a bug occurred as the duo had some downtime and a chance to work on the telephone pole addressing project. Of course that project had been completed thanks to Google Earth. But Jim had to go through the motions as-if not to alarm anyone that the job was done.

Jim drove to some remote, forested road in Sillmac which presented a couple miles of telephone poles. "Well, we've got some downtime. We might as well stay busy and do Ryan's pole project."

"Don't you mean *your* pole project?" asked Cody. "Ryan was asking me how that was coming along while reminding me to keep an eye on you."

Jim's face turned flush with outrage but kept his words to himself.

Then Cody apologized. "I didn't mean it like that. He just wanted to know."

"Don't worry about it." answered Jim. "Forget about it."

As Jim stepped out of the truck and over to a telephone pole with the newly-acquired GPS device, Cody followed while appearing to supervise. Cody watched as Jim activated the device to locate where he was standing. Once the detailed latitude and longitude coordinates were provided, Jim logged them into a notebook and walked back to the truck.

But Cody stopped Jim midway and asked, "What are you going to do with that?"

"The coordinates? I put them in a spreadsheet and then update the map with it."

"Aren't you going create an address tag for the pole?"

"Nope, the coordinates are way, too long for an address tag. It's only being used for reference."

The answer wasn't good enough for Cody. "Whoa! Wait until Ryan hears about this! From what I understand, you are to be conducting a detailed GPS survey of each telephone pole and them labeling them. Why aren't you following instructions?"

Jim sighed, "I was never told to label the poles. And how big of a label would we need to fit all those coordinates?"

Cody shook his head in disbelief and then reached for his cell phone. "Hang on; let me give Ryan a call!"

Cody's tattletale report to Ryan resulted in an immediate trip back to the Mapleview Cable office. If you were in Jim's shoes, being tattled on by a young cadet who is supposed to be in training and then ordered to come back to the office, how might your attitude be? Rest assured, nothing was said during that ride back to Mapleview Cable. Cody was the first to exit the vehicle and was sure to be many feet ahead of his supposed mentor, en route towards Ryan's office.

Moments after Cody entered the office and sat down across from Ryan's desk, Jim entered.

Ryan announced Jim's entrance. "Jim!"

Jim froze at the door, thoroughly fed up with his recent treatment at the job.

Ryan continued, "I was afraid it would eventually get to this." The he paused for a few seconds before continuing to speak. "Come on in and have a seat."

Jim did as ordered.

With everyone seated, Ryan initiated the meeting by asking Jim, "So what's going on out there? It sounds like we have a problem?"

Immediately, Cody spoke up. "I actually noticed a few things about Jim this morning. From what I gather, he's been slacking off and allowing excessive leakage to come out of the utility boxes. Then I noticed he's a violator of OSHA regulations by not placing a safety cone outside of his truck. Even worse, he's using safety equipment that is overdue yearly certification."

Ryan looked over to Jim, "Jim, how could you? I'm disappointed in you!" Then he looked back at Cody, "What's he doing with the telephone pole labeling project?"

"I guess he's getting the GPS readings at each pole, jotting the coordinates down in some notebook and entering them in the infrastructure map. But he's not labeling the poles."

Ryan turned his attention back to Jim, "Jimmy! This is not good! What's going on?"

Jim had been silent in recent times for too long and it was time he spoke up in defense for himself. "Can I talk, finally?"

"Yes, you may." reassured Ryan.

"First of all, you never said anything about labeling those telephone poles. Aside from that, those coordinates are very lengthy. I don't know what sort of label you would need to accommodate those long lists of numbers. As for the safety gloves that are overdue certification, you were already aware that the inspector was behind schedule."

Ryan raised his finger in interruption. "Yes, I already knew about the gloves. But suppose you can explain to me why you are violating OSHA regulations and not setting a safety cone out behind your truck?"

Jim now raised his voice. "Come-on, Ryan! We weren't dragging equipment out of the truck! I only pulled over to show Cody the inside of the utility box!"

"Still, Jim, if OSHA inspectors happened to be driving by, we would have been slapped with a fine. How old are you, now, Jim?"

Jim had been with Mapleview Cable for 18 years; started at 22. He was now 40, definitely a seasoned veteran in the business with seniority and worthy of some degree of respect, especially in the face of young men who were in their early to mid 20s who hadn't more than a year's experience in the company. He proudly announced with a challenging look on his face. "I'm 40!"

"Well, Jim, why don't you start acting your age?—someone who is 40."

"Excuse me?" answered Jim

"What?"

"You said something about my age!"

Ryan calmly sat back in his seat. "Jim, here's the thing: I've got you making up excuses for violating OSHA regulations; I discover you are slacking off in your job by allowing utility boxes to leak signal; and you are slacking off in your job by doing a project I assigned you, incorrectly. I would expect this sort of thing from someone like 20 years younger than you. I mean I feel like I have Cody babysitting you. How else would you want me think?"

Now I won't detail the remainder of that discussion as to how Jim tried in vain to explain why the excessive signal leakage from that box at the intersection of Mapleview Road and 6th avenue was acceptable. Nor will I detail his fruitless argument of how impossible it would have been to label the poles with lengthy GPS coordinates. Jim raised his voice throughout most of the discussion while Ryan spoke calmly in a patronizing manner, imposing his belief of being so many more years wiser than Jim. At some point it was decided that acquiring thousands of metal tags with lengthy GPS coordinates would require a purchase requisition; something that might be delayed with the soon-to-be company takeover.

And then Ryan made his executive decisions which ultimately ended the meeting. "So for now, Jim, just continue doing the project as you've been doing. By the time we get tags, Cody will be the official lineman technician and you can devote all your energies to nailing the tags up on the poles." And then he sighed, "Jim, I'd hate to do this to you, but when you come in tomorrow, there will be two final written warnings on my desk for you to sign."

"What?" Jim exclaimed. "You can't give me final written warnings. I've never received verbal warnings for anything!"

"Well, let's see; I had you in here one morning because you were sending cards in to the warranty center with vague diagnostic information. I caught you fooling around in a utility box a couple weeks ago that ultimately caused a serious outage. I believe you've received plenty of verbal warnings from me. Don't feel bad. Company policy says that after a year you will be eligible to have those written warnings erased from your employee file. But the new company might have a different policy when it comes to written warnings. Provided there's actually a chance for you to stay with us at the new company, your employee file might start fresh. But let me warn you; documenting your recent insubordinate behavior does not look good for you if they decide to clean house."

Despite how irate and thoroughly fed up Jim was with recent times, he now found himself pleading with his arrogant, young boss to be merciful. "Ryan, you can't do this to me; you just can't. Come-on, give me a break. Please don't write me up—not with the possibility of layoffs coming."

"Sorry Jim, I wish the situation were different. I can't allow your careless and insubordinate actions to be met without consequence. That's life. Be a big boy and take your punishment."

Jim turned numb at that moment and suddenly didn't care about anything. He stood up from his chair, threw his hands up and stormed out of the office. Never mind his obligation of training Cody for the remainder of the day. Jim simply needed to get away; far away from the office where he could be alone.

Chapter 64

The forest was the place where Jim needed to be; in particular, the very place where Ekaterina resided. This stolen moment made possible by storming out of the office and driving off from Mapleview Cable provided the perfect opportunity to look for Ekaterina. Jim parked on the side of Mapleview Road, climbed over the guardrail and into the forest. The narrow path created by him and Ekaterina was still there. It served as a comforting reminder that what Jim experienced in all those weeks actually did occur in reality.

Jim was destined to lose his job. Ryan and Cody inevitably had him on a schedule to constantly mess and fail. Today they succeeded in finding a way to write him up so that Jim would be gone when the new company cleaned house.

But then Doctor Millheimer's haunting words returned in Jim's imagination.

"How about false beliefs or strange delusions? Delusions are most often characterized with fantastic ideas such as the belief that people conspire against you, and are out to hurt you?"

Jim paid no mind to this possibility and continued hiking to the location of Ekaterina's cottage. Jim wasn't stupid! He lived long enough to know what Ryan had in store for him. Jim was slated to lose his job later that year.

This was the sort of thing that probably happened to witches as they realized what they had turned into. For many weeks, Jim was gradually called and inducted into magick. Ekaterina trained him. Now the world was changing around him. Most people in Jim's position would fall apart. But he was now a witch and much stronger than the rest of them.

"Sometimes you might think that you have some great power over everyone else."

No! Jim knew he had a power over everyone else. Jim's sanity and very life depended on understanding this! Now a short distance from the location of Ekaterina's cottage, Jim was disappointed to discover it remained invisible.

"Ekaterina! I know you are here! You can come out, now."

Then he realized the carelessness on his part. If Ekaterina was hiding for safety, Jim wasn't doing a good job in protecting her. She was probably in some magickal, invisible, parallel universe where she carefully observed Jim and everything he did. This was probably a test. Yes, of course! Why hadn't Jim thought of this before? Ekaterina probably waited patiently for him on the other side—that invisible, magickal realm where she invited Jim to go on Saturday afternoon. Would Jim pass the test? Could he enter this alternate dimension and find his new, loving witch-family?

"There is another delusion that seems to be a growing trend in society. Some people are under the impression that they are influenced by paranormal forces."

Jim ignored his imagination's resistance. He needed to believe! This was the crucial key in generating enough magickal power to cross over and find Ekaterina. He knew how to reach that invisible, magickal realm. He was to return to the special place where Ekaterina led him on Saturday—the place where the wind seemingly blew out of nowhere. From there Jim would find the magick portal and finally cross over.

Jim walked for some twenty minutes to Ekaterina's special place in the forest, all the while ignoring any suggestion from the imagined voice of Doctor Millheimer.

"How about hallucinations? Hallucinations are different from delusions in that rather than simply believing in some fantastic notion, the sufferer actually sees or hears things that are not present in reality. Do you experience this?"

If Ekaterina had only been a hallucination, then Jim wouldn't have known about the special spot in the forest. Ekaterina was real. His experiences with her were equally real. While continuing to maintain his belief in her, Jim climbed the final hill which ultimately led him to the place where he and Ekaterina stood on Saturday.

But where was the wind? It blew out of nowhere on Saturday; but now the air remained still with only the gentle trickle of water some distance below at the bottom of the ravine. "Ekaterina? Where are you?"

Maybe if Jim closed his eyes and concentrated on the wind it would finally appear. Then it would open the necessary magick portal and provide the means to join Ekaterina. Jim concentrated with all his might and imagined a strong wind blowing out of nowhere. But when he opened his eyes, there was nothing.

"Come-on, Ekaterina! You have to help me! I can't do this alone!"

But there was no answer and no help from Ekaterina. She was gone, probably forever. Jim had the opportunity to leave this world and live happily ever after with Ekaterina on Saturday afternoon. But he passed the chance up and walked away.

Or maybe it was something else. The voice of Ekaterina spoke in Jim's imagination. *"Just think about your girlfriend. What is she doing to you? You know what she is and what she's trying to do to you."*

* * *

Amber feverishly completed another mystical portrait in the candlelit attic of her home. It was that of Jim in the very place of nature where he was now at. Jim was heartbroken, confused and holding back that split second just before going insane. Tears rolled from his face as he lay in a disheveled mess at the very spot where the young Ekaterina had been last embraced. But unbeknown to Jim, the ghost of an old witch stood before him with a small cup positioned underneath his face and collecting his tears.

Finally; a heartbroken man's tears that had been cried for her! She could use them as needed.

The End

To be continued in the third book of Amber, house of witches.

Author Biography

Tom Raimbault is recognized as one of those authors who have difficulty distinguishing fantasy from reality. But as he feels, this is the crucial ingredient in writing dark fantasies and horror. Much of his writing sessions have occurred during the witching hour while the rest of the world sleeps. Tom arises from bed at two o'clock in the morning to ensure that he is partly in that unseen world behind the veil. From there he writes, for you, his most treasured place of fiction, Mapleview; and hopes that each book is a visual trip to his world of fantasy.

Halloween is an especially important holiday for Tom, and is celebrated each year on his blog with new short stories that portray the eerie world behind the veil, and those mysterious things that reach and call out to us.

Tom has developed a noteworthy style of storytelling that he calls "freaked out horror". With it he attempts to paint up the classic black and white Twilight Zone feel to relay the strange, the macabre and the bizarre. This style of writing expands into his bizarre tales of science fiction, alien abduction horror, and extra terrestrial romance fantasies.

Lightning Source UK Ltd.
Milton Keynes UK
UKHW041845030521
383075UK00008B/625/J